Praise for The Adventuress

'You cannot fail to be entertained by Nicholas Coleridge's latest novel . . . This clever retelling of *Vanity Fair* is not only hugely enjoyable but also has some spot-on social observations and splendid comic set pieces' *Tatler*

'A sharply written yet lighthearted satire of the British elite that works by undermining expectations' *GQ*

'Saucy' *Evening Standard*

The three plotlines are drawn exquisitely tightly until the satisfying resolution at the end of this indescribably pleasurable and entertaining novel . . . if any man were ever to steal the crown from our Jilly, in the sense that he delivers hugely readable, witty, sharp and sexy fiction, it would have to be *Condé*'s clever Nicholas Coleridge' *Lady*

'A fast-paced, enthralling depiction of an instinctive social climber who is forced to learn the hard way that the past always catches up with you' *Easy Living*

'Coleridge's latest novel is a satirical take on our obsession with status and celebrity. Cathy Fox is a woman who will not be denied . . . you'll love her brazen nerve and chutzpah' *Glamour*

Coleridge has an admirably pared-down style and an eye r the telling brand and place name, in a manner reminiscent of Tom Wolfe: few who pick up *The Adventuress* will be able to put it aside before they finish it' *Metro*

'Coleridge is at the peak of his powers . . . and here's another juici *Daily Mail*

'Fas *l Times*

WITHDRAWN FROM STOCK

D1392092

Nicholas Coleridge's acclaimed novels include *Godchildren*, *Deadly Sins*, *A Much Married Man* and *With Friends Like These*. He is also the author of two non-fiction bestsellers, *The Fashion Conspiracy* and *Paper Tigers*, and his books have been published in fourteen languages. Having worked as a newspaper columnist and magazine editor, he joined the Condé Nast magazine company in London as Editorial Director and has been Publishing Director since 1992, and President of Condé Nast International since 2012. He has been Chairman of the British Fashion Council, Chairman of the Professional Publishers Association and is Vice Chairman of the Campaign for Wool. He became CBE in the Queen's Birthday Honours 2009. His enthusiasms include long walks, sunshine and India, ideally simultaneously. He lives in London and Worcestershire with his wife, Georgia, and their four children.

By Nicholas Coleridge

FICTION

A Much Married Man
Godchildren
Streetsmart
With Friends Like These
How I Met My Wife and Other Stories
Shooting Stars
Deadly Sins
The Adventuress

NON-FICTION

Paper Tigers
The Fashion Conspiracy
Around the World in 78 Days
Tunnel Vision

THE ADVENTURESS

The irresistible rise of Miss Cath Fox

NICHOLAS COLERIDGE

An Orion paperback

First published in Great Britain in 2012
by Orion
This paperback edition published in 2013
by Orion Books,
an imprint of The Orion Publishing Group Ltd,
Orion House, 5 Upper St Martin's Lane,
London WC2H 9EA

An Hachette UK company

1 3 5 7 9 10 8 6 4 2

Copyright © Nicholas Coleridge 2012

The moral right of Nicholas Coleridge to be identified as the author of this work has been asserted in accordance with the Copyright, Designs and Patents Act 1988.

All rights reserved. No part of this publication may be reproduced, stored in a retrieval system, or transmitted, in any form or by any means, electronic, mechanical, photocopying, recording or otherwise, without the prior permission of the copyright owner.

Except for those already in the public domain, all the characters in this book are fictitious, and any resemblance to actual persons, living or dead, is purely coincidental.

A CIP catalogue record for this book is available from the British Library.

ISBN 978-1-4091-0921-1

Typeset by Deltatype Ltd, Birkenhead, Merseyside

Printed and bound by CPI Group (UK) Ltd,
Croydon, CR0 4YY

The Orion Publishing Group's policy is to use papers that are natural, renewable and recyclable products and made from wood grown in sustainable forests. The logging and manufacturing processes are expected to conform to the environmental regulations of the country of origin.

www.orionbooks.co.uk

This one is dedicated to my children and godchildren
Alexander, Freddie, Sophie and Tommy Coleridge
and
Helena Allan, Ione Hunter Gordon, Edie Campbell,
Cara Delevingne, Willa Petty, Ewan Wotherspoon and
Ned Dahl Donovan

Peterborough City Council	
60000 0001 14425	
Askews & Holts	Oct-2013
	£7.99

Acknowledgements

I would like to thank the following people who advised me on different aspects of this story: Neil Clifford, Paul Henderson, Katharine Barton, Fiona Shackleton, Julia Dixon, Shannon Tolar, Kit Hunter Gordon, Sarah Standing, Gary Read, Lizzie Norton, Nicky Eaton, Maya Monro-Somerville, Brian Greenaway, Karen Hibbert and Liz Hatherell. I would especially like to thank Georgia Coleridge and Jean Faulkner, whose observations and general cleverness improved things beyond measure. Chloe Southey kindly typed the manuscript, assisted by her sister Sophie Bradbury, and Emma Evans.

My editor at Orion, Kate Mills, gave countless invaluable editing points, as did Orion's Trade Managing Director Lisa Milton. Thanks also to Susan Lamb, Lucie Stericker, Loulou Clark, Louisa Gibbs, Gaby Young, Jemima Forrester and the team at Orion, and my American publishers, Tom Dunne and Karyn Marcus of Thomas Dunne Books at St Martin's Press. My legendary agent, Ed Victor, talks me up and reads my drafts faster than anyone.

The opening chapter of this novel was written poolside at Raas Haveli, Jodhpur; subsequent chapters at Wolverton Hall, Pershore; Firle Place; Le Bristol Hotel; Belvoir Castle; Villa Ezzahra, Marrakech; the Taj Mahal Palace Hotel, Mumbai; Marcus, By Forfar; Trenoweth, St Keverne; Ramathra Fort; Kentisbeare House and the Mandarin Oriental Hotel, Hong Kong.

Chapter One

On a blazing Saturday morning in June 1982, there drove through the great iron gates of St Mary's Boarding School for Girls between Petworth and Horsham in West Sussex a long procession of smart family motor cars. At least two hundred Mercedes Estates, Volvos and Range Rovers, fully laden with parents, brothers and sisters, picnic baskets and dogs, were forming up in lines around the perimeter of the sports fields. The keenest and best-prepared parents had arrived as early as eight o'clock, in order to bag the shadiest picnic spots under the horse chestnut trees, or beneath the spreading boughs of the holm oak beyond the long-jump sandpit. For ten long days England had been held in the grip of a heatwave, and the forecast for today was for temperatures reaching the high eighties. After several years of cold, rainy sports days, no one could quite believe it.

Just inside the gates stood groups of girls in their games kit, waiting for their parents to show up. The school grounds were primped to perfection. For days, groundsmen had been mowing, rolling and strimming, whitening the lanes of the running track, and erecting tea tents and Portaloos behind the sports pavilion. Exhibitions of pottery were set up on trestles, and mothers in summer dresses and fathers in blazers and panama hats strolled between them, admiring their daughters' handicrafts. By the open hatchbacks of cars, families were spreading rugs and unpacking picnics and cool boxes and jugs of Pimm's with mint and slices of fruit, and tipping water into dog bowls for thirsty spaniels.

Watching all this activity from her window beneath the eaves of the main school building stood Cath Fox. She was naked but for red satin knickers and she was smoking a cigarette, held between forefinger and thumb, blowing smoke out of the window in great nonchalant gusts.

Had anyone barged into her room at that moment, they would have seen three tattoos of various shapes and sizes on her back, thigh and upper arm: a spider's web protruding above the elastic of her knickers, a scorpion on a shapely thigh and the word *Callum* stencilled into a heart shape. Since arriving at St Mary's, Cath had been careful to conceal the tattoos from her fellow staff members. Old Ma Perse – or Mrs Violet Perse MA (Cantab) as the headmistress styled herself – would have been horrified, as would Cath's boss, Mrs Bullock, senior matron. But she had shown her tattoos and belly button piercing to some of the pupils – the ones she trusted – and it tickled her to see the look of fascinated shock on their sheltered little faces. Cath was the same age as the sixth form girls, but sometimes she felt twice that; they'd hardly lived, most of them still virgins.

From the window Cath could see the whole of the school grounds spreading out beneath her; a hundred and thirty acres of sports fields and parkland. She looked down at the cars parked round the fields and wondered what they must be worth, that many posh motors, not even locked and keys left dangling in their ignitions. Callum would have had a field day; not that she was telling that tosser where she was living now, no way.

She stepped away from the window and considered herself critically in the mirror. She'd got her figure back; if anything it was better than before. Her stomach didn't have a pinch of fat left on it. And her tits looked perky; not as big as they'd been, but they stood up nicely. She glanced down at her ankles and frowned: a bit porky. The pupils at St Mary's mostly had better ankles than she did, she'd noticed that about them. She liked her face though, which everyone agreed was attractive, though her hair was too mousy in colour. Her eyes were large and brown and ringed with mascara. Overall, she liked what she saw, she was OK, quite sexy, she knew that.

Slipping into a long-sleeved cotton dress which covered her tattoos, Cath headed downstairs. First she took the narrow flight from the attic to the dormitory floor where the girls slept, then went through numerous fire doors which led down to the mezzanine, and finally the wide carved wooden staircase hung with portraits of retired headmistresses which took you to the front hall. Before it had been turned into a school, the house had been the private mansion of some loaded aristocratic family, the Haddon-Carews, and it still felt more like a palace than a school to Cath. Her own school had been nothing like this, and that was the understatement of the year.

In fact, before she got the job, Cath hadn't known places like St Mary's even existed. She'd hardly ever left the Allaway estate in Wymering; the worst pre-war council development in Portsmouth, people said, long overdue for demolition. But now she was working at this posh girls' school, seventeen years old and a matron's assistant, folding and sorting laundry, pairing up socks, cleaning out basins, name-taping games kit, all under the controlling eye of that old witch Mrs Bullock. Cath hated the job but it provided a place to stop and a few quid in her pocket and it wouldn't be for ever. And it had its compensations.

Emerging into the sunshine of the front lawn, Cath wondered how she was going to fill her day. She was meant to be on duty serving teas in the marquee later on, but that wasn't until after speeches. There was a staff buffet going on somewhere, but Cath didn't fancy it; she thought she'd do better crashing one of the family picnics.

She strolled down the lines of cars and felt the approving looks of several of the fathers as she passed by. It was a pleasant feeling being looked at, even by dirty old goats in their fifties. Having seen their wives setting out the picnics, Cath wasn't surprised the dads preferred looking at her, and she swayed her hips as she paraded, to give them something to gawp at.

She hoped no one would recognise the dress she was wearing, which she'd pilfered from one of the girls' clothing cupboards earlier in the week. One of the advantages of tidying the dorms during lessons was having free access to their stuff. When she saw something nice from Miss Selfridge or Chelsea Girl, she took her pick. After all, most of the girls had more than enough already, didn't they?

Not far beyond the all-weather netball court, Cath spotted Annabel. Annabel Goode was one of the pupils Cath was friendly with, who'd been shown the tattoos. You could almost say they'd become mates, sort of, though Annabel only knew about the parts of Cath's life she'd chosen to tell her. Not the thieving or Callum and certainly not Jess. In any case, Cath had no illusions. Annabel and the other pupils at St Mary's came from totally different worlds; they could never be genuine mates, it wasn't going to happen.

Annabel saw Cath approaching and gave her a big, friendly smile.

'Miss Fox, hi, come and join us.' With her happy, open face, lustrous brown hair, English-rose skin and perfect white teeth, she was one of the prettiest girls at St Mary's, and one of the nicest. When old Ma Perse the headmistress required a senior pupil to show prospective parents around the school, she often chose Annabel Goode, because anyone who spent an hour or two in her company invariably decided to send their daughter there, hoping they would turn out like Annabel.

'I want you to meet my parents,' Annabel said. 'Mummy, Daddy, this is Miss Fox I was telling you about, the one who's our favourite matron.' Cath was introduced to Annabel's father, Michael Goode, a dark-haired man of about forty-eight and not bad looking, and her mother Felicity, a pretty blonde with an eager, submissive face.

'You know Miss Fox and I are actual twins?' Annabel told her parents. 'She was born on April the twenty-third 1965 as well.'

Michael Goode, who had assumed Cath was several years older than his daughter, looked surprised.

'Would you like to join our picnic?' Annabel asked. 'We've got way too much food. We've joined up with Sophie and Mouse's families and everyone's brought masses.'

'Please do join us, if you'd like to,' said Felicity, Annabel's mother, and Michael nodded encouragement and handed her a tankard of Pimm's.

Soon Cath was sitting on tartan picnic rugs with the Goodes, the Peverels and the Barwell-Mackenzies, who had parked their cars together and assembled tables and many fold-up chairs for their shared sports day picnic. Felicity Goode, who was known as Flea, unpacked two large serving dishes of coronation chicken, Mrs Peverel produced a fricassee of chicken and Mrs Barwell-Mackenzie a Pyrex dish containing cold roast chicken legs, bowls of tomatoes and hard-boiled eggs. Punnets of strawberries and cartons of Cadbury's Mini Rolls and Mr Kipling apple and almond tarts were set out on Pyrex plates. Soon Cath was introduced to Annabel's younger brother and sister, and Annabel begged Cath to show them her tattoos, since they had never seen a real tattoo before. With a sigh, Cath rolled up the hem of her dress to reveal the scorpion. But the children seemed less enthralled by the tattoo than the fathers, who leant forward the better to see it, with great exclamations of interest and encouragement. Michael

Goode was particularly impressed and wondered aloud whether he should get one himself.

'Please not, thank you very much, darling,' said Felicity, with a nervous frown.

'I wasn't actually asking your opinion, Flea,' Michael replied. 'I was asking Miss Fox. What do you reckon, Miss Fox, do you think it'd be an improvement if I got a tattoo done?'

Cath held him with a bold stare before bashfully dropping her eyelids.

'Up to you, Mr Goode. They look cool, if you choose the right thing.'

'What do you recommend then? A mermaid? An anchor on my arm?'

'What about a one-eyed trouser snake, Michael?' joked Mr Peverel, who was a friend of long-standing. 'Bloody agony to have it done though . . . can't say I'd be brave enough to get a tattoo myself.'

'But Miss Fox has one,' Michael reminded him. 'Sparky lady.'

'No, Dad,' said Annabel. 'She's got *three* tattoos, not just one. And a *piercing*.'

'Has she indeed?' replied her father, looking at Cath with renewed interest. 'This expensive school of yours must be more exciting than I realised, Annabel.' And he retrieved a corkscrew from the picnic basket and opened another bottle of wine.

Sports day was now officially the hottest day of the year. According to the car radio it had topped ninety degrees in Haslemere, which wasn't that far from St Mary's. The 1500 metres inter-house relay was cancelled, it being decreed too hot for such a long-distance race. An Airedale terrier almost died having been locked in a boiling Rover whilst its owners were watching the long jump. An elderly grandparent suffered sunstroke and had to be taken inside to lie down in sick bay. All over the playing fields, picnics were running low on bottled water and juice and having to fall back on alcohol.

At the Goodes' picnic, girls and their siblings kept peeling off to compete in events, and Cath accompanied Annabel to watch her younger sister, Rosie, take part in the brothers-and-sisters race. When they returned to the picnic, the three families were discussing their forthcoming summer holidays to Corfu, Sardinia and Cornwall. Cath was only too aware, from listening to the girls' conversations in the dormitories, that they all took glamorous holidays in the summer, with villas in the sun, or cottages at the seaside in Devon, Cornwall or Norfolk. Some of the girls went away all summer long, staying with schoolfriends in different locations.

'And what about *you*, Miss Fox?' Michael Goode asked. 'Are you getting away anywhere nice this summer, once you've got shot of the girls? I should think you'll need a good holiday by then.'

But Cath replied that she had no plans. If truth be told, she had no clue where she'd go or what she'd do – she could hardly go back to Portsmouth – but she didn't say that to Mr Goode.

'Tell you what,' said Michael. 'Here's an idea – why not come down to Cornwall with us for a bit? We were just saying we'll need someone to help us with the kids and the cooking. We'd pay you, of course. Wouldn't that be a good solution, Flea? Take Miss Fox to Rock as an extra pair of hands?'

Felicity looked like she wasn't convinced, but Annabel loved the idea. 'Oh, Miss Fox, *do* come, please say yes. It's so amazing in Rock, you'll love it. There's this great sandy beach and masses of our friends go. And you can surf. We take this house right by the beach.'

'I'd like that,' replied Cath. 'Cornwall, yeah, that'd be OK.'

And so the plan was made. Cath would join the Goodes in Rock for the first three weeks of July. She would be paid forty pounds a week and be expected to prepare breakfast, do some food shopping each morning, tidy round and keep an eye on the younger children, living as part of the family.

Annabel promised her she'd have an amazing time.

Michael advanced her money for her train fare to London, from where she would travel down to Rock by car with the Goodes.

If Flea had misgivings about the scheme, she could not think of any reasonable grounds on which to object to it, and so she kept them to herself.

Cath had many secrets, but some of her secrets were buried deeper than others. There were lifestyle secrets, like her tattoos and piercings she realised would make problems for her, should they become widely known in the stuffier quarters at St Mary's. Then there was the secret of her Thursday afternoons in Petworth, which she knew would get her sacked instantly if any of that ever came out, and would conceivably put her inside as well. Which would be an irony seeing as how she'd vowed not to end up like her dad, in and out of prison all his life. Last time she'd been in Petworth, the lady at the stall in the antiques market had given her a peculiar look and offered much less money than usual, which put Cath on her guard. Perhaps she should travel to Brighton next time, but it was a lot further to get to. But these were not the secrets that kept her awake at night.

She was sitting in the matrons' room, ostensibly unpacking baskets of clothes from the school laundry. There were several dozen pairs of knickers, bras, summer Aertex shirts, nighties, pyjamas, mufti – the St Mary's name for home clothes – all waiting to be sorted and placed on the foot of the girls' beds or in their lockers. She was no stranger to the lockers, having rifled through several of them earlier that day. The haul lay in her pocket now; a tangle of gold and silver chains wrapped inside a Kleenex tissue. There had been richer pickings than usual, since she'd targeted the fourth form dorms in which several girls had recently been confirmed. Cath had learnt how generous the girls' godparents could be at confirmations. She had three gold crosses on chains, two charm bracelets and a seed pearl necklace as proof.

You could say it was reckless but Cath saw it as a calculated risk. In her next break, she'd take the haul up to the attic and hide it under the loose floorboard behind the water tank. The water tank was next to her bedroom, but in the unlikely event of anyone discovering it, no one could pin anything on her. And they'd be disposed of soon enough in any case.

Sometimes, when she thought about it, she was amazed how simple it was to nick stuff at this school. There was so much of it lying around, like Aladdin's cave or Ali Baba's cave or whatever: clothes, jewellery, shoes, cassettes, fountain pens, all crammed into lockers and bedside cabinets. Mrs Perse had recently given the girls a lecture at assembly about stealing, after Cath had done over the first year dorms, but Cath had just sat there, gazing innocently into space.

It had started slowly enough, when she opened a package addressed to a girl named Nicola Sturridge. All incoming parcels at St Mary's had to be opened in the matrons' room, in case they contained contraband cosmetics or tuck. Cath had been intrigued by a Jiffy bag with a Cartier label, and thought she'd take a look while the girls were in chapel. Inside was a beautiful travel clock in a red crocodile case; you could see it was worth a mint. Before she'd thought twice, Cath had slipped it into her pocket and chucked the packaging. It was child's play, no one even knew Nicola had received a parcel.

A couple of days later she'd taken the clock into Petworth. Petworth was one of those stuck-up English market towns, full of genteel tea shops with spinning wheels and scones, and antiques shops flogging barometers and grandfather clocks. She walked round the whole place looking for somewhere that might buy the Cartier clock off her. After a couple of rebuffs, she found an antiques market selling old Victorian postcards, teacups and pincushions. One of the stalls dealt in jewellery, and the lady with her hair in a bun offered thirty quid for the clock in cash, no questions asked.

After that, it became a weekly fixture, visiting Petworth. It was what she did on her afternoons off.

She liked keeping busy, so as not to dwell too much on Callum and what might be going on at home. You could work yourself into a right state if you allowed yourself to. She hated her mum and couldn't get the picture of her out of her mind – she'd never forgive her, the dirty old tart. And she wouldn't forgive Callum either, even if her mum had initiated it as he kept on claiming. But Callum had looked like he was enjoying it well enough, that's how it had seemed to Cath when she'd discovered them together. Disgusting. How could he betray her like that? Especially considering the kid. It was Jess's *nan* he was shagging, for Christ's sake! Well, fuck them. She was well shot of the lot of them, she knew that.

But she did still wonder, especially at night when she couldn't get off to sleep, obsessing over their affair and what had happened with Jess. And she missed her brothers. She wondered how Doyle was getting along without her; he was all right, Doyle. And how Bodie was doing at his new school. And if she was honest she missed Callum too: she'd been with Callum three years, since she was fourteen, off and on. Well, she knew where to find him, at the door of Nero's, keeping out the scummers. That's where Cath had first seen him, the hardest bloke she'd set eyes on. It had taken her three Saturdays in a row to nail him; she didn't let on for weeks she was under age. A lot of people in Pompey had been jealous of her when she'd got Callum – there were enough women after him, everyone fancied nightclub bouncers.

Did she miss Jess? Cath wasn't sure you could miss a baby. Don't get me wrong, she thought, it's not like she had a *problem* with babies, it's just with Jess not being able to speak, or do little beyond cry all day, she didn't feel much for her one way or the other. And then Callum went and ruined everything, just when they were talking about getting married and making it official, for Jess's sake as much as their own, by jumping in the sack with her own mum.

The very next day Cath had left town. Far as she was concerned, she wasn't bothered if she never clapped eyes on Portsmouth or any of them ever again.

The bell rang for lunch and Cath headed down to the dining room. One of her duties was to supervise the girls' tables in the big dining hall, pulling them up on their table manners and looking out for anorexics. Cath thought it was rather funny, considering what she knew about fine table manners could be written on the back of a stamp. They hadn't eaten at a table at home more than twice in her life, not even at Christmas. The Fox family ate their meals on the couch in front of the TV; her dad had been in prison for the past three years in any case, eating off a Styrofoam tray in front of another TV in his cell.

Cath took her place at table 17. At the head of the table sat Colin Woodruff, the geography teacher with whom she sometimes had casual sex. He was an OK bloke with a Hillman Hunter and a fondness for village pubs, and he helped pass the time and kept her mind off Callum. At lunch, she listened to the prattle of thirteen-year-old girls about ponies, pop music and their impending summer holidays. All the places they were going to – Paxos, Malaga, the Algarve – Cath hadn't heard of before she arrived at St Mary's, but already they seemed almost familiar. Talking to the pupils was an education. Sharp as a needle, Cath knew she was absorbing a lot, about where families like these lived, their preferred counties, cars, servants, prejudices and assumptions. She even found herself picking up on their pronunciation and vocab.

Across the dining hall she spotted Annabel in animated conversation with her table of friends. They looked so carefree and innocent, Cath didn't know whether she felt envious or contemptuous. Annabel sensed she was being watched, looked up and saw Cath, smiled, and gave a pretty little wave. Annabel felt there was no one she admired in the world quite so much as Cath Fox, with the possible exception of her father. Cath was so pretty and wore clothes so well, and was way more sophisticated than any of the girls at school. She'd had proper boyfriends and worked in bars and sold candy floss at a funfair. In the evenings, before lights out, Miss Fox sometimes came into the dorm and perched on the end of their beds and talked to Annabel and her friends, and they envied the things she'd seen and done. When she'd first shown them her tattoos, it was a sign she trusted them. It was deliciously subversive.

Cath wondered what it would be like, going on her holidays with the Goode family.

Chapter Two

The bungalow in Rock, which the Goodes were renting for their eighth successive summer, had been built in the fifties opposite a favoured stretch of sandy beach, from which it was separated by a busy road. Originally constructed as inexpensively as possible as a retirement home for a postman and his disabled wife, it was now rented out during high season to families like the Goodes for four hundred pounds a week.

Several of the Goodes' oldest friends took similar houses in the town, with the same cast of characters assembling summer after summer. In the early years, they had arrived with toddlers and young children, and spent their days shrimping and crabbing in rock pools. These days they arrived with six-foot teenagers for surfing and windsurfing and evenings spent in local pubs. As Annabel explained to Cath in the car, 'There'll be about forty girls from St Mary's there, and their brothers. Last summer there were a hundred and fifty people we knew staying in Rock and Polzeath.'

The journey by car from Fulham to Rock had taken more than six hours, as they got caught in long tailbacks on the M5 round Bristol and later behind caravans on the winding Cornish roads. Annabel's dad's Mercedes Estate was the smartest car Cath had ever been in, but tightly packed with luggage, boxes of food, surfboards, snorkels and flippers. Cath, Annabel and Annabel's younger brother Tommy squeezed onto the middle seat with suitcases at their feet, Annabel's sister Rosie was on a backwards-facing jump seat in the boot, walled in with suitcases, until she felt car sick. Michael Goode had had to load and unload the car several times, first outside the Victorian terraced house near Hurlingham, later at a service station. By the time they arrived at Rock, tempers were ragged.

Flea kept apologising to Cath about the bungalow – 'It hasn't got much character, I'm afraid, but the location is perfect' – but Cath was impressed. It had three bedrooms with pine furniture, two shower rooms with toilets, a lounge with sliding glass doors onto a patio, and a big sun porch with oatmeal-coloured settees and wicker furniture. And the kitchen was nice too, with an extendable Formica-topped table to seat ten, built-in units round the walls and Formica tops on all the surfaces. Flea said, 'It's all a bit of a joke – especially the plates and cutlery – but we don't mind, it's only for three weeks. The children adore it here.' It was agreed that Cath and Annabel would share one bedroom, Rosie (feeling less sick now they'd arrived) and Tommy in another, and Michael and Felicity would take their usual front bedroom with the en suite. Cath thought one day she would like to live in a place like this, all clean and modern with an all-weather sun lounge, and wondered if she ever would.

Once they'd unpacked, Annabel was keen to show Cath the beach and see who was there, but Flea insisted on first introducing her to the two mini-supermarkets within walking distance, where she could buy the essentials. 'I've had to bring olive oil with us from London,' Flea said. 'It's all very basic down here. You can't even find avocados.' Michael, meanwhile, took the children to the hire shack to get wetsuits. 'I'll take you down there soon,' he promised Cath. 'You'll need a wetsuit if you want to stay in the sea longer than five minutes.'

Cath soon fell into the routine of the Goodes' family holiday. She prepared breakfast of cereal, eggs and toast for everyone, washed up, walked to the Spar to buy bread, milk and whatever else was needed, then returned to make the picnic with Flea in the kitchen. The picnic was the same each day – white doughy baps filled with ham and cheese, hard-boiled eggs, crisps and Penguin biscuits. Having glimpsed the more exotic picnics of the St Mary's sports day, Cath was slightly disappointed. Michael, meanwhile, drove to the butcher, fishmonger and off-licence to get steaks or sometimes lobster for the evening barbecue, and lager and wine for the beach.

Flea kept a list of provisions she needed Cath to buy and which she was expected to add to herself whenever she thought of something. Cath hated that part, because her spelling was rubbish. They'd never really done spelling at her school. So she wrote *Butta*, *Bred*, *Woshin powda*, and Rosie, Annabel's kid sister, thought she was a scream, assuming it was intentional and a joke. Cath blushed red, hating to be caught out. At St Mary's, she strived to avoid ever writing anything down, so no one would realise she was barely literate.

By midday the family set off to their usual spot by the high-tide mark, carrying the picnic, chairs, rugs and holdalls filled with masks, buckets and spades, and joined up with families of friends. The Peverels – Johnnie and Davina and their children, Sophie and Max – were there most days, and the Barwell-Mackenzies were shortly expected, back from Corfu. Some lunchtimes there were thirty people in the Goodes' orbit, including teenagers who came and went to swim and smoke.

In the evening, the same group reassembled at one another's houses for barbecues, at which the fathers, drinks in hand, stood grilling steaks and sausages, and the women set tables and lit storm lanterns, and the teenagers came and went to drink and smoke. Cath moved uneasily between the three groups – sometimes playing catch with Tommy Goode on the lawn, sometimes smoking a quick fag, fetching paper napkins or carrying piles of plates out to the barbecue where the charred meat would be served.

'You must get Cath to show you her tattoos,' Michael said when she passed by. 'I promise you, they're worth a look.'

And then the fathers would all stare at her, boggle-eyed, because there was something about Cath. In a garden full of pretty teenage girls, who they would never have thought about in that way, being the children of their oldest friends, Cath radiated sensuality and danger. She felt adult male eyes following her surreptitiously as she moved about the garden.

It amazed her how rich they all were. It was like money was no object. Annabel's dad had hired five wetsuits for the entire holiday like it was nothing, and bought a new surfboard for Tommy. And Flea had bought salt and pepper grinders and white serving plates at a shop in town, without thinking twice or even telling her husband. And when Cath went down to the Spar, Flea would hand her twenty quid and never asked for receipts, so she had quite a nice line going, putting a few pounds aside for herself.

And they all had these posh jobs Cath had never heard of before: Michael worked in commercial property and the other dads were stockbrokers and barristers, all driving big pricey cars. She hadn't a clue what it was they actually did all day but they were clearly doing very nicely for themselves.

When Cath questioned Michael about his job over breakfast, he looked delighted to tell her. He explained how he and his partners bought and refurbished office space before renting it out for more money, and how it was all about yield per square foot. He said they had more than forty London properties in their portfolio, which they acquired and disposed of at regular intervals. Most were offices, but there were shops and restaurants too. Michael said he was negotiating to buy the old Wandsworth ambulance station to turn into retail space and thirty residential units. When she looked interested and asked more questions, Michael said, 'Most people find my job jolly boring. Flea and Annabel yawn whenever I mention it.' But Cath's interest was sincere. She thought, *This is how people get rich.*

On the eleventh morning, Michael said to Annabel and Cath, 'All right, you girls, who's for a windsurfing lesson?'

Annabel had taken lessons the previous summer but Cath had never tried it before.

'We'll get you a wetsuit then,' he told Cath. 'You'll freeze without one.'

Michael and Cath strolled together the length of the beach to the hire shack, Annabel promising to catch them up in twenty minutes. The hire shack was a laid-back enterprise run by two blond surfers. Rails of wetsuits stood on sandy floorboards, with a modesty curtain strung across one corner as a fitting room.

'We need to find this young lady a wetsuit,' Michael announced. 'Do you know what size you are, Cath?'

Cath wasn't sure, so Michael and the other surfers picked wetsuits from the rail and held them up against her. 'It needs to fit comfortably so it doesn't rub,' Michael declared, his hands brushing against Cath's breasts.

Eventually she took a wetsuit to try on and carried it behind the curtain. A length of mirror was leant up against the wall and there was a chair for clothes. She stripped off and struggled into the rubber suit, tugging it up her legs and over her bottom and hips. It felt very tight, like squeezing into a washing-up glove. As she rolled it up towards her breasts, she became conscious of Michael peering at her through a gap in the curtain, eyes bulging with curiosity. Without saying a word, she jerked the curtain shut.

Michael rented a windsurfer and took them to a sheltered part of the bay, close to the headland. He taught them how to drag themselves onto the board and pull the sail up by the rope, hand over hand, and how to trim the sail by moving the boom back and forth. He held Cath around the waist and helped her up, and trod water next to her when she attempted to do it herself.

'Mind my asking who Callum is?' he enquired at one point, staring at her arm. 'I don't mean to be nosy.'

'No one who matters.' She shrugged.

'I feel like a spider caught in your web,' he said later, holding her waist on the tattoo above her bikini. 'I keep thinking my fingers will get caught.'

'It's the fly, not the spider what gets caught, isn't it?' Cath replied.

At what precise moment did she realise Michael fancied her? At the hire shack? The previous night at the barbecue? Or earlier still, during the car journey south or at sports day? Cath reckoned you always knew, even before anything happened. In her experience, most blokes were up for it anyway, given the slightest encouragement.

They were standing up to their waists, fifty yards out from the beach, Annabel clambering up on to the board and kicking her legs while Michael and Cath steadied it. Cath could feel the small roll of fat above Michael's swimming trunks pressing into her back; his face was very close to hers, the stubble on his chin where he'd missed a section shaving, the thicket of clipped dark hair in his nostrils. His arms were surprisingly muscular; not the gym-pumped biceps of Callum, but toned nonetheless. Annabel heaved herself upright and was holding onto the sail which slowly filled with wind and began moving across the bay. 'Well done, Annabel,' Michael called. 'Good girl . . . keep your balance, try a tack now . . .'

Alone in the ocean, with Annabel several hundred yards away into the bay, Michael and Cath paddled slowly back to shore together.

Cath asked, 'Mr Goode, with these restaurants you have, do you get to eat in them for free?'

Michael laughed. 'Sadly not. Though they do generally find me a good table when I want one.'

On the beach they could see Flea setting out the picnic with Davina

Peverel. Tommy Goode and Max Peverel were playing French cricket. Michael said, 'If you want to visit one of the restaurants, I could take you one day if you're interested. Let me know when you're next up in town.'

'Really? Thanks, Mr Goode. I might just take you up on that.'

'It's Michael, Cath,' said Michael. 'No need for this Mr Goode business. Makes me feel ancient.'

That evening, after the barbecue, Flea announced she was tired and would be having an early night. Annabel and a group of St Mary's friends were heading out to a pub called the Mariners, frequented by boys from Radley, Charterhouse and Eton. Annabel was keen Cath should accompany them – 'It will help us get served' – but Cath said she needed to finish clearing up, then take a shower and wash her hair which was matted from sea water. The St Mary's girls spent more than an hour getting beautified for their pub outing, while Cath made a big show of collecting up plates and glasses from around the garden before loading and setting off the dishwasher. Michael was in the lounge in front of the television with a can of Tennent's, watching football.

Cath took a long shower. She still found the concept of unlimited hot water novel and luxurious; in her parents' flat in Paulsgrove you had to feed the electric with coins and there were seldom any to hand. The utility companies had felt like the enemy, threatening to cut off supply at any moment. How often as a child had she stood guardian at the front door against bailiff or engineer, insisting her mum or dad were out while they hid away in the kitchen, to prevent the gas being disconnected, or the TV or settee being repossessed?

She washed with extra care, using the gels and shampoos that spilled out from Annabel's sponge bag with the pattern of strawberries on it. Then she slipped into the pyjama top and knickers she wore to sleep in, put her wet hair up in a towel turban, and went into the kitchen to make a cup of tea. She was waiting for the kettle to boil when Michael appeared in search of beer.

'I thought I heard someone in here,' he said. 'I couldn't think who it was. The teenagers aren't back yet?' Finding Cath in knickers and pyjama top made him awkward.

'They're down the Mariners,' Cath replied.

'And the younger ones?'

'Asleep. I checked them earlier. I think Mrs Goode's asleep too.'

'Said she's tired. God knows why, she's been on holiday for two weeks.'

'Want a tea? The kettle just boiled.'

'I've got a beer, but thank you for the offer. Not every day an attractive lady offers to make me a cuppa.'

Then he said, 'I hope you're not bored down here, Cath. There's not a lot to do, no funfairs or piers like you've got at home.'

Cath said she was fine. 'I'm enjoying myself.'

'Good. That's good.' He seemed distracted, which he was, having just spotted the spider's web tattoo rising above her stretched white knickers as she bent forward to add a teaspoon to the dishwasher.

'Didn't you want to go out for a drink with the others? Annabel and her friends love that pub, it's the place to meet boys, apparently.'

Cath shrugged. 'It's fine. They're a bit young, those lads, just schoolboys.'

Michael experienced a frisson of excitement, which he did his best to suppress. 'I hope Rosie and Tommy aren't exhausting you. You've been such a star, playing with them on the beach. Tommy thinks you're the bee's knees, with your tattoos and everything.'

In fact, Tommy Goode had shown no interest in Cath's tattoos; that honour belonged to his father and Mr Peverel.

Cath turned and faced him. 'Everyone's been really nice. Especially you, Mr Goode . . . I mean, Michael.'

'I'm glad you feel that. We want you to feel part of our family.' His eyes kept straying towards her knickers, the tattoos, the flat stomach. It was confusing: her sweet, pretty young face, but something hard-bitten and worldly, as though she was waiting for him to say or do something, make some move. 'As I say, the children love having you holidaying with us.'

She shrugged. 'They're nice kids. I'm lucky. The way I join in everything, not like a servant.'

'Don't be silly, Cath, it's not like that at all. You're more like . . . our fourth child.'

Cath sat down next to him at the kitchen table, her bare legs tantalisingly close. 'You're a nice bloke, Mr Goode, Michael,' she said, touching his knee. 'We can go next door and screw if you want to.'

Michael swallowed. 'Er, good heavens, Cath. That's very direct. I hardly know what to say.'

'You can say yes.'

His head flooded with lust. 'Well, if you really think it's a good idea . . . I mean, this is hardly the time or the place . . .'

Sighing, she took his hand and half led, half dragged him into the bedroom she shared with Annabel.

The floor between the pine beds was filled with a mound of Annabel's discarded clothes, a suitcase with more clothes lay open on her duvet. Cath pulled Michael's face towards her own and placed his hand on her spider's web tattoo as she dealt with his belt and the buttons of his trousers.

'Christ, Cath,' Michael kept saying. 'I didn't expect this.' And, later, 'Good gracious, Cath. Oh, my God . . . Good grief.'

Cath was grinding away on top of him, seconds away from climax, when the door handle turned and the doorway suddenly filled with people.

Michael jerked his head round to see Annabel and three of her schoolfriends staring at them in horror. Annabel emitted a piercing scream, and by the time Michael had extracted himself from underneath Cath, Flea, Rosie and a groggy-faced Tommy had joined the girls at the door, watching in stunned shock as he danced about from foot to foot, pulling his boxers and cords back on.

Chapter Three

The only thing Michael Goode publicly admitted to disliking about his new situation was lack of wardrobe space. His beautiful bespoke suits and sports jackets hung six-deep on coat hangers from hooks on the back of the bedroom and bathroom doors.

Aside from that one detail, everything was just perfect; he had a whole new lease of life and felt twenty years younger. As he explained to Johnnie Peverel when they met up for a boys' lunch at Foxtrot Oscar, he would never have planned things to turn out this way. It had all been very stressful and difficult, and was still very difficult with Flea and Annabel especially, but the truth was he had never felt happier, and he'd lost a stone and a half in weight, which he put down to the incredible sex. This wasn't to go any further, but Flea had pretty well given up in that department since Tommy was born. But Cath and he were at it like cats in a sack, two or three times a night, most mornings too, and he sometimes dropped home at lunchtimes for a quickie.

'Not wanting to make you envious, Johnnie, but Cath's something else. I mean, I've been married sixteen years and was in Hong Kong with the army, but I've never experienced anything like it.'

He could now see, from his newly imposed perspective, that his marriage to Flea had been growing stale for some time. In the long run, he felt sure, she would come round to the same point of view, and their separation would be for the best. Flea just couldn't see it yet, and was consequently being thoroughly unreasonable and obstructive about everything: the house, children, you name it. She wouldn't even allow him to collect his wine from the cellar in Napier Avenue, despite being virtually teetotal herself.

The early weeks had been the worst. Michael still shuddered

thinking about them. All through that first night after the family had surprised him and Cath on the job, Flea had wept and railed at him, demanding to know how long it had all been going on, and how could he even think of doing something like that *under our own roof* and in his *own daughter's bedroom too*? To which Michael had no answer, his avowals that it had never happened before and it had been a moment of madness being furiously dismissed by Flea, who could see it all now: the carefully contrived plan to bring *that girl* down to Rock and infiltrate her into the family holiday. It did not help that Michael also hadn't quite reached climax with Cath when they'd all burst in, so he felt irritable and bothered, and conscious of unfinished business rubbing inside his cords.

Annabel's schoolfriends had slunk tactfully away, no doubt to broadcast eyewitness accounts of what they'd witnessed throughout Rock, from whence it would spread down the various networks which criss-crossed their social world: the St Mary's school grapevine of pupils and parents, thence to their friends, neighbours, Michael's work colleagues, his cricket team (he played most Saturdays during the summer for a team called the Gentleman Players), his old army muckers (he had done national service as an officer in the Green Jackets), and so on and so forth, spreading onwards and outwards like a nuclear cloud until every person he had ever met, or would ever be likely to meet, would have heard about Michael Goode being caught in flagrante by his wife and children and their schoolfriends, going at it hammer and tongs with a tattooed au pair girl in their rented holiday house in Cornwall.

Annabel had dissolved into hysterics. Michael tried to comfort her but she'd shaken him off, not wanting him to touch her. Flea had eventually sent her off to bed but Cath was already asleep – sound asleep – in the shared bedroom, and Annabel refused to sleep in there with her and dragged her duvet to the sofa. This was the same sofa Flea had already told Michael to sleep on, so he lay down without blankets on the foam cushions in the sun room and slept not a wink. In the morning, Rosie and Tommy were found to have gravitated into the same bed, Rosie having cried all night long, but Tommy was seemingly unmoved by the night's events and asked to be taken to the beach. Flea worried his lack of emotion meant he had internalised the shock, which could have lifelong consequences.

Annabel refused to sit at the breakfast table with her father, or to touch the eggs and grilled bacon which Cath, bold as brass, was producing at the stove.

Flea, who normally breakfasted in her dressing gown, appeared in the kitchen fully dressed.

'I hope you realise this holiday is ending immediately,' she announced for Michael's benefit. She opened the cutlery drawer, took out a spoon, and slammed the drawer shut. Then she lifted a pan from the stove and flung it into the sink. 'We will return to London the minute we're packed.'

Tommy looked horrified. 'Why, Mum? We've got another whole week here, haven't we?'

Flea ignored him. 'And don't think she's coming in the car either, Michael. I'm not sitting for six hours on the motorway with *her* in the back.'

'I want to stay *here*,' said Tommy.

'We *all* wanted to stay,' said Flea. 'But your father's made that impossible. So we're going back to London. Hurry up and finish your breakfast, Tommy, and you can go and pack. A lot of your stuff's in the utility room.'

Michael began, 'Darling, is this really necessary? It's the children's summer holiday—'

'You should have thought of that, shouldn't you? Before behaving like that.' She slammed the lid on the bread bin. 'In front of the children too. I'll never forgive you. And with that common little trollop.' She glared at Cath.

Michael, exhausted, realised that in those few moments of ghastly discovery his life had altered, possibly irretrievably. He felt terrible remorse for the pain he'd caused to his wife and children, and longed to turn the clock back, to make things right again. That he had behaved wrongly he accepted absolutely. He had deep reserves of affection for Felicity and hated seeing her like this – the anger, her unhappy, hollow eyes. And he felt ashamed by the hurt in the faces of his beloved daughters. He wanted to throw his arms around them and comfort them.

But at the same time – and in some respects more urgently – he wanted to comfort Cath. He had no idea what it was that she was feeling. He didn't want her to think he had instantly cast her aside, or that his refusal to stick up for her against Flea ('that common trollop') meant he tacitly agreed with her assessment. He worried he must be losing Cath's respect, the action man of the previous day recast as henpecked, appeasing husband. Even in the midst of the crisis, he realised he was still strongly attracted to her. Lifting a slice of toast to his lips, he could smell her on his fingers. Watching her now, dabbing rashers of bacon with kitchen towel to remove the grease as Flea had taught her to do, Michael knew his infatuation was not over. His regret lay overwhelmingly in being caught, and in the effect upon his family, not in the offence itself. Given the opportunity to finish what had started the previous night, he would have leapt at it.

At Flea's insistence, he dropped Cath at Bodmin Parkway and purchased her a single ticket up to London. The ride to the station was mostly undertaken in silence. Michael asked, 'Can I get you a through ticket to Portsmouth?'

'London's fine.' She shrugged. 'There's nothing back home for me.'

'OK, London then. Have you somewhere to stay?'

'I'll manage.'

'I'm awfully sorry about all this.' He sighed. 'Jesus, Cath, I don't think Flea will ever forgive me. Or Annabel. It's crucifying. I don't know what'll happen.'

'Annabel's a nice kid,' Cath said. 'She'll get over it. My dad shagged anything that came along, whenever he got the chance.'

'Yes, well, I don't want you to think I'm like that. What happened . . . that was the first and only time I've been unfaithful to Felicity, I want you to know that.'

She made a face. 'Up to you. Not being bitchy, but most blokes married to Mrs Goode wouldn't be so choosy.'

They arrived at the station and Michael fumbled in his wallet for money for the ticket and to pay her wages for the holiday. 'Here's what we'd have owed you for the full three weeks. And I've added a bit extra.'

Cath accepted the money without saying anything.

'Will I see you, Cath? I don't know how to find you.'

'Me neither. I can't exactly show up at yours.'

'No, don't do that.' He blanched. 'Tell you what, there's a pub in the Fulham Road. The Goat in Boots. Near the cinema at the

Beaufort Street end. I sometimes drop by for a drink after work. Six p.m. most evenings. That's the best place to find me.'

'I'll remember that.' But she said it without conviction, and Michael drove back to Rock and his family with heavy heart.

Arriving home at Napier Avenue after the torturous no-speaks drive from Cornwall, Michael unloaded the Mercedes, assisted by Tommy who was the sole member of the family not crying, sulking or pointedly avoiding him. By the time they had stowed the surfboards, picnic blankets and beach equipment in their storage places, Flea had taken herself up to bed, the door firmly shut against him. Michael slept in his dressing room and wondered where Cath was spending the night.

Cath was, in fact, sitting up all night on a bench inside Paddington station. Having arrived there with her suitcase, she'd dragged it around the hotels in Praed Street behind the station but they'd all either been full or way too expensive. She wasn't paying nine quid for a bed in a fleapit! So she'd gone back to the station with its buffet and burger bars, where there were seats to sit down on, and wondered what to do. She knew nobody in London, had little money, and the city felt large and threatening and teeming with people in a hurry. She wondered what Annabel's dad was doing now, eating a nice hot meal probably, cooked by his bitch of a wife. She liked Michael, he was a nice man, but she didn't expect to see him again. Realistically, it wasn't going to happen, not if Flea had anything to do with it.

After it turned dark and the crowds thinned out, it became chilly and scary sitting there. Now her companions were mostly drunks and tramps. There was a pub in the corner of the station concourse with a jukebox playing records: Abba's 'The Winner Takes It All', and 'Don't Stand So Close To Me' by the Police. And, frequently, 'House of Fun' by Madness. 'Welcome to the house of fun, now I've come of age . . .' Yeah, quite.

She was afraid to sleep in case someone nicked her luggage. More than once, sleazy-looking blokes tried to engage her in conversation – 'You all right, darling?' – and she tried to avoid making eye contact. Every couple of hours she bought a paper cup of coffee from a stall. She thought about her mum and Callum in Portsmouth, and then a fury rose inside her, and she felt like thumping them. No way was she going back there; she'd sooner stop here in the station.

The next morning, bleary from lack of sleep, she got talking to some Dutch students who told her about a YWCA up near Russell Square where you could get a bed in a dormitory for two quid a night, plus a locker to leave your luggage. So she found her way on the tube and slept twelve hours, oblivious to the comings and goings of other backpackers, then bought a meal in Tottenham Court Road. She wondered what Michael was doing and whether to call him up, but what if Flea answered the phone? Or Annabel, who hadn't said goodbye when she'd fled Rock.

The morning after his return to London, Michael got up early and went into his office in Mayfair. His secretary was surprised to see him, ten days sooner than expected. He made some comment about needing to get back, shut his office door and spent the day waiting for six o'clock to come around. Sharply on the hour he parked himself at one of the wooden tables outside the pub and waited. In his late twenties and early thirties, Michael had been something of a regular at the Goat in Boots, but had scarcely entered the place in fifteen years. He had named it as a rendezvous to Cath because it was the first place he could think of that might work. Now he wasn't so sure. The pub was heaving with customers and he felt conspicuous sitting alone at a table and wished he'd brought a newspaper. He was worried, too, that a friend might spot him, and even try to join him, and how then could he explain Cath, if she showed up?

After an hour and a half he gave up and went home. Flea had already eaten supper with the children, the house had an atmosphere of mourning. He realised he hadn't eaten all day, so fetched cheese and salami from the fridge and turned on the television in the study. No sooner had he done so than Flea came in and switched it off. Her shoulder-length blond hair was scraped back from her face in an Alice band. Her once soft features now struck Michael as hard and accusatory.

'I want you to be straight with me,' she said. 'How long has all this been going on? I need to know.' There followed a circular argument full of denials and recriminations, of the kind already familiar and destined to become a nightly occurrence. Michael slunk off to bed, drained and alone, consumed by guilt and dreams of tattoos.

On the fourth evening at the Goat in Boots, Cath showed up with her suitcase. 'Mine's a Pernod and black, Mr Goode.'

His delight at seeing her surprised him. She looked shockingly sexy in a tight black sundress with the Callum tattoo on full view. He had almost forgotten how good her figure was.

They sat drinking outside at a wooden table until closing time, then ate at the Greek restaurant next door, Wine and Kebab.

'Have you somewhere to stay?' he asked her.

She shook her head.

He drove her to a hotel in West Kensington he'd noticed in the past, with a banner outside advertising rooms for low prices. It transpired that those particular rooms were all taken but a superior room was available, which Michael paid for. He carried her suitcase upstairs. The room stank of cigarettes but was otherwise fit for purpose, with a big sagging bed. There was a wardrobe with deep scratches down the front, and tea-making facilities on a tray: kettle and basket of sugar, sweetener and mini cartons of UHT milk. Cath, who had never stayed in a hotel before in her life, was thrilled by the novelty of it all, the en-suite bathroom and toiletries. Michael wrinkled his nose at the cigarette smell and hoped this wasn't all too sordid.

Of course, they both understood what would happen long before they had inspected the room.

'This time let's hope your wife and kids don't muscle in,' Cath said, leading him to the bed.

Chapter Four

Cath liked the new flat at once. The entrance lay between an electrical shop and a wine bar on Hollywood Road, the flat occupying the back half of the second floor, overlooking a vista of other people's backyards and gardens. Michael had found it through a contact in the lettings world, and they moved in almost at once, within a few days of their reunion at the Goat in Boots. Michael felt it was on the small side but Cath considered it spacious, with a lounge, galley kitchen, bathroom and bedroom.

For the first fortnight they scarcely had more than the clothes they stood up in, Michael having exited Napier Avenue with an overnight bag. That first weekend, whenever they weren't in bed, they were shopping for clothes. Michael took her to the King's Road, and later to Jermyn Street. Cath was entranced by the glamour of the shops and shopfronts, the wide streets, the imposing buildings of the capital. They drove along Piccadilly, down Pall Mall, past Buckingham Palace and Whitehall and the Houses of Parliament, then back through the stucco canyons of Belgravia and Kensington. At every turn, Michael told her about the different areas and the people who lived there. They passed expensive-looking restaurants in the Fulham Road which he promised to take her to, and pointed out the homes of friends and the pubs and bars he had frequented before his marriage. But after an hour or two, they always returned to the flat and their bedroom overlooking other people's back gardens.

In due course, and after many tense and protracted negotiations, Flea consented to the principle of Michael retrieving more of his clothes and certain specified belongings from Napier Avenue, and a time was agreed when she and the children would vacate the house for a couple of hours so this could be accomplished without any danger of interaction. Annabel was refusing even to speak to her father, let alone see him. Michael took Cath with him to his old abode, to assist him in loading up the Mercedes with his brogues, suits, golf bag and cricket bats, as well as certain pictures and team photographs which indisputably reflected Michael's taste more than Flea's, and would not detract from the completeness of the family home.

On her earlier fleeting visit to the house, Cath had penetrated no further than the front steps, so she had not appreciated the size and comfort of the Goodes' home. Now, as she followed Michael across the glazed tiled floor of the Victorian hall and into a succession of light, bright reception rooms, she knew she had never been anywhere so posh. The place was like something you saw on TV, furnished with matching sofas and armchairs, and small tables covered with tablecloths with patterns of rosebuds and exotic birds, and dozens of family photographs in silver frames; photographs of the kids on holiday in Rock, school photos of them in uniform – including one of Annabel in her St Mary's green cloak – one of Michael and Flea on horses in Arizona wearing cowboy hats. Each room was painted different colours: primrose yellows and powder pinks and sky blues. There were vases filled with flower arrangements, and china ornaments of dogs and pigs on the mantelpiece, and a big squashy stool covered with magazines in front of the fireplace. Some of the furniture was antique and smelt of beeswax, like the furniture in the shops in Petworth. French doors in the living room led out to a long narrow garden with a children's playhouse and a trampoline; the grass of the lawn had grown long, probably because Michael wasn't there to mow it. Cath picked up a framed photograph of a handsome man and a pretty bride on their wedding day, emerging from a church under a tunnel of swords held aloft by soldiers, and Cath recognised the bride and groom as Michael and Flea.

She followed Michael upstairs into the master bedroom with its glazed chintz pink and white bedspread, fastidiously arranged with cushions in size order, and a frilly chintz canopy above the bed like in a kid's book. Cath tried to imagine Michael and Flea doing it in that bed, but couldn't; not under the gaze of three sugary pastel portraits of their children in oval frames.

She thought of her old bedroom in Paulsgrove without even a proper bed, just a mattress on the floor and no bedside cabinets or lamps or dressing tables. And no frilly skirt thing round the edge of the bed to conceal the mattress. There was a proper word for them, it would come to her. *Valance*. That was it, a valance. Well, they'd never had those either.

Michael was loading up the car with boxes of files and a leather chair and lamp from his study. He lifted down from the lavatory wall framed photographs of school teams and a parade of officers in Catterick. Now he retrieved two large suitcases from a boxroom, opened them on the floor and began filling them with suits on wooden coat hangers and piles of ironed shirts from a chest of drawers. All his shirts were the same, Cath reckoned: whites, blues and pink stripes. She watched him place a pair of ivory-backed hairbrushes into the suitcase, then a bowl of assorted cufflinks, and half a dozen pairs of polished brogues into shoe bags, followed by spiked cricket shoes, rugby boots and golf shoes. Item by item, she watched Michael pack up twenty years of clobber.

She wandered into the bathroom, taking in the mirrored walls, the big white towels on a heated chrome towel rail, the neatly aligned hand towels. On a shelf beside the bath sat a green ceramic frog, the top of its head filled with bath crystals. Flea had more pots of moisturisers than anyone she'd ever seen; they were lined up around a box of tissues in a frilly cover on the vanity unit, with assorted atomisers of perfume and tiny heart-shaped silver photograph frames of the children. Cath turned the shower handle and a torrent of hot water cascaded down.

On impulse, she stripped off and stepped under the shower, having first pulled on Flea's pink and white shower cap. She lathered herself in gel and scrubbed herself with Flea's loofah shaped like the husk of a giant corn cob, and dried off with a fluffy white towel. Inspecting herself from all angles in a wall of mirrors, she decided London was suiting her: she looked lean and fit. Spotting a pair of nail scissors, she trimmed her bush, tufts of pubic hair floating down onto the pile carpet. Still wearing the bath cap, and naked apart from the fluffy white slippers she had stepped into by the bath, Cath strolled back into the bedroom. Michael was struggling to close the second suitcase, over-packed with skiing jumpers.

'For heaven's sake, Cath. You've not been using Flea's bathroom? She hates even the children going in there.'

'What d'ya reckon?' Cath said, giving him a twirl. 'Does Mr Goode like what he sees?'

Mr Goode did like. But he also knew Flea could arrive back in twenty minutes, and he had promised to be packed and gone by then, it was a condition. 'Get dressed, quickly, Cath. They'll be back any minute, we have to clear out of here.'

'But I've been preparing myself for you. I'm all washed up and smelling like the perfume counter in Allders.'

'Cath . . . Not now. We'll be back at the flat soon if we hurry.'

'I want you here, Michael. In your own bed. Now.'

'Absolutely not. Out of the question.' But she heard him waver.

Cath tugged back the perfectly smoothed bedcover and Flea's folded nightie flew out from beneath a pillow.

'She's going to know . . . she puffs up the pillows in a certain way . . .'

Cath opened her mouth and drew him towards her. As ever, when he spotted the Callum tattoo, Michael felt a surge of competitiveness. Whoever Callum might once have been in her life, he didn't wish to underperform him.

'This is madness,' was Michael's final caution as he slipped into his marital bed beside her.

Soon afterwards, he said, 'You should find one in the drawer there.'

Afterwards, Michael considered it unlikely the hastily remade bed would satisfy Flea when she returned. But, by then, he was intent only on quitting the premises before his wife showed up.

As they pulled away from the kerb in the laden Mercedes, he glimpsed his estranged family in the distance, turning into Napier Avenue on foot from the direction of the Hurlingham Club.

Cath loved her new life. Her previous lives in Portsmouth and at St Mary's already seemed hazy and distant, and could scarcely be compared to her present ritzy existence with Annabel's dad. Almost every night they ate out in Italian restaurants, sometimes with male friends of Michael's, and there was wine and sambuca and waiters who fussed over them and ground pepper over their pasta from giant pepper grinders. These restaurants, with names like San Frediano and Meridiana, were noisy and filled with glamorous people, but however full they were there was always a good table for Michael. On one of their first evenings, the head waiter had exclaimed, 'Hey, *ciao*, nice to see you again, Michael, and your beautiful daughter too,' and he bustled off and returned with complimentary glasses of Prosecco.

Sometimes they ate at a place named Foxtrot Oscar on the Royal Hospital Road where Michael knew the owner, another Michael, and in fact knew most of the customers too. They sat upstairs eating hamburgers and crab cakes and he pointed people out to her: 'That man's just bought the old Citroën garage on the Brompton Road in a three-million-plus deal'; 'See that blonde sitting with the Arab gentleman? She used to live with George Best'; and so on, all of which Cath found thrilling, making her feel part of the in-crowd. Sometimes they joined other tables for coffee and more drinks, and Michael always proudly introduced her – 'This is Cath Fox, my friend from Portsmouth' – and his friends accepted her as part of their set and congratulated Michael on his new date. 'I hear Michael found you sewing on name-tapes at his daughter's school,' they'd say. Or else, 'You should have seen the matrons at my old preparatory school in Broadstairs – nothing like you, sweetheart, worst luck.' As the evenings wore on, some of Michael's friends would surreptitiously place their hands on her knee, or higher, and she would playfully push them away – naughty, naughty, for taking advantage. They liked Cath because she was sexy and unexpected and made them laugh. It was amusing to see Michael with such an unsuitable woman, because he'd grown a bit dull with Flea.

Occasionally, when Michael introduced her to married couples he knew, Cath felt some frost, especially from the women. 'Give my love to *Flea*,' one of them said, pointedly, 'when you next see her.'

'Bitch,' said Cath when she was still within earshot, retreating with Michael to their own table.

Beyond making love and going out to dinner in restaurants, Cath's days were somewhat empty, but this did not especially trouble her. After sex, Michael slipped away to his office, and Cath dozed off back to sleep. The afternoons she spent exploring the shops of London, gradually becoming familiar with the geography of Fulham, Chelsea and Kensington. Having no money, other than when Michael accompanied her, she spent very little: she would see what was on the rails, try things on, and sometimes just sit on a bench in the King's Road, smoking a fag and watching the world go by. This perpetual shortage of cash, even for cigarettes, sometimes irked her. She considered finding a job but when she mentioned the idea to Michael he discouraged it – he liked his daytime trysts, which would not have been possible were she working. Once or twice Cath eyed the pewter dish filled with gold and silver cufflinks on his dressing table, but knew he would miss them if she sold any, since he liked to rotate them.

She did not put in much effort in Hollywood Road. You could not have described Cath as a home-maker, and it did not occur to her to wash or iron Michael's shirts, vacuum the carpets, or make the bed with any conviction. The sink was often piled high with coffee cups and plates, the fridge empty of food. When she'd visited Napier Avenue with Michael to collect his stuff, Cath had been transfixed by the huge gun-metal fridge-freezer in Flea's kitchen, like something out of *Dynasty*, its shelves filled to bursting with quiches, chicken and supplies. It struck her as unjust that Mrs Goode should have everything her way – the immaculate big house and full fridge – when she, Cath, did not. Michael seemed not to care, dropping off his laundry at Sketchley's and taking Cath out to eat.

Weekends were more eventful and Cath looked forward to them. They drove up to Silverstone to watch motor racing and had lunch with a lot of blokes in a VIP tent. They watched rugby at Twickenham and had tea in a VIP area. When the cricket season restarted they drove all over the south of England to different grounds where Michael's team was playing. Cath found she got on well with the girlfriends of the other players, less well with their standoffish wives. One Saturday the team played a match at Pulborough, close to Petworth, and Cath felt uncomfortable at the memory of that period of her life.

Another time the fixture was at Waterlooville, not ten miles from Portsmouth.

Michael said, 'Portsmouth's just down the road. We're very close. I can easily drive you in if you like.'

'Why would we want to do that?'

'You've got family there, haven't you? We could call on them, I'm sure they'd like to see you.'

'I'm not bothered.'

'Well I am. I'd love to meet them.'

'Too bad you're not going to.'

Guessing she might be ashamed of her relatives, he said, 'You've met my family, Flea and so on. It doesn't matter what they're like, I don't mind. It would be nice to meet them, that's all.'

'Shut up about it, won't you? You're not meeting them, OK. Not ever. They're not part of my life any more.' No way was she introducing Michael to her mum, or letting him find out about Jess. Or meet Callum. None of them.

'All right, darling. I was only asking. We don't have to visit them. But one day I'd like to, that's all I'm saying.'

'Don't even think about it. You're pissing me off asking. Just drive, OK?'

And Cath withdrew inside herself, refusing to say another word until they reached London.

Another source of conflict was Michael's children and their refusal to see him (apart from Tommy) which made him frustrated and sad. He blamed Felicity for withholding them, though she insisted Annabel and Rosie took that decision for themselves and she did not influence them one way or the other. Until visitation terms were agreed as part of a divorce settlement – Michael and Flea were only separated, the juggernaut of divorce yet to get rolling – Flea said she would not force the girls to see their father if they didn't wish to, and so long as he remained with *that girl* she doubted they would change their minds.

'You realise you're a laughing stock?' she told her husband. 'People are laughing about it all over London. She's the same age as your daughter, for God's sake. And covered head to toe in tattoos! And speaking of disgusting habits, please tell your teenage mistress not to cut her pubes on my bathroom carpet.'

Annabel secretly missed Cath, though their friendship had not been an intimate or equal one, more of a one-sided hero worship on Annabel's part, which added to her sense of betrayal. The two people Annabel most admired, her dad and her role model, were now shacked up together – in a *love nest* – and she couldn't, *wouldn't* see either of them. When Tommy went off to spend Sundays with his dad, Annabel quizzed him afterwards on every detail, particularly over whether Cath had joined them for any part of the day, such as tea at Tootsies; she wanted to know everything, to fuel her misery and feeling of displacement.

*

Only occasionally did Cath dwell on her old life in Portsmouth, and when she did it was like watching a slideshow of photographs of some event long ago, which she had certainly attended but which had lost its power to connect. Maybe part of this came because she'd managed to escape; no one else left the island city, she was like Liza Radley in that song by the Jam which they played all the time in Nero's. When she thought of Paulsgrove now, it was of the hard pubs along Allaway Avenue, the Portsdown Inn, the Beehive, the Clacton, where no one dared enter unless they lived locally; she thought of Arundel Street where the big stores were, Fosters, Colliers, Chelsea Girl, where she'd started her shoplifting with her mates; and the clubs she used to hang out in, Joanna's on the seafront, the Honky Tonk and Granny's in the Tricorn centre. And Nero's, obviously.

She'd stood on Portsdown Hill just before her sixteenth birthday – the view from the estate was of the whole of Portsmouth, the Solent, the Isle of Wight beyond – and watched the *Ark Royal* sail out of the harbour on its way to the Falklands. All the schools in Pompey had been closed for the day, that many kids were wanting to wave the task force off. But by then, of course, she was seeing Callum. And the baby was nearly due.

She could see him stood there now on the door at Nero's, the biggest club in the city, opposite Clarence Pier. Normally she steered clear because it cost a fiver to get in; she'd been in Joanna's along the front with some girlfriends hoping to pick up some skates for free drinks. But they'd chanced their luck afterwards at Nero's, and she clocked Callum at once – big with muscles and a cheeky grin. She knew several girls who'd got with Callum: he was a local legend. She knew her mum would kill her if she messed with him, which was funny considering what happened later. Anyway, her mum didn't find out for the best part of a year. She was working nights up at the Queen Alexandra hospital on Portsdown Hill, so she wasn't about to know. And her dad, who worked in the dockyard or at Vosper Thornycroft when he wasn't inside, wouldn't be out again for two years, even with remission. So that's how it had begun with Callum; first in the toilets at Nero's, thereafter at his.

She wondered who Callum was seeing now, there was sure to be someone, several probably. She hoped it wasn't still her mum. She wondered too if he saw anything of Jess. She doubted it. Jess wasn't his first kid, and he hadn't bothered with the others.

Almost the only time she missed Callum was in the sack. Michael was OK, she had no complaints, but Callum was a beast and a bastard, and they'd had some great times together for all that.

One aspect of living with Michael was that all the people they socialised with were much older than Cath was herself. It wasn't a huge deal because she'd always been with older guys – Callum had been twenty-six when they'd started, almost twice her age. Michael's friends were mostly in their early fifties and talked about things that had happened before she was even born. She got fed up listening to their old stories. It wouldn't have mattered if Michael had still been anything like the person portrayed in their tales of nightclubs and drinking. In fact, he was quite boring and predictable. When he took off his tie he rolled it up in this neat little coil like a rattlesnake, round and round, and laid it carefully in his tie drawer with all his other coiled neckwear. He said it prevented them from creasing.

When they walked together up the King's Road, Michael in his mustard-coloured cords, he would point out doorways which had long ago been the entrances to clubs he'd once frequented, and his eyes lit up at the memory. 'See that door there, Cath? You rang that intercom and went down some stairs into a basement called Francoise, known as Frankie's. Fantastic place, I went several times a month. Full of gorgeous women.' But these nightclubs had long ago closed down and been taken over by other ventures altogether, and Michael seldom had the energy to go clubbing now. On Saturday evenings after he'd played cricket, he carefully oiled his bat with linseed oil. And, by the start of their second year together, he became less forgiving of the untidiness of the flat, and testy at the lack of food in the fridge. He complained it was expensive eating out in restaurants every night.

The girlfriends of Michael's mates were twenty years older than Cath, and more insecure than they'd first appeared. At the cricket and motor racing, they confided in her that they longed for children, but it was difficult and they were trying to become pregnant without telling their lovers. Cath thought of Jess and the careless ease with which she'd been conceived. She reckoned her mum would be taking care of her. Sometimes Cath wondered what she'd be like now – she must be almost two, getting quite grown-up – and felt a moment's regret. But the occasions on which she thought about Jess were not frequent, and quickly passed.

As her birthday approached on April 23rd, Cath wondered what Michael might get her for a present. She had seen a pendant in an antiques market in the King's Road, a silver skull on a chain, which she intended to direct him towards. One evening, shortly before the birthday, he returned from work with a small gift-wrapped parcel in his briefcase; Cath spotted it when he removed the evening newspaper from it. Each evening he bought the *Evening Standard* at a newsagent close to his office, folded it in his briefcase, and read it when he got home. Although Cath was disappointed not to be getting the skull pendant, she was pleased he'd remembered, and wondered what the gold-ribboned box might contain. Later, Michael said, 'I've got to go out for a bit, Cath. I'll be about half an hour.'

'Where are you going?'

'It's Annabel's birthday on Friday, she's going to be nineteen. I'm dropping her a present through the letterbox at Napier Avenue.'

'Excuse me. You are kidding me?' Cath blazed with anger. 'You mean that fucking gift in your briefcase, all gift-wrapped, isn't even for me? It's my bloody birthday on Friday too, you realise. Not just Annabel's.'

'Darling, I'm so sorry. I was going to get you something nice, I promise.'

'I doubt that. You'd forgotten about it. You care more about Annabel than me.'

'That's not fair or true. Really, Cath. And I'll get you something good, you'll love it.'

'I'd better. I really had better.'

The next day Michael bought her the skull necklace. But the after-glow of the argument, and the things said in anger, took longer to blow away.

After that they started to argue and fight more often. There were scenes in restaurants when Michael complained again about the cost, and asked why she couldn't cook supper at home sometimes, like Flea used to. And Annabel reproached him for lack of vigour in bed. 'I got twice as good sex as this in Pompey.'

Cath had recently taken to using Michael's family membership at Hurlingham. Michael wished that she wouldn't since the club, with its acres of tennis courts and croquet lawns, was so close to the family home and unofficially understood to be Flea's territory in the separation. But Cath found Michael's membership pass, which permitted family to use the facilities, and Cath reckoned she was more than family, being his live-in partner. Besides, she loved to swim. In Portsmouth, she'd regularly swum at the leisure centre with its slides and water chutes. The pool at Hurlingham was more sedate but she enjoyed it. And it gave her a kick to see the faces of the other members at the pool staring at her tattoos.

She emerged from the ladies' changing room and padded through the shallow footbath which led to the pool. She was wearing her black bikini which showed her body art to best advantage: the spider's web up her lower back and the scorpion on her thigh. She lingered for a moment on the side, enjoying the hostile stares, and dived into the water.

She was on her second length when she spotted Flea glaring at her, hatred in her eyes. Cath considered ignoring her, but then, instead, gave her the finger.

Flea completed another length before hauling herself out at the steps. Look at the arse on that, Cath thought, watching her walk towards the changing room in her flowery costume.

Five minutes later, an official appeared at the side of the pool. 'Er, young lady, miss. If you could swim over to the side one moment. Are you entitled to use the club?' Cath said she was a guest of Mr Goode. 'I'm afraid it's family members only,' the official apologised. 'I'm very sorry, miss, but I'm going to have to ask you to stop swimming and get out.'

It was exactly one week later, shortly after her nineteenth birthday, that Michael told Cath he had decided to return to his family. He was full of apologies but he wanted to give his marriage a final chance. 'Flea and I go back a long way,' he said. 'I think there could still be something worth hanging on to.

'And there's the children to think of,' he added. 'The girls are still very upset, Annabel especially. I'm sorry, Cath, but I've got to give it another go.'

He said he would be moving back in to Napier Avenue that night. 'But this flat's paid for until the end of next month, so of course you're welcome to stay until then.'

Chapter Five

Jobless, manless and all but penniless in London, Cath evaluated her options. Michael had presented her with two old suitcases as a parting gift, to hasten her departure from Hollywood Road, and these now stood beside her on the pavement filled with the clothes she had accumulated during their twenty months together. In her pocket was £130 in cash, the proceeds from selling three pairs of Michael's cufflinks and his Rolex bracelet watch, which she had confiscated from his collection as a severance payment to herself, at the Antiquarius antiques market. She felt shocked at being dumped, not having seen it coming and having considered herself in control of the relationship. To lose Michael back to Flea was not just an affront to her pride but reawakened all her old insecurities, reminding her how vulnerable her situation was, dependent on the whim of a sugar daddy. She'd enjoyed her time with Michael, and he had introduced her to a world which, once tasted, she didn't wish to leave. How she would manage this, she presently had no idea. But the experience made her determined, and next time she wouldn't blow it either.

Meanwhile, the only people she knew in London were Michael's friends, plus Annabel whom she could hardly call upon. Fleetingly, she considered returning to Portsmouth, but no sooner thought than rejected the idea. She dragged her suitcases as far as Sloane Square and sat on a bench on the paved island and wondered what to do next. She reckoned her money could be made to last ten days if she was careful.

In the window of an Alfred Marks employment bureau she read postcards with jobs on offer, but had no wish to work in a shop or wash up. She had no skills or qualifications, no O levels, let alone A levels, she hadn't learnt to type. She doubted St Mary's would give her much of a reference if she asked for one since she'd bunked off without saying goodbye, and they'd know all about her and Michael Goode. She couldn't imagine Mrs Perse or Mrs Bullock having anything pleasant to say. She couldn't even get about London to look for a job, with two heavy suitcases weighing her down.

Eventually she took a bus to Victoria station and put her stuff in left-luggage. Feeling immediately lighter, she headed through the streets surrounding the station, past the sandwich bars, bureaux de change and mean-looking hotels. She walked wherever the mood took her, this way and that, until she hit Buckingham Palace Road and an area of better-heeled three- and four-star hotels. On impulse, she enquired at reception if they had any jobs and was directed to a rear entrance in a parallel street where she was told there were vacancies for chambermaids. The job came with shared accommodation on the staff floor of the hotel, the cost of which would be deducted from her wages. The assistant manager, a predatory slob named Paul from Wolverhampton, said it would be an experience having an English lass working at the Buckingham Gate Plaza, since the other chambermaids were all Spanish or Portuguese. He said, 'Maybe we can have a bevvy together after work one night,' and winked.

She spent the first day in training, was issued with a brown uniform and a cleaning cart, and worked under the instruction of a senior housekeeper, Ines, servicing the rooms. First they emptied the heavy glass ashtrays filled with cigarette butts, then showered away hairs of all varieties from the bathtubs, and replenished toiletries and soaps. It was standard practice at the Buckingham Gate Plaza to tip half-used shampoos and gels into a plastic jug, then refill the individual bottles. Ines reckoned some of the shampoos had been in circulation for years. At break times, they smoked in an underground staffroom, bottle glass at the windows and an iron grating at street level, through which you could see the shoes of passers-by on the pavement.

Cath shared a bedroom with a hairy Portuguese chambermaid named Dolores from Faro, who had been in London for four months, spoke no English and cried at night. The room was so hot from central heating – and with no thermostat to adjust – and the air so fetid from Dolores's garlic breath, Cath couldn't sleep; she tried to open the window but the frame was nailed shut and the parapet outside bristled with shards of glass to deter pigeons from perching. Across rooftops, beyond the Royal Mews, she could see into a corner of the gardens of Buckingham Palace, with its lake, specimen trees and acres of lawn. The curtains were so thin that the ceiling was lit up by the orange glow of streetlights from the road below.

By now she had become accomplished at servicing any room in the twelve minutes allowed, including changing linen on the beds and rearranging the hotel literature – room service menu, bar snacks menu – on the built-in desk unit. She learnt to strip sheets off the bed without noticing the stains and skids some guests left behind, and to flush the toilet without first looking in. So many guests had filthy habits, it reminded her of Callum. You had to beware stripping the bedcovers because many of the hotel's clientele smoked in bed and left ashtrays concealed in their rumpled bedding.

On the eighth evening, Paul the assistant manager took her out for scampi and a drink at a pub in Victoria called the Sportsman. He drank pints of Bulmer's cider and talked about himself, detailing his twenty-year rise from junior waiter at the Midland Hotel in Manchester, through escalating positions in Coventry, Belfast, Droitwich and Torquay, culminating in his present hire-and-fire authority at the Buckingham Gate Plaza. After the scampi, he purchased foil packets of dry roasted peanuts which he proceeded to eat entirely himself, tipping the crumbs into a greasy palm, and licking them into his mouth. A jukebox in the corner was blasting out 'Uptown Girl' by Billy Joel.

As he drained each pint, he became more boastful about the perks and opportunities that flowed to someone of his power and seniority, disclosing to Cath how he regularly cleared out the minibars in guest suites, removing dozens of miniatures of spirits from the premises, and how several of the hotel's chambermaids granted him sexual favours in return for sought-after shifts. 'You can't compare foreign beaver to what you get at home,' he said, leering at Cath and covering her chin with flecks of masticated peanut spittle, 'but it's horses for courses.'

At this point, he shifted his peanut-hand from his face on to Cath's lap, and told her that, if she played her cards right, she would soon enjoy shifts in the Saxe-Coburg bar or even in the Buckingham Carvery. Cath told him she'd rather not, thank you. Ugly with booze, Paul told her she was a fucking cock-tease, and no woman had that many tattoos without being a whore. His fat fingers lunged at her breasts. With lightning speed, Cath grabbed a fork from the table and drove it into the soft pad of his hand. Paul howled and told her she was finished at the hotel, fucking tattooed bitch. Cath didn't care. She stuck it out for two more days until she could collect her first week's wages, which were paid in arrears, and quit.

On her last day she took her break outside, walking the perimeter of St James's Park, then round the front of Buckingham Palace, up along the Mall and into Pall Mall and St James's. She remembered Michael driving her down those streets during their first weeks together, when he had pointed out the gentlemen's clubs with their pillars and steps. She passed an olde worlde wine shop called Berry Bros., all panelling and beams, which looked ripe for a refit, then retraced her steps up Pall Mall in the direction of Trafalgar Square. Halfway along the stretch she saw a notice on a window: 'Masseuses required. Apply within.'

The Pall Mall Steam and Fitness Club (estab. 1976) occupied the lower ground floor of a Georgian town house, the five upper storeys being given over to serviced offices. Cath entered down a steep flight of stairs with threadbare carpets and found herself in a long, low room with a reception desk and black leather settees. Upon these were sitting about eight women in white spa tunics, awaiting clients. Several elderly men in white towelling dressing gowns and slippers sat at the bar drinking wine or lager and chatting to a brassy Englishwoman who was shrieking with laughter. 'You're a *very naughty gentleman*, Ronnie,' she was joshing one of them. 'And I'm not answering that. What you need is a nice relaxing massage, so be off with you. Katrin, take the general away for a nice long massage – he needs it. Cabin number fourteen.' And then Katrin, who looked German or Polish, and about twenty-eight years old, helped the general, who must have been seventy, towards one of the numbered treatment rooms which surrounded the waiting area.

The lady behind the bar, who turned out to be the proprietor of the Pall Mall Steam and Fitness Club, was named Mona and came over to inspect Cath.

'Ever worked in a place like this before, dearie?' she asked.

Cath shook her head. 'I saw the notice outside . . .'

'That's no problem, you can pick it up quick enough. You legal?'

Cath looked blank.

'I mean, work permit, national insurance? You're entitled to work over here?'

'I think so. I'm English. From the south coast.'

'Hoped you were, dearie. My members ask for English, but it's a job finding them. What've you been doing before?'

'Working in a hotel. Before that at a school.'

'Schoolmistress? They'll like that.'

'I was a school matron.'

'Even better. When can you start?'

'Er, right away?'

'Lovely. You work alongside Magda today, she'll show you what to do. I won't pay you anything today, mind, today's tips only. But there should be something, my members love a four-hands. Now fetch yourself a tunic off the hooks and I'll introduce you to Magda. She's Romanian, but tells the gentlemen she's from Russia, which they prefer. It's still quiet this time in the mornings, but we're fully booked all afternoon long.'

Before she knew it, Cath had knotted a white tunic over her clothes, met Magda and was sitting on the black leather couch with the rest of the ladies. It soon emerged they were of every nationality: Thai, Filipina, Brazilian, a few Iron Curtain ladies. Two were British. They were also of various ages; the Brazilian masseuse, Sandra, said she was fifty, the Thai lady, Moon-Moon, was thirty-three, but the majority were in their twenties and had been living in London only a year or two. Magda, Cath's Romanian mentor, said she was officially twenty-three but actually twenty-seven and had been working at the club for four years, which made her one of the seniors. Her hair was dyed red and tied back from her face; her tunic short and worn with fleece-lined boots.

'Did you study massage in your own country?' Cath asked.

'Learnt it here,' said Magda with a laugh. 'At this place.'

As the time approached twelve thirty p.m., more clients began to arrive. Most looked smart and posh, Cath reckoned, wearing suits and nice watches like the dads at St Mary's. They disappeared into the locker room and re-emerged sometime later in towelling robes. One of the girls explained there was a sauna and steam bath in the locker room, and the punters generally liked to sweat in the heat for a while first, and take a shower.

One of the clients, like the general before him, seemed impossibly old and had trouble descending the stairs. Mona and Moon-Moon helped him down and, once arrived, he had to rest in an upright chair while he got his breath back and was brought a glass of water. Eventually he was supported by Moon-Moon into a cabin for his massage. Mona told Cath that the gentleman was one of the regulars: 'He's a lordship and comes down from White's Club up the road. Quite a character.'

Before long, Cath joined Magda for their first appointment. The bloke looked about fifty, Cath reckoned, with a tangle of dark body hair everywhere except on his head. Magda spread a roll of tissue paper across the massage table and made a hole in it for his face; the man hung his robe from a hook on the back of the door and lay naked, face down, on the table, while Magda switched on a cassette of Herb Alpert and the Tijuana Brass. She sprinkled baby powder across the man's back and began caressing his dorsal muscles with long, light strokes, running her thumbs up and down his spine, compressing the cable of his back muscles.

'I can feel lot of tension,' she said. 'You been working too hard?'

The man agreed this was the case.

'I can release some tension today,' said Magda, 'but you need proper course of treatment. Six treatments to release this much trapped tension. Two visit a week.'

The man replied he was far too busy, and far too tense, to contemplate six treatments in so short a time. Magda grunted and set to work on his thigh muscles.

Cath noticed that, as the massage continued, Magda's hands strayed closer to the man's testicles, whether accidentally or by intention it was impossible to be sure. A couple of times her fingers actually brushed up against his dick from behind. The client registered no surprise, simply lay there like a corpse. By the third time, Cath observed a physical stirring, which Magda enhanced with return sallies.

Cath had joined in the back massage and was busy digging into his shoulder muscles. Magda, meanwhile, had transferred her attention to the glutes of his buttocks. As she moved around the table, the client's right hand rose from its dangling, corpse-like position and settled on Magda's backside. She permitted it to rest there but when it probed further snapped, 'No touch. That cost ten pounds extra, OK?'

'OK,' grunted the man, persevering.

Cath now noticed that Magda was wearing nothing underneath her white tunic. She smiled at her own naivety; she hadn't realised it was that sort of place. She felt curiosity more than shock: she was a practical girl. It happened.

'Turn over now, please.'

Evidence of the effectiveness of Magda's prep work was there for all to behold as he rolled onto his back.

Magda lightly massaged his belly for a few minutes, during which he began breathing more heavily, until she asked, 'Is there any special area I can concentrate on for you?' At which he simply muttered, with something approaching urgency, 'Yes, yes please.'

'That's another ten quid, mind,' said Magda, setting to the task.

Minutes later she was cleaning him up with a fistful of tissues, and two ten-pound notes were being fished out of his robe pocket, quickly palmed away by Magda.

'So what you think?' Magda asked, when he'd gone.

'That always happens?'

Magda shrugged. 'Not every time. Some want happy ending, some don't. You can mostly tell. If you can't, best ask.'

'Nice money,' said Cath.

'A fiver goes to Mona,' Magda said. 'That's the rule anyway. You can judge it. She used to do shifts herself, so she knows if you cheat too much.'

Magda handed another fiver straight to Cath. 'And that's for you. Next time you lend me a hand.'

Chapter Six

Cath surprised herself how rapidly she assimilated into the culture and ethos of her new place of work. She got on well enough with most of the other girls, she liked the money, which was triple what she'd made at the hotel, let alone at St Mary's, and she found no difficulty coping with the club's membership, or indeed their members. On a good day she was giving eight or nine massages, six of which involved extras, and soon many of her clients were repeat customers. She did not know who they were, nor did she care. Some of the therapists liked to gossip about the gentlemen who came in, how this one was a successful QC and this one a committee member of the Royal Automobile Club opposite, but to Cath they were simply the source of the ten- or twenty-pound tips she squirrelled away in her tunic pocket. Before the end of her second week she had moved into a flat in Tufnell Park with the two English therapists, Tanya and Ros, and felt almost like an old hand, if that was the expression.

Mona declared herself delighted by Cath's progress, but insisted she change her working name to Kelly. 'We've already got a Cath who works weekends,' Mona declared. 'It'd be confusing. You be Kelly, dear, we don't have a Kelly. Kelly's like Cath in any case, near enough.'

She was a natural masseuse and her popularity grew with her ability to give a proper, vigorous treatment as well as the sensual augmentations which provided its climax. She was also the youngest and most attractive therapist, with her big, innocent eyes, partially offset by the worldly promise of the tattoos. Soon members began ringing to book her: 'Will Kelly be available at three?'

It amused her to keep new clients in slight suspense over whether a happy ending was on the menu, and oblige them to ask. She enjoyed the various euphemisms they came up with.

'I'm feeling particularly stressed today, Kelly, is there anything special you can do?'

'I'm jetlagged from New York, having problems sleeping . . . '

'Do you know any arousing Hawaiian techniques?'

Others were less subtle. 'What I need, Kelly, is my shoulders sorting out and a good rub down all over.' Or, even more directly, 'Give the old fella a nice pull for me, won't you, Kelly, there's a good lass.'

All of this activity flourished covertly at the club, seldom alluded to even in private between therapists. The nearest they came was the occasional note of caution: 'Good luck with the brigadier, he takes for ever.' If a client became noisy with heavy breathing or cries of ecstasy, the therapist hissed, 'Shush now, or they'll hear in the next cabin.' It was part of Mona's vision for the Pall Mall Steam and Fitness Club that, on the surface at least, it be seen as a bona fide gentlemen's establishment, like the others along the street. There was a strictly enforced dress code forbidding jeans, and pints were never served at the bar, only half pints. In similar spirit, the locker room walls displayed Edwardian photographs of shooting parties and tiger hunts, and a shelf of electro-plated nickel sporting trophies, acquired by Mona from a stall in Portobello Market.

Cath had been at the club a little over six weeks before taking her first booking from Lord Blaydon of Blaydon Cheyney. Charlie Blaydon was the octogenarian she'd noticed on her first day, being helped down the stairs and later supported into a cabin by Moon-Moon. Several of the girls knew 'His Lordship', as they referred to him, and were fond of the old boy, though they rolled their eyes about him in a meaningful way. Cath had observed him arriving a couple of times a week, generally after lunch, which he apparently ate at a club named White's, up the road.

'Kelly,' Mona called out one afternoon. 'Cabin eight with His Lordship please.'

Cath helped him into the cabin he liked, closest to the locker room, and then up onto the massage table. When he removed his towelling robe, his flesh hung in loose folds from a stooped back, his skin blotchy like parchment and criss-crossed with surface veins. As she manoeuvred him onto the bed, she smelt cocktails on his breath.

Unlike most of her clients, His Lordship liked to talk during his treatment, and was soon telling her about lunch at his club – 'I was being given lunch by my old fag-master, Angus Orr-Beaumont, and I always tell him "After the way you behaved, Angus, you owe me a bloody good lunch too," which, give him his due, he delivered on' – and about his house in Northamptonshire, Blaydon Hall near Kettering, and his 'damned nincompoop of a son-in-law' who was due to come and stay that next weekend with his daughter.

He was a lively old goat, Cath reckoned, who must once have been handsome. His eyes were rheumy but he had a full head of springy white hair. He mentioned his ancestors more than once ('We are Cavendishes on my mother's side') but also questioned her about herself.

'Where do you live, Kelly, my dear? In London somewhere, I suppose.'

'Tufnell Park.'

'Never heard of it. I know of a Tufnell Court in Shropshire. Up beyond Leominster.'

And, later, 'So you're Kelly. There was a Kelly up at Corpus with me. John Kelly? Robert? I forget now. Quite a common name, Kelly. There are Cheshire Kellys and Somerset Kellys.'

Cath was massaging his glutes when His Lordship said, 'Be a treasure and give me a few good spanks on my backside, will you?'

'Er, sorry?'

'Come on, m'dear, six sharp ones, don't hold back.'

Gingerly, she slapped his bum a couple of times. The muscle texture was so degraded, and his hip bones protruding so much, she was afraid of breaking him.

'Come on, Kelly, you can do better than that. Start again: six good hard ones, I said. Mona says you were school matron – you know what to do. You remind me of Miss Rash at my prep school in Westgate. I've wet my bed and you're disciplining me. Quickly now, six of the very best.'

Once she realised he was serious, Cath went for it. Soon the cabin echoed with loud, well-applied smacks.

'That's better, Kelly, good girl. Six more now, six crackers. I should think I'm getting a good rosy glow. I'm sorry, Miss Rash, I'm very sorry.'

Punishment over, Cath rolled him onto his back and was startled to find a full-blown tumescence where none had been before. In fact her earlier, tentative recces in that direction had produced no reaction at all and she had been wondering how Lord Blaydon's treatments normally concluded.

From there on, it was a matter of seconds to bring His Lordship to relief, and he seemed delighted by the experience, thrusting a crumpled five pound note into her hand. On the way out, he called to Mona, 'I like your new girl, Kelly. She reminds me of Miss Rash, only prettier. Please give me Kelly every time now, eh, Mona?'

When he was changed back into his suit, he called out to Kelly who was sitting on the black sofa, 'Goodbye, Miss Rash. 'Fraid I've got to go and vote in the Lords now. Important division on farm subsidies.'

Charlie Blaydon was good as his word and took Cath up as his new regular therapist. The severe-looking Thai lady, Moon-Moon, who had preceded her, was put out for several days by the defection, but then told Cath, 'Lordship gives rubbish tips, I don't care about him. Hims a very peculiar guy.' The tips, it was true, fell well short of the going rate, but Cath found herself almost looking forward to the old man's visits; their psychological dimension, which expanded with each treatment, interested her and made a change from the routine oiling-up and jerking-off of gruff businessmen. As he approached climax, Lord Blaydon exclaimed, 'I deserve a birching, sir,' or, once, 'I *will* clean your corps boots properly next time, Orr-Beaumont, I swear it.' He seemed pathetically grateful for her services, and kissed her before and after.

One visit, he said, 'There's something I've been meaning to ask you, Kelly, but I won't be offended if you say no. Would you ever care to have dinner with an old man one evening?' He appeared anxious in case he'd overstepped the mark.

'Sure I would. That'd be a treat. Will you take me to your club?'

'I'm afraid White's doesn't admit the fair sex but I'll book somewhere good, never you mind. Do you like fish?'

'Yes, no problem.' Cod and chips on Clarence Pier had been a favourite in the Callum days.

'Then I shall take you to Wiltons. I hope you don't find Wiltons tiresome?'

Cath replied she had never visited Wiltons. A date was set for Thursday and they would meet at the table at eight p.m.

*

She found the restaurant easily enough, scarcely a five minute walk from the Pall Mall Steam and Fitness Club, in the middle of Jermyn Street which she'd visited before with Michael Goode; it stood in a part of the street full of shoe shops displaying velvet slippers in their windows, some with fox masks or coats of arms embroidered on them, and shirt shops with monogrammed initials on the shirt fronts.

At the entrance to Wiltons she felt intimidated by the snooty receptionist who looked her up and down, and made her wonder if she was dressed the right way. She'd borrowed a low black dress for the evening from Tanya her flatmate, which showed off her breasts, with a red boa draped across her shoulders to cover up the tattoo. However, when she said she was joining Lord Blaydon, she was immediately ushered into the restaurant, past a long shellfish bar where a waiter was shucking oysters with a knife, and into a back section with semi-private booths. There she was greeted by Lord Blaydon who hauled himself to his feet to kiss her, and looked like a real lord for once in his nicely cut navy blue suit and silk tie.

'I nearly didn't recognise you there with your clothes on, Your Lordship,' she said, oblivious to the surprised look on the sommelier's face.

'Well, sit yourself down, Kelly, m'dear, and tell this fellow here what you'd like to drink.' A waiter in a white jacket was hovering to take her order.

'Snakebite and black, please.' The waiter looked blank, and Lord Blaydon said, 'Bring her a glass of champagne, George, and another of these pink gins for me.'

Cath looked round the joint with its green banquette seats and oil paintings of lobsters and shrimps on the walls, and was reminded of the Bridge Tavern in Old Portsmouth; except the punters here were way older and mostly men. An elderly geezer at an adjacent table wore a monocle, and everyone was dressed in dark suits and ties like they were going to a funeral. The geezer in the monocle, who had a head like a skull, peered at her disapprovingly, so she flashed him a big smile and he looked hurriedly away.

A waitress delivered menus and Cath gulped at the prices, they were having a laugh. But her host said, 'The oysters are very good here, if you enjoy oysters, and so is the smoked eel, though I don't know that ladies care very much for smoked eel. My late wife Betty couldn't stand the stuff so I always had to have it for luncheon at my club if I wanted eel, or here at Wiltons – same with potted shrimp. The ladies tend not to enjoy potted shrimp, I've noticed that, I don't know why. But if you *like* potted shrimp, by all means have it. Myself I am going to have the smoked eel with horseradish followed by potted shrimp with toast. Two first courses, because I find I become less hungry as I get older. But do please choose whatever you like the look of. Poached salmon? Dover sole on or off the bone. No need to have fish at all, of course. They do a mixed grill which some speak well of, if you're feeling hungry.'

Cath had wondered what they would talk about through supper – she could hardly tell him about her day at work, pulling cocks – but he turned out to be an easy conversationalist, especially when speaking about himself and his life. He told her at length about his home, Blaydon Hall, which he said was one of only two Hawksmoor private houses in England, the other being Easton Neston, the Hesketh's, of course. Cath, who had heard neither of Hawksmoor nor Easton Neston, nor the Hesketh's, whoever or whatever they were, was none the wiser, but understood it must be a magnificent place from the way he spoke of it.

'Does it have lots of rooms?' Cath asked.

'Well it does rather,' Lord Blaydon replied. 'Don't ask me how many though. I believe there are fourteen principal bedrooms, but there's the night nursery and the bachelor wing, of course. If you're interested in facts and figures, you must ask Mrs Stuart. She'd know, she knows everything about Blaydon, more than any of us.'

Later he told her about the park surrounding the hall and the various farms, and the quarry in Blaydon Hulse from where the original stone for the house had been taken and which was now run as a business concern by a local builder 'who's robbing me blind, I shouldn't wonder, but one's only happy to have someone prepared to take it in hand for one'. He told her about his paintings – 'Are you one for paintings?' – several of which he said had had to be sold for the roof. 'Those criminals from Sotheby's robbed me blind, of course. Though the other lot are no better.' Cath realised she was enjoying herself, and learning a lot too. It was interesting to hear about old paintings and big houses, even when they meant nothing to her. She liked the thought she was improving her knowledge.

'You must come down and see Blaydon one day, if you have an interest,' he said.

'I'd love that, Your Lordship.'

'Oh, do stop all this "Lordship this and Lordship that" business, Kelly,' he said. 'This is a social occasion. My name's Charlie.'

'And mine's Cath.'

'Kath? Katharine? Spelt with a K, one does hope.'

'Er, yeah,' replied Cath.

'Well, Katharine, you've been a very pleasant dinner companion. I've enjoyed myself talking to you – and looking at you too. You're a pretty girl. Much too pretty to waste time with an old buffer like me. But I hope we can do this again another time, if you'd care to.'

'I would. Very much.'

'Good. That's settled then. In the meantime I'm considering an afternoon visit tomorrow to Mona's esteemed establishment. You will be there? After lunch?'

'Yeah, my shift starts at eleven through till seven.'

'You see, I had supper tonight with a damned attractive young woman, who made me think all sorts of wicked and unworthy thoughts, which Miss Rash will need to address on the morrow. Goodnight, dear Katharine.'

Following the success of the Wiltons evening, Charlie Blaydon took to inviting Cath out on a regular basis. At first these excursions to restaurants, and later to the theatre, took place fortnightly, which then became weekly. They had dinner together at the Goring Hotel in Victoria and at Claridge's where, on Saturday nights, the hotel had an orchestra for dancing in the restaurant and Cath persuaded His Lordship to take her on to the dance floor for a few steps under the anxious watch of several grand tailcoated waiters. Charlie professed to have loved the experience ('I haven't danced for thirty years') but afterwards turned breathless and had to be taken home.

More successful were their theatre outings to musicals like *Les Misérables* and *Evita*, which Charlie found riveting. If he wasn't too tired they had drinks afterwards in hotel bars, when he told her how grateful he was to her for looking after him: 'You're like the daughter

I never had.' Cath learnt that Lord Blaydon's only child and actual daughter, Rosemary, married to a solicitor named Hugh Savill, was a source of annoyance to her father. 'They're waiting for me to kick the bucket so her dull stick of a husband can get his hands on my house.' Cath persuaded her mentor to sign up for a minicab account so she could deliver him home at the end of the evenings to his flat in Chelsea, and then be driven home herself to Tufnell Park. He complained like anything about the cost but eventually consented, afraid Katharine might otherwise curtail their excursions.

From Monday to Thursday, when the House of Lords was sitting, Lord Blaydon lived in a fourth floor flat in Burton's Court, a Chelsea mansion block overlooking a communal garden with views towards the Royal Hospital. Here he was cared for, after a fashion, by a Filipina maid, Conceptia, who lived in the second bedroom in return for basic cooking and cleaning duties but had other, better remunerated jobs all across Chelsea that she went off to every day.

Cath was disappointed by the flat the first time she saw it, having expected something grander. The furniture was rickety with cracked veneers, the sofas piled with old newspapers and post. The dark galley kitchen with its prehistoric Belling and buzzing fridge reminded her of some of the places she'd grown up in. The pair of Venetian market scenes, school of Canaletto, above the fireplace, needed cleaning and left her unimpressed. She went to take a pee but hardly dared lower herself onto the seat, which was wet with man drips.

The next time she went round, however, light flooded into the sitting room. Her earlier complaints about bathroom hygiene must have got through, because she noticed the seat was now undripped when Charlie accompanied her to view his school photographs, which hung next to the lavatory. Cath peered at the lines of boys, photographed in tiers in their housemaster's garden, while Charlie pointed out the faces of senior boys who had variously thrashed and abused him.

'Peterson's a fellow member of the Upper House now, sits on the cross-benches,' he said, indicating an eighteen-year-old in spongebag trousers.

Cath helped him down in the lift and across the road to Burton's Court garden, where they sat together on a wooden bench and watched children kick a football about.

'Tell me about your own family, Katharine,' Charlie asked.

'Nothing to say really,' said Cath. 'We're not important like your family. Me dad wasn't around a lot when I was a kid, he was in prison often as not. He's a right scoundrel, my dad. Mum worked up the hospital, cleaning and doing meals and that. This was in Portsmouth. What else can I tell you? I went to school. Spent Saturdays on the beach. Had a boyfriend in them days called Callum.'

'Callum? There was a Lord Callum, Irish title, I think. Antrim? Wicklow? Haven't heard anything about him in years. Could be dead, of course, he wasn't a young man, must be a hundred and ten if he's alive. Title probably extinct too.'

Having exhausted the potential of Cath's antecedents, Charlie reverted to discussing the Blaydons, who seemed to be related to every other posh family in England. Cath was becoming quite an expert, listening to him waffle on.

An elderly lady with a small dog on a lead approached, staring nosily at Lord Blaydon with his young, pretty, tattooed companion.

'Tell you what, Katharine, put your arm round my shoulder, won't you? We'll give the old trout a shock.'

When she'd passed by he said, 'Thank you, my dear. She's the chairman of our residents' association. That'll give her something to chew on.'

They sat together in the spring sunshine for half the afternoon, Lord Blaydon prattling on about his estate, genealogy and his schooldays, and Cath wondered what she thought she was doing there, unpaid companion to this peculiar old kink. But, in a strange way, she felt affection towards him, as well as considering how she might benefit from the connection. Of course, he was old enough to be her grand-dad and a funny old sod, which was an understatement, but he was kind to her and she felt safe around him, and enjoyed his company.

She returned him to his flat and said she had to be off now. She was on late shift at the club.

'Before you leave, Katharine, oblige an old man, won't you? It's only us here, Conceptia's out. Cleaning for some banking swell in Egerton Terrace for God-knows-what-an-hour. Mind giving me a sound slippering, Katharine? A dozen on the bare. I've got the slipper ready, here you see. Leather soles. Just like Miss Rash . . .'

*

It occurred to Cath that Charlie would be a lot more comfortable if he dismissed Conceptia and Cath herself moved into the second bedroom in Burton's Court as live-in companion. As she explained it to His Lordship, she was worried about him; he needed someone to make his coffee and ring up and order his cabs for him, and sort out his post and his paperwork for the House of Lords. If he gave her use of the back bedroom and a weekly salary, she would chuck in her job at the Pall Mall Steam and Fitness Club and devote herself exclusively to him. 'Think about it, Charlie. Having Miss Rash living here all the time, keeping a beady eye on your behaviour.'

Charlie Blaydon was entranced by the idea. His only worry was the awkwardness of telling Conceptia about the new arrangement; she had, after all, been working for him for twelve years. But Cath said she would take care of all that and speak to Conceptia right away, and Charlie needn't get involved. Which she promptly did: ordering her to pack her bags, clear her room and leave by tonight. Conceptia, who had never approved of Cath's increasing presence in the flat, nor been won over by her big eyes and pretty smile, swore at her and called her many unpleasant names, all of which Cath responded to in kind, only worse. But by the next evening, Conceptia had vacated the flat, leaving it to Lord Blaydon and his youthful nurse-companion.

'Look what I've bought you, Charlie,' Cath said, entering the drawing room with a long thin parcel. 'Housewarming gift. From Swaine Adeney Brigg.'

His Lordship unwrapped a swishy leather riding crop with a silver knob that Cath had found at the umbrella and equestrian shop opposite White's.

'I'm keeping this on the top bookshelf,' she warned. 'Don't touch. Miss Rash is the only person who can take it down.'

The abrupt change in the domestic arrangements at Burton's Court did not pass unnoticed in one quarter. When Charlie's daughter, the Hon. Rosemary Savill, was informed what had transpired by Conceptia, whom she had found for her father in the first place, she considered it totally unsuitable and rang Lord Blaydon at eight a.m. to tell him so. She was surprised to find the telephone answered by Cath: 'Lord Blaydon's London residence.'

'Who is this?'

'Katharine Fox, Lord Blaydon's personal assistant. Who is speaking please?'

'His daughter, Rosemary Savill,' said Rosemary, irritation rising in her voice. 'Please pass me to my father.'

'I'm sorry, Lord Blaydon isn't available at present. May I take a message?'

'For heaven's sake, of course he's there. Where else would he be at this time of the morning? That's quite enough of this. Give me Lord Blaydon, will you please.'

Rosemary heard muffled conversation, and eventually her father came to the telephone. 'Rosemary?'

'What on earth's going on? I've had Conceptia ringing me in tears, saying she'd been ordered to leave by a girl with tattoos. Is she one of those "punk rockers"? Was that her answering the telephone in that impertinent way?'

But Charlie Blaydon, who had no illusions about his daughter and was a wily old fox when he wasn't being a fool to love, said, 'You must come round and have a drink one evening and meet Katharine. She's a remarkable young woman – she's going to be a great help to me.'

Rosemary responded loudly enough for Cath to catch the full blast of her disapproval, but Charlie would not be drawn. 'Come and see us on Wednesday at half past six. Bring Hugh, if you'd like to. You can meet Katharine then and see she doesn't bite.'

On the dot of six thirty on Wednesday evening, the brass gates of the lift cage clanged open and shut again in the lobby outside Lord Blaydon's flat, swiftly followed by an overlong peel of the doorbell. Cath opened the door to an imperious 53-year-old memsahib in tweed skirt and cashmere cardigan, trailed by a weaselly, undersized, overly neat man in dark overcoat with velvet collar.

'Hiya, I'm Katharine.'

But the lady pushed past her into the drawing room, rapidly scanning its four walls as if expecting some of the pictures to have vanished from their hooks.

Cath had set out, on Charlie's instructions, a silver tray of bottles and glasses and two small bowls of Cheeselets and Ritz crackers, and she now demonstrated her usefulness by dispensing gin and tonics to the guests, and a pink gin for Lord Blaydon.

'Katharine makes excellent pink gins,' he told his daughter. 'Some people can't get them right, it's a knack. But Katharine got it straight away.'

Rosemary sniffed meaningfully and said, 'Well, I hope you're not drinking too much, Papa. It isn't good for you at your age.'

'Only thing that keeps me going, I shouldn't wonder. That and walking round the garden. Katharine's very patient with me. We've been out walking every morning round Burton's Court, she lets me lean on her.'

'That's very kind of you,' said Rosemary insincerely, looking at Cath for the first time. The girl was prettier than she'd been expecting, with no visible tattoos. She couldn't decide if she was now less or more worried. 'Tell me about yourself, Miss Fox,' Rosemary said. 'Have you trained in the care of senior citizens?'

'I was previously working in a health centre,' she replied, only slightly exaggerating the remit of the Pall Mall Steam and Fitness Club. 'Mostly taking care of older gentlemen. Previous to that I was a full-time matron. And me mum's been working for the NHS all her life.'

'I see,' said Rosemary, mildly wrong-footed by this information. 'And you appreciate Lord Blaydon is not a young man? He needs plenty of rest. We've had heart problems in the past, he takes pills for it.'

'He's told me all about that. I picked up his tablets from Boots after we'd been to the pictures.'

'You went to see a *film* together?'

'*The Living Daylights* at the Odeon. You enjoyed that, didn't you, Charlie?'

Rosemary's husband Hugh was meanwhile prowling round the sitting room surveying the various knick-knacks, candlesticks, clocks, letter knives and *objets de vertu* which stood on the various side tables. From time to time he lifted up a piece of silver, turned it over and examined the hallmark. Or else he peered at the artist's signature on a watercolour or small oil painting, or the leather bindings of volumes in the bookshelf.

Charlie was telling his daughter about some of his recent activities. 'Katharine and I went to a marvellous musical named *Evita*. You should go, it's got some awfully good tunes. And we went dancing at Claridge's. I recommend it. You should get Hugh to take you one Saturday, if you enjoy dancing.'

'And how are all your *old* friends?' Rosemary asked. 'Who have you been lunching with lately at White's?'

'Can't say I've been going there quite so often, not since Katharine moved in. No need. I've someone to make my lunch for me here now. I'm being very spoilt. Katharine fetched me some "pizza" the other day which we ate here in the flat. Have you tried pizza? It was a new one on me and jolly tasty it is too. An Italian invention apparently. All Katharine's idea. She's a very smart young woman.'

Walking back to their flat in Pimlico after their drink at Burton's Court, the Savills felt anything but reassured.

'This is even worse than I'd feared,' Rosemary declared. 'Much worse. You can see what she's up to a mile off, the little minx. She'll be asking him to give her presents of pictures next, you'll see, or family jewellery. I wouldn't put anything past her. We can only be grateful Daddy's beyond anything like *that*. He must be, surely? He's eighty-three years old, for heaven's sake.'

Chapter Seven

It was not long afterwards that Charlie suggested they go down to Blaydon Hall. Parliament was drawing to a close and with it Lord Blaydon's fitful obligations to the Upper House. And with the weather improving he was keen to show off his ancestral seat to his pretty companion.

They took the train to Kettering where they were met at the station by Reg Tew, a weather-beaten retainer almost as old as Charlie himself, at the wheel of a veteran Land Rover. Cath squeezed onto the front bench between Charlie and the gearstick, while they stalled and swerved the eleven miles to Blaydon Cheyney. For the final two miles they skirted a broken-down stone wall, with several sections collapsed altogether, which she was told marked the perimeter of the property, before turning under a castellated gatehouse and into the park itself.

The drive up to the house took for ever, meandering this way and that through sheep-chewed pasture, rattling across cattle grids, past ancient oaks – many toppled and left to rot where they fell – and sudden vistas of lakes, obelisks and pillared follies.

Eventually they crested a hill and there below in the cleft of a valley lay Blaydon Hall, eleven bays of windows glistening in the sunshine and a double horseshoe staircase rising to the front door from a gravel sweep. Cath had never seen anything so grand; it was like Buckingham Palace, but plonked down in the middle of nowhere. You wouldn't want to live here if you'd run out of fags and needed to buy some in a hurry.

Charlie said, 'They do know we're coming, Tew? Mrs Stuart's all prepared for us?'

'She is that, Your Lordship. She and Megan have been opening the place up for you. I drove Megan into Tesco's in Corby to buy your supper, and there's a fire laid ready in the morning room.'

As they drew up to the house, Cath saw it was in worse repair than it had appeared from afar. Long sections of balustrade had toppled forwards on to the lawn, and one spur of the horseshoe staircase was roped off and displayed a notice: 'Danger. No Entry. By order.'

She helped Lord Blaydon up the steps into a stone-flagged hall where he sat down to hyperventilate on a bench by the door; the journey home and the final ascent of the Hawksmoor staircase had taken their toll. Hanging from the walls were various moth-eaten military banners, brought back from campaigns long ago by Charlie's ancestors – many of whom Cath knew by reputation from his genealogical soliloquies – and plaster casts of ancestral Blaydons, interspersed with those of Roman emperors, incorporated into the architrave.

Soon they were joined by Mrs Stuart, who combined the roles of supervisory housekeeper with that of private secretary and house archivist, and who welcomed and appraised Cath with a certain beady reserve. It occurred to Cath that Mrs Stuart might have been briefed against her by Rosemary.

When Lord Blaydon had recovered sufficiently to continue, they progressed into an inner staircase hall, where a flight of one hundred and fifty shallow stone steps led upstairs. On the walls hung several dozen portraits, suspended six-deep from chains.

'I always stop here to doff my metaphorical cap to the first Lord Blaydon,' Charlie said. 'There he is, you see, splendid-looking fellow in the wig. Became a Gentleman of the Bedchamber to Charles the Second. Made all the money. Always pay my respects to Cousin William.'

It took Charlie a full ten minutes to climb the stairs, gripping on to the handrail while further supported by both Cath and Mrs Stuart, and trailed now by a fat cook named Megan who had joined the greeting party and carried Lord Blaydon's bags. When they eventually reached the landing they found themselves in a long gallery with windows at each end, lined with paintings of horses and classical and religious scenes, such as *Rome from across the River Tiber* and *The entry of Mary and Joseph and the infant Jesus into Nazareth*. Lord Blaydon's bedroom, which led off the long gallery, overlooked an ornamental lake bordered by yew hedges, and beyond to a vista of the parkland through which they had arrived. Having made it upstairs, he declared he would like to rest for a while, and was helped up onto a magnificent, lumpen four-poster with swags and coronets and yards of yellow silk, and a silk bedback, partly in shreds, embroidered with the armorial coat of the lords of Blaydon Cheyney.

'We'll leave you quietly to rest now, Your Lordship,' Mrs Stuart announced. 'I'll pop upstairs and tell you when supper is ready, then help you down to the dining room.' Then she added, 'I have prepared Nanny Frobisher's old bedroom for Miss Fox, and will show her where she's sleeping.'

But Charlie said, no, he didn't want Cath sleeping all that way away, he wanted her put in Lady Blaydon's bedroom which connected with his own, so she could tend to him, and tune his Roberts wireless for him as she did in London. Mrs Stuart, full of disapproval, began to protest that Lady Blaydon's bedroom had not been aired or prepared, but Charlie insisted. 'Put Katharine in Betty's old room. That's where I want her to be.'

While Lord Blaydon rested, Cath carried her suitcase – one of the suitcases she had been given by Michael Goode when she left Hollywood Road – into the adjoining bedroom and placed it on the bed. She located various switches by the door and dim bulbs flickered on beside the bed, as well as on a dressing table. This last was covered with silver-backed hairbrushes, pots of congealed cold cream and crystal scent spritzers; evidently relics from the occupation of Betty Blaydon who had died eighteen years ago. The room smelt airless, as though no one had entered it for many months, and slightly damp.

Three long windows framed by threadbare silk curtains stood shuttered and secured with iron bars, one of which Cath managed to force up, hauling back the shutters which folded into themselves with creaks and bangs, sending up motes of dust to dance and soar in the evening sunshine. She half wished she had her cleaning cart from the Buckingham Gate Plaza; she could have given the place the once-over in no time. She yanked open the doors of a mahogany wardrobe and found it full of old clothes on hangers and smelling of mothballs. The top shelf of the wardrobe held several large hat boxes, and Cath lifted these down and looked inside. Enveloped in tissue paper was a big purple hat decorated with pheasant feathers. Another hat was black with a heavy veil. She put on the purple hat and admired the effect in the mirror; she thought she looked quite the part.

At the foot of the bed was a rickety chaise longue, and Cath arranged herself gingerly upon it, half worried it might collapse beneath her from woodworm. She gazed around the room with its high, corniced ceiling and brown patch of damp above the window, and wondered what the hell she thought she was doing there.

She was Lord Blaydon's nurse-companion, that was her official job title. But her remit was already much wider than that: masseuse, dinner date, lover, pupil, dominatrix. And Charlie her mentor, protector, honorary godfather.

Wherever she looked, she saw antique furniture and oil paintings, silver framed photographs and china collectibles, all of which must be worth a fortune. She opened the drawer of a writing desk and it was stuffed with antique fountain pens and propelling silver pencils, none of which would be missed. Through the door to Charlie's room she could hear him snuffling and snoring; it was weird to think of this socking great place, hardly used most of the year, all belonging to the old man.

Above the fireplace was an oil painting of brooding countryside with trees and rocks, which reminded her of a picture in Charlie's dining room in London. They looked a bit the same. The one in the flat was done by someone called Claude Lorrain – she'd noticed that on the label – and when she checked the bedroom one, it was the same bloke. '*Landscape with Apollo and Mercury* by Claude Lorrain, 1660.' Cath felt quite pleased with herself.

Soon she heard Mrs Stuart waking Charlie next door, and they helped him back down the staircase for supper. This was served in a gigantic dining room with pillars at each end, at a table long enough to seat twenty-four people. Two place settings for Lord Blaydon and Cath had been laid at one end, with silver cutlery and side plates and a silver candelabra lit with candles. On a mahogany sideboard with clawed feet, supper was laid out. This was the supper that Megan the cook had purchased that morning at Tesco's in Corby, now decanted from its ready-meal packaging and presented on the Blaydon's best silverware. A silver tureen contained the shallow contents of two cartons of leek and potato soup. On a hotplate was a lamb and vegetable stew, freshly microwaved, tipped into a chafing dish. A silver cheese salver displayed a block of processed cheddar and a small red rind of Edam.

Charlie Blaydon seemed satisfied enough with the arrangements, and Cath helped him to a bowl of soup and carried it to his place. Mrs Stuart and Megan departed at this point, saying that everything should just be left where it was when they'd finished and would be cleared up in the morning. 'If you want coffee, Your Lordship,' said Megan, 'I've left hot water in the thermos on the side, and coffee and milk.'

After they'd gone, Charlie said, 'I never think there's much point having them hanging about watching me eating. You can help me upstairs, Katharine. It's very good of you to agree to come up to Northamptonshire with me, I'm very grateful. I'm afraid you'll be bored rigid but I shall show you something of the estate, if you'd like that. Most of it's in a shocking state, I'm afraid, so much has been let slip. It's too much to look after really. Too much for one person anyway. No doubt Rosemary and her husband – the lawyer – will take pleasure in shaking it all up, but I doubt they'll do much good. I wouldn't bet on them.'

As they sat together in the large, cold, underlit room, Charlie told her about the paintings. The dining room was hung with those family portraits not displayed on the staircase, and it became his routine over the coming weeks to focus on one or two of them each evening and expand upon them. 'Ah, Katharine, I see your eyes settle upon the third Lady Blaydon . . . She was born a Cake, of course. Our kinship to the Cakes, and thus to the Leicestershire d'Aubigny-Cakes and the Shenfields of Shenfield Saye, all derives from Lady Anne Cake . . .' Or he would say, 'Which brings us to Henry Cobold Blaydon, third son of the eighth Lord Blaydon, who never expected to inherit of course, and would never have done so were it not for the unfortunate conjunction of the Crimean War and a fatal accident out steeplechasing . . .'

Cath absorbed it all, evening after evening, until she knew many of his stories by rote, since Charlie had a tendency to repeat himself. When it became too much she screened it out, nodding and smiling at regular intervals while thinking about other things. Such as what Callum and her mother would make of all this if they could see her now sat in this room, and what age Jess would be – she'd lost track.

Most mornings after breakfast, if Charlie was feeling up to it, the Land Rover was brought round to the front of the house and they were taken on a tour of inspection of the estate. Half a dozen cottages in the hamlet of Blaydon Cheyney still belonged to the Big House, as well as the Blaydon Arms, though this had long ago been taken in hand by a pub conglomerate, Punch Taverns. When Cath wanted to go inside and take a look, the landlord scarcely acknowledged Lord Blaydon and the place was newly fitted out with a pine bar and a juke box playing George Michael's 'Careless Whisper'.

They drove to visit several farms where the tenant farmers showed them barns and farm buildings in urgent need of repair, complaining they were scarcely breaking even and asking to reduce their rents. Sometimes they were driven further afield to outlying farms and villages which had once upon a time been part of the Blaydon Hall estate but subsequently sold off. The Blaydon garage and car dealership no longer had any connection to the Hall, nor did the Blaydon dairy and farm shop.

Charlie had a tendency to become morose during these tours, but Cath had a gift for cheering him up. Where Lord Blaydon would instinctively see his glass as being half full, and the estate a decaying shadow of its former self, Cath encouraged him to recognise his good fortune. 'You're loaded, Charlie. You don't know how lucky you are, living in this amazing great palace. If me mates back home could see me now!' Her wide-eyed enthusiasm for his possessions coaxed Charlie from his gloom and he relished having an audience for his stories in this attractive girl, who laughed prettily at the exploits and antics of his ancestors. Even the food started to improve at Cath's behest. When Reg Tew ran over a pheasant on the drive, Cath talked Megan into plucking and roasting it and the experiment was judged a resounding success. In the old days, when a proper shoot was maintained at Blaydon Hall, there had regularly been roast pheasant in the dining room, but the habit expired with Lady Blaydon. Come the autumn, Reg was touring the woodland with his shotgun and bringing home a brace of pheasant for the table.

'Have you considered opening up your place to the public?' Cath asked him one evening at supper.

'Never. Wouldn't dream of it. And have half the burglars of Northamptonshire paying half a crown to case the joint?'

But Cath kept on at him, and made him visit several stately homes in the vicinity that opened to the public, and Charlie gradually became less hostile to the idea. Instead, he began to see the attraction of ready cash.

'And you can have a teashop,' Cath suggested. 'Doing teas and coffees and cakes and that. And tea towels and mugs.'

Charlie made a face.

'And the punters can pay extra for guided tours of the portraits. Tell 'em all about your relatives, who married who and how posh they all were, like they do over at Princess Di's dad's place. The one you say I don't pronounce proper.'

'Althorpe,' said Lord Blaydon, pronouncing it All-trop. The prospect of public ancestor-worship, with coach parties of hoi-polloi handing over good money to learn about his impeccable inbreeding, held undeniable appeal. He promised to think about it.

Each night after supper, after she'd helped him upstairs to his bedroom, Cath would make a private visit 'to tuck him in', as Charlie put it. She would arrive with riding crop in one hand and bottle of baby oil in the other, as the mood took him. If he was a good boy and took his medicine well, Cath would slip into bed beside him as a special treat and climb on top of him. Sometimes he dropped off to sleep while she was still at it, her task incomplete.

Chapter Eight

As the months passed, Cath encouraged Charlie to invite friends over to the house. She had discovered in Betty Blaydon's writing desk an address book dating from twenty years ago, filled with the names and addresses of neighbours as well as friends all over the country. It was evident from this, and from remarks made by Mrs Stuart, that the Blaydons had once been very social, regularly entertaining the county. But Charlie had become something of a loner, seldom any longer seeing anyone locally or in London, lunching only with a handful of old schoolfriends. His twice-weekly visits to the Pall Mall Steam and Fitness Club had supplied a large part of his human interaction.

Charlie was at first resistant to the idea of any form of socialising. He had left it so long, he said, he doubted anyone would remember his existence, or wish to come: 'Betty was always the draw.' He was ashamed by the condition of his house and wondered how the local gentry might perceive Cath.

But Cath said, 'Of course they'll come. You crazy? They'll all want a gander at a place like this, there's nothing else to do round here anyway.'

So it was agreed that Charlie would be At Home at Blaydon Hall in six weeks' time for drinks before Sunday lunch. Cath settled down with Mrs Stuart to comb through the old address book for feasible guests, having first established which were alive and which now dead, and eventually a list of seventy names was agreed upon and cards written out and posted off.

Cath was interested to learn from Mrs Stuart exactly how the cards and envelopes should be written and addressed, with all the correct titles, and which guests could be regarded as the most important.

As Cath predicted, the acceptance rate ran at more than 90 per cent;

the locals were filled with curiosity to see the house, the pictures, the park and Charlie Blaydon again in that order. Reg Tew, supervised by Cath, drove into Kettering to stock up on soda water, tonic and bitter lemon, and an expedition was made to the cellars to retrieve wine and spirits from the chaotic selection of bins and boxes. Charlie felt quite bucked by all this activity, and twice addressed Cath as 'Betty' before correcting himself.

The only invitees filled with misgivings were Mr and The Hon. Mrs Hugh Savill. Rosemary declared herself 'frankly amazed' at the prospect of her father throwing a party. 'What earthly point is there in that? It's not as if anyone's going to ask him back, not at his age.' However, she accepted the invitation by return, asking herself and Hugh to stay on at Blaydon Hall for Sunday night. Apart from anything else, it would enable them to check up on precisely what was going on down there; reading between the lines, it sounded like the punk rocker was becoming far too familiar with her father and starting to act like the house had something to do with her, which of course it did not. Rosemary was particularly disturbed to learn that Cath had installed herself in Lady Blaydon's old bedroom, which showed monstrous cheek; she hated the thought of that girl sleeping in her mother's bed, on her mother's pillows.

The day of the party eventually dawned, and the Savills were the first people to turn through the castellated gatehouse and draw up outside the house. Rosemary's antenna was on red alert to identify and condemn any change, large or small, in the home where she had grown up. She hoped Cath might have the courtesy not to join in the drinks party as a guest, which of course she was not, but be circulating with a jug or a plate of canapés, if she must be present at all. During the drive down from Pimlico, Hugh had worried her by saying that he hoped Cath had been issued with a properly worded contract of employment, otherwise she might later claim squatters' rights over her bedroom and be impossible to shift without extortionate compensation. Rosemary felt quite angry: imagine *paying* that girl to move out from her own mother's bedroom.

They found Charlie in the morning room where the drinks party would take place. Log fires were ablaze at both ends of the room, and a marble-topped table covered by a cloth was arranged with glasses and plates of food. The only discordant note, Rosemary saw at once, was a hideous arrangement of flowers in quite the wrong vase, comprising pink and white carnations with a fuzz of droopy greenery, which Mr Tew had bought at a service station in Kettering.

Her father, by contrast, looked infuriatingly sprightly and several years younger than at their last encounter at Burton's Court. They kissed each other, and Charlie said, 'You've driven a very long way for a drink, Rosemary, I hope you'll consider it worth it. Over a hundred miles. There used to be a convention when I was a young man: never more than ten miles for a drink, fifteen for dinner. Other than in Scotland, of course. And any distance for a ball, but there you had a house party to stay in, of course.'

'This all looks very nice and cosy,' Rosemary said, indicating the roaring fires. 'It's a long time since I've seen both fires going.'

'Ah, that's all down to Katharine,' he replied. 'She organised for a chimney sweep. Goodness only knows where she found one, she's a marvel. And here she is, look.'

Rosemary and Hugh turned to see Cath, and Rosemary's eyes narrowed. Was it really possible? For Cath was dressed in a black Hardy Amies cocktail dress which Rosemary was quite certain had belonged to her mother, and the purple hat with the pheasant feathers which Betty Blaydon had worn at several society weddings. The fact that Cath looked totally gorgeous in them only made it worse. Had she not known better, Rosemary might almost have mistaken her for a lady.

'Good gracious,' she exclaimed. 'Wasn't that my mother's frock? What on earth do you think you're doing?'

But Charlie said, 'I told Katharine to wear it. Doesn't she look wonderful? She discovered all Betty's old things hanging in her wardrobe and has been trying them on all week. We've been deciding what suits her.'

'I see,' replied Rosemary, seeing it all too clearly. 'Well, I don't think it's at all suitable. I hope none of the guests recognise Mummy's clothes, they'd consider it most peculiar.'

At that moment they heard the first of the non-family guests arriving, and the subject was suspended.

In what felt like the space of ten minutes, the morning room went from empty to full. Thirty old couples, most of whom had not stepped inside Blaydon Hall for two decades, were hobbling about greeting each other, frankly rather intrigued to be back inside the mysterious Hawksmoor house. Over the years, rumours had circulated about the fate of the Hall – Charlie Blaydon lived in only one room now, the pictures had been sold off, windows boarded up – so they were reassured to see that matters weren't nearly so grave as they'd heard: Charlie looked fit as a fiddle, and was accompanied by a pretty young woman who never left his side. Lady Naseby, who had known Blaydon Hall as a child, reckoned Cath must be Charlie's goddaughter, or otherwise a great-niece. The Mawsleys, from Prior's Culworth, also assumed her to be family, since she reminded them slightly of dear Betty. Lord Geddington, who was informed by Mrs Stuart that Cath was Lord Blaydon's nurse, said he hoped she might come and look after *him* one day when he required nursing. The Pagets from Preston Magna, who got cornered by Rosemary and Hugh early on and couldn't escape, were subjected to all Rosemary's bile on the subject of Cath, and how worried she was about her father being taken in by her. 'We can't *prove* anything,' Rosemary confided, 'but I'm watching her like a hawk.'

Cath was feeling quite the lady of the house. It was nice seeing the old place filled with people, even if they were all aged about a hundred. Charlie's neighbours, the men particularly, were very friendly towards her, saying she must bring Charlie over to visit. A grand old couple called the Mawsleys began telling her about their grandchildren, one of whom was at school at St Mary's in Petworth. Cath remembered Chloe Mawsley, a second year pupil, but said nothing of course. She kept half an eye on Mrs Stuart, Megan and Reg Tew, who were circulating with drinks, to make sure they were doing their jobs properly; her other eye was on Charlie to check he wasn't tiring himself. Over the months, she'd become quite fond of the old codger. It was nice seeing him enjoying himself.

Hugh Savill made a brisk inventory of the downstairs paintings, under the pretext of visiting the cloakroom. It was a frustration to him and Rosemary that, since Blaydon wasn't open to the public, they had very little opportunity to compile a catalogue of their future treasures. So each time they visited they made notes, recording all the paintings in the library, or on the stairs, or hung along a particular corridor. Their great fear, amplified by the arrival of Cath Fox, was that pictures or objects might disappear and no one be any the wiser.

Producing a notebook from his pocket, he wrote *Small 18th Century (?) oil of unidentified cathedral from across water meadow* and then *Portrait of gentleman in bottle-green frockcoat, artist's signature illegible.*

He returned to the morning room just as Charlie was clapping his hands for quiet. It took some time for this to be achieved, but eventually the party was brought to silence and everyone gathered around him at one end of the room.

'I'd like to welcome you all to Blaydon Hall and thank you for coming today,' Charlie announced in his posh, frail voice. 'I'm afraid I've rather neglected my obligations to hospitality since Betty passed on, for which I can only apologise. I've never been much use at this sort of thing. But now I am very fortunate in having Miss Katharine Fox here helping look after me. Some of you have met Katharine. I feel very blessed. This party was all her idea, you know, she organised everything. She's transformed my life, in so many ways.'

Cath, who was standing next to Charlie during this unexpected speech, spotted Rosemary in the throng, a look of steely hatred across her pug face.

'I don't know what I have done to deserve being looked after by such an attractive young lady. She reminds me of a certain matron at my prep school in Westgate, Miss Rash. I often tell you that, don't I, Katharine? She's very kind to put up with a doddery old fool like me – I consider myself a very lucky man.

'Katharine, I hope it won't embarrass you in front of all these people if I put you on the spot? But, dear Katharine, would you ever consent to become Lady Blaydon? There you are, you see, I'm asking you to become my wife. You needn't give your answer right away, you can think about it if you like.'

But Cath gave her reply as soon as he'd finished speaking. 'Of course I will, Charlie. I'd be pleased to. Whoever would have thought it?' And she smiled the sweetest smile, and kissed him on the cheek.

A ripple of applause broke out in the room, and several of the guests raised their glasses in congratulations. Several more turned round to gauge Rosemary's reaction, and saw her gawping. Lord Geddington felt a tinge of jealousy as the gloriously sexy twenty-year-old was embraced by the eighty-four-year-old geriatric. Linda Mawsley, whose mother had been a bridesmaid to Betty Blaydon at her wedding, muttered to her husband, 'Poor Rosemary. This is not going to go down well.' Lady Naseby spoke for them all, hissing, 'There's no fool like an old fool.'

It was fast approaching one o'clock and the guests began melting away to their own homes, leaving only the Savills and the newly affianced couple to have lunch together in the dining room. A brace of roast pheasants was standing on the hotplate accompanied by various microwaved vegetables in serving dishes, each flanked by silver-crested serving spoons the size of small spades. But Rosemary announced she had a headache and would excuse herself from lunch, and asked Hugh to take her upstairs and look after her. Charlie, too, felt fatigued by the double excitement of the party and his betrothal, so he and Cath soon followed the Savills upstairs, where Cath helped him into bed for an afternoon siesta before slipping in beside him.

Charlie soon dropped off to sleep, leaving Cath to consider the turn of events. The speed with which everything had happened – Callum, Jess, her flight from Portsmouth to St Mary's school, the year or so with Annabel's dad, then the hotel and massage parlour, culminating in her move to Blaydon Cheyney and sudden elevation to Her Ladyship of Blaydon Hall – was almost too much to take in. But as she lay there in the great canopied bed, listening to the wheezing and occasional coughs of the old man, her future husband, she felt a sense of security she had not experienced before. For the first time she would have a home to call her own, even if it wasn't the home she had ever quite envisaged.

Around teatime, she felt him stir beside her in the bed, and he rolled over in her direction, exhaling stale champagne breath.

'Miss Rash . . .'

'Charlie . . .' She reached over and kissed him, feeling the rough stubble on his chin press against her lips.

'You did say yes to me? I didn't dream it?'

'I did, Charlie. You asked me to marry you and I accepted.'

He groaned contentedly. 'I don't suppose Rosemary and her fool of a husband are very happy about that.' He chuckled. 'I should think they're in a frightful state.' And he began to cough.

Later he drifted back to sleep and it became dark outside. When he awoke he felt amorous; aroused, he said, by the memory of schoolday brutalities which had invaded his dreams.

Cath hauled herself on top of him, guiding him inside her, rocking to and fro. 'Yes, Miss Rash, yes, Miss Rash,' he kept repeating, and later 'Betty, Betty.' As Cath quickened her pace, he started panting, and coughing like a sheep in the night.

Cath was just pretending to have reached her own climax when Charlie emitted an agonising groan, clutching at his chest, followed by a series of twitches and jolts as she felt him buckle beneath her and then cease moving altogether.

She pumped away at his heart for a full four minutes, pummelling him with her fists and attempting a kiss of life before conceding the battle was lost and the thirteenth Lord Blaydon had departed this world.

Chapter Nine

Rosemary and Hugh moved with vicious decisiveness. Within thirty minutes of Lord Blaydon's body being removed from the premises by the Northamptonshire ambulance service, they had summoned Cath to the morning room and dismissed her from her employment.

'Obviously, with my father no longer with us, there is no position for you here. We have discussed this and think it would be best if you left immediately. We would like you to go to your room and pack up your belongings, and my husband has asked Mr Tew to drive you to the station.'

'I see,' said Cath. She stared at Rosemary Savill through narrowed eyes. 'So that's my lot, is it? That's all you've got to say to your future stepmother, as I nearly was, remember?'

Rosemary tensed. 'I don't think anyone is taking that very seriously, actually, Katharine. My father was a very old and confused man. There was never any question of his marrying you, you can put that thought out of your head. Isn't that right, Hugh?'

Hugh Savill looked very lawyerly and pompous. 'I can state, categorically, that you have no claim in law upon any part of the estate. Lord Blaydon's remarks yesterday did not constitute any sort of verbal contract. For a start, they were made under the influence of alcohol. Furthermore, Mrs Stuart is prepared to attest that he had lost most of his mental faculties, and was being placed under undue psychological pressure by you, Miss Fox. My father-in-law was a bewildered old gentleman, and we would have no trouble establishing that in any court of law, should the need arise.'

'He may have been old,' Cath retorted, 'but I can promise you he was still a perfectly good fuck. Once you'd got him going that is. You might like to know we was on the job when he keeled over—'

'A disgraceful lie – how dare you?' shrieked Rosemary. 'You are speaking of my father, a wonderful man.'

'Well, he didn't like *you*. Or your husband. He called you the vultures.'

'That's quite enough,' Rosemary said. 'We know exactly what your game is, Miss Fox. Oh yes, we saw right through you from the start, you little minx. My husband has drawn up some papers we insist you sign. If you do so, we might, just might, very generously consent to give you some money to leave here with. Give her the papers, Hugh.'

Hugh Savill produced two sheets of Blaydon Hall writing paper which were now headed *Compromise Agreement*, and contained several paragraphs of handwritten disclaimer in which Cath confirmed she had no further claim upon her fiancé's property or chattels.

'I require your signature here and here,' Hugh said. 'And here is a cheque made out to you for a thousand pounds in full and final settlement.'

'Far too much,' Rosemary muttered. 'Totally ridiculous. It makes me quite cross.'

Cath scrawled her name and grabbed the cheque. Then she glared at Rosemary with a look of pure contempt. 'And another thing. I bet your dad was a lot better in the sack than your sad prick of a husband, by the look of 'im.'

'Get out,' screamed Rosemary. 'Get out of my house, you horrible common little creature. We never want to see or hear from you again, do you understand me? Now, go and pack.'

'And just to warn you,' Hugh added, as she left the room, 'I will be searching through your suitcase before you leave, so don't try and take anything with you that isn't yours to take, or we won't hesitate to call the police.'

Barely ten months after she had first set eyes upon Blaydon Hall, Cath found herself back again at Kettering railway station, that particular episode of her life closed for ever. As she waited on the platform for the London train, she felt a range of conflicting emotions: rage, grief, remorse and thwarted opportunity. She felt sad and sentimental about the old man. OK, he was a kinky old sod, but she'd enjoyed their conversations at mealtimes when he'd told her about history and politics and architecture, and all sorts of stuff she'd never thought about before. He was a learned bloke. Through him, she'd picked up a lot about art too; she could recognise most of the important classical painters now, all your Stubbses and Van Dykes and Gainsboroughs and whatnot. And silver: Charlie had loved his antique silver, and taught her about Paul Storr and Paul de Lamerie and hallmarks and the different patterns on forks and spoons. She felt disappointed all this was over, just when she'd been getting the hang of it.

Where she'd go now, and what she'd do next, she had no idea. They'd probably take her back at the Pall Mall Steam and Fitness Club if she asked – Mona had said as much – but she didn't really fancy it. For a moment, she thought about her mum, and Callum, and everyone back in Portsmouth. She reckoned it'd all be exactly the same: they'd all be there, the old gang. And Jess. She did sometimes wonder about Jess; she'd be three now, coming up four, in fact. But it was only passing curiosity, she didn't feel motivated to visit.

The train was thundering through a particular pretty stretch of countryside, dotted with stone villages and church spires. Cath wasn't sure what she thought about the countryside. Too many empty fields with just one big tree plonked in the middle of each. And it got dark so early. The evenings were longer in the cities.

Cath put her feet up on the seat opposite and considered her position. The cheque for £1000 was in her pocket, drawn on Hoare's Bank; she would need to open a bank account in order to pay it in. Aside from that, she had £280 in cash which she'd saved up, and the half-dozen silver and gold propelling pencils she'd pilfered from the drawer in Betty Blaydon's bedroom and slipped into her coat pocket, which should raise another hundred quid. She was wearing Betty Blaydon's Hardy Amies cocktail dress underneath her coat, the one she'd worn yesterday for the drinks party. Hugh Savill had gone through her suitcase but hadn't frisked her, stupid old git.

The train passed through a series of new conurbations on the outskirts of Bedford around Biggleswade and then through another pretty stretch of green belt towards Leighton Buzzard.

Had she but known it, she was now passing within three miles of the village of Long Barton where her daughter Jess was happily playing in the back garden. From the train window, she could actually have made out the rooftop of Burdock Cottage where Jess lived with her adoptive parents. The little girl was rolling about on the lawn under the watchful eye of Kirsty Eden, her adoptive mother, and Kirsty's next-door neighbour Lizzie who had a daughter herself of the same age, Bryony. Jess had lived with the Edens for more than a year now, and already the memories of her previous life in Portsmouth with her nan and briefly with a foster mother, Sue, were fading. Kirsty and Robert Eden were Mum and Dad now, and the cottage and garden and little bedroom at the top of the house were her world.

Kirsty and Bob were surely the kindest and best of people; no greater contrast to the dysfunctional Fox clan would be possible to find. Poor, neglected Jess, abandoned by her mother at ten weeks, had been shuffled between her nan – Pat – and her dad, Callum. Not that Callum ever explicitly accepted that role, not in law anyway, and never allowed his name to be recorded on any official papers, such as Jess's birth certificate. Her teenage uncles, Doyle and Bodie, kept watch on her, sort of, while her nan was working up the hospital, and Callum's latest girlfriend, Renee, sometimes wheeled her round the shops in her buggy, when Callum told her she had to, having been lumbered with the kid by Pat on an afternoon. Callum's thing with Pat had long ago run its course but left Cath's mum with a slight moral hold over Callum, as well as a sense of grievance, which she did not hesitate to make use of.

When Doyle left school and signed up for the navy, and Bodie joined a construction company over in Havant, Pat lost her entire support network in one go. With no one to leave Jess with during the day, and Callum refusing to make any financial contribution to the kid's welfare, it was a mercy when social services took the child in to care. Initially intended to tide Pat over while she got herself straight, it was surprising how quickly Jess's removal from the family unit was accepted. Pat did visit her granddaughter a couple of times at the foster family which took her in, especially when social services provided her with a wait-and-return taxi for the journey. But on the second visit, perhaps guessing she might never make a third, when she said goodbye to Jess she thrust into her tiny hand the heart-shaped Ratners locket Cath had left behind in her room.

She said to Sue, 'I've left Jess with her mum's locket. We're not expecting Cath back, she may as well have it.' Sue promptly removed the jewellery from the little girl and placed it for safekeeping with her identity papers, and it was duly passed on to Kirsty Eden when Jess was put up for adoption. The cheap silver-plated locket contained a small photograph of Cath, taken in the photobooth in Woolworths at the Tricorn Centre. When Jess first came to Burdock Cottage, Kirsty studied it for signs of resemblance between daughter and mother and found them in the bright, beady eyes and pretty mouth. Jess's mum was nice looking. Kirsty shrugged. She couldn't understand how any woman could abandon a child, it was beyond comprehension.

When she thought of the heartache she and Bob had gone through, failing to conceive a baby, it made it even less explicable. Kirsty and her husband had met as students in Birmingham fifteen years ago, when Bob had been doing an accountancy and finance course at the university, and Kirsty teacher training at the college of education up the road in Edgbaston. They had met in a student bar and married four years later. By the standards of their contemporaries, they married young. Kirsty had been only twenty-two on the December day they'd tied the knot in the village church at Long Barton, half a mile up the road from where they now lived. Kirsty had grown up in the next village where her father was a GP and her mother acted as secretary to his medical practice. It had always been Kirsty's dream to have a winter wedding, ever since she'd been bridesmaid at a real 'white' wedding with snow on the ground. She had got her dream, even if it didn't actually snow on their own big day.

Bob was a couple of years older than her, and had worked in the finance department of Glaxo almost since college, based in their Milton Keynes office. In addition to being financial controller for a portfolio of pharmaceutical brands, Bob was president of the staff sports club and spent much of his free time organising and competing in inter-company rugby, track and swimming events. Bob had always adored sport. As the third of four brothers, he grew up in a family of team players. In Peterborough, where they'd been raised, it was the joke that there was scarcely an amateur team in the city which didn't have at least one Eden playing for it.

It had been a grave shock for Bob and Kirsty when they found they couldn't have children, because they had taken it for granted they would. Fit, young, sporty, non-smokers and light drinkers, except at rugby club dinners, it never occurred to either of them there could be any problem. But months of trying became years, and visits to fertility clinics were inconclusive. Kirsty even gave up her job teaching French in a local secondary school in case the stress and workload were somehow affecting her ability to conceive. Tests followed tests, and then a programme of the recently invented IVF which Kirsty found horribly invasive and emotional, and ultimately soul-destroying, since none of the implanted eggs survived for long, with each fresh hope followed by crushing disappointment.

By the time they conceded defeat they were almost too old to adopt, and this realisation placed strains on the marriage which might have broken one that was less stable than theirs. Kirsty was horrified by the prospect of a future without children, since even as a trainee she had always viewed teaching as a short-term occupation, assuming that one day she would be occupied with her own family. She could scarcely believe it when their adoption agency began questioning whether she and Bob were already past the age to take on the responsibility of a child, when they had so much love to give, and a warm home ready to welcome a child of whatever sex, colour, creed or race they were allocated.

Then, one evening, they were rung at home to be told that a three-year-old female, from a deprived inner-city background, might be available and were they interested? Three o'clock the next afternoon found them at an adoption agency in Portsmouth, and five months after that Jess Fox was brought home to Burdock Cottage to become Jess Eden.

Chapter Ten

As her train clattered through Buckinghamshire, Cath picked up a newspaper left on the seat opposite. It was *The Times*: a paper she associated with Michael Goode and dull as ditchwater. Charlie Blaydon had taken the *Telegraph* which was no better, and Cath had been pleased to look at Reg Tew's *Daily Mirror* when he brought one in to the kitchen. She turned the large grey pages of *The Times*, stopping only at a photograph of Princess Diana arriving at a film premiere, until she stumbled on a section named 'Crème de la Crème' with situations vacant. This caught her attention. The jobs were more elevated than the ones advertised in the window of the Alfred Marks Bureau, and she did need to find something. Most were for 'Executive PAs' to the chairman or managing directors of companies, but she noticed one from a magazine publishers seeking staff for their classified advertising department. The advertisement said you could earn *up to £9,000 p.a., including incentive bonuses*, and she tore out the page. The Imperial Magazine Group, it stated, was one of Britain's largest publishers of weekly and monthly titles, with headquarters in Shaftesbury Avenue in the West End.

She took herself to Tufnell Park where her old colleagues from the Pall Mall Steam and Fitness Club, Tanya and Ros, said she could doss down on the sofa until she got herself sorted. 'We haven't heard anything from you in ages,' Tanya said. 'We were talking about you at the club, wondering what's become of you. You were seeing that old perv, weren't you, Lord Wassisname?'

Cath shrugged. 'He snuffed it.' She didn't wish to discuss Charlie with the girls, or tell them how close she'd come to being mistress of a socking great palace with a hundred rooms. They might not take it right and, anyway, what was the point?

Next morning, dressed in Betty's Hardy Amies cocktail frock, she took the tube to Shaftesbury Avenue and found Expedia House, headquarters of the Imperial Magazine Group. Fifty storeys of concrete and brick soared into the sky, with two stone musclemen either side of the entrance shouldering a colossal stone globe. The lobby was like the concourse of a railway station, with soiled grey marble and a bank of turnstiles and half a dozen security men. The whole of one wall displayed the front covers of the company's 127 publications, several of which Cath recognised: she spotted *Cosima*, *Shine* and *Smile*, and lots of house magazines like *My Home*, *Beautiful Kitchens* and *Modern Living* (incorporating *Modern Food and Wine*). There were others she'd never even heard of before, such as *Your Gun*, *Your Pregnancy* and *What Carp*.

Removing the job advertisement from her purse, she approached one of the reception guards who told her to take a seat. It was almost twenty minutes before she saw him bother to lift a telephone and make a call and eventually she was told to take a lift to the forty-second floor where someone from Personnel would meet her. There were a dozen lifts constantly opening and closing, and Cath was intrigued by the procession of young women coming and going, and men in overalls pushing trolleys and carrying sheaves of proofs. On the forty-second floor she was instructed to fill in a form which asked about her qualifications, and which she struggled with due to her spelling. On impulse, under education, she wrote 'St Mary's School, Petworth' and awarded herself four O Levels and two As. Under references, she gave Lord Blaydon of Blaydon Cheyney and Michael Goode: she felt they owed her that, the buggers.

Sometime later, Cath was called into an office for an interview, and was surprised by how smoothly it all went. They asked no tricky questions and took her at her own evaluation. 'I see you were at St Mary's,' said the personnel manager. 'We've drawn several employees from St Mary's at IMG. They do quite well here.' Nobody questioned the new posher voice she put on, modelled on the accent of Rosemary Savill.

Having apparently passed this part of the test, Cath was escorted back to the lifts and down twelve floors to the Classified department. This turned out to be the largest room she had ever seen; there must have been three hundred women working at long benches, each with a telephone and files and order sheets. All were speaking into receivers, and as soon as they'd completed one call they picked up the next. From the windows in every direction you could see right across London. As she waited to meet a manager, she tried to figure out where she was, and was pleased to spot the Buckingham Gate Plaza Hotel where she'd worked as a chambermaid, and even the streets of Fulham from her days with Michael Goode. A lady in her forties named Jacqui Potts, who managed the Hearth and Home division for Classified, spoke to Cath for twenty minutes, running through the main points of the job, and then said, 'OK, when can you start? Tomorrow?'

'Yeah, that'd be fine.'

'Nice to have you on the team,' said Jacqui.

Cath rapidly got the hang of Classified. The Hearth and Home division consisted of seventy sales girls selling across fourteen different magazines, which between them brought in 19 per cent of the total departmental classified revenue. All this was explained to Cath during her half-day induction programme. The magazines she'd be selling into were the decoration and home-improvement titles, including *Beautiful Kitchens*, *Kitchen Extensions*, *My Home* and *Traditional Cottages*. One of her first tasks was to learn the relative circulations of all the magazines; some sold over 400,000 copies a month, others fewer than 50,000, each commanding a different price for lineage and for the dozens of small boxed advertisements which made up the pages.

By her second afternoon, Cath was making her first attempt at calling clients. First she consulted an index file, with a card for each advertiser that had taken space in the past. The card detailed which titles they had advertised in, what their business was, and most importantly what they'd paid for space before. The majority were regional bathroom companies selling taps and showerheads, or else tapestry kits, fireside fenders, tongs and bellows, or fire screens in the shape of cats and dogs. Cath was taught to dial the number, hear it ring in some distant shop or office and when it was eventually answered to chirp, 'Hello, how are you doing today?' To which the reply was generally, 'Oh God, this is all I need, being pestered for advertising. Last time I tried your magazine it didn't draw a single enquiry.' Or else, 'Actually, do you mind, we're very busy here right now, would you mind calling back at a more convenient moment?' Or, once, 'Sorry, we've wound up the business. I'm only here collecting my belongings.' Cath tried to use her poshest voice – her Rosemary Savill – but often forgot, which made her manager look at her askance.

Cath soon learnt that the majority of their hundreds of regular classified advertisers were carping malcontents. As they told it, nobody ever responded to the two-centimetre semi-display insertions they took issue after issue. They would happily spend forty minutes on the phone, trying to wheedle themselves a 10 per cent discount. They complained about their advertisement's position on the page – 'far too low' – and in relation to those other businesses they saw as competitors – 'Why were Blenheim footstools placed above us then? Don't think I'm paying you for *that*'. Most of all they were elated when a minor spelling mistake, or some elision in the typesetting, gave them a legitimate loophole to decline to pay altogether, claiming the trivial error invalidated their entire 'campaign'. The majority of Cath's advertisers were modest family-owned concerns, who resented the cost of advertising and directed their umbrage at the sales executives.

Cath nevertheless discovered she was good at the work. She had always had the gift of the gab, and enjoyed the challenge of ringing people she'd never met, charming them into booking ads. Each time she sold one, she came that bit closer to her weekly bonus. Cath particularly enjoyed the challenge of ringing cold prospects who might never have set eyes on *Kitchen Extensions* in their life, were impatient to get off the phone, and had no spare budget in any case, and slowly winning them round with cheerful banter and inflated readership claims until they finally succumbed and agreed to give it a try.

The only part of the job she found difficult was recording the bookings on paper, because her spelling remained terrible and she hated being shown up. In the evenings she practised writing out lists of words: KITCHEN with an E, SHOWER with an ER at the end.

More than once, Cath was in trouble with her supervisors for grossly exaggerating the circulation figures; it was considered fair practice within the department to embellish sales information by 50 per cent, especially if it wasn't put in writing, but Cath brazenly doubled or tripled it. On the other hand, she was soon achieving better results than girls who'd been selling for three or four years, and the name

Cath Fox moved near the top of the revenue blackboard, where the daily achievement of each sales exec was displayed for all to see.

Away from the office, Cath moved into a draughty flat in Wandsworth with three of her new colleagues, four roads back from the common. The place suited her because it was cheap, and she rubbed along well enough with her flatmates, without becoming close to any of them, finding them young and naive. Most had recently left a university like Manchester or Leeds, or some college of higher education, and were excited by the novelty of living in the capital and by their first jobs and new boyfriends. They spent their evenings in wine bars near the flat. Cath realised there were large areas of her life she could never share with them.

At the same time, she found herself intrigued by the dynamics of the Imperial Magazine Group. For her flatmates, their jobs were little more than a means of funding their social lives in town. Staff turnover in Classified was high, with half the girls moving on each year to enter other industries altogether, or to go travelling. A minority moved up within the company, promoted into Display where the money was better and targets less prescribed. Within a few months of arriving at IMG, Cath knew she wanted to be one of those people.

She had long ago seen through the manager who had employed her, Jacqui Potts. After Jacqui took her to task for telling a client that *Kitchen Extensions* sold 230,000 copies a month, when it actually sold 56,000, Cath lost all respect for her. Instead, she directed her coquetry towards Jacqui's boss, Dan Black, the 37-year-old departmental director to whom the Hearth and Home, Hobbies and Pursuits, and Young Women's weeklies classified managers reported. Beyond Dan, Cath knew, lay Rich Scarsdale, who was publishing director of the weeklies and specialist titles, but she had only laid eyes on him once in six months, when he had paraded through her office on a mid-year tour of inspection, glad-handing the line managers as he passed by. Far above even Rich Scarsdale, operating at a level which rendered him largely invisible within the organisation, was Tony O'Flynn, chief executive of the Imperial Magazine Group. He inhabited a lushly carpeted floor on the top storey of Expedia House, which he seldom left other than to have lunch. His chauffeur-driven Daimler was frequently double-parked outside the main door, waiting to deliver him to the Savoy.

As the months passed, Cath consolidated her reputation as a top performer. Three weeks out of five she brought in more revenue than any other girl in the department and secured the champion's bonus. Where most sales executives formulated their pages as they went along – pinning the ads onto drawing paper and devising a layout, before spray-mounting the fiddly artwork and boxes onto a production sheet – Cath preferred to hit the phones all day selling, then attend to the production and fix her spelling after work. This cleared her twice the selling time, enabling her to cold-call more prospects than anyone else. It didn't make her popular, but it did make her richer.

She was also resourceful, dreaming up new categories to bring into her sections. Her 'Modern Radiators' category, run across *My Home* and *Beautiful Kitchens*, took off like a rocket. As Christmas approached she launched a 'Yuletide Hampers' section. In the slower summer months, when revenue faltered, she introduced regional shopping specials around English market towns. One of her first focused on Petworth. Another success was a Cornish Riviera summer guide focusing on Rock and Polzeath, with small ads for the scuba shack where Michael Goode rented wetsuits and the smart kitchen shop where Flea bought salt and pepper grinders.

One evening, working late at her desk, she saw Dan Black crossing the deserted office. You could not have described him as good looking, but he had a certain cocky swagger, born of power, being the man in ultimate charge of three hundred Classified subordinates. From the way he swayed between the benches, Cath guessed he had been drinking. He had, in fact, spent the afternoon cultivating advertising agency contacts in a basement dive named the Cork and Bottle off Leicester Square, but he was not too drunk to overlook Cath, whose pretty face and perky figure had been drawing his attention since she arrived.

'You're working late,' Dan said, looming over her, exhaling alcohol.

'I'm here this late every night. I'm Cath Fox.'

'Dan Black. I head up the whole department.'

'I know. You're famous.' She allowed the sleeve of her top to slide from her shoulder, revealing the tattoo.

'Don't I know your name, Cath? I've countersigned your bonuses. You're a top revenue-generator.'

Cath smiled. 'It isn't that hard. We could double revenue from Hearth and Home if we wanted.'

'We could?' Dan gave her the half-fascinated, half-patronising look he reserved for pretty, ambitious babes on his payroll. 'And how do you suppose we can do that, sweetheart?'

'Fire Jacqui Potts. Replace her with me.'

'Really?' said Dan, noticing the tattoo for the first time and taking it as a good omen. 'Maybe we should go for a drink together, you and I? It seems we have things to discuss, Cath.'

Chapter Eleven

Cath reckoned that if it wasn't for the existence of Dan's wife and kids in Teddington, and for his on-off squeeze in the Production department, and for the fact he was a serial drunk and dickhead, she might easily have moved in with him. From their first evening together when they'd ended up in a bedroom at the Shaftesbury Palace Hotel (Dan had a barter arrangement in place, allowing him meals and accommodation in exchange for advertising space in the magazines), Cath identified him as the key to her self-advancement.

Carefully rationing her favours, and threatening to withhold them if he failed to fulfil his side of the bargain, she kept the pressure up. When Dan mentioned that Personnel was reluctant to make Jacqui redundant, because her severance after twenty years' service would cost too much, Cath ended their affair. When Jacqui was summoned to Personnel the following Friday afternoon, blissfully unaware of her impending fate, Cath's eyes followed her across the room, knowing she would never see her again.

On the Monday, Cath was named the new manager of the Hearth and Home Classified section and rewarded with a 60 per cent increase in salary. At twenty-two, she was the youngest person ever to head up a section. There was no spontaneous outbreak of rejoicing when her elevation was announced by Dan to the assembled staff. Later that same morning Cath received a message informing her that Mr Tony O'Flynn would like to meet her at twelve noon in his office on the fiftieth floor; as part of a new policy of staying in touch with the sharp end of the business, the chief executive liked to ratify promotions personally above a certain level, a process which normally took between one and three minutes.

At five minutes to noon, Cath began her ascent to the rarefied upper floors of Expedia House. She had never previously penetrated higher than Personnel, but now the lift doors opened and closed onto departments she never knew existed: Finance, Corporate Marketing, Investor Relations, New Projects. As the lift ascended, linoleum gave way to carpet tiles, then fitted carpet, and more of the staff were dressed in suits. Eventually she stepped out onto the fiftieth floor, where the chocolate brown shag pile was deep enough to sleep on. Teak-panelled walls displayed framed prints of birds and views of Horse Guards Parade. A faux-Georgian breakfront cabinet contained an array of silver cups and trophies, which reminded her of the locker room of the Pall Mall Steam and Fitness Club, as well as knick-knacks from the early days of printing such as hot-metal plates and hand-cut typefaces. A selection of the Imperial Magazine Group's less pitiful titles were arranged on a coffee table between a pair of shiny leather sofas.

A receptionist told Cath to wait where she was until Mr O'Flynn's secretary came to collect her. Cath was flicking through a copy of *Your Gun* when a pretty English rose of a girl with perfect white teeth and lustrous brown hair arrived along the corridor. Both girls started: it was Annabel Goode.

'Hello, Cath,' said Annabel, uncertainly. 'I was wondering whether it could be you, when they said your name.' She felt horribly awkward; it was the first time she'd set eyes on Cath since Rock, on the morning after she'd been caught in flagrante with her father.

'Yes, it is me. I didn't know you worked here.'

'I'm Mr O'Flynn's assistant. Well, his assistant's assistant. I've been here a year.'

'Is it good?'

'I love it. It's very busy. I mostly book his restaurants, and tell his driver to bring the car round to the front, and organise travel for Mrs O'Flynn and their children.' But Annabel found it hard to talk to Cath, and wanted to get away.

'I've been promoted,' Cath said. 'I'm going to be Classified manager for Hearth and Home.' But as she said it, she sensed Annabel wouldn't be over-impressed. The Classified department suddenly seemed rather remote and squalid, viewed from the lush uplands of the corporate suite.

'I'd better take you through to Mr O'Flynn,' said Annabel, leading her along a hundred yards of chocolate brown carpet.

They arrived at an outer office where Annabel's boss, a stern gatekeeper in pearls, was picking through a Rolodex of contact cards. Annabel's own smaller desk, Cath noticed, displayed a framed photograph of her parents, Michael and Flea, taken on a Cornish beach.

Annabel tapped on a heavy door and put her head round. 'I have Cath Fox to see you. From Classified.'

'You'd better send her in then,' said a terse Irish voice, in a tone which implied this encounter was the last thing he needed.

Behind a mahogany partners' desk, his red-socked feet resting on the leather-tooled surface, lolled Tony O'Flynn. A charismatic chancer from County Tipperary, he devoted half his daylight hours to jacking up his personal remuneration, the other half to closing down magazines which failed to produce a 30 per cent margin of profit on turnover. He was assiduously dressed in a blue and yellow windowpane check suit, with red polka-dot tie and matching handkerchief, and gold cufflinks the size of chocolate money. Ranged along the window ledge behind him, Cath saw a boast gallery of framed citations and awards naming Tony O'Flynn as Publishing Personality of the Year, Media Marketeer of 1983, and confirming his induction into *Campaign*'s Business Leaders' Hall of Fame.

Tony O'Flynn did not stand up to greet Cath but waved her to a chair across the desk. 'Remind me what it is you do exactly for the organisation?'

'I'm taking over as manager of the Hearth and Home Classified department.'

'I myself began my working career selling classified,' said Tony O'Flynn. 'Four pounds a week I took home then. Great place to start.'

'I've introduced a new section on radiators . . . and Christmas hampers . . .' said Cath.

'I myself established many successful categories before moving up to assume greater responsibilities,' said Tony. 'I remember those early days with great fondness, transforming the revenue stream of a small business.'

'Yes,' said Cath. 'I'm trying to grow departmental revenue by thirty per cent next year.'

'Go for fifty,' advised Tony. 'I myself grew revenues by seventy per cent in your position. Here at Imperial Magazines, I have grown topline revenue by . . . guess how much?'

Cath shrugged.

'Eight hundred and twenty per cent. And margin by six percentage points.'

'I'm impressed.'

'I shouldn't be telling you this, but I'm being named Media Innovator of the Year by *Financial Weekly*, a great honour, voted by industry leaders.'

'Congratulations,' said Cath.

'I can tell you're a bright girl,' said Tony. 'We need people like you at Imperial, a great place for hard-working young people to make a career. Well, we both need to be getting along now. It's been a treat for me reviewing your plans. Fifty per cent, mind. Good luck to you, miss.'

As she left his office, Cath heard Annabel ringing Tony O'Flynn's driver to bring the Daimler round to the front to drive him to Simpson's-in-the-Strand for lunch.

Chapter Twelve

Jess Eden, fast approaching her sixth birthday, was returning from her weekly art activity class where she had received a star for good behaviour and another two stars for helpfulness and craft. She skipped along the road with her friend Bryony, and their mums, Kirsty and Lizzie, talking about Jess's birthday party which would take place on Saturday. All the children from her class were invited, plus several girls from Brownies, and there was to be an entertainer named Silly Billy performing conjuring tricks with sausage balloons and a magic rabbit.

The two mothers walked along the pavement of the village street, Lizzie pushing a buggy with Bryony's toddler sister Hazel well strapped in, while the two six-year-olds tagged along behind. Kirsty had recently started to put on weight and had taken to wearing loose grey sweatshirts and exercise pants, inspired by the Jane Fonda fitness craze. Her friend, Lizzie, wore stone-washed denim and a cheesecloth shirt.

'Everybody is going to like my party,' Jess said. 'It's a dress-up party, isn't it, Mum?'

'Jess has got a new party dress,' said Kirsty. 'Silver and sparkles.'

'*And* my locket,' said Jess. 'I'm wearing my locket round my neck.'

'You and your blessed locket,' said Kirsty. 'I don't know what it is with you at the moment. Your special blanket and your locket and your special chair at mealtimes . . .'

'It's their age,' said Lizzie. 'Bryony's exactly the same. Won't go to sleep without her Cinderella pillowslip.'

Kirsty let the little girls run ahead, then confided, 'This thing about the locket is a new one. It came from her birth mother and I showed it to her recently, like they tell you to do, and she was so interested.

She keeps on at me, asking to see it. It's perfectly natural, I suppose, and I shouldn't be hurt, but I can't help feeling a bit upset. She stares at the photo of the "pretty lady" inside . . .'

'I shouldn't let it worry you,' Lizzie said. 'Jess is such a happy little thing. You've done wonders with her. When I remember what she was like when she first arrived . . .'

'I know,' said Kirsty. 'She's very affectionate now. We're lucky. I count my blessings every day.'

It was true that in many ways Jess was an easy child who enjoyed almost everything. She loved to cook with her mother, standing on a kitchen chair and cutting out biscuits with animal-shaped cookie cutters. Kirsty liked to bake her own bread, and Jess regarded it as a treat to knead the dough and form it into loaf-shapes. She loved swimming at the local baths and in the sea when they went to the coast for summer holidays. Kirsty did wonder whether her love of salt water was inherited, since almost the only thing she knew about Jess's birth family was that they lived close to the sea. Jess shrieked with pleasure when Bob lifted her up on his shoulders and carried her into the big waves.

But she could be insecure and clingy, which Kirsty ascribed to her old life. She seemed to have a fear of being left alone in any room. If Kirsty popped out of the sitting room for five minutes to check something in the kitchen, Jess would not be left in front of the television but insisted on coming too. She trailed her new mummy about the house from room to room. At night she wanted her door left open, for the light from the passage and the comfort of voices from downstairs. And she had a deep-seated phobia about being forgotten: if Kirsty was even five minutes late at the school gate (which she seldom was, being the most punctual of people), or Bob took longer at the shops than Jess had expected, she had a meltdown.

Aside from this neediness, and a normal six-year-old's vanity and love of dressing up, Kirsty considered Jess to be quite perfect.

The Hearth and Home Classified division began to post spectacular results. Nine per cent revenue growth in Cath's first month as manager was followed by 15 per cent in her third. Soon, Hearth and Home was outperforming all the other classified units within IMG, and gaining market share from rival home interest titles owned by competitor companies.

Results this good came at a price. In her first six months as manager, Cath fired eighteen members of her team and a further nine resigned before they were pushed. Two sales executives tried to bring workplace bullying claims against her, which had to be defused by Personnel, and there was a stampede of applications to transfer to different units within the department, beyond Cath's remit. Several times, Cath's boss and lover, Dan Black, had to take her out for a drink and tell her to cool it. But Cath didn't see it: the revenue was exploding – up 26 per cent this month – what more did he want? Would he prefer her to have stuck with Jacqui Potts' lazy team, who'd needed the biggest kick up the arse? Driven for success herself, fearful of slipping back into the poverty from which she'd clawed her way out, and which still seemed so real to her, she had little patience with middle-class sales girls who didn't understand the meaning of hard work. Her new regime of monitored cold-calls by the sales team with hourly targets for the number of calls made, and a daily, not weekly, bonus scheme, was working, wasn't it? Cath installed a new telephone system with headsets and newly invented computer terminals, which enable her to eavesdrop on any of her teams' calls. And woe betide them if they were ringing a boyfriend, or booking cinema tickets, rather than selling to a client.

Her take-home pay soared. Her personal bonus scheme shocked her bosses by paying out at a far higher level than they'd anticipated. Soon Cath was earning almost as much as Dan Black. With her success came a greater attention to her clothes, and she appeared each day in power-shouldered Alexon, and even an expensive Versace suit, and the highest of killer white stilettos. Having worn minimum make-up at St Mary's and Blaydon Hall, she now treated herself to scarlet lipstick and fragrances from the cosmetics hall at Harvey Nichols. She started reading magazines for their fashion and beauty tips, and was glued to *Dynasty* and *Miami Vice*; remembering how she used to dress in Portsmouth for a big night in Nero's, she shuddered. When Giorgio Beverly Hills was launched, she joined a queue halfway round the block to buy a bottle on the first day. And the smell of Poison by Dior trailed behind her in the office, leaving an unhappy reminder of where she'd just been.

After work, she began going for cocktails at Zanzibar in Great Queen Street and Morton's in Berkeley Square, and took clients – agency planners who booked series of classifieds for clients – to Kettner's and Langan's Brasserie. She was thrilled by these shiny new venues, bustling with successful, well-heeled people, and the novelty of being able to charge her drinks and meals to her company expenses. With Dan, she went to hot, noisy wine bars like Champers and the Loose Box, where she slagged off the other Classified managers to him, saying she should head up the entire department. To compensate for the time she spent out of the department at lunch, she discouraged her team from leaving the office over lunchtime, and if they missed their morning revenue target insisted they worked through their breaks to catch up.

It was not true to say – as many *did* say – that Cath Fox had no fans inside the company. Her lover Dan Black remained an ardent admirer, even when this was tempered by realism; Dan's boss, Rich Scarsdale, was a definite admirer and considered grooming her for serious further promotion, but was deterred by her reputation as a terrible people-manager; Tony O'Flynn referred to her, though not by name, in an interview in *Campaign*, flagging up strong gains in the home interest classified sector. Several of her subordinates, cowed by fear and the will to survive, swore blind they had learnt so much from her, and a few even began to dress like her, because Cath Fox was a role model for any feisty, ambitious, take-no-prisoners advertising moll. But the majority of Cath's teams detested her, and sat around in bars after work sharing war stories of injustices.

Nobody doubted how smart she was or how manipulative. Each Monday at nine a.m. she held a staff conference at which every salesgirl was expected to arrive with ideas for new classified categories. Cath sat behind her desk in her new glass-walled office, wearing her power-shouldered Escada jacket with gold buttons and braid trim, black leather miniskirt and reeking of Dior Poison, and her seventy-strong team squeezed in around her, standing against the walls. Then Cath picked on people at random for their ideas.

'So, Lauren, what are your innovations this week for growing *Traditional Cottages*?'

'Er, well . . .' You could see the panic and fear in Lauren's face as she tripped over her words. 'I was just thinking we could maybe start a pets section? Cat baskets, dog bowls, that sort of thing.'

'Did you?' said Cath. 'And how big was the UK pets sector last year in combined turnover?'

'Er, um. I don't exactly know, Cath.'

'Approximately then?'

'I'm sorry . . . I've no idea.'

'Not very well prepared, are you, Lauren? Do you consider yourself professional? Or are you only working here because you can't find anything else to do? Francesca?' She turned her sights by a hundred and eighty degrees. 'What are your ideas this week, Francesca?'

Pretty Francesca, who worked across *Modern Living* and *Kitchen Extensions*, and had spent the entire weekend with her boyfriend in Brighton, not giving a passing thought to the day job, stumbled, 'Maybe we could grow the food processor category? We don't get much from that at present.'

'And who are the top three manufacturers in the sector, ranked by profit?'

Fran stared down at her shoes. 'I'm not sure, Cath. Sorry.'

'See me after the conference, Francesca. I'm not convinced you have a future in the department.'

But sometimes one of the team came up with a good idea, which Cath did not hesitate to pass off as her own to Dan, or, better still, to Rich Scarsdale. Recently, Cath had begun to see through her boss and lover, wondering exactly what it was that Dan did to add value to the Classified department, beyond monitoring the performance of his three senior managers. She felt that at least half his lunches with industry contacts were non-productive and didn't lead to any actual business. Where once she had seen him as the gateway to promotion and salary increases, she now saw him as an impediment to those very things. She was pressing him to name her Head of Classified, a new position above both the other managers, but that was in effect Dan's own job, so no wonder he strung her along, procrastinating, whenever they spent an evening at the Loose Box.

Furthermore, he insisted on going home each night to Teddington. It was increasingly obvious he had no intention of ever leaving his wife Kim, or the kids, even though he assured her their marriage was effectively over. And yet each time he opened his wallet to retrieve his

Imperial Magazines AmEx, there was a photo of Kim grinning from a plastic window.

As Cath came to see it, she was being used by Dan at every turn: she was his biggest revenue-producer, which made him look good because of her hard work. She was fed up meeting him in hotels after work, especially since he made her run the free advertising – part of the barter for the room – in her own classified pages, which reduced the yield for bonus purposes. If he'd been amazing in bed it might have been different. But he was a distant second to Callum, only slightly ahead of Michael Goode, behind whom ranked Colin Woodruff, the geography teacher at St Mary's, and last, of course, Lord Blaydon.

With her new prosperity came a new place to live, and she rented a studio flat in a flashy new development next to London Bridge. The flat was her pride and joy, being clean and modern with a bleached wood floor and fitted galley kitchen with brand new electric appliances, and a tiled bathroom with glass shelves to display her growing collection of designer fragrances. That there was only one bedroom suited her – she hadn't enjoyed flat sharing – and she loved the mod cons, such as the intercom to the street entrance and the steel-lined lift. There was a tiny balcony overlooking the river, with space for a chair and table, where she sat outside on warm Sunday mornings with a coffee and croissant and the *Sunday Times*, scouring the newspaper's classifieds section for leads.

Not long after she moved in, Dan came round to inspect the place.

'This is all very nice,' he said. 'Cosy. We can meet here instead of in hotels.'

'Excuse me! We will not! I'm paying rent on this place, I'm not having you using it. Not for free.'

Dan looked amazed. 'You're saying you want me to *pay you*, each time I come over?'

'Why not? You'd be getting the benefit. Using the shower and that. Hot water costs money, it's an immersion heater.'

'You can't be serious. How much did you have in mind then?'

She shrugged. 'Thirty quid?'

'Jesus, Cath. You want me to leave thirty quid on the table? It'd be like visiting a knocking shop. One might as well call on a bloody tart.'

Cath stared at him. He just didn't get it. All her resentment flared up. 'And what am I supposed to be getting out of it then? It's not like you're God's gift in the cot, you know.'

He smarted. 'You can be such an ungrateful bitch, Cath. I've given you promotions, pay rises . . .'

'Yeah, and I've made you look so good. If it wasn't for my department and my results, you'd be nothing.'

'At least a prostitute doesn't pester for promotions all the time. I'm fed up with you, always asking for more, more, more. Nothing's ever enough for you, is it, Cath? I've had it up to here with you. You're not nearly so good as you think, you know that? Not in business, not in bed either.'

Cath called in sick next morning, skipping work for the first time ever, and lay in bed plotting revenge. Not since she'd discovered her mum's betrayal with Callum, or when Hugh and Rosemary Savill chucked her out of Blaydon Hall, had she felt so angry. How dare he? She considered ringing his wife – smug, grinning Kim – and telling her exactly what had been going on, just out of spite, to screw up his marriage. She could tell Kim about Dan's other ladies too for good measure, there was a long list.

Clearly she couldn't go on reporting to him – the sleazy waste of space – and she didn't see why she should quit her own job when her contribution was quantifiably better than his. She considered informing Rich Scarsdale about Dan's abuse of the expenses system but realised she'd been complicit in it herself.

She remembered all the meals and after-work drinks she and Dan had had together, and how he always pocketed the bill and claimed it as a client meeting. She could send an anonymous letter to Accounts. But, there again, the recipient of all this bogus entertaining was herself. She got up and stumped about the flat, still raging about Dan, and took a shower. Maybe she could expose him for sexual harassment in the workplace? Except the person he'd mostly been harassing was her, and she'd got a big promotion out of it. She went outside onto the balcony and stared down at the grey river, considering different ways of fucking up Dan's life. But none seemed to quite work.

An opportunity presented itself the following week. Imperial Magazines had taken five tables at the annual Media First Advertising Awards at the Grosvenor House Hotel. This ceremony, which celebrated innovation and creativity in the advertising industry, was attended, with varying degrees of enthusiasm, by anyone who was anyone in the media business. More than twelve hundred newspaper and magazine salespeople rolled up in black tie, accompanied by guests from media planning and buying agencies. The awards were notorious for their incredible length and for the volume of alcohol drunk during the evening. Most years there were incidents of bad behaviour, with brawls and name-calling between rival companies. It was said that, in his younger days, before he became so important, Rich Scarsdale had pulled out his cock and peed from the balcony onto the table of United Periodicals below.

For Cath to be included at an IMG table was a considerable coup for her. It came about because seven guests had dropped out that morning with a sick bug, and there had been a panic to fill the places. In desperation, Rich's PA had called her and Cath had leapt at the chance, saying she'd go home on the tube at lunchtime to collect her dress and make-up. She was excited by the chance to raise her profile within the company and the industry.

She nipped out in the afternoon to get her hair done at Upper Cut in Covent Garden, then spent an hour in the Ladies at work fixing her make-up at a row of basins. She had elected to wear a red Versace dress with a fish tail and plunging neckline; her new Butler and Wilson drop-earrings, bought that same lunchtime, completed the picture. She knew how gorgeous she looked when Dan spotted her by the lifts as she was setting off, and his jaw dropped.

The dinner was everything Cath hoped. The Great Room at Grosvenor House was the most magnificent banqueting suite she'd ever seen, five times bigger than the one at the Buckingham Gate Plaza. The tables of the different publishers stretched in all directions with their names displayed on stands; Mirror Group Newspapers, *News of the World*, *Sunday People*. There were far more men than women milling about, which made her stand out, and she felt the predatory stares as she waited for the meal to start. Her own table was on the edge of a cluster of Imperial Magazines' tables, with their top table nearest to the stage. From where she was sitting she had a clear view of Tony O'Flynn, who she hadn't seen since her promotion more than eighteen months ago; he was seated next to the Secretary of State for Trade and Industry, Michael Heseltine, and the chairmen of several advertising agencies whose faces she identified from *Campaign*, including Peter Marsh and Maurice Saatchi.

Cath was relieved Dan wasn't there. She hadn't addressed a word to him since their bust-up, nor did she intend to; she would communicate only by typed memo. She had told her secretary that if he rang, she was to say Cath was in meetings. As far as she was concerned, he was history.

The meal progressed and Cath was loving it. The publisher of *Your Gun*, seated on her right, and the advertising director of *What Carp*, on her left, were attentive and both probed her about joining their sales teams when they had a suitable vacancy, and suggested they should have lunch soon to talk about it. A photographer on a ladder, who moved from table to table during dinner taking group shots for sale, positioned her right in the centre of his picture, complimenting her on her dress. Although neither the crab mousse nor the breast of duck à l'orange with dauphinoise potatoes struck Cath as particularly good, she adored the awards ceremony itself, hosted by Jimmy Tarbuck, with all sorts of luminaries going up to collect prizes. It was during the twenty-eighth award – for Best Advertising Communication by a Regional Newspaper – that Cath had her idea.

She had been watching Tony O'Flynn all evening and realised this was the perfect opportunity to pitch herself to him. She was his guest, sort of, and she'd met him before, so why not just tell him she could transform the department and double the profits, if only he'd let her? Which was code, obviously, for sacking Dan who stood in her way.

Emboldened by a fourth glass of wine, Cath waited until the ceremony ended and edged over to his table. Many of his guests had left the minute the awards were over, so Tony was sitting at a half-full table. When she appeared at his side, he was non-committal, uncertain whether or not she was one of his 3,200 employees.

'Hi, I'm Cath Fox. I'm manager of your most profitable classified section. I just want to say a big thank you for inviting me here tonight and for giving me my job.'

Tony O'Flynn looked her up and down. In his younger days he had had an Irish eye for the ladies, and Cath was a corker.

'Well, it's my pleasure. And I'm glad to hear you're performing well for us. It's a nice little business, classified sales. Keep up the good work, miss.'

'We could do even better,' Cath said. 'We're missing a lot of tricks. I hope you don't mind me saying, I just know I can make a lot more money.'

Tony O'Flynn looked half interested, half irritated by this shameless pitch from the pretty girl in the red dress. She was evidently a Rottweiler, which he approved of, but equally this wasn't the time.

'You should speak with your manager,' he said. 'Or Rich Scarsdale, who oversees your division. But, tell you what, send me a note of your ideas, miss, if you'd like to. Send them up to my office marked for my personal attention. I'll read whatever you send me. Now, goodnight. I need to be with my guests here.'

Cath was elated. She had done it. Tony had given her the green light to send him her ideas directly. And when he'd read them, and seen her ambition for the department, he'd give her the promotion she deserved, no question. And Dan would be out the door, just as Jacqui had been.

Flushed with wine and her presence at the awards, Cath felt more confident of her abilities and more optimistic about her prospects than ever before in her life. She was the star manager in Classified, she had her own studio flat in London, she was fast-tracking at Imperial Magazines with a direct line to the Chief Executive. Who could have believed, when she quit Portsmouth not so many years before, she would travel so far? But she knew it was only the beginning. With her looks and her energy, were there any heights to which Cath Fox might not rise? That, anyway, was what passed through her head as she took a cab home to London Bridge, carefully keeping the receipt to claim on her expenses.

She woke up next morning slightly less confident. For a start, she was hungover. Furthermore, she had no idea how to set about writing the document she'd promised Tony O'Flynn. The very idea of putting anything down on paper made her anxious. She had never written any kind of business report and scarcely knew where to begin. She was OK giving orders to her department and sweet-talking clients over the phone, but she didn't know what was expected here or how to phrase it. And her spelling was rubbish. She still cringed remembering Rosie Goode, Annabel's kid sister, teasing her about shopping lists in Cornwall.

As it was Saturday, Cath resolved to spend the whole weekend working on the document. She bought a dictionary and a thesaurus, which the man in W. H. Smiths recommended, and which gave you better, posher words to use, and settled down to her task. After three hours, she'd hardly got anywhere. How were you meant to start? *Do you remember I* approached *you*, apprehended *you*, converged *you – at that meal, dinner*, gala, reception – *I was the lady, Cath Fox of the Classified department, Imperial Magazines Group, in the red dress who* graced *you at your table* . . . She tried to imagine Tony O'Flynn reading it in his vast office, and the thought made her nervous.

By Saturday night she was still on the first page.

By Sunday afternoon she was halfway down the third. *Let me have a shot and I can promise* – vouchsafe, vow, pledge – *to double revenue no problem. Just don't expect me to report to Dan Black no more, he does nothing, only takes people to lunches and drinks which don't achieve nothing except wastes your money. If I got promoted* – anointed – *to Head of Classified Sales with a big pay rise which I fully deserve, I can make you rich.*

She reread the document, upgraded a few words here and there to more elaborate ones, and retyped it one final time. Next morning she placed it in an internal company envelope and addressed it to Tony O'Flynn. Then dropped it in the basket for the internal post and waited.

For ten days she heard nothing, and was tempted to ring his office and check it arrived, but didn't relish the idea of speaking to Annabel. The existence of Annabel on the fiftieth floor irked her. She felt she was senior to Annabel in the company hierarchy, and must earn more than she did, and yet felt inexplicably intimidated.

On the eleventh morning she received a phone call from Tony's senior PA, telling her to report to his office at four p.m. Cath spent her lunch hour rereading her copy of the report and spritzing herself with fragrance. When she spotted Dan crossing the Classified floor, she blushed, knowing his days were numbered.

At five to four she took the lift up to the executive suite and was once again met by Annabel at reception. 'Mr O'Flynn won't keep you long,' said Annabel, as Cath loitered in the outer office. From the other side of the door she could hear male voices and laughter.

A buzzer sounded and Cath was told, 'You can go on through now. He's ready for you.'

She opened the door and saw Tony O'Flynn lounging on a black leather settee in the informal seating area. Also sat there, in black leather armchairs, were Rich and Dan.

'There she is,' said Tony. 'I've invited your managers to join us, because you've made some interesting suggestions, some of which they may want to adopt in the department. I've asked my assistant to distribute copies.'

Cath watched in dismay as Annabel handed round copies of her report, and Dan's face as he read what she had written.

Chapter Thirteen

Annabel did not mention her sighting of Cath to her parents when she went round for supper that evening at Napier Avenue. The name Cath Fox was not one that could be uttered in front of Michael or Flea, the entire episode – Michael's sexual sabbatical – having effectively been expunged from the records. No photographs of that final holiday in Rock were stuck into the family album. Nor did the Goodes ever return to Rock. In an unspoken change of policy, all subsequent summer holidays were spent in Tuscany or Sardinia, where the Goodes, the Peverels and Barwell-Mackenzies assembled in sunny rented villas or at the Forte holiday village at Santa Margherita di Pula, Cagliari. Nor did they risk taking a nanny or au pair. Instead, Flea, Davina Peverel, Annie B-M and their respective daughters rolled up their sleeves and got stuck in to the cooking and shopping, while the menfolk took charge of the poolside barbecues.

The Cath Fox episode was never referred to by any of these old family friends, in front of Michael and Flea anyway. In private, of course, they speculated all the time, wondering how poor Flea was coping. Annie B-M expressed the opinion that 'it could never be quite the same, because you can never rebuild the trust'. Only Johnnie Peverel, alone with Michael in a rental car on their way to collect a child from Pisa airport, dared ask what had become of 'that Cath girl?'

Michael shrugged. 'Not a clue. I doubt I'll ever hear from her again.'

'Would you want to?' Johnnie asked, leadingly.

'I'm well out of it. She wasn't an easy lady to be with.' Then he added, with a note of regret, 'Though she *was* rather amazing in certain respects.'

Later, as they approached the airport, Michael cautioned, 'Don't tell Flea we were talking about Cath, will you? She wouldn't like it.'

'Of course not.'

'We're getting along fine, Flea and I, most of the time. But it doesn't take much to set her off . . .'

Annabel was conscious of a change in atmosphere in her parents' marriage; it was as though the age of innocence had been swept away by the Cath saga, replaced by a new era of watchfulness. Although Flea tried not to monitor her husband's every movement, she could not help herself. When he told her he was meeting friends after work for a drink, her default reaction was one of suspicion. When they went to a drinks party, Flea's beady eye was never far from him, seeing who he was talking to, worrying if they were pretty. So Michael, understanding his wife's unease, and plagued by guilt, spoke mostly to the older, duller wives, which placed him beyond suspicion, but had the effect of making him feel cross and bored.

It was surprising how many avenues of conversation were now closed to them, and how many chance associations reawakened the spectre of Cath. Flea avoided movies with the theme of infidelity. Even the words 'Rock' and 'Cornwall' made her cringe. Annabel and Rosie avoided talking much about St Mary's because it had been for ever polluted by the connection to Cath.

Annabel had left St Mary's with six O levels and two modest A levels, both graded C, in French and Art. University being neither an ambition nor an option, and with her father shacked up with Cath in the Hollywood Road love nest, she returned home to support her mother through the crisis. How many evenings had she sat at the kitchen table in silent support while Flea cried bitter tears and chewed over Michael's betrayal? Sometimes she stated that she would never take him back now, however much he begged, sometimes that she'd take him back in a trice; she fixated on the absurdity of a girl like Cath – covered in tattoos – getting off with Michael, who was a laughing stock, they were welcome to each other. And so on and so forth, week after week, blaming Cath, blaming St Mary's for employing her in the first place, blaming Michael, even blaming poor Annabel for introducing Cath Fox into their lives on sports day. Flea, who scarcely drank a glass of wine from one month to the next, began drawing the corks of some of Michael's better bottles to hydrate her tearful monologues.

Annabel had enrolled at a secretarial college in a stucco terraced mansion in South Kensington, St James's in Wetherby Gardens, which taught her to type and furthermore gave her a cast-iron excuse to escape the house of despair each morning. Although she found the routine of learning to touch-type on the heavy typewriters with their leaden keys, followed by shorthand lessons in the dark room at the top of the house, rather dreary, there were compensations. At lunchtime she met up with old friends from St Mary's at the Hereford Arms pub, or with Sophie Pev or Mouse B-M at Dino's for spaghetti carbonara in the Gloucester Road. Her girlfriends had been fascinated by the shocking development of Annabel's dad living in sin with Miss Fox.

'Not being mean,' said Sophie, 'but it's so weird – your dad and Miss Fox. He's old and Miss Fox is our age.'

Annabel blushed. 'I can't really believe it myself. Mum's so upset about it.'

'You can't exactly imagine them doing it, can you?' Mouse said. 'I wouldn't want to, not with a man nearly fifty. Gross.'

And Annabel, who had actually witnessed them doing it, blushed deeper. 'I spotted them together last week, walking hand in hand along the Fulham Road.'

'*You didn't!* What did Miss Fox say when she saw you?'

'I was on my bike and pedalled off fast as possible. I won't speak to her. It would be disloyal to Mum.'

Having gained her secretarial diploma, Annabel did not immediately take a job in an office. Instead, she found a position as classroom assistant at a Fulham nursery school by Eel Brook Common, Miss Claire's, owned by a friend of Flea's. One of Miss Claire's cannier precepts was to provide short-term employment, regrettably unpaid, to a never-ending stream of pretty, kindly, well-adjusted English girls who helped supervise the toddlers in class, take them to the loo and tie and retie their gingham smocks. After the emotional stresses and strains of life at home, it was comforting for Annabel to spend her days finger-painting and cutting out shapes in Fuzzy Felt with blunted child-safe scissors. The children all adored Miss Annabel and gravitated towards her. Miss Claire, who had made herself a rich woman partly through the efforts of her unpaid classroom assistants, considered Annabel one of the best girls she'd ever taken on.

The atmosphere at home had not lightened, Flea's despair only increasing with her drinking. One of Annabel's more poignant tasks was to help her mother post off a hundred and fifty Christmas cards signed from Flea, Annabel, Rosie and Tommy, with no mention of Michael. It came as a considerable relief to Annabel when, in the days between Christmas and New Year, a friend rang from France saying she had broken her leg in two places, would be out of action for the remainder of the skiing season . . . and could Annabel possibly stand in? Annabel thus found herself on a plane to Courchevel to be a chalet girl for Supertravel.

Clean, cold alpine air, perpetual blue skies, the presence of dozens of cheerful young English boys and girls working for the season as chalet girls and barmen, all raised Annabel's spirits. A deep blanket of virgin snow enveloping and obscuring every contour and rooftop only added to her sense of a fresh beginning, a thousand miles from the anguish of Napier Avenue and a world away from the malign spectre of Cath Fox.

Besides, she was kept busy. Her position as chalet assistant required her, in return for her £15 a week, to help prepare and serve breakfast and supper for a house-full of punters, up to twenty a week, in one of the double-sized jumbo chalets that Supertravel operated, Chalet Cheva. She shopped, she stirred mince, she stirred pasta, she cleaned baths, she changed twenty sets of bedlinen on changeover Saturday, she melted ice on the front steps with pails of boiling water, she chatted up introverted punters and calmed down boisterous ones. She briefed each new wave of guests on how to hire skis and boots at Jean Blanc Sport and where to acquire lift passes, and which bars and nightclubs they would enjoy. Twice a week she baked coffee cakes with walnuts for the punters' tea. She shared a basement bedroom with two other English chalet girls, next to the drying machines.

Her kindness, her English-rose prettiness and perfect white teeth made her a favourite with everyone who stayed. She displayed the same concern for the well-being of her more plodding guests from Lancashire and Birmingham as she did for the confident Sloanes who made up the bulk of the clients. There was something so sweet and obliging about her, not one person in Courchevel ever guessed what a torrid year she had come through. In the nightclubs of Courchevel, she danced for hours fuelled by a single glass of wine and bottled water. Not considering herself to be very interesting, she preferred at dinners to ask people about themselves. If she had a fault it was an abnormally strong inclination towards hero worship. For years she had worshipped her father; at St Mary's, Cath Fox. Given the disillusionment she felt about both of them, it is hardly surprising she should have fixed upon a new candidate before long; or rather two candidates, who happened to show up more or less simultaneously.

Of the two, the less surprising was Rupert Henley. He was twenty-one years old, had been a pupil at Radley, was above-average handsome, grown up near Great Missenden, taken family holidays at Rock in Cornwall and visited many of the same places as Annabel but amazingly never met her before.

More fascinating was her hero-worship of Bruno Orcel. A sultry half-French, half-Spanish charmer of thirty-one, Bruno was by common consent the best-looking mountain guide in the resort, and the most dangerous. In seven consecutive winters as a Courchevel guide, he averaged nine conquests per season. His preference was for English girls, finding them more promiscuous. It certainly contributed to Bruno Orcel's success that so many of his past conquests warned against him, declaring him to be an untrustworthy, two-timing bastard who was amazing in bed.

It was Bruno whom Annabel met first, or rather spotted across the dance floor at a nightclub called La Grange. He was dancing with smouldering arrogance with an English chalet girl named Hattie Stratton to 'Money for Nothing' by Dire Straits, which happened to be Annabel's favourite song. Even at this distance it was obvious he was French, a Gitanes dangling from his lower lip. For reasons she was unable to articulate, Annabel found him enthralling.

'Who was that you were dancing with?' she asked Hattie, finding her in the bar.

'Bruno.' Annabel looked blank so she said, 'You *must* know Bruno. He's been out with *everyone*.'

Annabel spotted him again two nights later when one of her punters took her to Les Caves, where the entrance fee was half her weekly wage. This time he was loitering on a bar stool with a balloon of brandy, speaking to the barman. Annabel was bopping in a big mixed group of clients and chalet girls when Bruno joined them on the dance floor. Close up, he looked older and almost more attractive.

He danced assertively, hurling his partner around, pulling her towards him and casting her off again, never smiling. His jacket stank of cigarettes. From time to time he abandoned his girl altogether, dancing with his own reflection in the mirrored end-wall of the club, or bunking off to a black leather banquette for a smoke, eyes scanning the other dancers.

Conscious of Bruno as her audience, Annabel danced extra sexily, gyrating her hips and shaking her hair about. Every step she made, each gesture, was semaphored in the direction of Bruno. And the tactic worked. Soon Bruno was relaunching himself into the confusion of the dance floor like a great white shark closing on lunch. Slowly and deliberately, he came nearer, not once glancing in her direction, circling her, until she was mesmerised by his proximity. Suddenly he was dancing with her. The music changed to rock 'n' roll and they were cerocing – spinning and dipping and dropping; Annabel felt herself secure in his strong arms, with the mingling aromas of Eau Sauvage, brandy and Gitanes. The song ended and he asked, 'You are English?'

'Yes, I'm Annabel Goode, I work for Supertravel.'

'That is good, Annabel Goode. You are here for whole season?' He looked confused. 'I haven't seen you before.'

'I just arrived, I'm Cat's replacement.'

'Ah, that explains it. Well, Annabel Goode, I think we will have nice rendezvous before long. *Au revoir*.'

He walked away, leaving her flushed and confused, half relieved he was gone, half wishing he had not.

For the next three days Annabel looked out for him. When she ventured from Chalet Cheva to collect bread and pastries for breakfast, she was conscious she might bump into him anywhere in those snowy streets. She dropped in to Le Grange after supper in the hope he must have returned there. At the panoramic restaurant at the top of Saulire, she scanned every table.

Eventually she saw him, speaking intently to a French girl outside the newspaper shop. They appeared to be having an argument – she was raising her voice. Bruno shrugged. The girl spat her cigarette into the snow and squashed it with the toe of her boot.

The French girl left and Bruno noticed Annabel. His eyes lit up. 'So, here is our rendezvous.'

Annabel laughed. 'Yes, I'm just doing some shopping for the chalet.'

He stared at her, appraisingly. 'You would like to join me for coffee?'

'Er, I'd love that, that's so kind.'

He took her to a pine-lined bar where they were the only customers. She began telling him about her day and how a new group of English punters had arrived at the chalet. But he interrupted her: 'So, Annabel Goode, what I would like to know is *thees* – are you always really so good?'

'It's quite a silly surname, isn't it? People always make jokes about it.'

'I am serious. Are you good all the time, or can you sometimes be a *leetle* bit naughty?'

She blushed. 'Not always good. At school we once set off the fire alarm in the middle of prayers. Mrs Perse went ape, but no one ever found out who did it.'

'I like that,' said Bruno. 'I like to think of you English schoolgirls being a little bit, what is the word, *dees-ruptif*. That I like.'

There was a long pause when Annabel could think of nothing to say, and wishing she'd come up with a better reply than her story about school, when Bruno said, 'You must have a drink with me one night. You like to drink wine?'

'Yes, definitely. I love wine.' But she was thinking about Flea tipping it down her throat in Napier Avenue.

'Then come tonight. You know where I rest? Above the electrical shop in the small street behind Les Caves. You enter by the outside stairs to the first *étage*.'

'Er, thank you. But I have to do supper tonight, I'm working.'

'After you have finished, come. I expect you.'

Annabel spent the day in a daze. Bruno was, beyond question, the most attractive man she had ever met. He was entirely different to the boys she normally socialised with, being ten years older, foreign, and without the remotest connection to anyone she knew. She found this realisation rather liberating. Even with the group of strangers who'd arrived at the chalet this Saturday, it had taken no time to discover a myriad of coincidences: the Uppingham alumnus had a sister at St Mary's, the Oundle boy's cousins lived up the road in Napier Avenue, the Radley boy, Rupert, took his holidays in Rock. Rupert had been all over her at supper last night, flirting and pawing her and asking her out dancing. Annabel would normally have viewed him as borderline boyfriend material, but her head was filled with Bruno Orcel.

She fulfilled her duties that evening as efficiently as ever, preparing two large baking trays of mince-and-aubergine lasagne and a banoffee pie. She hung the punters' skiing jackets above the boiler to dry, and cheerfully deflected the advances of Rupert Henley, whose wandering hands were never far away. 'What's your problem, Bells?' he asked. 'Why are my magnetic charms failing me?'

Later he asked, 'Want to come to the Jump after supper?' The Jump bar being the hangout of choice.

'I'm fine, Rupert. Thanks anyway.'

'Come on, Bells. You're gorgeous. Join us for a drink.'

'Another night, maybe.' As soon as the guests left, she pulled on her ski jacket and boots and slipped off across the village.

She reached Bruno's street disconcertingly quickly. A flight of exterior stairs led up to a door above the electrical store; three lit windows overlooked the street. Annabel felt suddenly shy, unsure whether or not she dared go up, and dallied behind a line of parked cars and mounds of cleared snow. She could hear music from the flat – some alien French crooner – and this added to her feeling of unease. She wondered what she thought she was doing, arriving after supper at the apartment of a French playboy with a terrible reputation.

There was a light on above the door, and a bell. From the doorstep the music inside was louder. She rang and nobody came. She pressed a second time and this time heard it ring inside the flat. Then the sound of voices – Bruno's and a female voice – and footsteps. The door opened and there was Bruno, towel wrapped round his waist. He looked surprised to see her, then said, 'Oh Annabel. I am sorry, this is not a good time.' As he moved to close the door, Annabel spotted the French girl in the passage, stark naked.

Annabel felt crushed. She was overwhelmed by feelings of disappointment and humiliation. The sight of the naked, shameless French girl made her think of Cath Fox, holed up in another small flat smelling of sex with her father. She wondered why it was that bad girls got all the best men? All these thoughts churned inside her head as she trudged through the snow.

She knew, without one moment of considered thought, where she was headed and what would surely transpire. The bar felt warm and was packed with Brits, laughing and drinking, and Rupert spotted her entering before she saw him herself. His face lit up. 'Hey, it's Bells. What are you drinking? You look frozen.'

'Brandy.'

'A large brandy for the lady. We've got a table over here, Bells, come and join us.'

Annabel felt a deep sense of relief to be back in her comfort zone. Rupert was telling his mate Algy about some misadventure he'd had out shooting in Norfolk, while surreptitiously slipping his arm around her waist. Annabel did nothing to deter him; on the contrary, she had chosen him. He bought her a second brandy, then a third. She downed them gratefully; with each gulp, Bruno and the flat behind Les Caves felt less significant. Rupert was her man now.

They danced in a group to the jukebox. There was a song they kept playing over and over, 'Now that we've found love what are we going to do with it . . .' At some point the bar seemed to spin round. Rupert bought her another brandy. She kissed him and they snogged all the way back to Chalet Cheva, and Annabel didn't even feel cold, despite leaving her ski jacket on the back of her chair in the bar. At the chalet, they headed straight up to Rupert's room. 'Hey, Algy,' Rupert called to the friend he shared with. 'Be a hero and kip on the sofa downstairs, won't you?'

Annabel spent the night with Rupert and the night after that as well. The second morning being changeover Saturday, he had to leave by coach for Geneva at dawn. 'Well, see you, Bells,' said Rupert, guessing that their paths would one day cross again, their world being a very small place, but making no fixed plan.

'Goodbye,' said Annabel, kissing him lightly. 'I hope to see you in London one day.'

Chapter Fourteen

It was fast approaching Christmas again, Cath's least favourite time of the year. For a start, she had nowhere to go over the holidays and no family to celebrate with. The other girls in Classified were all heading home to their parents, or to their boyfriends' families, or some exotic beach, but Cath's diary stretched emptily in front of her. Portsmouth felt like another planet. She reckoned she'd hole up in her flat, watch a lot of Christmas telly, and try not to worry.

She worried all the time now. Ever since the disastrous meeting in Tony O'Flynn's office, she'd been worried. She couldn't believe he'd shown her report to Dan. It was obvious the chief exec hadn't read it carefully, merely skimmed through it, before summoning her managers to read it too. But Dan understood her treachery, and so had Rich.

Tony O'Flynn had said, 'The lady's come up with some interesting ideas. Plenty of food for thought here. I like that. Did I ever tell you, Cath, I began my own career down in Classified? It gave me an abiding respect for the sharp end.'

Dan and Rich, turning the pages of her report, kept looking at her, like she was a traitorous little slut.

'Well, I'll leave it to you gentlemen to progress on this,' Tony had said after eight minutes, signalling the meeting was over. 'Thank you for your ideas. We are committed to a perpetual programme of business innovation and reinvention here at Imperial. It is one of our stated corporate goals. A business which isn't moving forwards is moving backwards, isn't that right? Dan, may I recommend this young lady is given a special one-time bonus of fifty pounds for her initiative?'

They left the office together and walked back to the elevators.

Nobody uttered a word until the lift door closed behind them, when Dan simply said, 'Well done, Judas.'

Cath didn't get the reference, but got the drift. She did not reply. Her coup had failed.

'Fancy a drink, Dan?' Rich had asked. 'Cork and Bottle?'

'Sure,' said Dan. 'It's well needed, mate.'

The two men watched Cath get out at her own floor. That had been a week ago. Ever since, Cath had been waiting for the axe to land. Each time the phone rang, she thought it would be Personnel summoning her. She guessed she should start looking for another job but felt frozen in inaction. She wondered whether Annabel Goode would get to hear she'd got the bullet and reckoned she'd be celebrating. It irked her that Annabel had twice seen her on the ropes; first when Michael returned home from Hollywood Road, and now at Imperial Magazines. Cath found herself inexplicably freaked out by Annabel, with her piecrust frill blouse like Princess Diana. What right did Annabel have to disapprove of her?

Isolated inside her glass box, she knew the department were all talking about her. Normally she'd have been all over them, chewing them up for the slightest lapse in productivity, but she didn't feel up to speaking to anyone. She'd cancelled the Monday ideas meeting and stayed in each lunchtime. Fresh aspects of her predicament kept occurring to her: if she lost the job and bonuses, she couldn't afford the rent on the studio flat; without her corporate Amex, she could no longer frequent the bars and restaurants she loved. Rumours of her attempted coup were beginning to filter round the office; she guessed they'd all take Dan's side because he was a bloke and more senior. Never once did it enter Cath's head that she might have been in any way at fault, or had precipitated her own downfall.

That tonight was the Classified departmental Christmas party only added to Cath's tension. It was custom and practice at the Imperial Magazine Group for each department to celebrate Christmas, up to a strictly enforced financial limit per head, in whatever manner they chose. For weeks, different departments had been swaying about the corridors in Santa hats and reindeer antlers. Accounts had celebrated at Quo Vadis on Dean Street, *Your Gun* held a riotous dinner at Rules, the Mail Room and Messengers went bowling, *Cosima* caught the show at Raymond's Review Bar followed by a Chinese, Corporate went to the River Room at the Savoy. For Classified, Dan had organised a mass outing to the Roof Gardens nightclub in Kensington. There was to be a buffet supper for all three hundred of them, followed by free entry to the disco and a free bar. All afternoon, the ladies' washrooms were thronged with girls fixing their make-up and getting changed into the skimpiest evening dresses. Although an almost total absence of men in the department limited the scope, excitement ran high. The Roof Gardens, fronted by legendary French nightclub *maîtresse* Regine, was the hottest spot in town and haunt of celebrities.

Cath considered jacking the party. There wasn't much to celebrate and chances were she wouldn't still be employed by Christmas. But then she thought, fuck that, a few free cocktails might cheer me up – line them up, bartender – so she changed into the red fishtail gown she'd worn to the awards dinner, drenched herself in Calvin Klein Obsession, and climbed into one of the five coaches double-parked on Shaftesbury Avenue to transport the babes of Classified to the venue.

The Roof Gardens nightclub, occupying the penthouse and ornamental roof gardens of the old Derry & Toms department store, was accessed by a bank of steel elevators from a street-level lobby, in which several beefy bouncers behind a velvet rope did their best to prevent anyone at all from gaining entry. Tonight, however, the Classified girls were waved through, squeezing into the lifts two dozen at a time for the short ride upstairs. Cath rather wished she wasn't arriving as part of this obvious office party, because she'd been reading about the rock stars and personalities that frequented the Roof Gardens and would have liked to have presented herself differently. Upstairs, she was awed by the acres of black carpet, deep leather banquettes, chrome railings and pulsating strobes. The club was way flasher than anywhere Michael Goode had ever taken her. The bar must have been a hundred feet long, manned by the coolest-looking black guys; through the windows you could see palm trees and flamingos strutting about. Best of all, the place was heaving with blokes who looked rich, fanciable or both.

Cath filed into the private room where the buffet supper was set up, but spotted Dan in the throng chatting up her disloyal cow of a deputy. Whenever she made eye contact with her team, they melted away, avoiding her. She was the walking dead. They were probably thinking what a nerve she had showing up.

She headed to the bar and ordered a double vodka and cranberry juice and sat herself on a stool. Cranberry was the height of cool suddenly, everyone drank cranberry, there'd been something about it in *Cosima*. The DJ was playing music for dancing but the dance floor was deserted, though the strobes were on and banks of lights were reflecting off a silver ball. The song's lyrics were 'Cel-e-brate good times . . . *come on* . . . it's a celebration,' which Cath found ironic, since the only thing anyone was celebrating was her impending departure. Perched at the bar, she couldn't think of a time when she'd felt at a lower ebb. Not when Michael had fucked off back to his stressed-out wife; not even when Rosemary-bitch-Savill expelled her from Blaydon Hall. Then, at least, she'd had nothing of her own to lose. Now she was losing everything she'd sweated her guts out for, her promotions, salary, bonus, status, home . . . all of it most likely.

The place was filling up; it was three deep at the bar and she could tell that the waiters were resenting her the bar stool. The moment she drained a glass, they whisked it away and offered a refill. How many had she had now? Five? Six? She wasn't counting. There was a commotion across the room, flashbulbs flashing, people gravitating to look-see. Paparazzi sprinted across the bar, elbowing a path through the crowd. Someone asked, 'Who is it?' and a barman replied, 'Ryan James, he's a regular. He was here Saturday after the Chelsea game.'

Cath was excited. She wasn't a football fan exactly, but you couldn't grow up in Portsmouth without following it. She must have watched the Blues play at home at Fratton Park forty times, all her boyfriends took her there, Callum especially. Her brothers too. Doyle was a maniac when it came to supporting Pompey. Even her dad watched every match inside, when he was on privileges.

So she knew exactly who Ryan James was. He was a brilliant player – you had to give him that, even if he did play for Manchester United – and one of that handful of sports stars who'd made the jump from sports pages to the front half of the paper. Whenever he emerged from a nightclub, there was a photo of Ryan with some foxy blonde on his arm. According to what she'd read in the *Sun*, Ryan was paid fifteen hundred pounds *a week* by his club, which was silly money but intoxicating. As if by the pull of gravity, Cath relinquished her stool and joined the crowd of rubberneckers.

Ryan was lolling on a half-moon banquette, flanked by attractive women. Two open bottles of champagne and several bottles of lager were cooling in pails of ice. There were a couple of other blokes with him too, footballers by the look of them, though Cath didn't recognise them. Close up, Ryan was smaller than she'd imagined, compact and neat, with a little-boy face and hedgehog haircut. He and his mates were all dressed alike in Fred Perry polo shirts under dark Italian suits. No argument, the man looked fit.

She hung about, watching Ryan and checking out the two women with him, not considering them anything special, before parking herself at an adjacent table. Realising the tables in this area of the club were reserved for VIPs, and her status as part of the Classified Christmas party probably did not entitle her to sit here, she brazened it out, kicking back and lighting up a Marlboro, knowing she was slap bang in the sight line of Ryan James. As usual, she wished her ankles were slimmer.

Fifteen minutes later, Ryan started catching her eye. There had been a lot of horseplay going on at his table over a third bottle of champagne, with the footballers insisting on opening it themselves, shaking it up and spraying one another. The waiters and a manager stood impotently by, accepting it because they were celebrities. One of the women got her dress soaked and disappeared in a strop to the Ladies – 'You're pathetic, you'. Spotting Cath, Ryan rolled his eyes, as if to say 'women'. A waiter loomed at Cath's side, asking whether she had a table reservation. 'I'm sorry, you can't stay here, you'll have to move.'

But Ryan James cut in. 'She's with me. She's joining my table.'

'Thanks,' said Cath, following him to his booth.

'I've been watching you. What's that you've got tattooed on your leg? Looks like a beetle.'

'Scorpion.'

'You serious? They bite, don't they? They can kill you, scorpions.'

Cath laughed. 'Dunno about that. I had it done down the pier at home, chose it off the display. Hurt like hell getting it done, mind. The bloke who did it, it was his first day or something. Must of been.'

Ryan laughed. 'You know what they say about girls with tattoos?'

Cath shrugged. 'Go on then.'

'They're accustomed to big pricks. Isn't that right, Desmond? Birds with tattoos? Seen a lot of pricks.'

Des, his mate, roared with laughter.

'Only *little* pricks,' Cath said. 'Thousands of painful little pricks.'

'Sounds like City supporters,' Ryan said. 'Isn't that right, Desmond? Thousands of painful little pricks? Has to be City supporters.'

'Too right, Ryan,' said Des. Then, addressing himself to Cath, 'Hope you're not a City supporter, love?'

'No way, I'm from Portsmouth, I support Pompey. Used to. But I like Man U too.'

'Good girl,' said Ryan, handing her a flute of Cristal. 'Fancy dancing? I like this music.' He sang along to Wham as they made for the dance floor. 'I'm your man!'

Cath found Ryan dead easy to talk to. It was like she'd known him years already, because he was exactly like the blokes she'd hung out with back home, except Ryan was famous and had money. They'd been dancing together a couple of tracks when the paparazzi spotted them and invaded the floor taking pictures, so everyone else noticed them too. Cath stuck it to Ryan with both barrels, dancing like she used to at Nero's, oozing sex. He couldn't take his eyes off her, she was pleased to see. And she was happier still when several members of her Classified team arrived on the dance floor and found her in a clinch with Ryan James. It was gratifying to see the look of shock and wonder on their mean little faces. Pretty soon, half the department was bopping round them, angling for an introduction, which Cath had no intention of providing. She spotted Dan gawping at her and Ryan; in agony because he was a Man U supporter. She flashed him a smile and the middle finger. Loser!

She wondered what would happen to the photographs being taken of them and whether she might turn up in a newspaper. She'd always fancied being famous, even as a kid. When they finished with dancing and returned to the table, the paparazzi followed and took more pictures of her with Ryan, his arm draped round her. The two birds he'd arrived with did *not* look like happy bunnies.

Later they danced some more, and drank more, and it was after three a.m. before they left the club.

'You got somewhere to go, Cath?' Ryan asked.

'Yeah, but it's miles away, my place,' Cath replied. 'I need to find a cab.'

'I'm at the 'ilton,' Ryan said. 'You can come to mine if you want. I've got this great suite with a king size.'

Chapter Fifteen

Cath had never visited the north before. In fact, now she came to think about it, she hadn't been anywhere really apart from Portsmouth, London, Northamptonshire and Rock. In the past three weeks she'd travelled to more places than in the rest of her life. Ryan liked her to watch him play and she'd travelled to Sheffield, Wolverhampton, Burnley and Leeds. At every match he arranged comp tickets for her in the VIP stands, or in a box reserved for the team's wives and girlfriends, with everything laid on: food, drinks, whatever you wanted. It gave her the biggest kick to watch Ryan on the pitch, with all the club's supporters cheering him on, knowing they'd been shagging only a few hours before. Now she was up in Manchester, which was a breakthrough because Ryan's place was in Manchester, and she was stopping at his flat in Altrincham. For good, she hoped.

She could scarcely believe how much had happened in so short a time, since she'd spent the night with Ryan at his posh hotel. She and Ryan had really clicked in the sack, he was right up there with Callum in the shagging department, and they'd exchanged phone numbers next morning. Cath didn't know whether or not he'd call but she hoped so, and he was acting like he might. He'd had to catch a train next morning, though, and was tied up in training for the rest of the week, with no plans to be back down in town. Cath was disappointed to leave the hotel and filled her bag with toiletries from the en suite. It was a bit unsubtle crossing the lobby in her dress from last night, but she didn't care. Any of the girls behind reception would have leapt at the chance of having Ryan James.

She realised she'd be very late for work, especially once she'd gone home to change. She considered calling in sick but a part of her wanted to see their reactions so she tubed it back to London Bridge, pulled on her sexiest leather skirt and boots and made it in to the office by eleven.

Her arrival on the twelfth floor caused a sensation. As she told Ryan later, she'd felt like a celebrity with everyone staring at her as she paraded between their work stations to her glass box.

'Hi, Cath. Have a nice time last night?' called out cheeky Abi, and there were giggles. But Cath only raised her eyebrows meaningfully.

All morning long, people found pretexts to walk past her office. As news got out, staff from other floors made the journey to the twelfth, curious to see the girl who'd made it with Ryan James. When she stepped out later for a sandwich, someone stuck a poster from *Shoot* on her glass door, with Ryan in club strip squatting by a football and a lipstick kiss his on his face.

Shortly after lunch the first edition of the *Evening Standard* reached Classified. The department took forty copies a day to scour the newspaper's own substantial classified section for leads, and soon after it arrived Cath became conscious of something going on. Groups of salesgirls were clustering round the papers, and kept glancing towards her office. She paged through her own copy and gasped. There on page seven was an enormous picture of herself with Ryan. The caption said, *Man U lothario Ryan James had eyes only for a mystery brunette last night at Kensington's Roof Gardens nighterie. Hellraiser Ryan, 26, who earns* £2,000 *a week from the First Division club, earlier sprayed teammates with vintage Cristal champagne. His tattooed companion wore a figure-hugging red evening gown slashed to the waist.*

Cath was jubilant. She could scarcely believe it. The picture had come out great; it was the best photo ever taken of her, her face looked really pretty, her legs, tits, even her ankles. And Ryan was all over her, but not in a tacky way, Cath reckoned, more like they were just having a really good time together and he really fancied her.

She stared out into the department with a look of triumph. Every single one of the three hundred girls was staring back and you could practically taste their envy. Cath Fox had her picture all over the newspaper with a first division footballer. Did life come any sweeter? She hoped Dan had seen the picture – if he hadn't already, he surely would soon – and was kicking himself for being such a complete tosser. She hoped everyone in the company, on every magazine, would see her picture. She hoped the ladies in Personnel and Tony O'Flynn himself would see it, and realise what a star they had in their midst.

It so happened that a very large number of people who knew Cath – even more than she was aware of – spotted the photograph in that night's *Evening Standard*. Michael Goode, picking up his copy on the way home from work, didn't open up the newspaper until he had a large whisky and soda in his hand, and almost spilt his drink over Flea's pastel-covered sofas, such was his astonishment. He thought Cath looked marvellous and had a brief moment of regret before hurriedly removing the page from the paper and binning it, in case Flea should see it. No need to set her off again.

In the basement premises of the Pall Mall Steam and Fitness Club, the majority of therapists from Cath's era had long ago moved on and out, but a few still remained including the Thai masseuse, Moon-Moon, Magda the Romanian, and Mona.

'Isn't this Kelly, look, in the paper?' Mona said. Then, to the new generation of therapists, 'This lady, Kelly, she was one of our very best girls, very popular with the gentlemen. I always said that one'll go far, didn't I, Moon-Moon? And here she is, see, all over the newspaper.' Mona felt a burst of pride that one of her alumni had achieved such heights, and considered it encouraging for the newer ladies too, to see what was possible following a thorough training at her parlour.

Annabel Goode, flicking through her boss's copy at her desk on the executive floor, was amazed to spot Cath, and had to look twice to check it really was her. Then she rang another PA she knew in the building, who said that she was sorry but Cath looked like a hooker, where did one even *find* an outfit like that? Annabel hoped no one inside the company ever found out about Cath and her dad. She also prayed her mum wouldn't see the *Standard* tonight. If she did, she'd hit the bottle.

Paul, the assistant manager of the Buckingham Gate Plaza Hotel, thumbing through the newspaper on his lunch break, spent a long time ogling Cath's phenomenal tits and legs, but hardly glanced up at her face, so did not recognise his one-time employee and chambermaid who had driven a fork into his wandering hand at the Sportsman Pub in Victoria. He still bore the scar, which ached in cold weather, but it is unlikely he would have identified Cath in any case, with so many target females coming and going through the hotel.

Rosemary Savill was perfectly horrified, but not one bit surprised, when she spotted Cath's photograph. She looked at the *Evening Standard* every night, when Hugh brought it home, not that she really liked it, only opening it for the television listings and to read Patric Walker's horoscope, which she didn't believe in anyway.

'Hugh, isn't this who I think it is? The little tart who tried to marry Daddy? I know that face. And look who she's photographed with, some ghastly common footballer one's never heard of. And she wanted to be Lady Blaydon! Goodness, we did have a narrow escape. Horrid, horrid girl.'

Twelve days after she'd started going with Ryan, Cath handed in her notice at Imperial Magazines. Not that she worked her statutory notice period, she just resigned and was out of there. She told Dan's PA, 'You can tell your worm of a boss I've quit. And good riddance. He'll have to do some work himself for a change.'

The girl nodded. 'I'll give Dan your message when he's back from lunch.'

'Word for word, mind. And you can tell him Cath's still deciding whether or not to tell his wife about his behaviour. And unless he posts me my month-end bonus, I will too. So he'd bloody better.'

Then she walked out of the office for ever, gave a month's notice on her flat, and caught an afternoon train to Birmingham to join Ryan at the Holiday Inn. He was playing a midweek fixture at Aston Villa and asked Cath to be there for him. As Cath had discovered, he came over all phobic before a game and had a whole list of things he had to do, and couldn't do, to bring him luck. Such as he had to eat a well-done steak for his tea on the eve of a match, remove the laces from his boots and then rethread them, and have morning sex before the game. That was where Cath came in, and she was more than fine with it.

Already she was becoming accustomed to the routine of being a footballer's girlfriend. She knew where to collect her match tickets and where to find the seats in the stands. She'd got quite friendly with some of the other girls and learnt which ones to watch out for; there were a few snooty cows among them but Cath wasn't intimidated. Ryan was one of the top players in the squad and she was his woman.

She realised, from remarks made, that Ryan had had a brisk turnover of girls in the past. When she was introduced, people looked at her in a certain way, as though she wouldn't be around for long. But

Cath was undeterred because she knew from the off that she and Ryan were rock solid. It wasn't just a bedroom thing either. It was like he depended on her and needed her around, which was funny when you thought about it, considering who he was.

Once she'd moved into his Altrincham flat she felt even more secure, with her clothes from London hanging in his closets and her shoes lined up in the bedroom. His place was nice, though less flash than she'd expected: a two-bedroom new-build with wide balconies overlooking a canal. There was an underground car park where Ryan had parking spaces for his BMW and his Porsche, and a small entrance lobby to the block with a porter who supported Man U. He looked at Cath knowingly the first few days she was there, as though he'd seen her sort before.

Her days, it had to be said, were rather empty because Ryan went to train three mornings a week at the club ground at Broughton. He invited Cath to come and watch if she liked, which she did a few times but there wasn't a lot to see: just the lads jogging round the pitch, doing fitness exercises and five-a-sides. It was interesting to meet Bryan Robson and Paul McGrath and the other players she'd heard of, but there wasn't much else, just standing about in the cold, and not many of the other girls turned up, so Cath didn't either. Instead, she spent the mornings in bed and having long baths, enjoying the sensation of not working. She realised it was the first time since leaving Blaydon Hall she'd had any time off, and that she didn't have to fight her corner any more. She'd slogged her guts out for the magazines and now it felt good to put her feet up for a bit. It made a nice change not having to submit any end-of-week figures – the Friday numbers – or preside over the Monday morning ideas meeting. Instead, she tidied round the flat a bit – Ryan was a shocker when it came to clearing up his stuff – though really she mostly relied on Ryan's mum for that.

Ryan's mother, Barbara, lived on the other side of the city in Wythenshawe but arrived several times a week on the bus to give Ryan's place a good clean. Ryan had forgotten to tell Cath about this arrangement, so it was a bit of a shock when she heard a key turning in the lock and this bustling Mancunian midget with dyed red hair and clacking false teeth showed up in the bedroom carrying a bucket and mop. She didn't seem surprised to find Cath sitting up in bed with her wet hair in a towel, and said, 'Hiya, luv. And who might you be, if you don't mind me asking?'

'Cath Fox.'

'Well, pleased to meet you, Cath, I'm Ryan's mum. Don't mind me, I'll start in the lounge, there's plenty to be getting on with through there. I'll try not to disturb you too much with my vacuuming.'

Cath put on a bathrobe and followed her into the sitting room where Barbara was polishing the mirror glass on the coffee table.

'I've just made myself a nice cup of tea,' Barbara said. 'If you'd like one, luv, it won't take a second, the kettle's boiled.' She quickly returned with a mug for Cath which she placed on a cork coaster on the table.

'So you do Ryan's flat then?' Cath asked.

'I hate to think what it would look like if I didn't. I don't see Ryan going round with the duster. And his lady friends never seem to do much. Sorry, luv, I'm not casting aspersions. But he does need his old mum. Anyway,' she said, 'I enjoy coming over. Who'd have thought our Ryan would have a place like this? When I've finished my work I sit down on the couch and put my feet up and watch television, and have to pinch myself, knowing it all belongs to my lad.'

Cath wasn't sure she fancied the idea of Barbara coming over so regular, like it was her own place with her own front door key. Before she left, Barbara said, 'I have enjoyed chatting with you, Cath. I hope you'll be here next time, which will probably be Thursday. Tell Ryan I've taken his washing, including his match strip. Ta-ra then, Cath. See you later.'

Cath quickly learnt that Ryan's family played a big part in his life. His dad, Alf, who worked in the facilities department at the Wylex electricals factory, was another lifelong Man U supporter who got comp tickets through his son and sat with the players' wives at games. Like Barbara, he was a frequent visitor to the flat, undertaking small DIY jobs and tinkering with the electrics. Ryan's kid brother, Dean, a sixteen-year-old school leaver shortly to embark on a course in sports management at Wythenshawe Tech, completed the family group, and his bovine, spotty face was another fixture at the Altrincham flat.

It was clear that the James family's life had been transformed by Ryan's success, and all three lived vicariously through him. Barbara kept scrapbooks, already running to two volumes, of everything written about him; each mention in the *Manchester Evening News*, match programmes and anything, however small, in the national newspapers. On her third visit to the flat after Cath moved in, Barbara brought the scrapbooks round to show her, and they paged through them, side by side on the black leather couch, looking at all the cuttings about Ryan.

'Here you are, see,' said Barbara. 'There's Ryan playing for his school team. And there he is again at Middlesbrough, before they transferred him to United.' There were cuttings of Ryan with a succession of different girls, mostly bimbos Cath reckoned, and she narrowed her eyes. But Barbara didn't notice: she was proud of any mention of Ryan in the newspapers.

On the final page, Cath saw the photo of her and Ryan taken at the Roof Gardens.

'Oh wow, there's me,' Cath said.

'Look at Ryan,' said Barbara. 'Proper Jack the lad, bless him.'

It surprised Cath on the first Sunday morning with Ryan when he mentioned they were going round to his mum's for breakfast. 'I always go round Sundays for a fry-up,' Ryan said. 'She does the best fry-ups, Mum does, the full works.' They drove over to Wythenshawe in Ryan's red BMW and sat at the kitchen table with Alf and Dean, while Barbara dished up bacon, eggs, sausage and fried bread, and the boys dissected the previous day's game, pass by pass.

Cath had been conscious of Ryan as a famous footballer before shacking up with him but it was only after she moved into his orbit that the full extent of his celebrity was revealed to her. They seldom went anywhere without someone asking for an autograph; a crowd of fans was generally waiting by the players' entrance at Old Trafford, and others at the training ground at Broughton. Even at the Chinese at the end of the road the waiters asked Ryan to sign menus and took photos of Ryan and Cath at their table with all the kitchen staff gathered round. In the tobacconist where Cath bought mags and fags, they had a big display of Panini soccer stickers with Ryan pictured on one of them: Manchester United's midfield ace.

Cath found all this intoxicating, especially when Ryan's reflected glory embraced her too. A picture of her taken in the stands appeared in the *Manchester Evening News*, identifying her as 'RYAN'S NEW DATE KATE.' After that, she started getting regular mentions:

'Ryan James's new squeeze, Katie Fox, was out on the town with her midfield beau last night. They are pictured leaving the Moss Trooper pub, Altrincham, following post-match celebrations. Says Katie, "I used to be a Portsmouth City supporter but now my allegiance is only to Man U. And Ryan of course."'

She quickly became accustomed to the sensation of being stared at in the stands by supporters. It was a nice feeling, being famous. She preferred the away games – when Ryan drove her himself and they put up at a Holiday Inn or Hilton – to the home matches when Barbara, Alf and Dean insisted on sitting with her. On Saturday nights she was expected to accompany Ryan for marathon drinking sessions at the bar of the Four Seasons, out by the airport.

Behind the glamour of his sport, Ryan was a simple soul. Beyond his teammates, he kept up with only two friends, Kev and Gary, both from his old school. Kev was a plumber and Gary did bar work. Cath soon learnt that Ryan's reputation as a hellraiser, regularly promoted by the press, was misplaced; apart from occasional outings to nightclubs where he ordered champagne, his evenings were spent in front of the TV. She discovered he was financially naive, giving scarcely a thought to his money and only too happy for his girlfriend to take over talking to his bank and getting his savings onto a higher rate of interest. He was shy of meeting bank managers and avoided confrontation with officials, or even garages. As a result, whenever one of his cars went in for a service, he was overcharged. With Cath involved, this changed overnight, and Ryan's reliance on her increased all the time.

Having been waited on hand and foot by Barbara since birth, he was barely housetrained, and Cath didn't know what state the flat would have got into if his mum didn't come over. His clothes lay in heaps by the bed, outside the shower cubicle, wherever he stepped out of them; he seldom took a plate from table to sink, or properly flushed in the bathroom. When Cath complained, he said, 'That toilet never flushes, you should ask Dad to look at it.'

Probably because the newspapers referred to her as Kate or Katie, Ryan and his family picked up the habit too, and so did the other players. When Cath was finally introduced to Ron Atkinson, Ryan's revered manager, he squeezed her hand and said, 'Nice to meet you,

Katie. Ryan's a lucky feller.' When Cath organised for credit cards in her own name on Ryan's account, Kate Fox was the name printed on the plastic.

Chapter Sixteen

Dean James, Ryan's kid brother, sat on the leather couch in Ryan's living room, staring at the TV and stuffing his face with snacks. Whenever the James family paid a social call on Ryan and Cath, they first stopped by at the convenience store to buy provisions: cheese and onion and smoky bacon crisps, individual pork pies, pasties and cheese puffs, cans of lager and bottles of Lucozade and Irn-Bru. Dean's escalating delinquency was a problem to which no one had a solution. He had thrown in his course at Wythenshawe Tech and, ever since, been hanging about the parks and shops of Manchester getting into trouble; or else spending his days round at Ryan's place, watching TV and eating junk food. As the months passed, he became fatter and his face and neck spottier. Cath came to find him a slightly creepy presence in the flat. More than once she sensed his eye pressed to the keyhole when she was taking a shower.

As she approached her first anniversary of moving in with Ryan, Cath increasingly came to regard the James clan as her surrogate family, which in certain ways they resembled. Barbara had spent twelve years as a dinner lady in a local school, and before that in the kitchens of the University Hospital of South Manchester; Cath's own mum had done school dinners before getting the job up the hospital. Fleetingly, Cath wondered whether her mum still had that job, and whether she ever saw Callum, and what had become of Jess. The existence of Jess made her uneasy. She'd never told anyone about her daughter, and never would. It wasn't anyone's business. Ryan's mum had asked her a weird question recently about whether she wanted kids one day, and she'd almost replied without thinking, 'I've had one of them already, Barbara.'

If ever Barbara asked about her family, Cath was evasive. 'Me dad's long dead, when I was a kid,' she told her. 'And me mum's moved abroad with her new man. To Spain. They live in Spain, in a flat like Ryan's place.'

'Like *Ryan's*?' said Barbara, offended anyone should live anywhere quite so desirable as her famous footballer son.

Armed with Ryan's credit card, Cath took to treating herself. Soon she knew all the boutiques as far afield as Macclesfield and Chester, though her favourite was Blanche in Wilmslow. Emulating the other players' girlfriends, she had highlights put in her hair and went several shades blonder. She joined a health club, Herriots in Manchester, and got into aerobics and step classes. She began visiting a sunbed centre in Altrincham – Tropical Bronze – where you lay in the nude between ultraviolet panels like a giant sandwich toaster and came out brown from head to toe. She knew it was a good look because, the night after she'd first visited, she'd been with Ryan at a club called Millionairz 'n' Playerz in Prestbury and the in-club photographer took dozens of pictures of them, it was mental, and they ended up all over the newspapers.

Experiences like these made Cath feel very close to Ryan, and lucky to be with him. One afternoon, waiting for her sunbed appointment, she noticed a tattoo parlour in the same arcade of shops. There and then she had a new tattoo applied to the back of her neck, just above the shoulder blades: the initials RJ encircled by barbed wire. When her hair hung down, it would be concealed, a secret token of her commitment to Ryan. And she loved his surprised reaction the first time he saw it, when he was shagging her from behind.

'You see, Ryan. I got it done so you know I'm yours for ever. What do you reckon?'

'Dunno,' replied Ryan. 'It's OK, I s'pose. Better than the beetle, scorpion, whatever.' But he seemed quite chuffed she'd made the gesture.

One evening while they were sat round the television – Ryan, Cath, Barbara, Alf and Dean – Ryan mentioned, 'Oh, Katie, we're playing away in Portsmouth next Wednesday.'

'You're playing Pompey?'

'Testimonial match. I thought you'd be interested, seeing as how you support them.'

'Used to.'

'Used to then. I'm driving, if you fancy coming.'

Cath didn't know what she thought. She had blanked her home city for so long, the idea of visiting was unsettling. Too many ghosts. It was as though she'd parcelled the whole place up – seafront, Clarence Pier, Nero's, Callum, her family, Jess – and placed it in a locked room in her head, never to be entered again.

But she was curious. It was years since she'd left the place on the spur of the moment, without saying goodbye. She felt herself to be a different person to the Cath Fox she'd been back then. In fact, she wasn't even Cath, she was Kate or Katie. And she looked different: new hair, new gear. And she lived with Ryan James in this dead posh flat.

A part of her was intrigued to see what it was like now, the city where she grew up. Nobody ever leaves Pompey, that's what they always said. But she had. She wondered if her old crowd was still hanging round the same old pubs and clubs and the Tricorn Centre.

It would be risky going back but realistically she wasn't going to run into anyone. They'd be staying in a nice hotel and she'd be sitting in a box. She remembered looking up at the directors' boxes from the terraces and wondering what they were like inside. Well, now she'd be sat in one as a VIP.

'OK, I'll come,' she told Ryan.

'That's nice, Katie,' Ryan said. 'Dean, have you scoffed all the smoky bacon? There were three packets there too.'

They drove south from Manchester to Portsmouth in six hours and checked into a hotel, the Fareham Seacrest, with the rest of the team. As Portsmouth began appearing on road signs, Cath found herself becoming anxious. She checked her appearance in the passenger mirror. She'd had her highlights redone specially and boosted her tan at Tropical Bronze. She was wearing her new beige Armani suit with the shoulder pads which showed off her figure. She'd had the hem lifted three inches for Ryan's benefit; he loved her in short skirts. In the unlikely event of running in to any of her old mates, chances were they wouldn't even recognise her, Cath reckoned.

They joined up with the other players and their partners for tea in the hotel coffee shop, and Ryan ate his usual steak for good luck.

Afterwards, someone suggested an outing to Nero's, which they'd heard was the best club in town, but Cath said she wasn't feeling great and wanted to turn in, and Ryan agreed he wanted to get his head down too, so they went up to their room. From the window, Cath could see the orange glow of downtown Portsmouth, all the way to the harbour. It was weird to think that her mum – and Jess – were probably less than three miles away.

In the morning they fucked for luck, and afterwards, filled with bravado, Cath suggested they drive through the city in the red BMW and see something of the place. She directed him along the seafront, past the pubs, the arcades with the one-armed bandits, Nero's, Joanna's, nothing seemed to have changed. If anything, it looked more rundown than she remembered. More of the shops were boarded up and part of the dockyard too.

'Let's park up and walk on the sands,' Ryan suggested, but Cath said no, she didn't have the right shoes. She expressed a wish to drive to the top of Portsmouth Hill, above the town, ostensibly to see the view over the Solent but in fact to drive by her old flat where her mum in all likelihood still lived. When they arrived, Ryan wanted to get out of the car but Cath said, 'No, best not get out, it's a rough area.'

'Yeah?' said Ryan, looking at the deserted streets bordering the estate. 'Looks safe enough to me.'

'Stay in the car, Ryan. I'm telling you.'

He looked at her, surprised. 'You all right, Katie? You've been acting funny all morning.'

'I'm fine. I just don't want to get out, OK?'

'All right, it's no big deal, Katie. I was only asking.'

'Well, *don't* ask. Stop questioning me all the time. You're getting like your mum. She's always on at me about me family. I wish people would stop asking.'

'It's fine,' Ryan said, placating her. 'I'm sorry, Kate, I didn't mean to pry.' He looked at his watch. 'We should be heading over to the ground in any case. Frogmore Road? You know where that is?'

Cath knew. When she'd calmed down, she said, 'Thanks, Ryan. And sorry for having a go at you. Coming back here, it feels odd, dunno why. Can't explain.'

*

They located the players' car park and Ryan went off to the dressing rooms. Cath collected her match ticket and headed to the box in the centre of the stands. There were forty tip-up seats for visitors and a function room behind set up with free drinks and platters of finger food and sandwiches. Several of the other girls had already arrived, and Cath bagged places at the front with Anita and Hayley, girlfriends of players Wayne Corrigan and Midge Long. Below, the terraces were starting to fill up with supporters. Cath took pleasure in looking down on the section where she once used to stand, and now she was sat up here in an executive box. She hoped people were staring at her, envying the occupants of the boxes, like she used to herself.

Fans were streaming in through the gates. Hayley had heard the game was a sell-out, which was hardly surprising, Manchester United was always a draw; recent seasons hadn't been glory ones for the club, but Man U was Man U. Cath's seat was opposite the tunnel from which Ryan and the squad would emerge. Cath always loved that moment, when this great roar of approval went up for her man and the lads, when they came out onto the pitch.

She went inside to fetch herself a drink and some food, and was piling up a paper plate with prawn sandwiches and samosas when she saw him and her heart turned over.

There was no mistaking him, even though it was only his back she was looking at. He was standing in the passage guarding the door to the box, checking tickets and doing security. She knew that frame anywhere: *it was Callum.*

Muscles bulged beneath his jacket. His hair was buzz-cut close to the skull in a number two, exposing neck muscles like lengths of plaited cable.

Cath felt a wave of panic. If Callum spotted her, she'd be finished. What if he approached her in front of the other girls, talking about what they'd had . . . and about Jess? It would get back to Ryan for sure. She hastened to her seat and kept her head down – she didn't think she was visible here.

But, at the same time, she couldn't help looking round. Seeing Callum again had a strange effect on her. The last time she seen him he'd been shagging her mum and she'd told the cheating bastard to get lost, she never wanted to see him again. She'd meant it, too.

Now she wasn't so certain. She'd always had a thing for Callum, right from the first time she'd seen him outside Nero's and he'd let her in past the rope. Seeing him again, she felt a definite stirring. He was an animal, Callum, and untrustworthy, but he was all man, and she realised she still fancied him.

The game was going well for Man U. They went one up in the first ten minutes and scored again just before half-time. Ryan was on form and set up the second goal, and the girls were all congratulating her. But she couldn't get Callum out of her head. She saw him enter the buffet room and help himself to a plate piled high with sandwiches. His nose looked different, like it had been broken, and she thought he'd lost another tooth at the front too, but he was fit, with the same cheeky expression and crooked grin. She wondered if he'd recognise her, with her new hair and suntan.

The whistle sounded for half-time and everyone gravitated towards the buffet for more refreshments. But Cath hung back at the seats. She stared down at the terraces, watching the supporters surging towards the exits, and it crossed her mind Doyle and Bodie might be out there somewhere, or even her dad. Everything felt unsettled and confusing, she didn't know what she felt about anything, except she regretted coming back to Portsmouth. It had been a big mistake.

'Cath?'

Slowly, she turned, knowing who it was.

'Oh, hiya, Callum.'

'I thought it was you. You've dyed your hair.'

'Coloured it, yeah. And you've been in a fight, your nose is mashed.'

'You disappeared, Cath. No one knew where you'd gone.'

'You know why. And I don't want to talk about it, all right?'

'Aw, come on, Cath. You're looking brilliant, babe. That thing with your mum, it didn't mean anything, I was doing her a favour, that's all. She came on to me, you know that.'

'I don't want to hear. Anyway, all that's finished, it's history. I've got a new life now.'

'So how come you're sat up in a box? You entitled to be in here?'

'I'm an invited guest, I've got a ticket. You don't have to chuck me out. Anyway, I didn't know you worked at the ground.'

'There's plenty you don't know, Cath. You've been away. But, yeah, I do security, just on match days, otherwise I'm down at Nero's.'

'Got yourself a nice girl?' Cath heard herself asking.

He shrugged. 'Yeah, there's women. But I still miss you, Cath.'

'Well, you blew it, didn't you? Not still seeing my mum, are you?'

'That was stupid, I told you that. Haven't seen her in ages. Not since she put Jess into care.'

Cath flinched. 'What? She gave her away?'

'Gave her up for adoption. I told her not to but she said she couldn't manage.'

Cath made a face, then stepped back, ending the conversation. 'OK, well it was nice seeing you, Callum.'

'You moved back into town then, Cath?'

'No, miles away up north. I'd best be going.' People were starting to return to their seats, and she could see Hayley watching her with Callum and wondering who he was. 'The game's about to restart.'

'I want you, Cath.' Callum was staring at her, just like he used to, the big muscle-bound yob with the broken nose.

'Don't be an idiot, Callum.'

'I'm serious. I want you, right now. Come on, Cath, you know you do too, I can tell. A quickie for old times' sake.'

'You kidding? You're disgusting, you. Anyway, where?'

'Toilets. I've got a key to the directors' toilets.'

'You've got a nerve. If you think I'm doing it in the effing toilets . . .'

'You've done it before. You liked it then. Come on, babe.'

She felt herself weakening and followed him out into the corridor. Callum produced a key and unlocked a door into a private washroom, furnished with lavatory, basin and hand towel, which Callum said was the VIP toilet.

'This is horrible,' said Cath. 'I can't believe we're doing this.'

'You what? It's *fancy*, babe. Remember the toilets at Nero's?' And then he scooped her up and positioned her on the edge of the basin. Cath raised her arse and yanked down her own knickers as she leant back against the taps.

To Cath, it seemed like the past seven years had never happened at all, as Callum the nightclub bouncer and father of her child revived his old animal magic.

Chapter Seventeen

The Earl's Court flat in Trebovir Road which Annabel shared with her old schoolfriends Sophie Peverel and Mouse Barwell-Mackenzie occupied one part of the fourth floor of an Edwardian mansion block. From the sitting room windows and a narrow brick balcony which ran the width of the front of the building, there were views across a dank, shrub-filled communal garden, much frequented by drug users at night. The bedrooms at the back overlooked the extractor fans and overflowing rubbish bins of various Chinese and Thai restaurants. Annabel had been only too delighted to join her friends at 16 Segrave Mansions following her return from Courchevel, and they were all still here several years later. Segrave Mansions had been the scene of numerous classic parties and countless dinners, and several romantic escapades which, looking back on them, brought blushes to their cheeks, such as the time Sophie Pev brought that Lloyd's underwriter – Algy? Angus? – back to the flat after the IncredaBall at the Dorchester and was so mortified next morning that she slipped off to work before he'd woken up, leaving him to have breakfast in his dinner jacket with her two flatmates; and the time that Mouse (who was notorious for having *no* taste in men) picked up an Australian backpacker in the Europa Stores on the Old Brompton Road and kept him in her bedroom for an entire weekend, and never even found out his name (or claimed she didn't) and for weeks afterwards he kept turning up at Segrave Mansions and pressing the entryphone and Mouse pretended to be out.

How much longer the flat would survive was now in contention, since Sophie was stepping out with a stockbroker who might shortly be relocated to their Hong Kong office, and she might follow him out; and Mouse was constantly and noisily sleeping with Hector

Murray, the future Earl of Arbroath in about fifty years' time, and everyone was predicting wedding bells. In fact, Annabel could hear them through the wall now, working off their Saturday-morning hangovers in Mouse's single bed. Annabel was ironing in the sitting room while eating a bowl of muesli and turning the pages of *Smile*, one of Imperial Magazines' tackier celebrity weeklies, full of pictures of soap stars and Princess Diana. Lately, Annabel had been seriously considering quitting her job at Imperial. She had put up with her boss, Tony O'Flynn, for four years, and wasn't sure how much more of him she could take; the magazines they published became trashier and trashier, until she could scarcely bear to bring them home.

She flicked through a photo shoot of Prince Andrew and Fergie's new ranch house in Sunningdale, then turned over to a spread of party pictures. She spotted Cath at once, even though she looked different. Her hair had gone five shades blonder and she had either just returned from holiday in Barbados or tipped a jumbo bottle of self-tan over herself. Her skin had gone a strange orangey-caramel. She was wearing a beige suede cowboy jacket and was wrapped round her footballer, Ryan James, who Annabel had to admit was quite dishy if you liked footballers. The caption said they'd been photographed at some northern nightclub, Millionairz 'n' Playerz, which Annabel thought said it all.

It had been a great relief to her when Cath departed the company. Even though they'd been on different floors, and seldom crossed paths from one month to the next, it made her uncomfortable knowing she was there and that they might run in to each other in the lifts. From time to time, Annabel had needed to add Cath to the distribution list on a group memo, and her fingers always hesitated above the keys, before typing out the name Cath Fox.

Cath's abrupt resignation to live with Ryan James caused much gossip in the office. Several of the Classified team had been envious of her, though others had said, 'Poor Ryan James.' Annabel doubted it would last in any case. Her dad had seen through Cath in a few months, it would be the same with the footballer.

Having finished her ironing, she wondered what to do this weekend. Unusually, she had made no plans. There was no one special in her life at present. Pretty Annabel was never short of suitors, but for some reason never quite went for the reliable, considerate and suitable men who pursued her – she didn't know why. She allowed herself to be taken out on dates, up to the point when some greater commitment was sought and expected, but then hesitated and prevaricated, and the suitable suitor eventually backed off wondering where he'd gone wrong.

Motivated by guilt, she decided she should go round and visit her parents. It was several weeks since she had seen them and she was feeling bad about it. The truth was, the atmosphere at Napier Avenue was frequently terrible and visits didn't hold much appeal but Annabel knew her parents would be there alone. Her sister, Rosie, was on a post-Exeter University trip round Cambodia and Vietnam with her boyfriend Mark, and their brother, Tommy, was in his final year at Stowe. So she took a deep breath and invited herself to lunch.

She arrived to find Flea in the kitchen preparing a mozzarella, tomato and rucola salad. An array of goats' cheeses was also arranged in readiness for lunch on a plate thermo-printed with illustrations of exotic French cheeses. As usual, the Napier Avenue kitchen was pristine, with every cupboard door free of fingerprints, and the granite surfaces free of debris. Through each step of the cooking process, Flea liked her kitchen to look like it had never been used.

Something about the studied manner in which her mother was slicing tomatoes alerted Annabel to the fact she'd been drinking. When she'd been at the bottle, especially before lunchtime, Flea compensated by undertaking every action, and forming her sentences, with special care, so as not to stumble and give herself away. And so she crossed the kitchen and kissed her daughter with the deliberate caution of an invalid. 'Hello, darling, how lovely to see you. It's been a long time.'

Annabel thought she detected wine on her mother's breath, partially disguised by peppermint. A tell-tale box of Tic-Tacs was visible next to the spice rack.

'Sorry, it's been incredibly busy at work and lots going on. How are you? And Dad?'

'Your father's here somewhere. He's here this whole weekend, no cricket, no golf, so he's very grumpy and bored and not being very nice.'

At that moment Michael strode into the kitchen. He looked handsome, Annabel thought, in his raspberry red corduroy trousers and blue guernsey, for a man closer to sixty than fifty. Despite being half a dozen years older than his wife, Michael seemed younger than Flea these days.

'Hi, darling. I thought I heard your voice. I was in my office paying bills and on the telephone.'

At mention of the telephone, Flea became suspicious, associating the device with the means to infidelity. She asked, too quickly, 'So who were you ringing, Michael?'

Michael looked pained. 'If you must know, I was speaking to Johnnie. Johnnie Peverel. Arranging lunch for next week. That's all. Hope that's OK with you.

'So what's *your* news, darling?' he asked, turning his back on his wife. 'Everything going all right at work?'

'Sure, fine. Not sure I'm intending to stay for ever, but it's OK.'

'And what about men in your life? Any dashing new heart-throb on the scene?'

Even for her father, this was quick. Normally Michael waited until halfway through lunch before quizzing her on her love life. His questions were always phrased in similar terms: anyone 'dashing', anyone 'exciting'? Michael Goode took it for granted his elder daughter was seeking someone as close in spec to her father as humanly possible. The preferred candidate would be smooth, handsome, a wearer of raspberry red cords.

Annabel laughed. 'You're so nosy, Dad. And I'm afraid the answer's still no. Still looking for Mr Right.'

'Johnnie says Sophie's moving out to Hong Kong with her boyfriend; he's being sent there by his firm. Can't remember his name. Johnnie says he's all right, whoever he is, doesn't mind him, without being totally thrilled about it.'

'He's called David. They've known each other two years. He's nice.'

'He's a lucky chap, Sophie's a very attractive girl.'

Flea frowned. 'I wish you'd stop commenting on what every woman looks like, Michael, as if you were some kind of connoisseur. I don't like it. It's not as though your record in that department is very savoury.'

'Well, I married *you*, didn't I, darling?'

'You know what I mean, I don't have to remind you.'

The atmosphere moved from chilly to antagonistic. 'Flea, I merely observed that Sophie Peverel is an attractive girl, which she is. She is also my goddaughter. Is it a crime these days to notice someone's pretty? It doesn't mean I'm intending to run off with them.'

'It wouldn't be the first' – *firsht* – 'time, let's face it.'

'Oh, for goodness sake. That was ten years ago . . . '

'Seven, actually.'

'Seven then. I think eight. And I've said I'm sorry, I've said sorry dozens of times, hundreds. Sorry, sorry, sorry. There, that's three more. But you won't leave it. I can scarcely remember the girl's name, for heaven's sake.'

'I can. Cath Fox.'

'OK, Cath Fox. I haven't seen or heard of her in years.'

'Then it may interest you to know,' Flea said, picking her words carefully, 'that your old mistress – the one who left her horrible hairs all over my bathroom carpet – is now the girlfriend of some professional footballer. I was having my colour done and flicking through that new magazine – *Hello!* – at the hairdressers, and there she was with him. I recognised her at once, even with peroxided hair. And she's calling herself Kate these days. So that's the sort of girl *she* is – a footballer's girlfriend, very classy.'

Michael, who knew nothing of Cath's latest incarnation, only said, 'Forget it, Flea. It isn't helpful, going on like this.'

'I'm sure you *would* like to forget it,' said Flea. 'I expect you'd like us all to forget it. That would be very convenient for you, I see that. But we haven't forgotten, have we, Annabel? When your father ran off with your school matron. It wasn't a lot of fun for *us*, even if it was for you, Michael. So we haven't forgotten about it, no.'

The Goodes sat down for their Saturday lunch, and Annabel saw her father watch Flea uneasily as she removed a second bottle of rosé from the fridge door and place it in front of her on the table.

Annabel felt demoralised as she left Napier Avenue and bicycled home. With no fixed plans for the rest of the day, no friends to see, no man, she wondered how she was going to fill the time. She headed up the New King's Road and cut across Parson's Green towards North End Road. Outside the White Horse pub there was, as usual, a large crowd of drinkers spilling onto the pavement and leaning against cars. The

White Horse had a reputation as a 'Sloaney' pub, much frequented by estate agents, army officers and upmarket car dealers and their birds. When she'd been living in Napier Avenue, Annabel often met friends there after work, especially in the summer when they served Pimm's in half-pint tankards with huge tufts of mint.

She was pedalling by when she heard her name called: 'Annabel! Bells!' The voice was vaguely familiar and she stared into the thicket of young men in covert coats and tweed jackets.

Then she spotted him: Rupert Henley. 'Hey, Bellsie, over here.'

Rupert looked virtually unchanged since Courchevel – hair slightly shorter, face slimmer. He was standing in a group of fit-looking male friends, holding half pints of Bloody Mary. Annabel wished she wasn't astride a bicycle: never a good look, she felt. It was the first time she'd seen Rupert in years, since his departure on the dawn coach to Geneva following their two-night stand at the Chalet Cheva.

'Hello, Rupert.' She dismounted and kissed him.

Seeing him again, she felt nothing beyond mild embarrassment and curiosity. She did not blame him for making no effort to stay in touch, not even a telephone call, having made no effort herself.

'Guys, this is Bells. Annabel Goode . . . we met skiing in Courchevel on this crazy chalet holiday.' Then he introduced his companions, 'This is Jamie, Jamie Pilcher. And George Palmer. We're soldiers, in case you didn't realise.'

'You're in the army?'

'Been stationed out in Germany for two years, in Münster. Just got back to London, thank God.'

He said that his regiment, the Irish Guards, was headquartered at Wellington Barracks next to Buckingham Palace, and that it was a relief to be able to speak to proper women again, because the women in Germany were all German.

'That's typical bloody Rupert,' roared Jamie, joshing him. 'Always thinking about bloody frauleins. Classic. I hope Rupert didn't cause you any grief in Courchevel, Annabel? He's a total caveman when it comes to women. You do realise?'

'Er, no, he was fine,' Annabel replied, blushing. She was surprised to find herself rather attracted to Jamie, who was a taller, more drawling, more handsome version of Rupert, with thick brown hair swept back across his forehead, and with a dangerous edge she found exciting.

The third man, George, she scarcely registered; he was quieter and less confident than his brother officers, with a kind face. He watched her attentively during her conversation with Rupert and Jamie, but hardly joined in.

Rupert and Jamie were full of the joys of regimental life. All three men were captains though Jamie was also adjutant and thus technically senior to his two friends. Their conversation centred around various hilarious misadventures while training in the pine forests around Soltau. There was something at once commanding and adolescent about them; one minute grave and self-important with the burden of leading platoons of semi-educated squaddies into battle, the next delirious with the high jinks of the officers' mess, and pranks involving tequila, a firework and the regimental Irish wolfhound.

Jamie insisted on buying her a glass of wine, and sending George inside to fetch it, while he rather obviously chatted her up. 'Do you ride? No? I'm surprised, I thought you might from the way you were handling your bicycle. Nice seat.' And, later, 'So you grew up near the Hurlingham? We're putting on a charity ball at Hurlingham next Saturday. In aid of the victims of the Russian invasion of Afghanistan. Going to be a hell of a rave, live band, dodgems, you name it. You're coming as my date.'

'I am? Er, thank you. I'll need to check what I'm doing.'

'I'll take that as a yes, then. Anyway, you can confirm tomorrow, yes or no.'

'How do I get hold of you?'

'You don't, I get hold of you. I'm collecting you from wherever it is you live at seven thirty for drinks.'

'You are?'

'Assume you like cocktails? Trader Vic's at the Hilton. Big boys' drinks, kick like a mule.'

'Sounds great,' she said, uncertainly.

'So where do I find you?'

Annabel gave her address in Trebovir Road. 'I share with my flatmates, Sophie and Mouse.'

'Harem in deepest darkest Earl's Court, eh? Very enticing. See you there then.'

*

Annabel didn't quite know what to make of Jamie Pilcher. He was sleek and super-confident, which she found oddly attractive, accustomed as she was to working in the magazine company surrounded by flabby divas and ingratiating hypochondriacs. Captain Pilcher was tall, fit and smooth. He had a way of looking at her which was unnerving, as though he was sizing her up like a cheetah sizing up an impala as a potential lunch. He mentioned he had a flat in Pimlico, on Cambridge Street, within walking distance of his barracks, and a widowed mother living near Oakham in Rutland. As she bathed and changed to go out, Annabel decided that Jamie wasn't her kind of man, she didn't trust him, and wondered why she'd agreed to go. But when the intercom buzzed and she heard his barking voice – 'I'm calling for Annabel Goode' – she hastened to the lift, not wanting to keep him waiting.

He drove at speed up Cromwell Road in his shiny blue Audi, perfectly clean inside and out; the handiwork, he mentioned, of his batman, the same man who shone his shoes. His cheeks smelt over-poweringly of Eau Sauvage. He said he had a black Labrador, Monty, who didn't appreciate London so lived with his mother in Rutland. 'You have to meet Monty,' he said. 'Though he does get jealous when I bring new women home. It's like a test: does Monty approve?'

'How daunting. Being judged by a Labrador.'

'Don't worry, I'm sure he'll give you the tails-up. He loves gorgeous brunettes.'

He parked the car in a mews behind the Hilton and they entered a long, dark bar with a Kon Tiki theme; wooden Pacific Island sculptures and dugout canoes suspended from the walls. It was difficult to see anything, though Jamie seemed to know the way. She trailed him to a circular table at the back, already filled with army officers and girls and covered with cocktail glasses. She spotted Rupert and the other one, George, in the gloom.

'Oh, I gather you had a fling with Rupert in that ski resort,' said Jamie, as they approached the table. 'He says you're a cracker in the cot.'

Annabel blushed crimson.

'Don't tell Rupert I said that,' Jamie went on. 'He's proprietorial about his exes.'

A Thai waiter arrived, tilting his pad under the pencil beam of a downlighter and trying to capture the list of conflicting orders being thrown in his direction.

'That's two Brandy Manhattans, waiter, one Havana Zombie . . . and, Alice, what was yours? Another Harvey Wallbanger? No? Oh come on, don't wimp out – waiter, that's another Harvey Wallbanger for Alice and . . . Rupert, Piers . . . you ordered?'

'Yah, Prohibition Punch please, one Sidecar and, Rosie, fancy another Slow Comfortable Screw Up Against the Wall?'

'Bet she does,' roared Rupert. 'And another of those Hawaiian tropical punchbowls for the table with ten straws.'

Jamie and Annabel squeezed onto the end of the banquette where, in the abrupt, random manner he favoured, he quizzed her about her life to date. It felt like being questioned by a research company in the street: 'School? Jobs? Father's occupation?' Annabel found herself wanting to please him with her replies, as though it was another test to be passed. But sometimes she found his questions uncomfortably probing: 'Had plenty of boyfriends, Annabel? I assume so, fabulous-looking girl like you.' To which her reply was, 'I don't meet that many men, sadly. St Mary's was all girls. The teachers at Miss Claire's were all female and the magazine company is mostly women too.'

'So nobody in your life I need be aware of?'

'No,' she giggled.

'Shame. I enjoy a contest. All my best women were taken off other blokes. Not in the regiment, obviously. Civilians. Fair game.'

The waiter returned with further multicoloured cocktail orders – verdant green crème de menthe, bright pink cassis, golden champagne cocktails – until the tabletop was filled with every variety of liqueur. Annabel soon felt flushed and light-headed, and wished there was food. Two small saucers of chicken satay and prawn crackers quickly disappeared.

Across the table she saw Rupert flanked by two tipsy blondes, and wished he hadn't told Jamie about Courchevel. The officer seated on her other side, George Palmer, whom she'd hardly noticed during her conversations with Jamie, asked her if she'd like a glass of water, and fetched it for her from the bar. He told her he'd been at school at Wellington with Jamie but was a couple of years younger; Jamie, he said, had been head of the corps – the Combined Cadet Force – and a schoolboy hero. George himself, he said, had joined the army with mixed feelings, really wanting to be an artist, but his father wouldn't pay for him to go to art school. Annabel found him an interesting and sympathetic man but was soon drawn back into Jamie's orbit by the stronger pull of his character.

'OK, team,' Jamie said eventually. 'It's past eleven o'clock, some of us are on exercise tomorrow at six a.m. Say goodnight to the ladies, please. Annabel, I'm dropping you back at your harem. George, take care of the tab and we'll settle up tomorrow.'

He then drove Annabel at great speed back along Cromwell Road, weaving between the traffic, seemingly unaffected by the half-dozen divergent cocktails inside him.

'So, Annabel,' he said on the pavement. 'See you next Saturday at Hurlingham. Should be a classic night.'

Jamie called for her at Trebovir Road and this time came up to the flat. Annabel had been looking out for him, watched his Audi pull up at the kerb and Jamie crossing the pavement in full regimental mess kit. Weaving between the backpackers of Earl's Court, he looked seriously incongruous but heartstoppingly handsome in cutaway red jacket with black lapels and gold braid, and tight black trousers with red stripe down the outside. She could hear the clink of spurs on shiny black boots.

Looming into the flat, he seemed to fill the place. Hector Murray, the future earl, shrank in stature by comparison. Both Soph and Mouse were spellbound by the dashing captain and Mouse gave a thumbs-up behind his back: 'Go for it, Bells.' He told the flatmates he'd been in Rutland for twenty-four hours 'visiting my dog and my mother', which reinforced the general impression that Jamie Pilcher was a mighty fine prospect.

Annabel had spent all of the past week wondering what to wear, and had even taken advice from the fashion department at *Cosima*, going through rails and rails of clothes with them, though ultimately rejecting their recommendations as too weird and trendy. In the end she'd bought a new taffeta ball dress in a lilac shade which worked with her colouring, and which she wore with black lacy tights. Eighty per cent of the guests would have army connections, Jamie said, and the ball was expected to go right through to dawn. When Annabel mentioned she was stressing over her outfit, he'd said, 'I really wouldn't worry, sweetheart, you'll look gorgeous in anything.'

They arrived at Hurlingham to find four hundred people milling about on the lawn, girls in long taffeta dresses, men in black tie or mess kit. It was a warm June evening and the flaps of the marquee were open on one side, forty round tables laid in readiness for dinner and the shallow stage for the band. A dodgems rink and smaller tents, set up as bars and casinos, dotted the perimeter: people were already clustered around the green baize of a roulette table, and Jamie said that at a previous army ball he had won a thousand pounds in an incredible run of luck, and taken the lady of the moment for a weekend in Paris. Annabel felt a twinge of jealousy, hearing of the existence of this former girlfriend.

Jamie escorted her around the lawn, introducing her to officers and to his commanding officer, who asked her if she was anything to do with Michael Goode and was delighted when she replied he was her father, since they'd been stationed out in Hong Kong years before. Annabel noticed how the younger officers were especially nice to her, fetching her drinks and complimenting her on her dress. She felt very well cared for in the company of these attentive army officers, with their good manners and good looks.

Dinner was called and she found herself on a table comprising many of the same group from Trader Vic's. She was seated next to Jamie, with Rupert Henley on her other side – he had one of his tipsy blondes from last Saturday next to him. George Palmer, the watercolourist, gave a shy smile across the table. There was a beaky redhead named Rowena who worked as a secretary at Strutt and Parker, and a voluptuous girl, Rosie, with breasts tumbling out of a black taffeta ball dress, on Jamie's other side. Jamie was wonderful company. He pointed out officers at adjacent tables, telling her scurrilous stories about them and making her laugh. Charlie, he said, had narrowly missed driving a Chieftain tank slap-bang into Stonehenge during thick fog on Salisbury Plain. But sometimes Jamie came over all serious and sincere, telling her how much tonight's charity meant to him personally, because two British officers he knew well had lost their lives training the mujahidin in Afghanistan during the Soviet invasion and how crucial it was to help in any way one could. He asked Annabel whether she thought any of her magazines could write helpful articles about the charity, and Annabel felt ashamed since Imperial's magazines mostly wrote about pop stars, royalty and diets.

A salmon and leek roulade was followed by a mound of beef shaped like a doughnut and finally bread and butter pudding with caramelised toffee sauce. Rupert, who had been drinking solidly throughout dinner and flirting with his blonde, turned to Annabel and asked, 'So, are you going out with Jamie?'

'Well, he's brought me tonight which is very kind of him. But I don't think that means we're going out together.'

'You know what I mean. Have you slept with him yet?'

'No! We only met last Saturday. This is only the third time we've seen each other.'

'Don't leave it too long. Jamie doesn't hang about.'

'Really, Rupert. And thank you for your interest.'

'Anyway, I'm sure you've heard all about Jamie. His legendary wanger.'

'What?'

'Apparently it's huge.'

'Honestly, Rupert. I'm blushing. I don't know what to say.'

'Gasp, I should think, when you finally get to see it. Don't say you weren't warned.'

It was time for speeches and a succession of fundraisers and soldiers approached the microphone. A major from a tank regiment thanked everyone for coming and supporting such a wonderful charity before handing over to a twittering professional fundraiser who thanked the major and numerous people in the back office before introducing another soldier who had visited Afghanistan and had actually met the mujahidin leader General Rashid Dostum and witnessed the situation at first hand, who then handed over to the ball's co-chairwomen who stood together in their taffeta ball gowns thanking everyone all over again and hoping they would have a fabulous time tonight, and then explained various complicated procedures involving envelopes and table heads and lucky tickets and pledge cards by which further donations could be made. In the course of these long speeches, Annabel became conscious of Jamie's hand resting on her knee, and later creeping upwards onto her lap. It was not altogether an unwelcome development, though Rupert's earlier information gave her pause for thought, and she wondered what exactly she did think about Captain Jamie Pilcher.

His hand was now straying under the hem of her dress, which had bunched up on her knees, and she couldn't decide whether to remove it or ignore it. She stared straight ahead, pretending to pay attention to the speeches. Once or twice she caught the gaze of George, seated opposite, and was glad he couldn't see the captain's encroaching hand.

When his fingers began probing the edge of her knickers, Annabel firmly pushed them away and brushed down her dress. She was conscious of Rupert watching the unfolding show from the sidelines and smirking.

Jamie swung round to his other side following this rebuff, murmuring something to Rosie who shrieked with laughter and the speechmaker was temporarily put off her stride.

Having turned his back on Annabel, Jamie proceeded to ignore her during the laborious serving of coffee. Then, when dinner started to break up and the band came on stage, he led Rosie away to dance. Annabel could see them bopping to a cover version of Thin Lizzie's 'The Boys Are Back in Town', with Rosie swinging her big tits around the dance floor. Annabel began to wonder if she'd been too prudish.

At the end of each song, she expected him to return to the table. But each track segued into the next, and Jamie and Rosie remained on the dance floor, boogying together conspicuously.

Annabel was determined not to look pathetic or rejected, despite having nobody to dance with. George the watercolourist came over and asked if she'd like a bop but she smiled sweetly and turned him down, thinking Jamie would come back soon.

'See?' Rupert said, as he swept his blonde off to dance. 'You've blown it, Bells. Jamie hates being kept hanging about.'

The band was playing a medley of Abba songs and the audience was lapping it up. 'Sooper Trooper,' they sang along, militarising the lyrics. Afterwards, hideously chirpy, came 'Tie a Yellow Ribbon Round the Ole Oak Tree'.

'Sure you don't want to dance?' asked George.

'Really, I'm fine,' replied Annabel with a sad smile.

It was puzzling, she could no longer see Jamie anywhere on the dance floor. For the best part of an hour he and Rosie had been larking about at the front but now there was no sign of them. Probably they'd moved deeper into the throng. She'd like to have checked but didn't want to look like she was spying.

The band struck up a new tune which raised a cheer. Annabel recognised it at once, since its irritating lyric had been lodged inside her brain for several years. 'Oops, upside your head,' and at once the crowd began forming into a conga, clutching each other's waists and sitting on the floor like a rowing crew, swaying back and forth. 'Oops, upside your head say oops, upside your head . . .' Caught up in the general rush of spectators towards the dance floor, Annabel only confirmed that Jamie and Rosie were no longer there.

Now she felt such an idiot. Rupert was right: she had blown it. There he was, the perfect man, seated right next to her, and she'd driven him away as she always did. What was wrong with her? All her friends had boyfriends, a few were married already, or soon would be, two were actually mothers of small babies. And yet, faced with a dream man with a Labrador, she'd blown it.

She would gladly have gone home but without Jamie had no transport. So she wandered about the lawn, watching the gambling, watching out for Jamie. Each five minutes felt like an hour. The dodgems were doing brisk business. Two dozen cars swerved and collided, driven by officers in mess kit. Girls in taffeta dresses were shrieking. Annabel watched while two cars had a full-on collision, rebounding into the cars behind. She saw Rupert bump violently into the car in front: 'Up the arse.' Then she spotted Jamie. He was steering one-handed with his arm draped over Rosie's shoulder, cupping her left breast. Rosie was lighting up a fag and leaning into him. Annabel retreated to the casino and longed to be home.

Five minutes later she felt a tap on her shoulder. 'Annabel! I've been looking for you everywhere. Where the hell did you disappear to?' It was Jamie with a look of relief on his face. 'No one knew where you'd gone.'

'I've been out here watching the gambling.'

'Which reminds me. What's your lucky number, sweetheart? I want to place a big bet on it.'

'My lucky number? Er, sixteen? It's our flat number.'

'Sixteen it is.' He was leading her by the hand back to the roulette table. 'Twenty quid's worth of chips please on black sixteen.'

'That's crazy,' Annabel said. 'That's so much.'

'You make me feel lucky.' The silver ball spun and clattered inside the wheel, before coming to rest on three red.

'Oh no, now you've lost twenty pounds,' cried Annabel.

Jamie shrugged. 'You know what they say: unlucky at the tables, lucky in love. Now, I've been waiting to dance with you all evening, darling. Stay with me this time and don't run off again.'

As they made it to the dance floor, Annabel very nearly believed him, and an hour later, having danced non-stop, was almost reassured that her suspicions had been entirely misplaced; Jamie was the most chivalrous of men and a brilliant dancer, and she wondered how she could ever have doubted him.

Captain George Palmer, soldier and watercolourist, was hopelessly smitten with Annabel. From the moment he had seen her outside the White Horse pub, he was besotted. He loved her pretty face, her smile, and more than that felt that he recognised in her an inner goodness, a sweetness of character which touched him.

It was perpetual torment to have to stand by and watch his friend make a play for her, especially when he knew that friend to be unworthy. It pained him to listen to Jamie speak disrespectfully of her as a future conquest. And it pained him more when he'd heard Rupert tell Jamie that Annabel was good in bed.

At the same time, he was conscious that his own sensitive personality would never be enough to win her. He was too bashful, too sincere in his affections; George already knew, from bitter past experience, that these fine sensibilities invariably lost out against the direct action of a philanderer. All these thoughts played on his mind as he stood behind his easel in St James's Park, painting a view of Horse Guards Parade. Each afternoon, regimental duties discharged, he would carry his watercolours into the surrounding parks and streets and work away, painting views of the Household Cavalry parading past Whitehall, or a vista of Buckingham Palace or the bridge across the Serpentine. Other times he chose as subjects random buildings around the barracks, such as the Queen's Gallery or the Victorian Gothic façade of the Buckingham Gate Plaza Hotel. Even during regimental exercises in Germany, his blocks and tubes of paint travelled with him and he would be found mixing the burnt umber, raw sienna and yellow ochres with water on his palette, attempting to capture the spirit of the Soltau forests. When he looked back at his efforts he was seldom satisfied, though liked to believe he was improving, little by little. One day he hoped to reach the standard where he could hold a small exhibition, though that day still felt a long way off. When he'd mastered watercolours, he wanted to try his hand at oils. And, most of all, he'd like to paint a portrait of Annabel Goode.

It should be firmly noted that Annabel did not end up in bed with Captain Jamie Pilcher on the night of the Hurlingham ball; she was not that kind of girl. In fact it was a further five weeks before she was persuaded, after supper at Ziani's in Radnor Walk, to return with him to his Pimlico bachelor pad in Cambridge Street, where their relationship would move on and up to the next level. Here she found herself in a second-floor flat crowded with pieces of brown furniture, sagging armchairs and a regimental tin trunk employed as a coffee table. On the walls, regimental prints and a watercolour by George Palmer of a black Labrador. In the bedroom, a large wooden bed with a wooden headboard, its sheets and blankets in an unmade heap, was the inevitable destination for besotted Annabel who was about to encounter his legendary wanger for the first time

Afterwards, while Jamie smoked a cigarette and considered whether or not he could be fagged to drop her home, or ring for a cab, he remarked, 'I enjoyed that, Annabel, you're a great girl. Rupert was right. Let's do that again sometime soon.'

Chapter Eighteen

While Annabel was attending her first army ball with her dashing captain, and Cath renewing an old friendship with Callum, poor Jess Eden, recently turned teenager, did not consider her life to be exciting at all. In fact, as she confided to her best friend Bryony, she didn't know of a single other person her age who led a duller life, in a duller place, with more boring or annoying parents, than she did here in the village of Long Barton in Bedfordshire.

It was a place in which precisely nothing happened unless you counted the Brownies, which she had outgrown, or the church choir, which she wanted to quit but her parents wouldn't hear of it, or the various embarrassing village events such as the annual fun run ('the no-fun run') in aid of the hospice, and the hog roast in the garden of the Crown and Cushion with its tombola and bouncy castle. What made it so unfair was that most of her schoolfriends lived in towns like Biggleswade and Leighton Buzzard, and were allowed to go out wherever they wanted at weekends, shopping, cinema, whatever, without needing to be driven everywhere and collected and having to declare exactly who they were seeing, whereas she was trapped in Long Barton like a prisoner, and her parents treated her like she was still ten or eleven or something, when nobody else's parents did.

And what made it doubly unjust and ridiculous, as Jess saw it, was that she did everything to please them. She had got a place at the Bishop Ottley School for Girls in Leighton Buzzard, where there were ten girls trying for each place, and her school reports confirmed how hard she was working. She swam for the school Under 13s and had achieved a faster time in front crawl than anyone, apart from the swimming captain. Her summer project on the Story of Chocolate had been commended for a High Mistresses' prize and won her a £10 book token. Now Jess wondered what the point of it had been, all that work researching South American cocoa beans and wasting a whole day being driven by her dad up to Cadbury World at Bournville to do research, if her parents still didn't trust her and wouldn't let her go clothes shopping with Bryony in Milton Keynes on the bus. And it wasn't even that anything bad would happen, they were only going to Top Shop, Miss Selfridge and River Island, which were all in the pedestrian precinct; their friends went every weekend and it wasn't a big deal.

Nowhere on earth is quite so dreary as a small English village in Bedfordshire. On Saturday afternoons she and Bryony would walk together along the pavement, past where the new housing petered out, to the Esso garage on the main road and buy soft drinks and Pringles and celebrity magazines. They would then walk back to the bus shelter where there was a bench. Jess's favourite mag at the moment was *Smile*, which had all the juiciest gossip about Kylie and Madonna and Take That and photos of celebrities caught off guard, such as George Michael papped inside a supermarket – just imagine going into your local Tesco and actually finding him there, it would be the most amazing thing in your life.

But it wasn't going to happen in Long Barton, which didn't even have a Tesco. Seated on the bench, part-shielded from the wind by the glass-sided bus shelter, Jess and Bryony paged through the latest *Smile*. Jess paused at photographs of footballers' wives and partners taken in the stands at Manchester United, and all the ladies looked so beautiful and well-groomed with their suntans and highlights, and dressed in all the latest designer styles, that the two teenagers felt quite downcast.

Kirsty and Bob Eden were not, in fact, nearly so boring or unusual as their adoptive daughter would have the world believe. Kirsty was, to be sure, a woman lacking in glamour and eccentricity, which is what Jess most wished for in a mother. The list of topics in which Kirsty was uninterested was long and, Jess considered, damning, and included soap stars, pop stars, hair dyes, celebrity magazines, cosmetics, jewellery and ear piercing (Jess was one of only three girls in her class at Bishop Ottley's without pierced ears). The subjects in which Kirsty *was* interested – namely the church, the Women's Institute, cooking and education – struck Jess as deadly. Similarly, Bob was interested in little beyond rugby, swimming and his job. Admittedly, he supported Jess in her swimming but that was because swimming was one of his own hobbies. He was tight with money and it distressed her that she had fewer new clothes than practically anyone in her school, and Bob always backed up her mum on her stupid rules about ear piercing and not wearing lipstick. The Eden parents were, in short, an honest, slightly serious couple, who made countless contributions to the village and the wider community. They personified what politicians term 'ordinary, decent, hardworking British families'. But if you were selecting a couple with whom to enjoy a hilarious, gossipy dinner, you almost certainly would not fix upon Bob and Kirsty Eden as your first choices.

Recently, Jess had begun to speculate about who her real parents might be, and whether they were still alive somewhere. It was pretty obvious, given the gulf between herself and Kirsty and Bob, that her birth mum and dad would be a lot more exciting; film stars most likely, and certainly very rich. She daydreamed that one evening, when they were all sat round doing homework, this great big stretch limo would pull up outside Burdock Cottage and a uniformed chauffeur get out and open the car door, and out would step Julia Roberts or Princess Diana saying, 'Darling Jess, at last I've found you . . .'

Jess kept her precious locket in a musical jewellery box in her bedroom, and it had become a tradition that she take it out once a year on her birthday and wear it to her party. She was afraid to wear it more often because the chain was so thin and cheap (something she chose to ignore in her daydreams) it might snap and get lost. But she often stared at the tiny photo of her birth mum, no larger than a two pence coin, faded and fogged under its perspex frame, and wondered about her. You could tell she was a very beautiful lady. At her thirteenth birthday supper at TGI Friday's in Leighton Buzzard, where her mum and dad treated her and six classmates, Jess unhooked the clasp and passed the locket round the table, inviting her friends to take a look. She never made a secret of being adopted, considering it rather special. One of her schoolfriends, Holly, thought the lady looked like Carol Vorderman off *Countdown*, which was an exciting prospect, and might account for why Jess was so bright at school.

Kirsty laughed it all off and tried not to feel hurt, knowing it was natural for an adopted child to speculate about such matters, though she did feel a little bit sad inside. But afterwards, in the car home, Jess snuggled up to her in the back seat, and said, 'Thanks, Mum, for an amazing party. And thanks, Dad, for taking us and paying. It was really kind of you. My friends had a really nice time. And you weren't even that embarrassing tonight either.'

Chapter Nineteen

Back at Ryan's Altrincham flat, Cath filed the latest Callum encounter in Portsmouth in a secret place inside her head. Outwardly it was as if nothing had happened. Which, as Cath reasoned to herself, nothing really had; you couldn't say she'd done anything underhand, because she'd been with Callum before she'd met Ryan, so it wasn't like she'd been messing with some new bloke. Anyway, she'd already mentioned the existence of Callum to Ryan, sort of.

It was true that Cath occasionally referred to a nightclub bouncer in her past. She'd discovered, in the first few months of living with Ryan, that he was turned on by hearing details about her ex-boyfriends. Sometimes, in bed, he would ask her, 'So you lost it to an effing bouncer at a club door, did you, Katie?'

And Cath would reply, 'Yeah, but he wasn't a patch on you, Ryan. You're way better, he didn't have your skills and ball control.' And then she ran her fingers through his hedgehog hair and squeezed his tight little arse, and made sure she worked him up into a nice hot sweat, which was what he liked and expected from their lovemaking.

'So how do I compare to your club doorman then, Katie?' he would ask in the moments before his climax, and Cath who was adept at faking it, gasped, 'Don't stop, don't stop. You're the best, Ryan.'

But the truth was, she had found the reprise with Callum unsettling. It had been quite a shock seeing her old lover, in ways she hadn't expected. For a start he was uglier than she remembered. Losing a tooth at the front hadn't helped, and she discovered he was missing a few others deeper inside his gob too. His neck had grown thicker with a roll of fat, but his biceps and triceps were rock hard, as was every other inch of him. He smelt horrible – she had forgotten his distinctive smell – the smell which had hung about his flat of sweat, drains, Brut and lager. After Ryan, with his neat little features and almost feminine complexion, Callum was fourteen stone of gristle, with stubble like sandpaper on his chin. But when he had lifted her up on to the sink in the VIP toilet, he'd reawakened in her a lust she'd almost forgotten existed.

Not that she was under any illusions. Ten minutes of huffing and puffing and thrusting in a toilet cubicle was hardly going to change her life. Callum was a dirty illiterate beast. Noticing her latest tattoo, he'd asked, 'Why've you had BJ put on your shoulder?'

'It's RJ actually, my friend's initials.'

'Oh, I thought it meant Blow Job.'

The episode with Callum – the whole visit to Portsmouth – only reminded her of why she'd left, and the distance she'd travelled since then. It had taken three days of baths and showers to wash the smell of Pompey out of her hair; that first evening back in Manchester, sleeping next to Ryan, she kept thinking she could smell Callum in the bedclothes and was worried Ryan might smell it too. But Ryan was miles away, sleeping the untroubled sleep of the innocent. And Cath, remembering certain aspects of her time with Callum, found herself frisky and unable to switch off.

Her life with Ryan had, by now, assumed the comfortable routine of a mature marriage. Ryan's days were occupied with team training to maintain match fitness; Cath's with gym training to maintain bedroom fitness. She still accompanied him to many of his away matches, and was by now familiar with half the Hiltons and Marriotts of England, as they criss-crossed the country from stadium to stadium. Ryan was having a strong season and his reputation and pay soared; when a new club contract became due, Cath played an aggressive role in jacking it up, far beyond the level at which Ryan himself would gladly have settled. He kept saying, 'I'm enjoying me game and I like the club, Katie. I don't want to transfer anywhere else.' But Cath planted rumours that Liverpool and Everton were both after him, which prompted Man U to come through with their enhanced offer. As Cath explained it to Ryan, Barbara, Alf and Dean on one of their frequent visits to the flat, it was important for Ryan to be paid fairly, it was a question of respect. One day, when the ban was lifted on English clubs playing abroad, and the whole Heysel disaster thing was forgotten, there would surely be bigger triumphs for Ryan to come. He could achieve international status.

Flushed with success at doubling her boyfriend's pay, Cath felt she was owed a reward, and spent more time than ever in the boutiques of Wilmslow and Manchester. Increasingly, she liked to shop in a posse with the other players' girlfriends, and she and Anita and Hayley became favourites with the boutique owners who invited them for exclusive previews when the new stock of designer labels came in, plying them with complimentary glasses of champagne. Cath was thrilled when a local magazine, *Manchester Life*, commissioned a specially taken group photograph of the wives and girlfriends of the two rival Manchester clubs; they all assembled in a studio, with hair and make-up professionally done, and were photographed in their best designer gowns, surrounded by the carrier bags of their favourite local boutiques. The result was undeniably classy, even if some of the other ladies let the side down with fat arms. Cath ordered herself ten copies of the issue. It felt like an achievement, to be photographed in her own right without Ryan being the main focus of the publicity for a change.

From time to time, on those days when Barbara came over to do the flat, and Dean accompanied her to watch TV on the leather settee, it did occur to Cath that she should find some occupation, a job or even study something at college. She remembered how she'd enjoyed learning stuff when she'd been with Charlie Blaydon, and how he'd always been on about his portraits and rare silver candelabras. She'd found all that quite interesting. But it wouldn't be the same studying it at Wythenshawe Tech compared to lapping it up at Blaydon Hall.

And, anyway, she saw herself as Ryan's unofficial manager these days, so what with that and the retail therapy, she hadn't got the time.

It was in this capacity as Ryan's business manager that Cath pulled off a second coup.

She spotted in the newspapers that the American fragrance Kick for Men was shortly to be launched in Britain and was searching for a sportsman to feature in its advertising. With her knowledge of perfumes, Cath had already heard of Kick, which had been massive in the States and was right up there with Fire and Ice by Revlon and Davidoff's Cool Water. She put in a call to an old advertising contact in London and obtained the address of the Kick offices, then posted off some photographs and cuttings about Ryan.

Several weeks later, she heard back. Kick for Men's Marketing Director was interested and wanted to travel up to Manchester with their advertising agency to take trial shots. When Cath excitedly told Ryan the news, he was dubious: 'No way am I appearing in any perfume advertisement, Katie. Do you think I'm a poof or what?'

But Cath reassured him. Kick had been launched in the States by major league baseball and football stars. 'Trust me, Ryan.'

Eventually he consented to meet the people and hear what they had to say.

They met in the lobby of the Four Seasons and afterwards took Polaroids of Ryan in the hotel car park. Even Cath was surprised by how many people had travelled up to Manchester; three young women from Kick for Men's marketing team, an American marketing chief from the parent company, UniGlobal Corporation of Atlanta, and four more from the London advertising agency – account director, photographer, his assistant and a creative director. Ryan turned silent and shy, leaving Cath to do the talking. Which she was good at. Ryan felt very grateful to his girlfriend, listening to the way she bigged up his talent to the visitors. All he needed do was nod from time to time. And he was amazed when he heard Cath tell them he'd had previous overtures from rival fragrance companies, which they'd turned down because the fee was too small.

The American boss Doug Maggiotti was serious and measured, describing the phenomenon of Kick for Men in the States, where it had been the number-one selling fragrance for over a year. He explained it had been a breakthrough product for UniGlobal Corp, hitherto the world's largest manufacturer of detergents and household brands but now diversifying into the cosmetics and fragrance market. Kick for Men had exceeded its business plan by a factor of twenty, and was being launched in seventeen new markets around the world. The original Kick for Men aftershave had been followed by a comprehensive roll-out of brand extensions, including a prestige cologne, body wash, deodorant, exfoliator and soap on a rope. Ryan's eyes glazed over when the marketing manager described the unique formula with its top notes of peppermint and citrus and middle notes of sandalwood, cedarwood and mimosa, but Cath was quite the expert, talking about her lifelong love of perfume and all the different brands and their advertising campaigns.

Outside in the car park, Ryan was willingly compliant, tilting his face this way and that for the photographer, and smouldering without smiling into the camera lens as instructed.

'How was that then, Ryan?' Cath asked him after the delegation had packed up and gone. 'You all right?'

'Wasn't so bad,' he replied, sounding surprised. 'I quite enjoyed meself, Katie. Not so bad as I expected.'

Six weeks later, Ryan and Cath drove down from Manchester to UniGlobal's UK headquarters in Slough where Ryan was formally signed up as the advertising face and brand ambassador for Kick for Men. Cath handled the entire negotiation, having sent Ryan out to wait in reception while she did the business. UniGlobal's lawyers were unprepared for her tenacity, and the focus she put on every last clause in the contract. After four gruelling hours, Ryan was brought back into the room to sign the revised deal. He would appear in all print and point-of-sale material, as well as feature in a TV and cinema commercial and make twenty-five personal appearances in department stores. Afterwards, when Cath told him what he'd be paid, he was gobsmacked; it was the same as he made in the whole season playing football.

The Kick for Men agency returned to Manchester, this time in even greater numbers, and spent three full days photographing and filming Ryan at Old Trafford. The sixty-second commercial showed him dribbling a football past half a dozen opponents to delirious cheers of the crowd, before powering it into the back of the net. Cut to Ryan in the dressing room, emerging from the shower with dripping hair and towel round his waist, anointing his cheeks with Kick for Men. A voice-over in Ryan's surprisingly squeaky tones declared, 'I always get my daily kicks . . . Kick for Men . . .' Cut to product with ball-shaped flacon and silver metallic packaging.

The advertising done and dusted, neither Ryan nor Cath heard anything for several months, beyond requests for dates for personal appearances. In the weeks following the launch, Ryan was booked to sign autographs and bottles of fragrance in a dozen cosmetics halls of House of Fraser, and Cath carefully scheduled these to fit in with Ryan's match schedule. Wherever he was playing, they would drive down the previous day and he would do his bit for UniGlobal.

It was Ryan's brother Dean who was first to catch the TV commercial. He'd been stretched out on Ryan's leather settee, digging into a tub of KFC, when it came on during the break. Dean shouted out, 'Oi, Mum, quick, look at this,' and Barbara, who'd been rinsing out the bath, hurried through and saw the end of it. After that they sat together all afternoon waiting for it to air again, which it did several times. When Cath got home from shopping, she found Alf and Ryan sat there too, having just viewed it in the break in *Coronation Street.* All agreed Ryan came over brilliant. 'I always get me daily kicks,' said Dean imitating him. 'It was quite good, that.'

Ryan quickly got fed up with people quoting the slogan back at him. His teammates ribbed him incessantly: 'Had yer daily kicks yet, Ryan?' Even in the Chinese restaurant they joked about it. Ryan found it embarrassing but Cath told him, 'You crazy, Ryan? You're famous.'

As the campaign rolled on, there were posters of him in the department stores and in Boots, and pyramids of Kick for Men in the malls. *GQ* ran a six page promotion for the Kick range, featuring Ryan and five teammates wearing Italian suits. When he turned up at House of Fraser in Birmingham to sign bottles, the queue stretched out along Corporation Street. There was even a skit about Ryan and Kick for Men on *Drop the Dead Donkey*.

As Ryan's fame escalated, so too did Cath's. *FHM* named her as one of their sauciest soccer sexbombs: 'Gentlemen, stand up and salute our first division hunnies'. Soon stories started to appear speculating on whether Ryan would shortly pop the question to long-term girlfriend Katie Fox. If Cath herself had any hand in this, Ryan was oblivious; the idea of getting hitched had never previously occurred to him, and slightly scared him.

The marriage question took an unexpected turn when the phone rang one evening while Ryan and Cath and Ryan's family were all sitting round the TV.

Ryan hated answering the phone and always left it to Cath, so it was she who told him that *Hello!* magazine was calling and wanted to speak to him.

'No, you talk to them, Katie,' he said. 'I don't feel like it.' He wondered how they'd got hold of his number, cheeky devils, when he'd gone ex-directory.

The whole family listened to Cath talking to them. 'No, sorry to disappoint you, but Ryan and I definitely aren't engaged to be married. No, honest, God's honest truth, I'm not messing with you. He hasn't even asked me.' Cath made a face at Ryan as if to say, 'I'm trying to get this nutter off the line.'

The caller persisted and Cath suddenly exclaimed, 'You what? You'd pay for the whole wedding and wedding party if we ever do decide to get hitched? You're not serious? You'd pay for *all* of it, dinner, tent, band, the works? And you'd pay us a hundred grand in cash on top?'

She saw Ryan's family staring at her with assorted expressions of astonishment and greed. Alf and Barbara's mouths gaped open.

'Well, like I said, we've got no plans, sorry to disappoint,' Cath went on. 'But I hear what you're saying and I will pass on your message to Ryan. Thanks for calling, no problem.'

She put the phone down and Dean said, 'Are they serious? They'd give you a hundred grand just to get married? I'd marry *anyone* for *half* that.'

Barbara said, 'That's crazy. Why would anyone pay that?'

Cath shrugged. 'Sell magazines, I reckon. They probably think if they put Ryan's wedding in a magazine they'd sell lots of extra copies. It's a business decision.'

'But a hundred thousand quid . . .'

'That was their opening offer,' Cath said. 'They'd have to pay a lot more than that . . . That's if we was even engaged, which we aren't.'

'Maybe you *should*,' said Alf. 'To be honest, I'm speechless. That's ten years' wages where I work.'

'Let's not talk about it,' Cath said. 'It doesn't seem right, putting a price on marriage. If we ever do get hitched, it'll be for love, not because some mag's paying us two hundred grand or whatever, and paying for the wedding on top. I dunno, it might feel funny.'

'Jesus,' said Dean. 'I mean, Ryan, it's not like Katie's a total dog or something. She's fit. I'd ring 'em back and take the cash. You'd be mad not to.'

Ryan went very quiet and thoughtful, and said, 'Well, you might be right, Dean. We'll have to talk about it, won't we, Katie? You can't just say no, not without considering it.'

Chapter Twenty

Without knowing how, Captain George Palmer found himself the great promoter, protector and manager of the love affair between Jamie and Annabel. Determined not to see Annabel hurt, he cajoled his friend into behaving decently towards her, reminded him to ring her, prompted him to send flowers. 'How's Annabel?' he would casually ask, and if Jamie replied he hadn't spoken to her for a few days, George gently suggested he call her.

'How was Annabel?' he'd ask again later, to check the call had been made.

On her birthday, it was George who made suggestions to Jamie for suitable presents, and on Valentine's Day it was George who ordered the roses which arrived at Segrave Mansions, ostensibly sent by Captain Pilcher. When Annabel's face lit up with delight at these romantic gestures from the man she adored, Jamie never revealed the part played by George, and for George it was compensation enough that his sweet Annabel had not been neglected. He gladly did whatever he could, while smiling rather bitterly that he, of all men in the world, should be the person upon whom responsibility for the romance should have devolved.

George thought constantly of Annabel, far more constantly than did her lover. He thought of her during the morning jogs when he led his platoon through St James's Park. He thought of her as he stood behind his easel, attempting to capture on paper some particular vista. It pained him when, after dinner in barracks, Jamie declared, 'I can't decide what to do now. Play snooker or ring Annabel and get her round to the flat.' He took it for granted Annabel would make herself available at a moment's notice; and she did indeed always do so. Annabel understood Jamie's duties were terribly exacting, so of course she must slot in around him.

After a week of not bothering to make contact, Jamie would assure her, 'Sorry, sweetheart, the regiment's been on exercise in the Brecon Beacons, survival training. No means of calling you.' And Annabel, relieved she hadn't been dumped, was immediately forgiving. And George, knowing there wasn't a word of truth in what Jamie had just said, and that he hadn't even left London, redoubled his efforts to protect her.

It was George who convinced Jamie to take Annabel on a regimental skiing party to Val d'Isère, and George who suffered so acutely as a result, with Jamie and Annabel sharing the bedroom next to his own in the chalet. It was George who hung back each day to ski with Annabel, while Jamie, who was a reckless skier, raced ahead down every black run without a backwards glance at his girlfriend. And it was George, with the motive of further cementing the love match, who invited Jamie and Annabel and several other friends for a weekend at his parents' house near Thatcham in Berkshire.

The Palmer family home, Mallards End, lay at the conjunction of small lanes in one of the last parcels of rural Berkshire. A tile-hung Victorian farmhouse surrounded by barns and outbuildings, it had been purchased by George's father, Colonel Simon Palmer, when he'd come out of the army seventeen years earlier. Since then, the colonel had commuted into London most days where he was senior partner in a security company, Lionbrand, providing protection and bodyguards for Middle Eastern and African heads of state. As such, he had succeeded in transferring his military ethos directly in to commercial life, retaining many of his regiment's former squaddies and sergeants on the payroll, as well as discharged SAS and security guards. George had, from earliest childhood, been slightly in awe of his bullnecked father, with his boundless regard for army life and instinctive suspicion of everything else.

It had been Colonel Palmer who selected Wellington College with its military associations as the public school for George, and who had insisted he join the Irish Guards, his old regiment, firmly vetoing all talk of art college. As it happened, George's mother Mary was herself an accomplished amateur watercolourist, and it was evidently from her that George had inherited his talent. Colonel Palmer had nothing but praise for Mary's hobby, and many times carried her easel in Oman and Cairo; their sitting room walls were covered with framed examples of her work. He simply did not regard the career of a professional artist as a suitable one for his son.

Ordinarily, George was circumspect about bringing parties of friends home; he felt comfortable introducing them to his mother, but his father could be overpowering. This weekend comprised mostly army friends which made it simpler, and he both looked forward and rather dreaded the prospect of Annabel being under his roof.

They arrived in convoy in two cars, Jamie and Annabel in Jamie's Audi and George with Rupert and Rupert's new girlfriend, Chloe, in George's Golf. All down the motorway Jamie accelerated ahead, weaving from lane to lane, then waited to let them catch up, incredulous at their slowness, before speeding off ahead again to the next junction. Each time, George tried to gauge Annabel's expression as she smiled out from the passenger window of the waiting car. Was she embarrassed by Jamie's showing off? Her face indicated unconditional adoration.

They pulled up outside Mallards End where Colonel Palmer waited in readiness to direct the parking. He was dressed in a tweed overcoat and carrying his gnarled walking stick carved from Omani cedarwood, a gift from the emir whose security he provided. It was one of his foibles that no vehicle should be parked directly in front of the drawing room windows, spoiling the view, nor should they be parked at an angle which wasted space and looked unsightly. So whenever guests were expected he would position himself on the sweep of gravel and issue, with many extrovert hand signals, instructions on precisely where to draw up. He beckoned Jamie's Audi into position, then George's Golf; he liked all arrivals to be spaced to an exact distance so that passenger doors could be fully opened without touching the adjacent vehicle, but no wider.

George saw that his father was in high spirits. It pleased the colonel to have his home filled with serving officers. When Annabel was introduced he perked up further because he had an eye for a pretty girl and Annabel had the look he favoured.

They went into the sitting room which was the room the Palmers habitually occupied, other than for drinks before dinner which took place in the more formal, seldom-used drawing room. The sitting room was filled with sagging armchairs and threadbare Persian rugs, and a very old television with an aerial on top. Mary Palmer had arranged glasses on a tray with an ice bucket and bowls of crisps and Cheeselets.

Annabel was admiring Mary's watercolours with the artist, who was identifying wadis and mountain ranges in the Oman and mosques in Cairo and Yemen. These were interspersed with views of Salisbury and Hereford Cathedrals, the second of which she had painted when Simon had been briefly attached to the SAS in the city. The paintings reminded Annabel of Mary herself, being soft and English and rather faded. Annabel pointed at a watercolour of an impressive façade and said, 'I love that one. Where's it of?'

'That's not one of mine,' replied Mary. 'That's by George. Good, isn't it? He was only sixteen when he did that. It's the front of Wellington College.'

'Jamie was at Wellington,' said Annabel. 'He loved it there.'

'I'm not sure George did very much. Too hearty for him. He'd probably have been better off somewhere else. But he did start his painting there, that was one good thing.'

'He's very talented. You both are.'

'George is better than I am. He has the potential to be really good. I hope he's finding enough time to practise, he says he is.'

The colonel, who had been half listening to their conversation, now joined in. 'Well, I hope George isn't carrying his paintbox everywhere when he's supposed to be on duty.' Turning to Jamie, he said, 'George isn't painting all day long, is he? He told me he'd taken his paints on exercise to some German forest, which alarmed me. Good thing the Russians didn't choose that moment to flood across the borders. They'd have been met by George with raised paintbrush and jam jar of water.'

'I think we're probably safe enough,' Jamie replied. 'George isn't our only line of defence. And he did a brilliant painting of Monty, my black Labrador. Caught his expression in one.'

'Had a black flatcoated retriever myself once,' said the colonel. 'Mary painted him several times, tried to, but he wouldn't stay put. Fidgety hound. And always hungry. Which reminds me: lunch. Mary, *lunch*. A lot of ravenous young men here, feeding time, I suggest.'

The colonel seated Annabel next to himself, and put Chloe,

Rupert's new blonde, on his other side. Throughout lunch, he lobbed questions at Annabel: 'Now, what do you get up to in life, pretty girl like you? Live up in town, do you?'

'Yes, I do.'

'Bad luck. London's all very fine but I wouldn't want to sleep there overnight. What about your people? Where do your parents live? Where did you grow up?'

'Er, in London. Fulham.'

'I see,' he replied doubtfully. 'Well, so long as you've got some green space to breathe in. But can't say I'd fancy it myself.'

He asked her about her job but lost interest once he'd established that Imperial Magazines published neither *Country Life* nor *Shooting Times*, and he had heard of none of their 127 other titles. 'There are far too many magazines,' he pronounced. 'Who has time to read them all, I wonder? They're mostly just full of advertisements in any case.'

Later, when Annabel mentioned that her father had done his national service in the Green Jackets, the colonel said, 'Goode? Michael Goode? I've heard that name. Well, there was a Michael Goode who ran off with his daughter's school matron, a punk rocker. But I don't suppose that was your father.'

Annabel blushed crimson. 'Actually, it *was* my father, but it was all a long time ago. My parents are still together and very happy.'

'Good heavens. Forgive me. I always heard your father was a splendid chap, apart from the punk rocker business. Anyway, glad to hear your parents stuck it out, so much simpler for all concerned when one can.'

Lunch ended, the party got changed into boots, coats and caps, and embarked on a walk through the Berkshire countryside. They headed first along a rough track behind the outbuildings, then across a footpath through a vast, flat, empty field, in which stood the now decaying stumps of corncobs and kale, planted as ground cover for pheasants. From time to time a hare or partridge would explode from the vegetation, and Jamie and Rupert would lift their walking sticks to their shoulders and shout 'Over!' or 'Ground game,' and pretend to bag them.

Annabel found herself walking in step with George and told him about her restlessness at work, and how after four years it might be time to move on. 'I get on fine with Tony O'Flynn, my boss,' she said.

'He's perfectly OK, but incredibly vain and selfish. I've noticed it even more since meeting Jamie, who's so straight and upright. Army men are different.'

'Yes, he's a great guy,' said George. 'A complete one-off.' But he was thinking how much kinder and more appreciative he would be to Annabel, were she his own girlfriend. 'The better you get to know him, the more you'll see what really makes him tick.'

'Oh, I know him so well already,' replied Annabel. 'It's only been six months but it feels like we've been together for ages. Like we knew each other in a previous life.'

George, who really had known Jamie Pilcher in a previous life, at Wellington, and was alarmed by Annabel's unquestioning devotion, only said, 'Jamie's a very confident guy. He knows exactly what he wants and goes for it.'

'That's why I feel so lucky,' replied Annabel, oblivious to the veiled warnings. 'That I met you all outside that pub. What if I hadn't bicycled past on that afternoon? Jamie and I might never have met, and then I wouldn't be staying this weekend at your house.'

There were moments on the walk when George almost submitted to the temptation of declaring his love to Annabel, or of signalling his affection obliquely. But he could find neither the right words nor the opportunity, nor the courage. Instead, as they tramped through the grey Berkshire countryside, they spoke about Annabel's flatmates, watercolour painting, and a dozen other subjects, but never George's feelings towards his companion. Annabel found herself confiding in him about her parents and the difficult atmosphere at home. 'When I get married, I hope it'll never end up like that.'

'I'm sure you're not planning on getting married yet,' George said quickly.

'A lot of my friends have. If the right person came along and asked . . .'

'Probably best not to rush into anything.'

Annabel turned, surprised. 'Jamie and I have talked about it actually.'

'Really? Obviously Jamie's great. I'm just saying some people get married without knowing each other properly, and end up with really incompatible people.'

'I'm so relieved you approve of Jamie. That's so good to hear since you knew him at school and now in the army.'

'Er, yes.' George felt the conversation had spun away irretrievably. 'Yes, well, the important thing, so far as I can see, not that I'm an expert or anything, is to find someone completely trustworthy and loyal, and you know is a great long-term bet.'

'That's so true. You've exactly summed up what I feel about Jamie.'

They arrived back at Mallards End and were removing their boots by the back door. Annabel said, 'That was a lovely walk, George. It was really helpful talking to you. Everything feels clearer now.' And she went upstairs to her bedroom to find her man.

George went up to his own room to change. The bedroom in which he slept on visits home was his old childhood room, the walls decorated with posters of a blond tennis player scratching her bottom, and various optical illusions and labyrinths titled Zonk and Spirograph. Interspersed between the posters were several of his adolescent watercolours of fruit bowls and trees.

George heard footsteps approaching Annabel's room and the creak of her door opening and finally shutting. Soon there followed the unmistakable sounds of a couple making love. George first heard the squeak of bedsprings, then the headboard thump-thumping against his wall and muffled cries of satisfaction. At one point Jamie's voice was clearly audible, 'Keep doing that, don't stop, damn you.' Soon afterwards, George heard the sound of taps being run for a bath, and Annabel's laughter, and Jamie's footsteps striding about the room. George did his best to block out all this activity leaking through the wall, but was at the same time too hideously fascinated to leave his room.

Eventually he headed downstairs where his parents plus Rupert and Chloe were already gathered in the drawing room for drinks, with a fire blazing and the colonel presiding over decanters of gin and whisky and bottles of Schweppes tonic and bitter lemon. Chloe requested a vodka and tonic and the colonel, who did not believe in vodka, was explaining to her why he did not regard it as a proper English spirit – 'a Russian invention to blot out their miserable existence' – and consequently did not provide it at Mallards End.

On seeing George, the colonel asked, 'Do you think your other friends are all right? They know it's dinner soon?'

George shrugged.

'I do like Annabel,' the colonel went on. 'Very pretty girl.' Then he added, 'Your mother and I were just saying, you should find yourself a girl like Annabel. Exactly the sort to go for.' Turning to Rupert, he said, 'Perhaps you can help George? Find him an Annabel of his own?' Rupert undertook to keep his eyes open for similar women.

'I would have snapped Annabel up in an instant, when I was forty years younger,' said the colonel. 'I should think all the young men were after her.'

Rupert's face took on a self-satisfied expression, having been there himself.

George, agonised, busied himself pouring drinks.

Shortly before dinner there was the sound of Jamie and Annabel coming downstairs.

'So sorry we're late,' Jamie declared. 'We've had rather an eventful last hour.'

George stared at Annabel who had never looked more beautiful, eyes shining, complexion slightly flushed, in a long turquoise evening dress. Jamie stood beside her in his maroon smoking jacket, velvet slippers with shamrocks, hair slicked back from the temples.

'Annabel, do you want to tell them?' he said, wrapping his arm around her waist.

'No, you do it,' replied Annabel, blushing.

'All right, well, I'm very proud to tell you that this evening I asked Annabel to become my lawful wedded wife. And I'm even happier to announce that she has accepted me, and well, that's about it actually. We're engaged.'

There was a gasp of delight from at least four of the people present, and soon George was dispatched to fetch a bottle of champagne from the cellar which was opened in celebration, and Jamie said, 'God, Annabel, I haven't even asked your father's permission,' and it was agreed he would do so on the way back into London the next evening.

'I think it's splendid you got engaged under our roof,' said the colonel. 'And of course Annabel's father is going to be delighted.'

'Don't tell Dad you asked me to marry you in the bath, will you?' said Annabel. 'I don't want him knowing that bit.'

Chapter Twenty-One

Annabel had no idea there would be so much to organise, and for months resented every letter and memo she typed for Tony O'Flynn since these interrupted her wedding preparations. From her desk at work she compiled lists of wedding guests, lists of dressmakers, lists of bridesmaids and pages, cake makers, florists, hairdressers, shoe shops. From the moment they'd become engaged, life became a round of duty drinks with relations – Jamie's as well as her own – with everyone expecting to meet the affianced couple. She spent a weekend up in Rutland to be introduced to Jamie's mother, Bridget, and his Labrador, Monty, and seemed to win the approval of both. It surprised her when Bridget let slip that Jamie had been engaged once before, four years previously, but the wedding had not gone ahead. She was dismayed because Jamie had never once mentioned that episode, but her fiancé made light of it. 'Trust me, sweetheart, it was all a bit of a joke. It was never serious like we are.'

'But who was she?' Annabel persisted.

'Just a local girl. Suki. It was ages ago, before the regiment was sent out to Germany.'

Bridget Pilcher was a widow, her husband having died when Jamie was ten years old. Annabel quickly decided she was rather nervous of her, with her bluff manner and outdoors complexion. Her cheeks were threaded with broken veins and her hands large and callused. In widowhood, she had started a riding school from the stables adjoining her farmhouse and kept other people's horses at livery. Her days were spent giving riding lessons and taking Jamie's dog, Monty, for long walks.

'D'you ride?' she asked Annabel.

'Only my bicycle.'

'Then I shan't bother asking whether you hunt. What about dogs? Are you a doggy person?'

'My parents have a miniature long-haired dachshund.'

'A lap dog! Well, keep it away from Monty, he might eat it. Won't you, you naughty, naughty hound? You might eat a little miniature sausage dog for breakfast. What a wicked boy you are, Monty. Like master, like dog. You need a good long walk, you do, tire you out a bit.'

By the end of the weekend, Annabel felt quite tired herself, and sure of two things. Her future mother-in-law was a very strong personality who worshipped her only son, considering him the most attractive young man ever to walk on God's earth. Well, Annabel thought, I can't blame her for that, since we are both in full agreement. But she felt marginalised in Bridget's devotion to Jamie, which seemed to allow no place for her. Furthermore, Bridget made it plain she had little interest in decisions surrounding the wedding, and hardly minded how or where it took place, providing she was told the date well in advance so she could organise someone to feed and water the horses.

Annabel's own mother took the exact opposite position, declaring the strongest opinions on how a wedding should suitably be conducted. Bucked up by the arrival of Jamie in their midst, who she said reminded her of Michael when she had first met him, Flea developed a new lease of life. Scarcely a day now passed when an envelope did not arrive at Segrave Mansions enclosing pages clipped out of *Brides* magazine with ideas for dresses and cakes. She became obsessed with the precise wording and engraving of the wedding invitation, harassing Annabel for decisions on the style of card and envelope, the typography, and whether or not a slip of paper should be inserted along with the invitation directing guests to a wedding list. Flea felt emphatically that there should be two lists, one at Peter Jones, the other at the General Trading Company, and Annabel had to intervene with great tact to prevent her mother from actually selecting all the presents herself.

Annabel's father also found Captain Pilcher strongly to his liking. 'You've chosen well,' he told his daughter when they were out walking Mollie the dachshund in Battersea Park. 'Jamie's exactly the sort of man I would have picked out for you myself.' Michael had a sense that all was right with the world when Jamie turned up for Saturday lunch in Napier Avenue wearing a pair of raspberry coloured cords and a blazer with regimental buttons.

Annabel did not altogether look forward to her fiancé's regular visits to her parents' house for kitchen lunches and suppers. Of course, she was delighted they approved of her handsome husband-to-be, and it was nice to be able to provide Jamie with home cooking as a change from the officers' mess, especially with his own mother living so far away in Rutland. But Annabel came to dread the inevitable moment, towards the bottom of her third glass of wine, when Flea's social drinking tipped first into loss of inhibition, then loss of coherence and finally self-pity. With the first and second glasses she was sweetly hospitable, sharing with Jamie her latest research on wedding florists – 'Two lovely girls who go along to Nine Elms and do all the flowers themselves for half the price of Pulbrook & Gould' – and ideas for the wedding cake. But by the third glass she began to slur and became over-attentive to Jamie, directing all her conversation at him to the exclusion of the others, and moving her face too close to his own. By her fourth and fifth glass, her mood lost its lightness and she became belligerent. At one supper, when she had drunk more than usual, she started telling Jamie about Michael's affair with Cath Fox, and neither the reproving glances of her husband nor the imploring looks of her daughter could deter her.

'With Annabel's school *matron*, you say?' said Jamie, struggling to keep up with the unfolding tale.

'Oh yes, she was covered in tattoos from head to foot. She's become the girlfriend of some well-known footballer now, according to my *Daily Mail*, you can just imagine.'

Despite Flea's urgent declarations that she wanted to organise the wedding, Annabel found it easier and certainly more relaxing to do everything herself, while allowing Flea the illusion she still had an important hand in it all. So it was Annabel who liaised with the chaplain at the Guards Chapel in Wellington Barracks, and Annabel who selected the canapés for the reception afterwards in the officers' mess, and Annabel who identified the Fulham dressmaker who would make the organdie dresses with satin yellow sashes to be worn by the bridesmaids, and the organdie shirts and silk knickerbockers for the pages.

*

Cath found negotiations with *Hello!* even more complicated and protracted than they'd been with Kick for Men, and by the time everything was signed and sealed it felt almost an anticlimax getting engaged. In total, she'd had ten long meetings with *Hello!* executives and lawyers, including one with the magazine's Spanish owners, and there were dozens of clauses still to be agreed. *Hello!* wanted guarantees that at least ten of Ryan's Man U teammates would turn up for the big day and be photographed with their wives and girlfriends, and requested lists of all their other celebrity friends who'd be invited. When Cath confessed they didn't really have any celebrity friends, *Hello!* said not to worry, they could provide these themselves.

Cath hadn't realised *Hello!* would be taking over all the arrangements, choosing even the wedding venue and guests, but it didn't bother her. It meant she didn't need to think about it herself, since they supplied a team of planners. She'd never forget the look on Alf and Barbara's faces when, after weeks of negotiations, she finally revealed the agreed deal: 'Two hundred and fifty grand, plus the dress paid for and a limousine ride to the ceremony, followed by a free five-star Caribbean honeymoon.'

'You're amazing, Katie,' said Ryan. 'I dunno how you did that, I'm gobsmacked.'

'Well, there's one important thing you can do yourself and all,' replied Cath. 'Any idea what I'm talking about?'

Ryan looked blank.

'You'd better ask me to marry you, now I've done all this work.'

'Oh, yeah. Right, well, I dunno what you're meant to say, Katie. But if you'd like to get hitched, I'm up for it.'

'Pathetic,' said Cath. 'You're hopeless, you. You can practise how you're going to ask me properly before tomorrow. *Hello!* are coming round to photograph our engagement. Six pages in next week's issue. It's part of the deal.'

As the date of the Pilcher–Goode wedding edged closer, it seemed to Annabel to become all-encompassing. Not a lunch hour was unfilled when she wasn't seeking out satin ballet shoes for the bridesmaids, or proofreading the words of hymns for the service sheets, or speaking to the lady in High Wycombe who was making the three-tier wedding cake. Christmas came and went – her last Christmas as a single woman – and Annabel felt a moment of sentimentality, celebrating in Napier Avenue in their particular family way. Her younger sister, Rosie, was hugely excited by the wedding and had actually broken up with her own long-term boyfriend, Mark, as a direct result, when she realised he would never be her choice of a future husband. Rosie was now fully employed in selecting her outfit for the big day. Tommy Goode, in his first year at Leeds University, had located a second-hand morning suit at Age Concern on Fulham Broadway, and was hoping the prominent urine stain on the trouser fly could be removed with dry cleaning. As for the wedding dress itself, Annabel was in a slaver of indecision, wanting something fairy-tale like Princess Diana, but not having the budget and worried by how much the wedding was costing her poor father. She had visited half a dozen designers, and the more possibilities she was shown the more confused she became.

Although Captain Jamie was less engaged in all these preparations than was his future wife, it could not justly be said that he played no part at all. Already, he had appointed Rupert Henley as his best man and George Palmer as chief usher, and options were being weighed for the mother of all stag events. Rupert was determined to devise something truly memorable, and was full of schemes for an ushers' weekend in Amsterdam or Malaga, or failing that paintballing at a place in the Buckinghamshire woods – though paintballing could be considered somewhat coals to Newcastle for professional soldiers – or, failing that, an epic night on the town in London.

Other aspects of the wedding left Jamie cold. He did not enjoy the Saturdays when Annabel dragged him round the shops looking at wedding presents; to Jamie, one saucepan was much like any other, and he quickly became claustrophobic in the Peter Jones giftware department choosing tablemats and waste paper bins. But he made Annabel cry with laughter when they bought a new Vi-Spring double bed for his flat in Cambridge Street, where they would make their first home, when he ordered her to lie down next to him in the middle of the bedding department to test the mattress, and kept pawing at her in front of the shop assistants.

'That was *so embarrassing*,' Annabel said afterwards. 'All those people staring at us.'

'They're just jealous,' Jamie replied. 'Thinking what we'll be getting up to on that bed.'

George faced up to the fact of the engagement as stoically as he could. Outwardly thrilled for his friend, and afforded a special role at the heart of the arrangements since the engagement had taken place in his own home, he was privately devastated. It took all his self-discipline to conceal his agony. When a Saturday in May was chosen as the date of the wedding, it felt more real than ever. When Jamie invited him to become chief usher, George flinched at the ceremonial part he must play in the proceedings he dreaded.

On a Saturday one week prior to the wedding, the much anticipated stag party took place. Rupert had booked the private room behind Julie's restaurant in Holland Park, and it was here that a dozen army officers, plus three of Jamie's old non-military mates from Wellington College, assembled. Rupert, as best man and master of ceremonies, refused to divulge the full programme of the evening's events, merely telling them to expect 'a very memorable night' and to request £120 from each person to cover the cost of dinner and cabaret. 'After that, we'll be playing off-piste and responsible for our own tabs.'

As dinner progressed and the wine flowed, the atmosphere became boisterous. Rupert kept looking surreptitiously at his watch and made calls from a phonebox in the passage, and eventually reappeared in the private room with two girls in moth-eaten fur coats, carrying a bag of props and a ghetto blaster. 'Gentlemen, may I present our cabaret tonight . . . this is Roxy and this is Aimee . . . I just want to say I've personally checked out their act and they're incredible . . . but keep your hands to yourself, gentlemen, because they're both *lesbians*, so they don't welcome audience participation, got that, Jamie? So, ladies, over to you.'

George found himself increasingly despondent. The cabaret left him untitillated. He felt sorry for the women but at the same time revolted and manipulated as they performed their routines. The other stags were lapping it up, roaring their approval when Aimee slipped out of her fur coat. An even greater roar erupted when Jamie attempted to join in the act, until Roxy switched off the music and threatened to leave if he didn't sit back down again. George felt heartily relieved when the cabaret drew to its close and the ladies' driver, a big bruiser named Callum with a mashed nose, arrived to take them on to their next booking.

After that, Rupert announced they were going to the Pinstripe Club in Soho, and a minibus was waiting outside. George thought he might slip quietly away but Rupert wouldn't hear of it. 'No wimping, I've booked us all tables.'

The Pinstripe Club turned out to be a basement dive in Beak Street reached by a treacherous flight of stairs beneath a Korean restaurant. Inside, you could just about make out tables and booths, several occupied by businessmen being entertained by hostesses. A bar displayed several dozen brands of malt whisky and pails of champagne on ice.

The arrival of so many tall, fit young men, evidently part of a stag outing and thus prime targets for fleecing, did not pass unnoticed amongst the hostesses who converged on them like wasps to Fanta.

George was startled by how pretty some of the girls were. He had expected raddled old slappers but these were young and rather gorgeous. They mostly seemed to come from Nottingham.

He watched with amusement the way they ordered flute after flute of champagne, seldom drinking more than a sip, and the cigarettes came in cartons of two hundred and were added to the communal bill. When Jamie placed his hand on an escort's knee, Bethany told him, 'Sorry, you are only paying for my conversation and companionship. If you want to touch, that costs extra.'

'Understood, sweetheart. Charge it to our bill.'

'I don't know what I'm going to do with you,' breathed Bethany.

'But I know exactly what to do with *you*, sweetheart,' said Jamie, steering her towards him.

In no time, every stag including George was entwined with a different escort on velveteen banquettes. After several more drinks George reckoned his girl, Shelley, looked quite like Annabel, with the same pretty complexion and eyes, except she came from Nottingham. When they kissed, her tongue tasted of cigarettes.

'I think I'm falling in love with you,' he told Shelley late in the evening.

'I'll take that as a compliment. Mind if I order more smokes?'

Just after four a.m., the lights were abruptly turned on and a manager they hadn't seen before said the club was closing for the night, and who was paying the bill?

'George Palmer,' croaked Jamie, prone on a banquette.

George stared at the long, semi-itemised bill for £3,145 as he scrabbled for his cheque book. The cigarettes had cost £90 a carton.

'Fuck, Bethany was hot,' declared Jamie as they staggered up to street level. 'I've a good mind to give her one before Saturday.'

Every two weeks Cath met up with the *Hello!* team to hear how the wedding plans were shaping up. Sometimes she travelled down to London for the day, other times they came to brief her in Manchester. A locations manager was scouring Cheshire for a suitable venue, which needed to be close enough to Manchester to pull in the celebrities while guaranteeing complete privacy. A stately home or exclusive hotel was the preferred option, providing a prestigious backdrop for the photographs.

Meanwhile, someone named the Marquesa was supervising the guest list, assisted by three researchers. Cath, never normally intimidated, felt quite anxious when the Marquesa quizzed her about her family, asking her which members would be attending the ceremony.

'None, sadly,' Cath replied, reddening. 'They've all passed away. I've no living relatives.'

And when she was asked for her guest list of friends, she struggled again. She'd lost touch with the Classified department at Imperial Magazines, and she wasn't exactly going to ask the girls from the Pall Mall Steam and Fitness Club. In other circumstances she'd have liked to have invited Annabel Goode and some of the pupils from St Mary's, but it obviously couldn't happen. Michael Goode could scarcely be invited either. And she wasn't inviting Callum. Which really only left the marketing team from Kick for Men, and the other footballers' wives like Anita and Hayley, plus her aerobics teacher and the ladies from Tropical Bronze.

At the third planning meeting, the *Hello!* team showed her their draft guest list and Cath's eyes were on stalks. Half the cast of *Coronation Street* had apparently agreed to come to her wedding, plus the news presenters from *Look North* and an anchor from *Grandstand*. They also said they were negotiating with the agents of two famous pop stars and a game show host, and there was an outside chance of getting George Best.

*

As the date of the great James–Fox nuptials drew closer, the list of requests from *Hello!* grew longer. They had an idea that all Ryan's teammates plus the three ushers – Ryan's friends Kev and Gary, and kid brother Dean – should be dressed in matching pearl-grey morning suits for the big day, with dove-grey cravats and top hats. Cath had a job persuading them all to do it, and then chasing round getting their measurements. Then *Hello!* requested she recruit ten girlfriends as maids of honour, in matching pink frocks, so she signed up eight of the footballers' wives and girlfriends plus her aerobics teacher, Donna, and Dannii off reception at Tropical Bronze. The bridesmaids presented another problem, since Cath knew no small children. For one guilty instant, she thought of Jess and what a shame her nan had put her into care, she'd have been roughly the right age. But the *Hello!* people said it was fine because a couple of kids of the *Corrie* cast would adore to be flower girls, and the *Hello!* stylist's twin daughters were co-opted to make up the numbers.

As for Cath's dress, everyone agreed it had to be something drop-dead spectacular. 'You're such a pretty lady, Katie,' said the stylist. 'I'm seeing fairy tale, I'm seeing fantasy, I'm seeing Fergie Duchess of York, I'm seeing Cinderella . . . we're hoping to get two covers out of this, two issues of the magazine back to back, so it's got to jump out at you.'

In the end, they settled on a couture dressmaker named Hollywood Dreams who set to work on something epic in white silk, embellished with spangles and sequins and the letters K and R embroidered into a twenty foot train. The same interwoven letters would also appear on Cath's shoes and woven into the fabric of Ryan's white waistcoat and light blue cravat. When Cath first saw the sketches of the bride and groom's outfits, with Ryan in pearl-grey topper and herself with a tiara on her head, she couldn't believe it, it was all so perfect.

What was that saying? About living well being the best revenge? Well, look at her now. She felt a moment of regret that her old mates from Nero's, and her neighbours from the Allaway estate in Wymering, and the girls from Classified and the massage parlour couldn't all be present to see her, the centre of attention and queen of style. But Cath never looked back for long. She was more worried about how Alf, Ryan's dad, would appear on the day in the photos, and whether Dean would fit into his morning suit. He seemed to have gained a stone, and she doubted his waistcoat would do up.

Everyone agreed that Annabel made the most beautiful of brides at her quintessential English wedding. If you had a party of foreigners in tow, and wanted to show them a perfect example of how these things are conducted in a certain stratum of upper middle class England, you could not have done better. As she processed up the aisle of the Guards Chapel on the arm of her father, trailed by six tiny attendants in organdie dresses, yellow sashes and knickerbockers, there was only one adjective which came close to describing Annabel, and that was *radiant*. Her dress, with its ruffles and ruches and fifteen foot train, owed more than a nod to Princess Diana, and many in the congregation expressed the opinion that Annabel looked every bit as ravishing as the Princess of Wales had on her own wedding day.

Even afterwards, when experience made her reconsider the wisdom of the marriage itself, Annabel would remember the day as one of the happiest in her life.

It began shortly after dawn with the arrival of the hairdresser and make-up artist who set up shop in her parents' bedroom and bathroom in Napier Avenue, and were soon attending to the whole family, blow drying Flea and Rosie's hair as well as the bride's before taking the scissors to Tommy, who'd travelled down from Leeds and looked like a caveman, and even Michael who fancied a final trim. Then the wedding dress lady turned up with her assistant and the dress in a special clothes bag, and the make-up lady caked Annabel with far too much foundation, making her resemble a Japanese geisha, and it all had to be scraped off again. Soon afterwards, the bridesmaids and pages started to arrive, accompanied by their mothers or au pairs, and the whole house was heaving with people and small children running about from room to room. Flea was driving her hairdresser mad by wandering off, mid-appointment, to make coffee for everyone and jugs of squash for the children, and Michael offered stronger drinks to the fathers of the pages, even though it was still only eleven o'clock. When Flea poured herself a glass of wine, Annabel frowned. Flea had a second glass before changing into her Caroline Charles suit and pinning on her brooch.

How they would ever all be ready on time, Annabel had no idea, and she began to feel quite worried. But somehow, barely twenty minutes after the hired limousines arrived outside Napier Avenue to take them to the church, the bridal party, the bridesmaids and pages, even the mother of the bride, were ready to depart. Mollie the miniature long-haired dachshund was fed and watered and shut in the kitchen, and the wedding party set off on its three mile journey to the Guards Chapel.

Cath awoke at dawn in an enormous four-poster and lay there for a while, savouring the moment. The ceiling and curtains of the bed were ruched rococo-style in yellow silk, secured with purple rope tie-backs, and she felt like a princess. She hadn't slept in such a grand bed since her days with old Charlie Blaydon at Blaydon Hall, except that this bed was way more comfortable, with no lumps and bumps. It felt strange waking up alone without a feller next to her. That was something that hadn't happened in a long time.

The *Hello!* people insisted she spend the night before the wedding at the hotel, to have her safely on site, so here she was. She gazed round the cavernous bedroom with its mullioned windows and Fragonard-style tapestry of a girl on a swing, and three velour settees. When she'd arrived last night the manager of the hotel had assured her it was their best suite.

Eventually she drew back the brocade curtains. Outside, she couldn't get over the activity. A huge silk-lined marquee was erected on the lawns, and dozens of caterers and florists were buzzing about, shifting tables and putting together the final touches for the wedding breakfast. It had been genius to festoon the inside of the tent in Manchester United colours of red and white, to give it a football theme.

She could see several of the *Hello!* people on the lawn with their clipboards, checking everything, and there were security men at all the gates and entrances, making sure no rival press slipped in. Apparently there was even going to be a helicopter hovering overhead throughout the day, blocking the airspace, to prevent any unauthorised paparazzi from flying over and getting any shots. The entire wedding was exclusive to *Hello!*, and they'd even had to warn the guests not to bring cameras with them, they'd all be frisked on the way in.

The Mere Grange hotel was a sixteenth-century hunting lodge built for the Earls of Wilmslow, substantially rebuilt in Jacobean-Tudor style in the twenties by a prosperous Mancunian cotton broker, and converted last year into an exclusive hotel. With its high walls, romantic moat, on-site church, picturesque shrubberies and rock garden, and ample parking, it was a perfect venue. A chauffeur-driven limousine had collected Cath from Ryan's Altrincham flat and she'd been greeted at the hotel steps by a line-up of Mere Grange staff and presented with a welcome bouquet, all recorded by the *Hello!* photographer. The porter who'd carried her suitcase asked for her autograph, and told her he was a big Man U fan and was wearing Kick for Men.

Breakfast was delivered to her room and shortly afterwards the hairdresser and make-up team arrived. Cath had invited Hayley and Anita to join her in the suite, as her senior maids of honour, and the hotel sent up flutes of Buck's Fizz which they were photographed drinking, all sat round in their hotel bathrobes. Outside in the marquee they could hear the band for the reception tuning up, and the helicopter began flying overhead, so it was difficult to hear themselves speak.

By eleven o'clock the girls had their hair up in rollers and the manicurist arrived to do their nails. The photographer got some hilarious shots of the three of them with their new false nails, clinking glasses of bubbly.

At one point Hayley took a phone call from her partner, Midge Long, to report on last night's stag party. Cath hadn't been too happy about Ryan's stag night, especially it taking place so close to the wedding, but none of the other dates worked with their training. Anyway, it sounded like it had all been quite tame, a few bevvies down the pub and then an outing to Millionairz 'n' Playerz. Wayne Corrigan had arranged a strippergram to turn up dressed as a policewoman, and she'd pretended to arrest Ryan before stripping down to her garters. The only casualty seemed to be Dean who'd got sick on lager and tequila chasers and had been up half the night over Ryan's toilet.

Still in their bathrobes, Cath and the maids of honour nipped outside for an inspection of the marquee. Waitresses were spreading red and white tablecloths and caterers delivering the gold candelabras with their gold candles. The long top table where Cath and Ryan would be seated with the celebrities had already been set with red and gold serviettes, little gold bags of sugared almonds, bottles of Kick for Men as table gifts for the male guests and a selection of beauty products for the women. Party bags for the celebs were filled with miniature bottles of spirits from the drinks sponsors and a copy of last week's *Hello!*.

On the centre of the stage where the speeches and cake-cutting would take place, Cath saw the two enormous thrones on which she and Ryan would be seated, with red and gold cushions embroidered with the initials K and R in gold thread.

The bridal procession drove through the great iron gates of Wellington Barracks and drew up outside the Guards Chapel. The wedding dress lady and her assistant smoothed the train of its crumples, then Annabel took hold of her father's arm, the organist struck up Handel's 'Arrival of the Queen of Sheba', and they began their long march up the aisle.

Everywhere she looked, in every pew, Annabel saw the smiling faces of her friends, all incredibly smart in their wedding finery. The church was packed with girls in amazing hats, men in tailcoats and soldiers in uniform. A hundred yards ahead of her on the altar she could see magnificent displays of spring flowers, and further posies suspended from the end of each pew, matching the little baskets of narcissus carried by her bridesmaids.

In the sea of faces, she kept spotting people from different parts of her life. There were schoolfriends from St Mary's, whom she hadn't seen for years, several accompanied by husbands she hadn't even met. There were chalet girls from Courchevel, from her days at the Chalet Cheva, and her fellow classroom assistants from Miss Claire's nursery school. Miss Claire herself stood formidably in an aisleside seat in navy blue Peter Jones suit and matching hat.

It had been a relief to Annabel that her boss, Tony O'Flynn, had declined the invitation, claiming a prior engagement, and sent her a casserole dish as a gift, chosen from the list by his senior PA and charged to the company. But ten of Annabel's friends from Imperial Magazines were in the church, wearing outfits borrowed from *Cosima*'s fashion cupboard. And it gave her a shock to spot her old headmistress from St Mary's, Mrs Violet Perse, standing shoulder to shoulder with her matron, Mrs Bullock, who had once employed Cath Fox.

During the build-up to the wedding, Annabel had several times thought about Cath. It was hard not to, since Cath's forthcoming wedding to Ryan James was all over the magazines. Annabel thought it an odd coincidence that she and Cath were getting married on the same day. Cath looked incredibly glamorous in her engagement photos, and Ryan's face was everywhere in those adverts for aftershave.

As she neared the front of the church, she started spotting her best friends and family. There was Sophie Peverel with her fiancé David, both of whom had flown in specially from Hong Kong to be at the wedding. Sophie was wearing an eye-popping fuchsia-pink suit made by a Chinese tailor in Kowloon. Sophie's parents, Johnnie and Davina, were seated in the same pew along with the full Barwell-Mackenzie clan, including Mouse with her boyfriend Hector Murray, the future Earl of Arbroath, who still hadn't popped the question and was consequently a mild cause for concern.

Now Annabel passed a pew filled with cousins, the Goodes of Castle Cary in Somerset and the Goodes of Lambourne in Berkshire. Her uncle Simon, her father's younger brother, trained racehorses and seemed to have ballooned in weight, tailcoat straining at its seams. Across the aisle she spotted George Palmer's parents, Simon and Mary, in whose house she'd become engaged, and Rupert Henley's girlfriend Chloe. Annabel's mother, sister and brother were stationed in the front row, and Jamie's mother, Bridget, in the pew opposite, along with Jamie's Labrador Monty, a yellow silk bow tied round his neck.

And there, waiting by the altar rail, stood Jamie, flanked by Rupert his best man. Both looked sleeker than ever in morning dress. Annabel couldn't help thinking how peculiar it was that the only two men she'd ever been to bed with were standing side by side waiting for her. Sensing her approach, Jamie turned round and mouthed the words 'Hi, gorgeous' and Annabel felt herself the luckiest woman, to be marrying her tall handsome soldier.

The service itself passed in a blur. Afterwards, all Annabel could remember was concentrating on getting out the words of her vows in the right order, and hoping the wedding ring would slip onto her finger which had swollen in the heat. Of the vicar's homily about marital love, she registered not one word; she was too busy hoping the bridesmaids and pages were all right, fidgeting on their little chairs at the front. Sophie Peverel read a passage from Kahlil Gibran's *The Prophet*, and George Palmer read a Shakespeare sonnet Annabel had once studied at school, about love being the meeting of true minds. He read it beautifully and with great feeling, so Annabel felt she was hearing the words properly for the first time. She had become very fond of George, regarding him as one of Jamie's nicest friends. As a wedding present he had offered to paint her portrait in oils, so they spent many hours closeted together in a room at Wellington Barracks which George co-opted as a studio, and had many lovely conversations.

She remembered the congregation belting out her favourite hymns, 'I Vow to Thee My Country' and 'Jerusalem', and then, in the batting of an eye, the service was over and they were married. Now she was retracing her steps up the aisle, this time on Jamie's strong arm. As he passed the front pew, Jamie grabbed Monty's lead and so departed the church with his faithful wife on one arm and faithful hound on the other, and the congregation felt quite emotional because they made such a charming sight.

On the steps of the church an honour guard of soldiers awaited with outstretched swords forming a tunnel above their heads, and they emerged the other side into bright sunshine and the lens of their wedding photographer. For long afterwards, this dramatic tableau of the newly-weds and their dog, saluted by the regiment, stood on the desk in the Pilchers' sitting room.

By the time Annabel and Jamie reached the officers' mess, half a dozen waiters stood ready with outstretched trays of champagne, and waitresses were emerging from the kitchen with plates of canapés made by the mess chefs. Annabel felt quite overwhelmed as so many friends queued up to congratulate her on her dashing new husband. She wished she'd had more time to speak to them all – especially her old St Mary's friends – but cousins and aunts kept barging in and needing attention. Sophie Peverel said, 'Did you know Cath Fox is getting married today too? To a footballer. I read about it on the flight from Hong Kong, but she seems to be called Katie now.'

'Yes, he plays for Manchester United. But don't speak too loudly about Cath. Mum's still totally paranoid.'

Annabel was keeping a worried eye on her mother, who was holding out her glass to every passing bottle. Annabel recognised the warning signs; Flea was locked in frenzied conversation with Jamie's mother, Bridget, who was looking at her strangely.

Colonel Simon Palmer and his wife Mary loomed up, basking in the reflected glory of having provided the setting for the engagement. 'I hope you'll be very happy, my dear,' said the colonel. 'I'm sure you will be. But I want you to promise me something: introduce George to someone nice. You must have a nice friend.'

Annabel promised but by then her father had appeared telling her it was time for speeches and the cutting of the cake, and she was hurried away to the shallow stage where cake and microphone awaited.

First up was Michael Goode who said how proud he was today of his beautiful daughter (loud cheers of agreement from the whole room) and how delighted to welcome Jamie into the family, even though Jamie had already attained a higher rank in the army than Michael ever did.

'You know you're becoming old when your darling daughter marries a more senior officer.'

Then Jamie made a short speech thanking the bridesmaids and pages, and thanking Michael and Flea for giving birth to such a ravishing daughter.

'And I bet you *will* ravish her too, you dirty beast,' someone shouted out to jocular laughter.

And finally Rupert Henley took the microphone, announcing that there were 'a few secrets about Jamie which ought to be revealed' (further cheers from the floor) and proceeded to tell several long, rambling, unfunny anecdotes which fell just the wrong side of good taste. 'Anyway, ladies and gentlemen, Jamie has done one sensible thing in his life by marrying the gorgeous Annabel. Who I can assure you from *personal experience* – but my lips are sealed on that matter – is really, really good news, or rather Goode news, so please join me in drinking a toast to the bride and bridegroom.'

'The bride and bridegroom,' intoned everyone, raising their glasses. 'Bride and groom.' Jamie and Annabel now approached the cake with Jamie's unsheathed sword, preparing to cut the first slice.

It was at this moment that Flea felt her legs give way beneath her, and she collapsed onto the floor.

*

Afterwards, Cath felt the whole occasion had sped by in a blur.

The wedding service itself had been specially shortened, but with all the photography going on it still took more than an hour and a half to get through it. Cath walked up the aisle with her maids of honour, and then had to do it all over again so the photographers could get the shots they needed from all angles. The exchange of rings had to be performed three times, as did the signing of the register. Cath felt she'd been sat there all afternoon in that hot little vestry, while they snapped them from this side and that.

The choice of hymns and readings had been entirely left to *Hello!* and the vicar since, to be perfectly honest, neither Cath nor Ryan had any particular requests nor knew many of the tunes. As kids, neither of them had been great ones for church.

Cath was elated by the celebrities at her wedding. Obviously she and Ryan were celebrities themselves, but having the *Corrie* cast present was something else. She kept turning round from the altar to check they were all right and still there: Brian and Gail Tilsley, Terry Duckworth, Curly Watts, even the Barlows. In the second pew, she recognised a couple of the stars from *Brookside* and the weather lady from *Look North*. The *Hello!* people had been very cagey when she'd asked how they'd persuaded them to come along, saying it was part of a wider deal with the television station.

Having no family members present herself, the celebrities had all been seated on Cath's side of the church which was nice, since it made it look like she was the one with famous friends. Across the aisle, on Ryan's side, she could see Alf in a lounge suit, gasping for a fag by the look of him. Barbara looked magnificent in her new outfit printed with a pattern of autumn leaves and a hat like a cake-stand. As for Dean, he was white as a sheet and sweating like a pig. He was leaning forwards against the pew and you could see the *Hello!* photographers trying to keep him out of their pictures.

Cath felt that, aside from Dean, the whole event was a triumph. She couldn't wait to see it published in the magazine. Her ten maids of honour looked like film stars in their pink dresses. It had been a masterstroke that they should all carry matching pink feather fans. Dannii from Tropical Bronze had taken so many suntan sessions for the big day, she'd practically turned black.

Further back in the church she spotted the Kick for Men marketing team, and several executives from UniGlobal's head office. Even Doug Maggiotti had flown in from Atlanta. She was glad he was here because it would reinforce to him how famous Ryan was in England, and should lead to a pay rise when Cath came to renew the contract.

When she exchanged vows with Ryan, repeating after the vicar, Cath found it a very welcome surprise. She hadn't appreciated she'd be copping a half share of all Ryan's worldly goods, but it said as much in the wording. As they stood at the altar as husband and wife, she seemed to see Ryan anew, and it passed through her mind how random life can be. Had he not died in bed while they were on the job, she would have married old Charlie Blaydon and been Lady Blaydon long ago. Had she not gone along to the Classified's Christmas party at the Roof Gardens, she would never have met Ryan, let alone been stood here now as Mrs James. With his spiky haircut and cheeky grin, and all dressed up in his sparkly waistcoat and cravat, Cath felt satisfied in her choice of man. Sometimes she felt more like his mother and publicity manager, but she didn't mind. He was a lovely bloke, even if she had to do everything for him.

The service finally over, it was out onto the hotel lawns for the formal photographs. Bride and groom, family group, bride with maids of honour tossing bouquets in the air, groom with his ushers, on and on it went. Then there was Cath and Ryan with the cast of *Coronation Street*, and Ryan with his Man U team mates all giving a joyous thumbs up, and Cath and Ryan with the manager, assistant manager and sommelier of the Mere Grange hotel. The only frisson came when Ryan's Auntie Val produced her instamatic and started taking photos on the lawn. Two security guards quickly confiscated the camera and ripped the film out the back. Cath noticed that Dean looked rougher than ever, laying into the champagne.

But now it was time for dinner. Once the guests had been shepherded into the marquee and settled at their tables, there was a fanfare of trumpets, and the hotel's Master of Ceremonies announced, '*Laydees and gentlemen*, may I present your bride and groom . . .' and there was an eruption of applause as Cath and Ryan paraded into the tent. They weaved their way between the tables, preceded by photographers walking backwards. A follow-spot was trained on them every inch of the way, making Cath's dress and Ryan's waistcoat sparkle in its beam. Ryan's teammates and girlfriends were raising their glasses and whooping, and even the waiters and waitresses cheered the celebrity couple. Several guests remarked they'd never seen a bride so stunning as Katie looked that night, eyes darting coquettishly in the spotlight, as she took her seat alongside Ryan at top table.

The meal was gorgeous, Cath reckoned, even if it wasn't to everybody's taste. She could see Alf and Ryan's Auntie Val struggling with the prawn, lobster tail and avocado starter. The medallions of veal with samphire in an orange and port wine jus got left by virtually everyone, even at top table. But the *mousse de quatre chocolats* was a triumph, with its entwined initials K and R piped on each plate and decorated with white chocolate sprinkles. The sous chef of the hotel was presented on stage to take a special bow in his chef's toque, and be photographed by the magazine.

Now it was time for speeches. Cath and Ryan took their places on stage on their gilded thrones, while a succession of Ryan's teammates, sponsors and family approached the microphone in turn. Midge Long assured the guests that Ryan was 'a really nice bloke and a really good mate'. Doug Maggiotti told them how many flacons of Kick for Men had been sold internationally and how, thanks to Ryan, it was currently the number one men's fragrance in the UK. He added that Katie Fox was 'one of the best-looking ladies with a great head for business on her shoulders,' and wished the couple all the happiness in the world.

Finally it was the turn of Dean, who was to propose the toast to bride and groom. This had, in fact, been written for him by Cath, and transcribed in capital letters on to cards.

Cath had never been happy at the prospect of Dean on stage, but Alf had refused the job, saying he couldn't speak in public, and there'd been no other family member available.

Now Cath saw her worst fears fulfilled. Dean lurched up to the platform, speech in one hand, balloon of brandy in the other. His hair and forehead were damp with sweat, mouth and shirt smeared with chocolate mousse.

'Ladies and Gents,' he began. 'Ladies and Gents . . .' but got no further.

For then, in one hideous projectile belch, he covered microphone and stage in vomit, before subsiding onto the floor with a thud.

Chapter Twenty-Two

Only six months after her much-publicised wedding we find Cath Fox, or Katie James as we must now learn to call her, sitting in the passenger seat of a metallic-sky-blue BMW 3-series being driven across Cheshire by a new gentleman in her life. Terry Brady was, by general consent, the best connected estate agent in the north-west and the man to whom a generation of footballers, television stars and successful local businessmen turned when in need of a new home. So exclusive were Terry's services that he did not bother with official premises with photos of properties in the windows; instead, he worked from his private home in Alderley Edge, with two sports cars parked up in the driveway and a dream client list on his Rolodex. Nor did he accept every client who asked. According to Terry, he turned away as many as he took on, because with the level of personal service he liked to provide he couldn't accommodate everyone. Cath hadn't expected to be refused – not after appearing on two consecutive *Hello!* front covers – but it was still a relief when he said yes.

She had not thought it necessary to mention the house-hunting to Ryan, since she was merely taking a look at what was out there. And Ryan probably wouldn't like the idea of moving. Everything to do with properties and contracts and money put him into a panic; he would rather stay put in a two bed new-build than go through the anxiety of buying a bigger place. But Cath would take care of all that, she reckoned, like she always did; once she'd identified the perfect property, she'd break it to him at the right time.

Obviously it made sense to move. They could well afford to. What with Ryan's Man U contract and the Kick for Men contract, and the *Hello!* money just come through, they were loaded. *Cheshire Life* had whetted her appetite with pictures of amazing mansions, all within easy commute of Trafford Park, and Terry Brady advised her not to hang about and get in quick while the market was still below its peak.

If she were brutally honest, Cath knew her desire for a better, larger home had been partly stimulated by an article in the *Sun*. They had done this double-page feature on footballers' homes, saying where all the players lived, and because of her and Ryan's new-found fame and being in *Hello!* and all that, they'd included Ryan's place. Looking at it, you had to admit theirs was the worst of the lot, especially put next to Gazza's place with its private grounds and some of the other players with their swimming pools and fountains and impressive driveways. When Cath pointed this out to Ryan, he shrugged. 'I like it here, Katie. There's only the two of us. And we've got the parking spaces in the garage' – *the garridge* – 'and it's easy for me mum to come over.' Cath didn't mention that, far as she was concerned, the sooner Barbara was replaced by a proper paid cleaning lady, the happier she would be. She was fed up having Barbara round all the time.

The *Hello!* pictures still thrilled her, they were everything she'd hoped and more. Even months later, she could flick through those issues for hours at a time. There had been thirty-six pages of pictures in week one and a further twenty-two in week two: she'd counted! Over eighty shots of her personally. For weeks afterwards, wherever she'd been, people asked her about it. And then there'd been the honeymoon coverage, ten double pages of her and Ryan sitting around in Barbados on the beach, resting on their bed cover in their luxury cabana, helping themselves from the buffet at the poolside restaurant. They'd even set up a photoshoot of them pretending to play golf at a local links, with an electric golf buggy on hand, and a caddie serving them champagne on the green. Cath relished every minute, but Ryan had got quite moody towards the end, saying it wasn't a proper honeymoon because they hadn't been left alone the entire time.

Now it was back to reality. Ryan was hard at his training, the football season had restarted, and it was all a bit of an anticlimax really. If it wasn't for house-hunting, Cath didn't know what she'd have done to fill the day. As it was, she was tearing all over the county with Terry Brady in his BMW viewing these jaw-dropping mansions in Hale, Knutsford and Mottram St Andrew. If she could only live in a place like one of these, she'd be truly happy.

*

Annabel adored her honeymoon, it was the most romantic, incredible holiday of her entire life. For a start, she had Jamie completely to herself for thirteen glorious days and nights. In London, his army duties intruded at every turn. Other times he had to go up to Rutland at short notice to see his mother and sort something or other out for her. He always prioritised his mother, even when it meant missing a dinner party with Annabel's friends, which said wonderful things about his values.

Africa was incredible. Annabel had never travelled outside Europe before and was thrilled when Jamie finally told her where they were going. He had made a big thing of keeping the honeymoon under wraps, insisting she bring two suitcases to Heathrow, one packed with warm-weather clothes, the other with cold-weather. Only at the check-in desk did he reveal Nairobi as the destination. She had hoped it would be somewhere hot, because her prettiest outfits were for hot weather.

As it happened, Jamie had booked a five-day safari in the Masai Mara, followed by a week on a beach near Mombasa. To Annabel, it was the perfect combination of adventure with relaxation. The stress of the wedding and coping with her mother had left her exhausted. It was a dream to spend time alone with Jamie, just the two of them, with no interruptions or responsibilities.

They spent a truncated night at the Muthaiga Club in Nairobi, then rose at dawn to reach the domestic airport for an air taxi west. Annabel found it the most exciting thing, boarding the tiny twin-engine Cessna with only two other passengers. She couldn't get over seeing her name printed on her boarding card as A PILCHER, MRS. She placed it carefully into her purse, along with her boarding stub from the outbound Nairobi flight, to keep for ever.

They came down at the smallest airport she'd ever seen, just a dusty landing strip and a hut. A jeep was waiting to meet them, to take them to the camp which was apparently two hours further into the bush. It was all so civilised. Before they set off, the driver opened a cool box and offered Tusker beers, gin and tonics, Cokes and water. Jamie sank a couple of beers and Annabel was persuaded to have a gin and tonic which went straight to her head, so she felt quite woozy when they finally bumped off along the miles of mud-coloured tracks criss-crossing the Masai Mara. Through the open windows they caught glimpses of animals, mere spots on the horizon, which their driver, Tembo, took pains to point out. And if they passed a buffalo or antelope at closer quarters, or even a rare species of bird on the road, Tembo stopped the jeep altogether, waiting five or more minutes for the signal to proceed, giving them time to absorb these wonders of nature.

Jamie struck up a conversation with Tembo, questioning him about the possibilities of shooting an elephant or other big game during their stay, but Tembo was discouraging. It turned out he was a naturalist more than he was a driver, and devoted his life to protecting game from poachers. A disapproving mist descended on the car. Behind Tembo's back Jamie made throttling gestures in the back seat, before smiling at Annabel in the loveliest, most attentive way. There was no question about it, Jamie was very handsome. With his thick brown hair slicked back across his head, strong jaw, open khaki shirt and Hackett chinos, he resembled a ranger from *Born Free* or *Daktari*. Annabel felt a wave of love and gratitude towards her new husband, for bringing her to this magical place, for arranging every detail so beautifully, the flights, the hotels (she was unaware this had been the work of George Palmer), for rescuing her from her old existence in Segrave Mansions and plunging her into an exhilarating new life. She took Jamie's hand and squeezed, and he squeezed back, then leant over and kissed her. He took her face in his large masculine hands and kissed and kissed her, all the time making sure Tembo had a good view in the driving mirror. Once or twice the jeep swerved across the track as Tembo lost concentration. 'No, Jamie, no,' and Jamie roared with laughter. 'You're right, we mustn't provoke the naturalist, Annabel. He's probably very interested in mating rituals.' Then, addressing the back of Tembo's head, 'Tell me, Tembo, have you got any good *mating rituals* lined up for us? Is that part of the programme?'

Tembo shrugged. 'We go on morning game drive, evening game drive. Sometimes we find leopard, water buffalo, samba, blackbuck.'

'But will they be *mating*, Tembo? That's the thing. You see, we're *honeymooners*. Just married. We need to get ideas.'

Tembo drove on, pretending not to understand.

'Stop it,' hissed Annabel, embarrassed by her husband's banter.

'Tembo, another question,' said Jamie after a while. 'Serious question about natural history. Is it true the white rhinoceros has the longest, thickest dick in the jungle?'

Tembo hesitated, working out how to respond to the guest. 'When fully engorged, the pizzle can extend to half a metre.'

'Whoa. And how does that measure up to a giraffe, Tembo? What's the betting a giraffe's is longer but thinner? Less girth.'

'That is correct.'

'And buffalo? Short and stubby but very effective. Like a jack hammer. Isn't that right, Tembo?'

'Probably, sir.'

'But, in your professional judgement, you're saying the rhino has the biggest and best all-round tackle in the jungle?'

Tembo nodded. 'Rhino is very big animal, very dangerous.'

'But you haven't seen *mine* yet, have you, Tembo? You just wait, down by the old watering hole at sunset. Willy parade. Captain Pilcher versus the big beasts. Annabel, you're the judge. She's biased, Tembo, which is understandable. Newly married. Rutting season in full swing.'

They arrived at the barrier of the Masai Mara National Reserve and were issued with permits. After that, the tracks became sketchier and Tembo moved into lower gear as the jeep traversed steep gullies and dried-up riverbeds. Eventually they arrived at a small encampment of huts and tents close to the wildebeest migration route. This was Mara Delta Safari Camp, run by a former Irish Guards officer contact of Jamie's; his beshorted figure could be seen looking out for them, and clapping his hands for the camp boys to bring beers. Soon their luggage was carried to the final tent in the line. 'I've put you here for extra privacy, seeing as you're on honeymoon,' said Richard, the Guards Officer-turned-camp manager.

Annabel truly felt that those five nights in the jungle camp were amongst the happiest of her life. The first two mornings they were awakened before dawn, given a mug of tea, then they clambered into jeeps for a game trawl. Jamie was still agitating to be allowed to shoot something, but Richard told him it was out of the question – 'They'd put you away for ten years if you shot a rhino.' At the end of each drive they drew up in a jungle clearing where a luxurious breakfast had been laid up on linen tablecloths, with cooks serving bacon and eggs, and fruit salad in cut-crystal bowls, and it felt like bliss, sitting there in that remote spot with the birdsong and sunshine and the vague threat of a lion strolling past at any moment. Annabel took film after film of photographs but when, back in London, she had them developed, 90 per cent were of Jamie and the rest of breakfast. 'Didn't you see any wildlife at all?' asked her father, with a twinkle in his eye.

After the first couple of mornings they began skipping the game drives, and lay in their tents instead. Annabel wrote long letters to her parents thanking them for the wedding, and a letter to Jamie's mother, her mother-in-law, which was somehow trickier. And then she made a start on the two hundred thank you letters for wedding presents. She was determined not to make them formulaic, because people had been so kind, but they did begin to sound all rather alike. However, she wrote an especially long one to George to thank him for his portrait of her, which really was the most lovely picture. Annabel reckoned it was very over-flattering but George denied that. It had taken him ages to do – six sittings – which made it doubly generous. She told him all about the jungle camp and the flight in the Cessna. 'You *have* to come here one day yourself. Ask Jamie who can tell you how to book it and all the details.'

The only mildly annoying thing was Jamie's refusal to write any thank you letters himself, declaring it was woman's work. But Annabel couldn't be cross with him for long, even when he dawdled by the campfire at night, talking army talk with Richard, when she longed for him to join her and zip up the tent flap. However late it was, and however much Johnnie Walker he'd drunk, he always made love to her. Once, in his confusion, he called her 'Suki', which Annabel remembered was the name of one of his old flames. It was disturbing, but Jamie just laughed. 'I don't know how that slipped out. We've totally lost touch.'

After five days, the routines of camp life become rather soporific, and they did less and less, just slept and hung about awaiting the next gargantuan meal. It became embarrassing dodging Tembo and the other naturalists, who were determined to coax them out on game drives, when they preferred to doze by the algae-infested dip pool. Annabel began to wonder what her wedding photographs were like and became impatient to see them, and wished she'd brought more books to read.

On their final afternoon at Mara Delta Safari Camp, a party of elderly Brits showed up, two retired couples in baseball caps and binoculars. By the pool, Annabel noticed one of them flicking through *Hello!*. Even at a distance she could read the coverline: *World Exclusive! Ryan and Katie's Big Day – 36 pages of intimate pictures from their celeb-filled nuptials.*

Having stared across the pool at Cath's beaming face, Annabel strolled round and asked if she might borrow it, 'only when you've finished it yourself, of course'.

'Have it now, dear. I've done with it. I bought it for the flight out.'

Back on her sun lounger, Annabel was transfixed by so many pictures of Cath. She looked dazzling, even prettier than Annabel remembered, with masses of lustrous brown hair. There were pictures of her flashing her ring at the camera, and pictures of her getting ready, clinking glasses with two frankly rather naff-looking women, not being bitchy, who it said were also married to famous footballers. Ryan James she knew about, of course, because of his aftershave ads, and he was obviously good looking, though completely different to her dad. Annabel thought how weird it all was, that Cath had been her matron at St Mary's, and had then lived with her father, and was now all over *Hello!* married to a northern footballer. Well, good luck to her. Annabel took in every detail of Cath's wedding: the dress, the marquee, the *mousse de quatre chocolats* and decided she wouldn't have chosen one single thing about it, but hoped Cath would be as happy as she was herself. She remembered how they'd all admired Cath at school, and how much more worldly she'd been than any of them. It was funny she was called Katie now. And there was hardly a trace of her tattoos in the photographs. Perhaps *Hello!* had airbrushed them out?

Jamie joined her by the pool. 'Who's the bride in the monster meringue?'

'Cath Fox. Well, Katie James now.'

'Not the lady your mother bangs on about? Who shagged your dad?'

'Jamie, shushh. For heaven's sake, we never mention that. But yes. Same Cath.'

'She's bloody fit. No wonder your dad gave her one. I mean, no disrespect to my wonderful new mother-in-law, but he would have been mad not to.'

Chapter Twenty-Three

All the excitement of Cath's wedding to Ryan James, which Jess Eden would have relished more than any other guest, she learnt about only at second hand in *Hello!*. Her friend Bryony's mum Lizzie sometimes took *Hello!*, and then passed them on to Jess, and it so happened that Jess, having nothing better to do that week, read this issue especially carefully.

As she approached her GCSEs, she had suddenly to take her school work seriously, or so they kept brainwashing her at Bishop Ottley School for Girls. She was a sharp and quick-witted pupil, top or close to top of her class in most subjects, and already there was talk of her getting a place at a good university, if she worked flat out. Her mother, Kirsty, with all her interest in education, was thrilled at the prospect, and sent off for prospectuses from Bristol, Newcastle and Durham, and even Oxford and Cambridge, and left them around the living room to inspire Jess. All it achieved was to annoy her daughter. Jess wasn't sure she even wanted to go to college, she'd had it up to here with studying. Her dad, Bob, said why not go to Birmingham where me and your mum went? It was a nice city in which to spend three years. But Jess couldn't wait to work on *Smile* or *Sugar* magazine and go to celeb parties and get freebies. She was also receiving a lot of attention suddenly from boys in the upper sixth. There was a sexiness and sassiness to Jess which slightly worried Kirsty and Bob.

Gazing at Katie James in her wedding pictures, Jess reckoned she was incredibly good looking. And all her grooming, her make-up, eyebrows, hair, her amazing tiara; Jess really, really wanted to have a wedding like that herself one day. It must be so incredible knowing all these celebrities like Katie did; it was amazing how all the celebs were really good friends with each other, and just went to parties and film galas all day long and got photographed wherever they went.

Jess wondered if Katie James had gone to university. You couldn't exactly imagine celebrities at college or school. If she couldn't get a job on *Smile* or *Sugar*, Jess wanted to be a hairdresser in some big town, a really glamorous job where you got tips. Secretly, she also enjoyed science, so as a back-up she could go to uni and work at Glaxo like her dad. Anything, so long as she didn't have to live at home.

Even as she drove through the front gates, Cath knew it was the house of her dreams. Everything about it shouted prestige. The gates themselves set the tone, with decorative black ironwork highlighted in gold paint, and pillars on each side topped with stone chessmen. The drive curved through a small shrubbery, offering complete privacy as Terry the estate agent pointed out, and there ahead of you stood Prestbury Manor, surrounded by lawns and screened from the neighbours on both sides by mature laurel hedges.

Cath's first thought was that it reminded her of the Mere Grange Hotel where she'd got married, though the manor was built several hundred years later; an Arts and Crafts mansion in the vernacular style dimly influenced by the work of Lutyens. Like her wedding hotel, it had mullioned windows and a medieval-style front door with great iron rivets and a big iron key, which made Cath think of the Sheriff of Nottingham's castle. And, like the hotel, it had a large square hallway with wood-panelled walls and a fireplace you could step inside. Cath could just imagine herself greeting her guests in a hall like this, especially at Christmas with a fire going in the grate and holly and ivy strung over the mantel. Temporarily forgetting that her social circle with Ryan was rather limited, she envisaged herself as lady of the manor, giving all these exclusive parties.

The rest of the house pleased her no less. As they moved from reception room to reception room, it was all there. This room, with views across the lawns, was the lounge, that one the dining room. The largest space was a snooker room already equipped with full-sized snooker table, which the present owner was willing to sell by separate negotiation. Cath could just see Ryan in there with all his mates, and it would keep them out of the lounge too.

Obviously the entire place needed seeing to, even Terry conceded that. They'd need a new kitchen, new en suites, new everything really.

But, as Cath reasoned, she had the time and the taste, and Ryan had the cash, so what was keeping them? All right, it was a big place, but she'd lived in bigger before. She'd like to have told Ryan about Blaydon Hall but didn't know how she'd explain that particular episode. Instead she set about the task of persuading him to unlock his wallet.

As she'd predicted, it wasn't easy. Ryan was immediately hostile to the whole idea; he didn't fancy living out near Prestbury, considering it posh and stuck up, nor was he blowing that kind of cash on a mansion. He worried about money because he lived in fear of being dropped from the squad; the slightest note of criticism from manager or trainer and he'd fret for days.

'Come off it, Ryan, you're one of their top-paid players. I did the contract, remember?'

Ryan shrugged. He looked pathetically inadequate at moments like these, not knowing what to do or say.

'And there's all the Kick money coming in,' Cath went on. 'Your UniGlobal contract has two more years to run.'

'I guess,' said Ryan, unconvinced. 'They might give it to Eric Cantona instead.'

'You have a *contract*, right? I negotiated it, it's watertight.'

But Ryan didn't see the benefit in moving. It wasn't just buying a new house which scared him, they'd be needing furniture too, a new three-piece suite and suchlike. And how could Barbara get out there to clean? She'd have to change buses four times.

Cath was rattled. She'd expected Ryan to need persuading, but this was much worse. Furthermore, she'd as good as told Terry Brady they were buying the place; she'd even agreed the price.

Determinedly, she went on the sexual offensive. Each afternoon when Ryan returned from training she was waiting for him. She stopped wearing the designer gear she adored and which Ryan found intimidating, and instead welcomed him home in tight jeans and a T-shirt. She made breakfast in the nude and supper in the nude. Sometimes, when he unlocked the front door, Ryan found her stark naked on the couch. Twice a week she visited Tropical Bronze, topping up her honeymoon tan, and her bush was waxed closer and closer to the main event which kept Ryan permanently enthralled.

It took Cath three weeks of boisterous shagging to get her own way.

Her friend Hayley kept commenting on how fabulous she looked and asking for her secret, suspecting her of finding some new Slendertone machine, but Cath just rolled her eyes mysteriously. 'We *are* newly-weds, Hayley.'

On the evening of the twenty-second day, Ryan conceded defeat. 'Katie, about that house you're always on about. I've been thinking, maybe it would make a nice investment.'

'You think so, Ryan?'

'Yeah, I was talking with Gary and he says bricks and mortar is a good bet. Better than putting it in the bank.'

'Well, if you're quite sure.'

'I can see the sense in it.'

'OK, you're the boss, darling. I'll get the agent to prepare the papers for you to sign. Now, have a good day's training. And maybe we can go for a Chinese later?'

'Yeah, that'd be nice,' said Ryan, brightening up at being excused sex and having a chicken chow mein instead. 'Thanks, Katie, I quite fancy a Chinese.'

The more time she spent over at the manor, the more Cath became excited by its possibilities. There was plenty to be done – new schemes occurred each day – but the salesmen in the kitchen and bathroom showrooms were helpful, and now she had the keys to the property she was always over there meeting tradesmen and letting them in. It was funny how one thing led to another because the bloke who was measuring up for the granite worktops had a mate who did landscape gardening, and the next day he came over and they had the concept of extending the patio out on to the lawn, and creating gravel borders in place of some of the flowerbeds, and planting clumps of pampas grass on strategic sightlines. And then the designer from the bathroom company turned out to be best mates with a kitchen fitter at Clive Christian kitchens, who came up with a much better scheme than Cath had thought of herself, so all the black granite had to come back out again.

The finished kitchen was amazing, with cream custom-built units with corner pillars, and slide and glide drawers, and all the walls sponge-painted in pale creams and peach. The *pièce de résistance* was a peninsular island unit with space for ten people to eat on special custom-built stools.

Cath was never so proud of anything as that kitchen. When the builders had left for the day, she'd linger at the manor till it got dark outside, and she'd lower the peach blinds which matched the sponge-painted walls, and dim the lights, and just stand there looking at it, knowing it was all hers. Or would be, once Ryan had paid for it. Which was another problem, because Ryan had no idea, not the faintest concept, what these things cost. To Ryan, if you said you were doing a new kitchen, he'd think, right, that's two hundred-odd quid for the oven, a hundred for a fridge, so much for a cupboard to store the pots and pans. But Cath had always dreamed of having a fabulous kitchen. As a kid, all their kitchens had been pits, with greasy battered hobs and grill pans. A *Dynasty* kitchen was the fulfilment of a dream.

Bills were arriving each day and she daren't even take them home to Altrincham, she left them on a window sill at the manor. And still she couldn't stop ordering more stuff: she wanted it all to be perfect.

The lounge, she decided, would follow a similar colour scheme to the kitchen, all creams and peach, with gold and gilt accents around the edges of the lampshades and the rim of the coffee table. The carpet was cream, the new leather settees cream, the curtains peach and teal matching the peach and teal cushions on the settees and window seats. From a store in Altrincham she purchased a gilt-edged mirror and art deco ornaments and a Chinese bowl. Above the fireplace, in pride of place, hung an enlarged colour photograph of Cath and Ryan on their wedding day, which had been the cover of *Hello!*, mounted onto backing board. In the gaping hearth of the fireplace, she placed an arrangement of dried corn and 'baby's breath', an idea she'd noticed in other celebrities' homes in *Smile*. When all the new furniture was arranged in its proper place, the large room still looked underfurnished, and Cath didn't know what to do until she had the idea of buying a white baby-grand piano.

More than anything, Cath loved the process of 'dressing' the room, dreaming up the little style touches which made it personal. There was a built-in niche with shelves in the corner by the piano and Cath was at a loss over what to display in it, until she remembered her collection of fragrance bottles, so she created a shrine to her favourite perfumes, all the different shaped bottles and flacons, with Kick for Men in pride of place even though she preferred her Diors and Chanels and Gaultiers.

None of these artistic flourishes, however, were going to pay the bills. It was getting quite embarrassing with tradesmen chasing her for money. Cath was at her wits' end when her luck turned. She was speaking with her contact at *Hello!* and mentioned they were in the throes of moving house. The *Hello!* assistant editor was immediately interested, questioning her on what size and style of mansion the new place was. 'You know, Katie, we might like to run an At Home feature with you and Ryan. Especially if you can get Ryan's teammates over for drinks.'

'Is there a fee?'

'I'll need to speak to my editor, but lots of our celebrities love showcasing their new homes. It helps get discounts from their suppliers if they know they're going to be in the magazine.'

Cath was on it. Armed with the currency of editorial mentions in *Hello!*, she soon secured 50 per cent reductions on the outstanding invoices and higher discounts on new ones. She hadn't previously given much attention to the dining hall, but now had the panelling replaced with wall to wall mirror, maroon paintwork, a black ash dining table and potted palms in planters. The crystal chandelier, once installed, was bigger than it had looked in the shop but definitely a statement piece.

Upstairs, she went overboard. Ever since she was a tiny girl, when the Ladybird *Cinderella* had been one of her few books, she had dreamed of a fairy-tale bedroom like Cinders, with a princessly four poster. She found the bed – a vast mahogany number – in Macclesfield at Arighi Bianchi and had it swathed in blue and yellow drapes to match the festoon blinds at the windows. Fitted closets with Venetian doors occupied two entire walls, with built-in vanity.

Understanding that the success of the *Hello!* shoot depended upon pictures of Ryan and his teammates hanging out in the snooker room, Cath went to endless lengths to create a photogenic man-den. Soon the walls were painted red and white in Man U livery and covered with memorabilia, photos, caps and framed news cuttings. The old black leather couch looked fine against the red walls. A circular corner bar came complete with bar stools and optics. In the opposite corner stood the largest TV screen money could buy, sat on a black ash unit.

As the project neared completion, Cath forbade Ryan from visiting because she wanted him to see it finished as a glorious surprise. This suited Ryan who was hard at it with training. Ryan's dad had his nose out of joint, not having been asked to lend a hand, and Barbara was beginning to think Cath was getting above herself. It was all very well putting on airs and graces but Ryan was the famous one, not her. She couldn't get over Cath saying she'd prefer to pay a professional cleaner at the new place rather than have Barbara come over.

At last the day of the great shoot arrived. Cath had the idea of combining it with a house-warming, which made it easier to persuade guests to show up, and at least six lads from the squad were coming along. Ryan's schoolmates Gary and Kev would be there of course, and Donna from aerobics and Dannii from Tropical Bronze plus Alf and Barbara and Dean, if they were still speaking to her. If it had been down to her, she wouldn't have invited them to the house-warming at all.

Cath felt incredibly proud as she went round the house putting finishing touches to each room. The *Hello!* stylists insisted the dining table was fully laid with china and glass for the photographs, and Cath was pleased she'd splashed out on the gold goblets which glinted under the chandelier. The vintage jukebox for Ryan's den was delivered just in time and was pumping out Rod Stewart classics. Ryan seemed chuffed – 'You've done a grand job, Katie' – and uncomplainingly spent the afternoon being photographed with Cath in every room, in five changes of clothes.

The doorbell chimed. The very first guests to arrive were Ryan's family, Alf carrying his toolbox in case any last minute DIY was required. Barbara went from room to room, hardly knowing what to say. Inside she was flushed with pride at her son's trophy mansion but didn't want to give any credit to Cath. Instead she made carping comments to show she wasn't over-impressed. 'I wouldn't have put cream carpet in the lounge, it'll show every mark.' And, later, 'Get the white piano. Who'll be playing on that, I wonder? Elton-bloody-John!' Cath banished Dean to the snooker room where he slumped in front of the TV on his old black couch, remote in one hand, beer in the other.

Now all the guests began showing up at once, rapping on the medieval doorknocker. Donna and Dannii arrived clutching bunches of chrysanthemums which annoyed Cath because the colours didn't match the decor. Kev brought Milk Tray, Gary brought Lambrusco and the Man U boys presented Ryan with a rolling pin as a house-warming gift because they had this running joke he was a henpecked husband. Ryan took it in good part and placed it on his new bar.

Soon champagne corks were popping and lager cans cracking, and the *Hello!* photographer roamed about forcing the guests into unnatural groups and interrupting the flow of the party. Ryan and his teammates were pictured lining up breaks on the snooker table.

As the evening wore on, Cath felt unaccountably dissatisfied, she couldn't say why. The manor was everything she'd dreamed of. It had taken more graft getting it together than she'd possibly imagined, and here it was at last, being photographed for *Hello!*. She seriously doubted there was a more prestigious home in Prestbury. Momentarily she remembered the flats she'd lived in as a kid in Portsmouth, and how far away they seemed. But having obtained the house of her dreams and the man of her dreams, it felt anticlimactic.

Hayley and Midge kept assuring her how nice the place looked. Everyone was giving her compliments. But for some reason she couldn't settle; she drifted from room to room not wanting to engage with anyone for long, like she was channel hopping on the telly. She caught her reflection in the dining room mirrors, stopped, examined herself critically and decided she looked good. More than good. Versace was the Big New Solution in her life. Ryan would have a fit if he knew what she'd splashed out on tonight's outfit.

So this was it then, was it? She'd finally arrived. Here she was, stood in her dream home with *Hello!* covering the house-warming and half Manchester United gathered round the bar. So this is what it feels like?

She spotted Ryan in the snooker room, looking ridiculously young and slightly out of things, while his mates cued discs on the jukebox. Alf had his powerdrill out, straightening picture hooks. So this was it? From here on in, happily ever after. Mrs Ryan James, the envy of Prestbury. She reckoned she must be tired, that's what it was.

She sat on the old leather couch and remembered the role it had played in her relationship with Ryan. They'd spent a lot of time on that couch when she first moved up north, and more again when she'd wooed him into buying the manor. But she'd always associate the couch, above all, with Dean. She fervently hoped that, with their move out to Prestbury, they'd be seeing a lot less of him.

Thinking of Dean, she couldn't see the hooligan anywhere. Earlier, he'd been sat right here watching TV. She couldn't spot him with Ryan and the team, and he wasn't with Alf or Barbara either. The whereabouts of Dean began to play on her mind. She hoped he hadn't gone upstairs or started messing about with the jacuzzi. You could damage the mechanism if you switched it on without water up to a level, they warned you about that.

'Seen Dean anywhere, Barbara?' But she hadn't, not recently anyway.

With mounting foreboding, Cath traipsed back through the house, checking each room. She almost didn't notice him slumped on the piano stool by the baby grand, head in his hands over the keys. His face was partially obscured by the white piano lid, raised on its supports.

'Dean? You OK? Dean?'

He made a gurgling noise and Cath quickened her step. 'Sorry, Katie,' croaked Dean, mopping his mouth with his sleeve.

At that moment Cath made two vows which no force on earth would induce her to break: first thing tomorrow the piano would leave the house for good, and Dean wouldn't step back inside the manor ever again, not while Ryan and she were still man and wife.

Chapter Twenty-Four

Annabel almost wished they'd received fewer wedding presents. People had been so incredibly generous, they'd ended up with virtually every item on both gift lists and Jamie's Cambridge Street flat had no storage. The new Peter Jones Vi-Spring double bed occupied most of the floor space in the bedroom, and stacked up under the windows were all these boxes of presents: Le Creuset casserole dishes (six), asparagus steamers (three), more tumblers, wine glasses, bath towels and dinner plates than she could imagine needing in a lifetime. As for her clothes, the wardrobe was crammed to bursting with Jamie's suits and military clobber, and she didn't like to ask him to shift them, so her stuff was stored beneath the dining room table in suitcases.

She adored having their own place, even if it still felt like Jamie's bachelor pad. She quickly civilised it in numerous small ways, installing a full length mirror in the bedroom, new lampshades in the sitting room, toothglasses in the bathroom, and sorting out the chaos of the kitchen drawers. Annabel took pleasure in throwing out handfuls of rusty spatulas, toasting forks and barbecue tongs, replacing them with sparkling new cutlery from the wedding gift haul. Jamie made it clear he expected a proper cooked breakfast each morning, which Annabel was only too willing to provide, before setting off for her own job in Tony O'Flynn's corporate office. For all its shortcomings, Annabel was profoundly happy with Jamie in their Pimlico flat.

Any newly married couple recognises the process of shake-down which inevitably takes place in their combined social circle. Generally there are casualties on both sides; individuals who, for one reason or another, do not win equal approval from both partners and gradually slip off the joint roster. Inspired by her pretty new china and ovenproof dishes decorated with a pattern of dragonflies, Annabel was keen to entertain at home. Jamie's dining room was capable of seating eight people, providing they filed into their places consecutively. A series of dinner parties was embarked upon, with Annabel attempting a higher level of cuisine than she'd achieved in Courchevel or Segrave Mansions. She took her responsibilities as a new wife seriously, and did not want to disappoint Jamie or his friends. She borrowed Prue Leith's *Cookery Bible* from Flea and bought Raymond Blanc's *Cooking for Friends* from the office book sale.

It so happened that, at their first three dinners, the guests were comprised entirely of Jamie's old circle. It was felt that Jamie's commanding officer and his wife should be among the first to receive hospitality, which in turn demanded other army guests, so that first party took on an exclusively military flavour. The second dinner was to congratulate Rupert Henley upon his engagement to Pippa, which naturally implied more army guests, and the third was a reunion dinner for Jamie's pals from Münster days. Annabel did not resent it; she enjoyed the high spirits of military men, even though she wasn't sure they fully appreciated the delicacy of her cheese soufflés or mixed summer berries in brandy snap baskets.

One consolation was having George Palmer at all three dinner parties, because he was so nice to her and noticed the food she'd slaved so long over; she always tried to have him seated next to her if she could. Jamie had hung both of George's paintings in the dining room: the portrait of Annabel and the one of Monty the Labrador. 'Both my great loves,' said Jamie.

It wouldn't have surprised Annabel if there was a portrait of Jamie's mum, Bridget, hanging there too; he was spending so much time up in Rutland, sorting out the riding stables and matters related to his late father's probate. Jamie was a saint when it came to his mother.

It frustrated Annabel how tricky it was to fix a suitable date to give a dinner for her own old friends. She longed to introduce them to Jamie. Apart from at the wedding, neither Sophie nor Mouse had met him properly. It was Annabel's ambition to show off her man, her new abode and new china to her best friends from her single days. After all, she had had a life pre-Jamie, and wanted her husband to be part of that.

Not without difficulty, a Thursday night was identified when Jamie could be available. Sophie Peverel and her man, David, were over from Hong Kong, and Annabel had already invited Ginnie, a friend from her Miss Claire's teaching days, and her husband Richard. Mouse B-M had sadly split from Hector Murray, the future Earl of Arbroath, so was back to square one, and Annabel asked George Palmer to balance up the numbers as spare man.

As usual, Annabel did much of the prep-work the previous night, even setting the table using their best new tablemats depicting uniforms of the various Guards regiments, and four glasses for each person for red and white wine, pudding wine and water. She managed to sneak off early from Imperial Magazines, and for once felt everything was more or less under control: the cheese soufflés in their ramekins, coq au vin in the casserole, a *tarte aux pommes* waiting to warm through in the oven. She made place cards, each individually decorated with appropriate doodles: chopsticks for the Hong Kong guests, paintbrush for George, a tank for Jamie. Then, having checked the table one final time, she went off for a long soaky bath.

When Jamie hadn't returned home by seven o'clock, she began to wonder where he was. By seven thirty she was worried. By ten to eight, she was frantic. Guests could start arriving any minute. Where on earth was he? He could at least have rung. She wondered whether or not to open the wine, normally Jamie's job.

The doorbell and telephone rang simultaneously. She raced to the front door, beckoning Sophie and David inside, and just caught the phone. Her husband sounded a long way away.

'Jamie? Where are you? Sophie and David have arrived.'

'Rutland. I'm sorry, darling, something's come up. I tried to call you earlier. My mother's had a fall. I'm going to have to jack tonight. I'm sorry, Annabel.'

'Is she OK?'

'Is who OK?'

'Your mother.'

'Yah, fine. Will be. Obviously not fine at the moment. She's in hospital.'

'How awful. Can I do anything? Send flowers? Which hospital is she in?'

'What's that? Sorry, darling, terrible line. Can't hear you. Anyway, apologies about tonight, wish I was with you all. Got to go, doctor approaching.'

Annabel felt deflated. The whole point of tonight was for Jamie to meet her friends, and now he wasn't coming. It seemed unfair to blame Bridget but it was awfully disappointing just the same. She couldn't help feeling Jamie might have told her earlier, and that it would happen on the night when her own friends were coming.

Now the doorbell rang and rang, and soon the sitting room was filled with guests. It was wonderful to be with Soph and Mouse, and to see Ginnie and Richard, even though it meant explaining what had happened to Jamie. George opened the wine while Annabel removed a place from the table, and there was nothing to be done except get on with it. Soon the flat was full of laughter and it felt like her single days again with her old friends around her. Even Mouse, heartbroken over Hector, cheered up as the evening wore on. 'I meant to ask you, Bells. Have you been following Cath Fox's latest adventures in *Hello!*?'

'Her gracious new home, you mean? Riveted by it. Cream carpet and cream leather sofas . . .'

'Not forgetting the bar.'

For years, ever since Cath's affair with Michael Goode, Annabel's friends had been circumspect about discussing Cath with her, it was too sensitive a subject. But now, so long afterwards, and with Cath reinvented as a footballer's wife, she was decontaminated as a topic and the focus of legitimate fascination.

Soon Annabel, Sophie and Mouse were regaling the table with Cath stories. 'Those amazing tattoos, what were they, I can't remember? Was it a scorpion she had on her thigh?'

'And a spider's web. Right above her panty line.'

'Wasn't she having a thing with our geography teacher? The one with the teeth?'

'Mr Woodruff. No Ryan James, he.'

'You can't think he's good looking? Ryan James, I mean?' asked Sophie.

'Certainly do. Really cute,' said Mouse. 'Quite fancy him myself.'

'What's her secret? Cath Fox. Is she very attractive?' George asked.

'Sexy,' said Sophie. 'There's something about her. Men go mad for her.'

'She's smart too,' Mouse said. 'Picks things up quickly. At St Mary's, she was always asking where people went on holiday and where they lived, she liked knowing stuff. She came from somewhere like Birmingham originally.'

'Portsmouth,' said Annabel.

'Precisely,' said Mouse.

The guests went home shortly after midnight, though George lingered to help clear the table and load the dishwasher. 'That was a fantastic evening, thanks for including me. Your friends are great fun.'

'It's a shame Jamie wasn't here, I so wanted him to meet them.'

'Another time. I'm sure he'll get to meet them soon.'

But Annabel wondered. For reasons she hardly dared explore, she doubted her husband would ever really want to know her friends. He was an incredible man and she adored him, but she did sometimes worry he might be a little bit self-centred.

Whatever reservations she harboured about Jamie were soon overtaken, however, by a piece of wonderful news. Within a fortnight of the dinner party, she realised she might be pregnant. And six weeks later it became official: with her family and friends, the HR department at Imperial Magazines, all briefed on the joyous news. Now, of course, there could be no room for doubt or conjecture, since the fact of her pregnancy, and the new life growing inside her, changed everything, and brought with it excitements and responsibilities which displaced all others.

Chapter Twenty-Five

Ryan still liked Cath to accompany him to away matches, but Cath was increasingly prepared to travel only to those games where she could get there and back in the day. After four seasons as a WAG in the wagon train, the novelty of staying at Holiday Inns had worn off and she would sooner sleep in her own statement bed at Prestbury Manor. She would support him up to Liverpool, Newcastle and Glasgow, and as far south as Wolverhampton, but no further, not unless Ryan was playing a London club and she could combine it with a shopping spree along Bond Street.

Otherwise, she wasn't bothered. The prospect of being sat in a VIP stand and free food in a function room had lost much of its initial appeal, unless it was an important fixture when the paparazzi were out in force. Then Cath was pleased enough to turn up, showing off her new gear; but the games got quite tedious with the same crowd of people always there, and Alf and Barbara on at her to get them comp seats in a box. She had stuck to her guns about Dean no longer being welcome at the manor, and this created additional friction between Cath and her parents-in-law. Barbara told anyone who asked, 'Ryan's Katie is a right stuck-up cow.'

With house and garden finally completed, and no builders or landscape designers to occupy her days, Cath started to wonder what came next. She was twenty-nine years old and, as she'd demonstrated over Ryan's contracts, no fool. What was it Doug Maggiotti called her? A sharp cookie. She'd pulled a blinder renewing Ryan's Kick for Men contract, with a 40 per cent hike in fees for fewer days' commitment. She'd taken it to the wire but never once doubted they'd capitulate. The new sixty foot billboard of Ryan outside Manchester Piccadilly station was the talk of the north.

One thing she'd come to appreciate was how relatively easily one could become the talk of the north. For all its sprawl and satellite conurbations, Manchester felt like a small place, hardly bigger than Portsmouth. She felt she knew every boutique and department store inside out, had eaten in every classy restaurant. When *Cheshire Life* interviewed her as a local celebrity she regretted doing it because the article made her sound parochial, like she had nothing to say. Which was hardly surprising since all she did was exercise classes and sunbed sessions, and have coffees with Hayley and Anita behind the chessmen gates and pampas grass clumps of her new home.

She looked back on her years of struggle selling classifieds and felt almost nostalgic. Who would now believe she once ran a department of eighty salesgirls? And was identified as a fast-track executive? If she hadn't sacrificed her career for Ryan by moving up north, would she not be a main board director by now with salary and perks to match?

Her relationship with Ryan still had its moments, she wasn't exactly complaining, but sometimes he got on her nerves. On Sundays he sat at the kitchen table reading sport in the *News of the World* while Cath made him his Sunday fry-up, which was the only way to stop him driving over to Wythenshawe for a fry-up with Barbara. In the afternoons, Gary and Kev came over to play table football in the den, so Cath generally went off shopping or to Tropical Bronze. Ryan was delighted by the power hose she'd installed for washing his array of cars, and could happily pass an hour or two with the nozzle pointed at the tyres of his Porsches and Ferraris, blasting away every trace of dirt. When Cath tried to entice him abroad for a beach holiday, he was anxious about the food and the heat and not speaking the language. 'I'd sooner not, Katie.'

One Saturday afternoon Cath was sitting in the VIP stands at Old Trafford watching a game against Liverpool, when a man she dimly recognised from the newspapers entered the box, accompanied by a small posse of retainers. The man looked mid-fifties in age, of below average height, with a strong aura of power and energy about him. He was dressed in sweatpants, bomber jacket and baseball cap. He stood at the front of the box for a moment, surveying the pitch, while his people tipped down his seat for him and swept it clean of crumbs. Then he removed his cap, revealing himself as totally bald.

It took Cath a minute or two to recall his name; it was a tricky foreign one, she knew that. Then she got it: Randolph Jaworski. He was an American, she thought, she couldn't precisely remember, but she knew he owned newspapers and television stations; a media tycoon and multimillionaire. She seemed to remember reading he also owned the Miss World contest, or Miss Universe or something. Cath found she couldn't take her eyes off him.

She was fetching a drink at half-time and found herself standing next to him.

'That's a very interesting tattoo you have there on your neck, miss,' Randolph Jaworski said to her. 'They're my initials: RJ. I trust you put them there in my honour?'

Cath laughed. 'Of course. What else? I have the initials of all my heroes inked on myself.'

'You mean you have *other* heroes? That distresses me. I hoped I was the only one. I'm Randy, by the way.'

'Me too,' replied Cath. 'Just kidding. And I know who you are, though I wouldn't like to pronounce your surname.'

'Jaworski. It's Polish. My folks emigrated to the States. Won't you come and sit with me, miss, and explain me the rules of this soccer game? I'm kind of mystified what the hell's going on down there on the field.'

She spent the whole of the second half talking him through each shot, telling him about the players and explaining the different divisions and leagues and clubs. Randolph mentioned he was considering buying a club himself. He already owned an American-football team in Florida, and had become interested in English soccer.

When Cath mentioned it would cost him a packet to buy a club, Randy demurred, saying the multiples in England were quite reasonable 'certainly compared to valuations back home in the area of sport'. In any case, he said, sports management in Europe was in its infancy – 'I'm not sure folks over here even know what it means' – there were vast untapped opportunities in merchandising and licensing.

Cath agreed. 'I manage contracts and licensing for one of the first division players, actually. I recently renegotiated his contract with UniGlobal Corp of Atlanta. He's the UK face of Kick for Men. The men's fragrance?'

Randolph Jaworski said he was familiar with UniGlobal Corp,

being friends with the CEO there. 'So you're a licensing and contracts specialist?'

'I wouldn't say specialist. But I do quite a bit of it. I handle contract negotiations with Manchester United mostly. I learnt my negotiating skills when I was running a division of Imperial Magazines, the publishing company down in London.'

'Well, maybe you should head up our licensing if we are ever successful in acquiring a club.'

'Maybe I should,' said Cath. 'But I warn you, Randy, I don't come cheap.'

'If you came cheap,' replied Randolph, 'I wouldn't be interested.'

Randolph Jaworski was intrigued by Cath. For a start, she was very easy on the eye. And she was tactile: when explaining some refinement of the soccer game, she held his arm or brushed his back, but in a guileless way he found refreshing. Her eyes were bright and alert, her figure fabulous, he found it hard not to stare at her breasts. Since the end of his second marriage a couple of years back, Randolph was open to offers. But his schedule necessitated so much international travel that opportunities for meeting new ladies were fewer than you might expect, given his great power and wealth. He liked to complain that his time was spent at the whim of his senior executives, who demanded his presence on different continents to sign off this deal or that.

'So, miss, you live here in Manchester?'

'Prestbury. In this lovely old manor house. Not too far from the city.'

Randolph shrugged. 'I can't say I have a clear picture of your English cities. I come to London quite frequently, we own media properties there. And I've visited Edinburgh' – *Edinburrow* – 'and some places outside of London in the countryside.'

From time to time one of Randolph's aides came over to check he wasn't being bothered by his pretty companion. But Randy waved them away. 'We're doing fine here. And fetch us a couple of sodas, will you? And sesame pretzels if they have them.'

'Your home is in America?' Cath asked.

'Houston is my principle residence, not that I get to spend much time there. There's an apartment in New York, and I keep a place on Mustique for vacation time. And an apartment in Florida for the football. And it's looking like I'll need to find someplace permanent in London, given the time I'm needing to spend over here.'

'You own newspapers, don't you? I've read about you.'

'When my parents arrived in the States they eventually settled in Chicago where my father started a weekly newspaper, published in the Polish language. He ran articles about the Polish community in the city, and stories from back home in Poland, and generally served the community. They carried a lot of classified advertising aimed at the Polish diaspora. From that one small publication grew several more, and I've spent the past thirty-five years building and diversifying our franchises. We have more interests in television these days. But newspapers – and classifieds – remain highly material to us.'

'I used to run a classifieds business,' Cath said. 'I had eighty salesgirls under me.'

'You, miss, are a constant source of surprise and wonder. You are evidently a formidable young lady. And I can't keep calling you "miss".'

'I'm . . . Cath,' said Cath.

'Is that short for something? Katharine? Kathleen? I like the name Kathleen.'

'That's me. I'm a Kathleen. But known as Cath.'

'OK then, Kathleen. Well I've enjoyed speaking with you today. And I hope you'll permit me to stay in touch. With your expertise in contract negotiation and classified advertising, we will likely wish to retain your services.'

Chapter Twenty-Six

Cath was pleasantly surprised but not exactly astonished to receive a telephone call a couple of days later from Randolph Jaworski's corporate office, inviting her to a business meeting down in London. His senior executive assistant, Ann Saltzman, was solicitously polite and considerate, offering a car to meet Cath at Euston station, but at the same time managed to signal that Mr Jaworski's schedule was very busy and his options few and restricted. If Cath was unavailable at the time proposed it would be many weeks before an alternative could be found. Cath quickly found herself accepting the preferred slot and catching a train south from Manchester Piccadilly. For some reason she omitted to tell her husband about her appointment with Randy Jaworski, stating she had a routine business fixture with UniGlobal regarding Ryan's sponsorship contract.

Randy did not yet keep a London office, preferring to monitor his British investments from a suite at the Connaught Hotel, the sitting room of which had been equipped with boardroom table and fax machines. When Cath was shown in, two assistants were retrieving long coils of paper from two fax terminals, cutting and sorting them into page order. From their conversation, she understood these were overnight revenue and viewing figures from a TV station in Chicago.

'Kathleen, my apologies for keeping you, I was detained on a call.' Randy emerged from the bedroom, vibrating with surplus energy, dressed in a navy blue suit. He looked richer and more formal than at their previous encounter at Old Trafford. He shook her hand and told his assistants, 'Kathleen is going to put a rocket under our UK operations.' Then he said, 'Show her some of our Midlands publications, I asked for a selection to be sent over.'

Soon Cath was sitting at a table leafing through regional newspapers which apparently belonged to Randy. They had titles like *Kettering Argus* and *Corby Bugle and Advertiser*, full of smudgy columns of small ads for cars and properties for sale, second-hand fridges and conservatories. As she turned the pages, ink came off on her fingers.

'So whaddya reckon?' Randy was standing over her awaiting her judgement. 'Are they doing their jobs right, these folks?'

'I'm just looking. I can see some categories they don't seem to be going after.'

'Such as?'

Into Cath's mind came an image of the retail parks encroaching on Charlie Blaydon's estate, all looking for staff.

'I don't see many retail sit vacs,' Cath said. 'Jobs in Tesco, Asda . . . all them. I used to live in the area, there's loads of potential in recruitment.'

Randy was making notes on a leather-edged notepad. 'What else?'

'Er, tanning shops, nail salons. I don't see hot tubs or jacuzzis.'

Randy jabbed his finger onto the desk. 'I knew our people were making a hash of this. Didn't I say that, Ann?'

'You did, Mr Jaworski,' replied his senior executive assistant. 'You've not been satisfied.'

'And now Kathleen's confirmed it. Everything I've been saying.'

Encouraged, Cath grew bolder. 'House improvements – local builders, kitchen fitters, garden services. They should be booking way more than nine pages in your Corby paper, Randy. It has to be underperforming.' Cath was enjoying herself. Her sharp eyes were missing nothing. And she was enjoying the feeling of impressing Mr Jaworski, winning his approval.

'You know what?' Randy said. 'Ann, call the people up there and tell 'em I want to see 'em. Tomorrow. Down here in London. Kathleen, I'm appointing you special consultant, I want you to show 'em where they've screwed up. You don't have a problem staying overnight and meeting with my executive team tomorrow? Good. Ann, fix Kathleen a suite at the hotel and a table someplace to eat tonight.'

'You haven't forgotten you're flying to New York tomorrow morning, Mr Jaworski?'

'Change it, this is more important. I can take a later flight to JFK.'

Cath spent the afternoon shopping, being driven around by Randy's car and chauffeur, Makepiece. She found the experience delightful, telling Makepiece the stores she wished to visit and having him wait for her outside, and helping her load carrier bags into the boot. Makepiece told her he was Mr Jaworski's regular chauffeur whenever he was in London, that he was a generous tipper but you never knew how late he would be at night. He mentioned he had been parked up outside Annabel's, the Berkeley Square nightclub, until three in the morning.

She loved her suite at the Connaught with its antique furniture and yellow silk sofas, which felt more mellow than Prestbury Manor. She ordered a cup of tea and it arrived in a bone china cup, with teapot and silver tea strainer on a tray with a cloth, and she perched on the settee while the waiter poured it for her. She could get used to this! Ryan always fished out the teabag with his fingers and dropped it on the nearest surface.

Later she joined Randy in the lobby and they were driven to Wilton's for dinner. 'I love Wilton's,' Cath declared, based on her one dinner there with Charlie Blaydon when she'd been working down the road at the Pall Mall Steam and Fitness Club. 'They have the best fish in London.'

'The place for fish, Kathleen,' Randy said, 'is San Francisco. There's a little place I know on Fisherman's Wharf. We must try it sometime.'

Cath found Randy endlessly fascinating. She felt she learnt more new things, and enjoyed more stimulating conversation over that first dinner than in the past five years with Ryan. She couldn't get over all the different businesses he was involved with. He mentioned he'd invested in a movie animation company developing cartoon characters in collaboration with Disney, and a Grand Canyon theme park in Arizona. He asked her opinion on his Miss Teen America beauty pageant, which he was considering disposing of, and gave every impression of valuing her opinion. He referred to his companies as 'assets', as in 'we've been investing in television assets in New Jersey'. He made reference to the existence of a Gulfstream jet, and to a media conference he had attended in Sun Valley, Idaho, at which Rupert Murdoch and Sumner Redstone of Viacom had been fellow delegates. He advanced a theory that newspapers as an industry were in structural and irreversible decline but that, like the Texan oil business, there were still considerable profits to be extracted, providing you set about it in the correct way.

'That's why I'm excited by your observations concerning our classifieds division. We haven't spoken compensation yet but I'm open to pay you what you want. If you shake up South Midlands Newspapers, there will be further opportunities elsewhere, in the States and Eastern Europe. We are looking to acquire newspapers in Poland, which is something my father would have loved for us to do.'

Cath couldn't see how any of these enticements could possibly coexist with her life in Manchester with Ryan, but she didn't wish to halt the flow of possibilities. She loved Ryan and their house and everything, but this was exciting.

'Tell you what,' Randy said. 'If you're not busy at the end of the month, come with me to Chicago. I'd like for you to meet my CEO over there, he's a smart guy. You can swap notes and tell him how you're transforming classifieds.'

Over coffee, he said, 'Kathleen, you have to forgive me, I've been talking too much about myself and my business. I have a tendency to do that. My ex-wife complained about it in her deposition.'

'No problem, I was interested. You're a really interesting man, Randy.'

'I'm not sure everyone would agree with you there, but thank you for the compliment. But I want to know more about you. Like how an attractive, smart young lady ended up living in Manchester, which I'm reliably informed is the Cleveland of the United Kingdom.'

Cath gave him a version of her life story which instinct told her he'd appreciate. How she'd been educated at an old-fashioned girls' boarding school in the countryside, and became engaged to be married to a rich, older man when she was in her twenties. 'I like my men like my wine, a little more mature,' she said. She described running the classifieds division at Imperial – 'I was the youngest senior manager in the history of the company' – but how she'd given it all up for love with a celebrity sportsman.

'This is Mr Ryan James, right?' said Randy. 'He's quite a well-regarded player over here, I'm told.'

'He's a great player,' Cath replied. 'He's still exciting to watch in a match.' She allowed the sentence to hang.

'But not so exciting anyplace else? That's frequently the way with sportsmen. My first wife was with a professional golfer when we began dating.'

'Ryan's like my brother. He enjoys cleaning his cars with a hose . . .'

Randy laughed. 'Sounds to me like the ideal choice of starter husband. My first wife was a wonderful woman, I have nothing but the greatest respect for her. She's been a fine mother to our daughter, Candy. But I couldn't stay married to her. Some people take you so far but can't go the distance. As my business became more interesting, she couldn't keep up, couldn't make a contribution, not intellectually, not socially. My second wife, Krystal, was another story altogether. Now that's one episode I have no wish to repeat. A tricky lady.' He waited while the waiter poured more wine. 'Well, they say you learn from every experience. What I learned from that one is that a prenup is only as good as the attorney who drafted it.' He blew crossly. 'She's one wealthy lady now. But she couldn't help me in business. If you put the newspapers down in front of her and asked for her assessment like I did with you earlier today, she wouldn't know where to begin.'

In the car back to the hotel, Randy put the moves on her, as she guessed he might, and she pushed him away with a pretty laugh. 'Mr Jaworski, we have only just met.' And later, she turned him away at the door to her suite. 'You sleep well, Mr Jaworski. I have to make my notes for tomorrow morning's meeting.'

But the next day, following the meeting at which she was appointed Special Advisor to the Chairman of Jaworski Media with a brief to monitor and improve the classifieds performance of South Midlands Newspaper Group (SMNG), Cath reckoned she had denied her tycoon boss for long enough. Her performance in the bedroom that afternoon was everything he could have hoped, being aggressive, uncompromising and thorough. Seldom before had Randy experienced such a satisfying lover.

Cath hardly knew what she'd taken on, only that her life had assumed an impetus she hadn't experienced in years. She could now see that her existence in Manchester had been stultifying. Already she regarded it in the past tense. Ryan, Dean, Alf and Barbara, even her friends Hayley and Anita, all struck her as unbearably parochial. Even her new house, so recently the source of pride and joy, looked all wrong. She stared from the window onto the empty lawn, pampas grass drooping under a leaden sky.

All these thoughts ran through her head as she made the train journey between Manchester and Kettering. In the three weeks since her encounter with Randy at the Connaught Hotel, she had made the journey four times. From the station she would take a minicab to the headquarters of SMNG in a business park on the edge of Kettering, where the classifieds heads of the various local newspapers were gathered in her honour. That they resented her sudden insertion in their midst was an understatement; they stared at her with scarcely concealed hostility, unreceptive to each suggestion. When Cath pushed her ideas for pet care and hot tub categories, they said these had been tried before but hadn't worked; when she pushed recruitment advertising, they said it all went through Job Centres and there was no budget.

Only Cath's natural determination stopped her from giving up. That and the regular reports she faxed to Randy, currently travelling between Houston and Chicago. He responded to each report with staccato instructions: 'Kathleen – you may need to fire the whole lot of them. Do any of our competitors employ viable candidates? RJ.' Or else, 'Don't ask, tell them. You are their boss.' Once he rang her in Prestbury from his Gulfstream flying above Utah. As they spoke, Cath watched Ryan through the kitchen window, directing his power hose at the wheels of his new Ferrari.

She told Ryan very little of her assignment in Kettering, and he lacked curiosity, hardly seeming to notice her trips south, which anyway took place while he was training. He was disappointed when she missed away matches but spent the time with his parents and Dean instead. When Cath announced she was going to Chicago for a few days' work, Ryan asked her to bring him back a White Sox cap. The States was one of the few countries he wouldn't mind visiting one day.

Cath adored every second of the Chicago trip, beginning with the first class ticket Randy's office organised for collection at Heathrow. She only wished her friends could see her sat up at the front, with stewards fussing round her with hot towels and menus like she was a celebrity or high-powered business executive. Which she virtually was, of course, her home having been exclusively featured in *Hello!* and herself in her role as Special Advisor to Randolph Z. Jaworski: Chairman of Jaworski Media Corp. For Cath, there was no disconnect between the reality of her job to date – coaching resentful classifieds salespeople in a Midlands business park – and her entitlement to a

VIP seat in the snout of the plane. As the oxygen and second glass of complimentary champagne kicked in, Cath imagined herself helping Randy sort out his whole business empire.

The suite at the top of the Four Seasons Hotel Chicago had three toilets, a private dining room and views across Lake Michigan. This time there had been no question of a second bedroom, Cath moved straight in with the boss. They ordered goujons of sole and French fries from room service which arrived in a trundling food wagon, and afterwards Randy asked Ann Saltzman, his senior executive assistant, and Maria Hernandez, his second assistant, to leave them, saying he had confidential discussions to pursue with Kathleen, and the two ladies removed themselves from the suite with many a knowing look. Randy said he had been closing significant acquisitions on opposite coasts of the country, and the focus and energy this entailed had left him feeling sexually agitated.

'Then you came to the right place,' laughed Cath, who always responded best to the direct approach. 'I've been looking forward to it ever since last time.'

'By the way, I had your return flight cancelled. You're coming to New York with me at the end of the week, and I'll fly you back across the pond Sunday.'

'Mmmm . . . That's wonderful. I've always wanted to see New York.'

'And who the fuck is Callum?' Randy asked, staring at the heart-shaped tattoo.

'Just some guy I knew, long ago.'

'Well kindly reassure me his dick was smaller than mine, right?'

'Way smaller,' Cath lied. 'No comparison.'

'I've a good mind to marry you, Kathleen. I like you. You know something, I might just do that.'

A week spent in the slipstream of Randolph Jaworski and Cath could scarcely recall what life had been like before.

Luxuries which struck her as remarkable at the start of the trip, such as presidential suites, constant room service, town car limousines, even the corporate jet, achieved something approaching normality. The ease with which she acclimatised surprised even herself. Deducing that Randy wished her to be impressed, but not awed, by the lifestyle he showed her, she took pains to reference Blaydon Hall – 'one of England's stateliest statelies' – and hotels like Claridge's where Charlie had treated her to dinners. She implied she had been a board director at the Imperial Magazine Group and helped identify acquisitions for them. On the flight from Chicago to New York, Randy asked her to run her eye across several media properties being touted by investment banks, and Cath found no difficulty in formulating a point of view, favouring this opportunity over that. Randy was impressed. He congratulated himself on finding a sexy, sassy new lady who was a blast in bed and understood the subtleties of the media business.

She loved the Manhattan apartment on the Upper East Side with its contemporary art collection and views across the park, and the office building on the Lower West Side with views over the Hudson River. In the mornings, she joined Randy in the small gym adjoining his den in the apartment, where he worked out with weights. Afterwards she accompanied him to the office where she was loaned an executive office of her own and conducted reviews of the various American newspapers in the Jaworski portfolio. There were more than sixty of these, large and small, ranging from metropolitan dailies to weekly shoppers and freesheets distributed in malls. As she told Randy, 'Some of them don't feel that exciting. You should sex them up a bit. Advertisers would love it, I'm telling you.'

In the evenings, Randy took her to dinner at restaurants like Le Cirque and the Four Seasons Grill Room where the tables were occupied by celebrities and other tycoons, none of whom Cath had heard of, but she didn't let on. Randy introduced her on the way to their table to Ron Perelman of Revlon and Barry Diller of Fox and later to Leonard and Evelyn Lauder, who Cath had certainly heard of, being a big customer of Estée Lauder products at Allders in Manchester. When she mentioned this fact to Mr Lauder, his face lit up and he told her he'd inspected the new cosmetics hall there only seven months earlier. 'Kathleen is our new vice president for special projects,' Randy told everyone. 'We're expecting great things.'

Randy was impressed by Cath's curiosity, by the way she interrogated him with questions, always eager to learn. She quizzed him about cable television and where the profits derived from, and the business models for his various operations. It pleased him she was so interested and receptive, which neither of his previous wives had been. And rehearsing the details of his businesses enabled Randy to show off to her, explaining how he'd turned round this division and how he'd created value at that, and how poorly a particular asset had been managed before he acquired it.

For Cath it was like the college education she never had, but at an infinitely higher level. Not only in business but culturally she knew she had much to learn. She found the paintings in Randy's apartment incomprehensible, but from remarks he made understood them to be valuable. One afternoon she took herself off to the Whitney and the Solomon R. Guggenheim and MoMa, and located other examples of work by artists in Randy's collection, and later toured the galleries in the streets surrounding the apartment building, finding paintings by Basquiat and Clemente. Over dinner she said, 'I saw a wonderful Basquiat at Richard Feigen today, but I prefer both of yours.' She told Randy that when she'd been engaged to be married to the English lord, she'd helped catalogue his collection of old masterpieces, but recently her taste had moved more to the contemporary. In Randy's den she chanced upon an issue of *Forbes* with its annual list of America's Top 400 Richest People, and devoured it. Several of the tycoons she'd been introduced to were in it, and it was comforting to discover Randolph Z. Jaworski's name on the list at $860 million.

By the time he flew her back to London's Northolt airport in the Gulfstream, and they'd made love on a leather couch at 45,000 feet, Cath felt like an entirely different person to the one who'd left Manchester only seven days before.

It was a welcome diversion to be house-hunting again, especially with a considerably enhanced budget. In fact, no budget. Randy sketched out what he required in terms of space and location but was happy to leave the decision to Cath. 'Someplace near the centre. You know what works, Kathleen. With space to entertain.'

Having devoted several months to viewing multimillion-pound properties, none of which quite hit the spot, Cath settled on an apartment in a portered block behind St James's Street, in a cul-de-sac opposite the Stafford Hotel, with views across Green Park. It was the closest equivalent she could find in London to Randy's Manhattan apartment.

What with her regular meetings in Kettering, and trips accompanying

Randy around the States and Europe, and days spent viewing properties from Eaton Square to Hyde Park Gate, Cath scarcely had a moment to focus on the mayhem she had left behind with Ryan, and all the awkwardness of the divorce she'd demanded from him. Alf and Barbara predictably took massive umbrage at her treatment of their son, and were bad-mouthing her all over Manchester, not that Cath cared, she'd never liked Alf or Barbara. They were making a big deal out of how she hadn't told Ryan face to face but served a lawyer's letter on him out of the blue. But the fact was Randy had wanted her to travel to Warsaw with him and she couldn't be in two places at once, and it was better to lay it all out clearly in a letter so Ryan could take it in. The way Cath saw it, she was being very reasonable in her demands, asking only for half the market value of Prestbury Manor and her agent's cut of his Kick for Men sponsorship fees for the next five years. Beyond that, he was welcome to it: furniture, knick-knacks, the lot. There was nothing she wanted.

She was worried when they printed a negative story about her in the *Daily Mirror*, saying how she'd dumped Ryan, because she didn't want Randy getting any wrong ideas about her. But it was simple enough to keep the newspaper from him, and anyway he was besotted. In the mornings, when he was sweating and straining in the newly installed Nautilus gym, Cath would stroll into the room in T-shirt and knickers, doing her best to distract him, until he rejoined her in the bedroom.

It gave her a frisson to know that less than five minutes' walk from the St James's flat was the Pall Mall Steam and Fitness Club, still apparently going strong. She had been driven past it several times and there was the familiar shady entrance. She was half tempted to call in and see if Mona was still working there, and any of the girls, but caution prevailed. That episode felt like a long time ago now, nothing to do with her present life.

She didn't bother collecting her clothes from Manchester. Partly because she didn't fancy the hassle of returning, but also the styles she'd left behind no longer felt appropriate. She'd observed at the parties Randy took her to in New York that the ladies dressed more simply in beige and camel, and nobody wore shoulder pads or power suits. She embraced American *Vogue* as her new style primer, and Prada and Donna Karan as labels of choice. And the highlights she put in her hair became more subtle.

Concluding that none of the sixteen classifieds chiefs in the South Midlands Newspaper Group were up to the task, Cath had them all dismissed. The regional CEO, Brian Boyce, considered it madness and argued strongly against, but Randy backed Cath so the restructure was actioned. Randy seemed thrilled by his girlfriend's unilateral brutality, and shortly afterwards promoted her to a larger role across his American publications, which meant she would no longer visit Kettering.

Instead, they fell into a routine of spending eight months of the year in the States and four months in London, though they never stayed put in one place for long. Under Cath's supervision, Randy's house in Shadyside, Houston was stripped of all traces of her predecessor until nothing remained of Krystal's regime. And the vacation home in Mustique, built in the Indonesian style with satellite pavilions, quickly became Cath's favourite of Randy's properties. The only shadow across her life was her tattoos, which she increasingly regretted. No one in the social circles in which she now moved had tattoos. At the poolside parties where the women lunched in diaphanous wraps over bathing costumes, she never spotted a single tattoo, and wondered about having hers surgically removed. But the clinic she consulted warned it wouldn't be easy, since the spider's web and Callum heart had been crudely applied and the ink leaked into her epidermis.

And all the time Randy cajoled her to marry him, exasperated the divorce from Ryan James was taking so long. 'What is it with you Brits? It takes longer to get unhitched than the marriage lasted.' At Randy's suggestion she switched to more rapacious lawyers, who threatened Ryan with worse and worse penalties unless he consented to Cath's terms.

Cath, meanwhile, grew daily more accustomed to her lover's jet, as it flew them around the States reviewing his far-flung newspapers. Generally it landed at some second-tier airfield capable of receiving private planes, then a limousine ride into town, dinner with the local manager and executives, followed by a morning of meetings reviewing every aspect of operations. Randy positioned himself during these encounters as an impatient catalyst for change, pushing his managers to innovate and expand. But, before long, Cath came to be seen as the more deadly of the two. If she formed the view that a commercial director was underperforming, or some aspect of the advertising sell lacked vigour, then heads would roll. 'Randy Jaworski's a little over-hyper sometimes and needs careful managing,' his people told each other. 'But this new lady of his, Kathleen, she's trouble. Take care.'

Then there was the St James's apartment to decorate and furnish, with its numerous bare walls requiring art. Fat glossy catalogues arrived from the auction houses, and invitations to fairs and private views from all corners of the world. One of the tasks of Maria Hernandez, Randy's second assistant, was to compile monthly schedules of the important sales to ensure they were fully briefed. Often Cath would make the initial inspection of any potential purchase to gauge whether it was worth Randy's time. Prices for contemporary art which initially astonished her soon seemed commonplace, until a small canvas estimated at between $180,000–$240,000 struck her as inconsequential.

One afternoon she dropped by at Sotheby's where the big autumn contemporary sale had just been hung. She had marked several items as being potentially of interest.

Cath looked particularly smart that day, having had lunch with Randy at Harry's Bar, and she swept past the girls at the front desk. Twenty minutes later, as she swept back out again, her business done, a voice called out, 'Cath? Cath? It's Annabel.'

She stopped and there, perched behind a stack of catalogues at Sotheby's reception, was Annabel Goode. Cath hadn't clapped eyes on her in years, since the days of Imperial Magazines, but she seemed almost unchanged: the same pretty face and lustrous brown hair, held back from her forehead by an Alice band. She dressed the same too, in stripy tailored shirt and navy blue skirt, almost like she was still a pupil at St Mary's.

'I nearly didn't recognise you,' Annabel said. 'You look fantastic, Cath. Have you been viewing the contemporary sale?'

Cath nodded.

'It amazes me people would pay so much money for some of that stuff.'

'Well, we're considering bidding on a few lots ourselves,' Cath replied.

'Oops, sorry. Well, if you appreciate it, it's probably worth it. I didn't realise Ryan James collects modern art. We should put you on our mailing list.'

'Ryan and I are no longer together,' replied Cath.

'Oh, sorry. Put my foot in it again. I didn't know.'

'It doesn't matter. Hey, is there somewhere to grab a coffee round here? It's good to see you, Annabel, it's been ages, can you get away for a bit?'

Annabel fixed for a girl named Fiona to cover for her and they found a table at the Sotheby's Café next door. Anyone seeing the two young women together, stirring their cappuccinos, would have wondered what they could possibly have in common, the sophisticated beauty and the guileless Sloane. Cath thought Annabel looked rather tired. Her shirt was rubbed at the collar, and her nails needed a manicure.

'So what's going on in your life, Annabel? You quit Imperial?'

'Over a year ago. I've got a baby now, a little boy, Henry. He's eight months. So I'm mostly looking after him. My job here is only part-time.'

'Congratulations! I didn't know about the baby, that's great. I didn't even know you'd got married.'

Annabel looked crestfallen. 'That's rather a sore point. It didn't work out. I was married to a soldier but he left me, two weeks before Henry was born.'

'Shit. What happened?'

Annabel shrugged. 'He got back with an old flame called Suki. It's all been quite confusing and upsetting. And I thought everything was fine, I had no idea there was a problem. Not until he left.' Then she said, 'I bet you didn't know we both got married on the same day, Cath? I read all about yours in *Hello!*, it looked incredible, star-studded. Ours was much less glitzy, at the Guards Chapel.' A look of misery crossed her face. 'The weird thing is, I'd still say my wedding was the happiest day of my life, even though it was all a total disaster – the marriage I mean.'

'I didn't know that, about us having the same wedding day. Weren't we born on the same day as well? Or did I imagine that?'

'April the twenty-third 1965. Taurus. Not that I believe in astrology.'

'It's a strong sign, Taurus the bull. Taurus women are good at coping with life's knock-backs.'

'I need that at the moment, what with looking after Henry and the whole Jamie thing. And my parents have split up again, Dad's moved out on his own.' And then, remembering the Cath parallel too late, said, 'Sorry, I didn't mean to bring that up. Anyway, there's no one else involved this time.' And then, hurrying on, she asked, 'What about you, Cath? I hope it wasn't too hideous, splitting with your husband?'

Cath shrugged. 'There's someone new in my life now. Everything's fine. We travel a lot.'

'Lucky you. I can't go anywhere because of Henry. Where does he live, your new man, I mean?'

'All over the place. New York, Houston, Florida. It's complicated.'

'I don't suppose you're coming to the St Mary's reunion?' Annabel asked. 'It's going to be our year and the years below and above. They're holding it on a boat on the Thames. You can bring husbands and partners, if you have one.'

Cath laughed. 'You know what, I kind of doubt we will be there, even if I was invited, which I'm sure I'm not. I don't think it'd be exactly Randy's sort of event, not really.'

Chapter Twenty-Seven

When we last heard properly of Annabel, she had just learnt she was pregnant and was filled with optimism about her new life ahead. If Jamie's joy was more muted than her own, Annabel scarcely noticed. Flea was delighted at the prospect of becoming a granny and dug out all Annabel's old baby clothes, which she had carefully kept in a linen cupboard at Napier Avenue. Although most were now discoloured and pitted with moth holes, and had to be quietly chucked, Annabel pretended to be delighted by the treasure trove of Babygros and bibs, and also by the handpainted cot and wicker baby basket Michael retrieved from the cobwebbed loft.

Her pregnancy raised the issue of where they might live, once the baby was born, since Jamie's bachelor pad was too small. Jamie was reluctant to start searching until after the birth, claiming it would be bad luck. Without telling him, Annabel began scrutinising the free property magazines that dropped through the letterbox, alert for suitable two bedroom flats from Pimlico to Putney. She paid particular attention to the lower end of the New King's Road, in the Victorian streets beyond Parson's Green, since it would be close to her mother, and the child, whichever sex it turned out to be, could one day be enrolled at Miss Claire's nursery school.

As the due date edged closer, and the fact of her pregnancy began to show, Annabel gave up her job in Tony O'Flynn's office, commencing her maternity leave months before the birth. She assured the office she'd be back, but the truth was she didn't know what she'd do. She'd never seen herself as a career girl. And Flea, who had never worked herself, said she couldn't see any point in Annabel trudging off every day to an office in the West End and leaving the baby with some Polish or Bulgarian nanny – it wasn't like Annabel was 'some high-powered Nicola Horlick-type businesswoman earning squillions, thank God.'

Jamie remained disengaged from the drama of pregnancy, declining to take part in the baby classes Annabel signed up for. In any case, he was spending a lot of time up in Rutland. Annabel wished he was more interested but understood that her fit, masculine army officer was quite unlike the touchy-feely dads of the antenatal classes, and on balance she preferred him that way. Carelessly chauvinistic, forthright in the bedroom, Jamie devolved all domestic obligations to his wife. Watching him take part in Trooping the Colour, from the section of the stand reserved for wives and families, Annabel considered herself supremely lucky in her choice of husband, and thought how much prouder she felt of him than she could ever have been of any banker or estate agent.

Between her friends and her mother, Annabel felt supported. It was lovely when Sophie Peverel announced she too was pregnant, by her man David, and they were now planning a quickie wedding in Hong Kong, which she was desperate for Annabel and Jamie to fly out for. George, too, kept in touch. He knew when Jamie was detained in Rutland, so sometimes asked Annabel if she was up for seeing a movie. They shared similar tastes in films and particularly enjoyed *Shakespeare in Love* – George told Annabel that Gwyneth Paltrow slightly reminded him of her – and *You've Got Mail* with Tom Hanks and Meg Ryan, who also made George think of Annabel.

Then, one Sunday evening, came the first of what came to be known as the double bombshell. Flea rang her in Cambridge Street, sounding sozzled, to announce that Michael had left her. Her story was garbled and incoherent, but it emerged that Annabel's parents had hit another bad patch – 'He hasn't said one nice thing to me since Christmas' – and Michael had announced during Sunday lunch he was moving out that afternoon. He wouldn't tell Flea where he was going but insisted no other woman was involved. Annabel hurried round to Napier Avenue to find Flea midway through a third bottle of red wine, and the remains of the Sunday roast still on the table. She cleared the dishes, stacked the dishwasher and set it off, all the time ignoring Flea's slurred entreaties to 'leave them, you're the pregnant one, you should be sitting down not doing everything'. And then made her escape back to Cambridge Street before her mother could repeat everything over again.

Michael rang her the next morning from his office, explaining he needed 'a little break from your mother'. He hoped this dramatic step would force her to confront the issue of her drinking. Recently Flea had stumbled when drunk against a footstool which had rolled into the gas log fire, setting the upholstery ablaze. She insisted she was only a social drinker but Michael had discovered over a hundred and fifty empty wine bottles behind the summer house in the garden. 'Johnnie Pev has offered me a bed for a week or two, and I'm looking for somewhere to rent.'

Annabel listened to all this with a sinking heart. She didn't blame her dad, she had witnessed Flea's issues with alcohol often enough. But she felt depressed at the thought of her father moving out to a gloomy rental in his early sixties. It didn't seem right.

One month later came the second, greater bombshell. This was so devastating Annabel hardly knew how to respond, being entirely unprepared for it. Jamie had been on a ten day training exercise in Cyprus, from which he warned her it would be difficult and perhaps impossible to call. He arrived back in London on a Sunday night (why did all bad news arrive on a Sunday night? Annabel wondered) and she had prepared a welcome-home supper of lasagne, with layer upon layer of minced beef and béchamel. He looked less brown than she'd expected, given the heatwave in the Med. But no sooner had he sat down than Jamie said, 'Annabel, we need to talk.'

A note in his tone chilled her, and she was suddenly alert.

'There's no easy way to put this, but I don't think this marriage is working out. You probably feel the same.'

'Jamie, what on earth do you mean?'

'We're not a hundred per cent clicking. Different expectations probably.'

'But, Jamie, we're having a baby in two weeks. And I love being married to you, I love you. If something's wrong, tell me. We can make it work. If you want me to be different—'

'Of course not. You're a super girl, Annabel, one of the best. But we've married the wrong people, that's all. There's no point pretending everything's OK when it isn't. Much better to be honest and straightforward, even if it's painful.'

Annabel began to cry during this little speech, and kept begging Jamie not to talk like this, as though everything they had was already of the past. 'We've hardly been married a year. Marriages take time, everybody says so. I've been trying not to cramp your style.' She was in pieces now. 'I haven't even taken any cupboard space in this flat, I didn't want to inconvenience you.'

'Well, I do have a lot of suits and uniforms which need to be on hangers or they lose their shape.'

'And how can we even be having this conversation? With our baby about to be born.'

'Actually, that's precisely why we do need to talk. Because I'm not going to be around when the baby arrives. Look, please don't become hysterical, I need you to listen calmly. There's another woman involved.'

'Who?' Annabel asked quickly.

'It doesn't matter, it's not relevant. You've never met her. She's an old friend from way back, and when our marriage went off the boil I started seeing her again. Initially because I wanted someone to talk to – because I felt ignored at home – and later things developed.'

'Is that why you've been away so much? Tell me honestly.'

'Partly, yes. And you need to know that Suki's pregnant too. She's had a much more difficult pregnancy than you, poor thing, so she's needed me with her. She almost lost the baby at four months.'

Annabel listened in dumb astonishment, scarcely able to follow the unfolding tale. Each new fact hurt her more deeply.

'In fact, Suki's due date's a few weeks after yours. She's having it up in Rutland, and the plan is she'll move in with Mum for the first few months who'll help take care of the sprog.'

'Your mother knows about this?'

'She's known Suki for years, they get on really well. Suki used to help out at the riding stables, before doing her stint as a DJ on the Costa Smeralda.'

'I see. So you're telling me our marriage is finished. And you're off with this Suki person? Is that it? And what, may I ask, is supposed to happen to me and to our baby which hasn't even been born yet?' She was suddenly furious. 'And another thing, Jamie, I don't need any lectures from you about being honest and straightforward, you two-timing creep. So all the time you've been pretending you've been visiting your witch of a mother in Rutland, and I'm supposed to have been impressed by what a dutiful son you are, you've actually been screwing this Suki person and getting her pregnant – which was jolly clever of Suki, I don't think – and all with the knowledge and approval of my mother-in-law, who having shown no interest whatever in *our* baby – one measly telephone call, during which she told me you'd like to be fed more red meat – is now setting herself up as unpaid maternity nurse to this Suki slapper . . . So I don't need any lectures in morals from you, James Pilcher, you slimy, hypocritical . . . cad.'

Annabel was exhausted by this outburst which was the longest sustained speech of her life, and certainly the most ferocious. But Jamie only said, 'Steady on, Annabel. I mean, I know you're upset but there's no need to get personal. Especially about my mother. And Suki's a great bird. It's not her fault. You'd really like her and I'm sure you'll meet each other one day and get along fine. In fact you're bound to, because the two sprogs will be half-brothers, half-sisters, whatever, so you're all going to have to rub along. Not that I expect you to see that when you're stressed and upset.'

'Well, thank you,' replied Annabel, suddenly steely calm. 'That's good to know. And very reassuring. I'm sure Suki and I will become bosom buddies . . . *not*. Now will you kindly please get out of here before I pick up this tray of lasagne and batter you with it? Because that's what I'd like to do. And the only reason I haven't already is that I don't want *our child* to have their mother spending the first fifteen years of its life in jail for murdering their father . . . even though my plea of provocation would probably be accepted. And another thing, I shall be putting every single one of your suits, dinner jackets, mess jackets, uniforms, camouflage, all of it, into black bin liners and placing them outside the front door tomorrow. So if you want them, I advise you to take them. Otherwise the dustmen will collect them. Now get out, Captain Pilcher. Get out of my life before your toxic presence damages my baby.'

Annabel gave birth one week early, barely ten days after this conversation, at the Chelsea and Westminster Hospital. Apart from the midwife, she was entirely alone during the birth, though Mouse Barwell-Mackenzie came round to visit half an hour afterwards, quickly followed by her father. Michael hadn't been there five minutes and was opening a bottle of Moët when Flea turned up, forty minutes early, and Michael felt he ought to go, leaving the champagne behind which Flea quickly dealt with. As the level of the bottle went down, Flea's joy at her first grandchild took a maudlin turn, and soon she was extemporising on the unreliability of husbands, and how she and Annabel were both in the same boat, abandoned by their menfolk. Annabel wished she would hurry up and leave.

George Palmer was a more welcome visitor, arriving with fruit and chocolates for the mother, and a plastic Viking sword for the baby boy. 'He'll love it when he's older,' Annabel said. George's reaction to Annabel's abandonment was rather complicated, combining shock at such appalling behaviour by a brother officer, concern for Annabel, and something close to elation. Soon he was making himself invaluable in numerous small ways, collecting extra nightclothes and essentials for Annabel from Cambridge Street, and obtaining the registration form for Miss Claire's nursery school. When George asked what names he should put on the form, Annabel replied, 'I've been thinking about that. I'm going to call him Henry. Not for any reason, I just like the name. Henry Michael George Pilcher. Michael after my father, George after you, if that's OK.'

'I'm honoured. Shouldn't you check with Jamie first though?'

'I don't see why. I haven't told him Henry's been born yet. I suppose I should. He isn't exactly interested.' George undertook to make the call – 'I think you do have to inform the father' – then strode out into the Fulham Road to buy pizza for them both, since Annabel wasn't loving the hospital food.

Annabel was overcome with gratitude to George, for so many separate kindnesses she didn't know how she could ever repay. Everything in her life was a mess but George was a rock. Nevertheless, during that second bleak night in hospital, when the physical exhaustion of the birth caught up with her, Annabel cried and cried, humiliated in her abandonment by her husband, and blaming herself for the failure of the marriage. There was nothing she would not have promised, if she could only get back together with Jamie.

Twelve days after the birth, with mother and baby settled safely back in Cambridge Street, Jamie did finally condescend to meet his son. The visit was rather brief since he had been unable to find residents' parking so had left his Audi on a meter with inadequate coins. He was rather put out when Annabel didn't have a ready supply of twenty- and fifty-pence pieces to give him, so spent much of the visit peering out of the window for parking wardens. His first comment on seeing his son was, 'Christ, he's an ugly customer. But then babies usually are.' He expressed mixed satisfaction at Annabel's choice of the name Henry – 'More of a dog's name in my experience' – and mild annoyance that his own father's name, Hector, hadn't been included. 'On second thoughts, Suki's having a boy herself. His cock showed up on the scan. We can use Hector for him, which is actually better.' He told Annabel he had 'no problem' allowing her to carry on living at Cambridge Street 'for the time being', implying this was a generous concession on his part. Before leaving, he removed several favourite paintings and prints from the sitting room walls, which he carried down to the car to take to Rutland, along with a quantity of wooden shoe trees.

Henry grew, thrived, was duly christened (Godparents: Sophie Peverel, Mouse Barwell-Mackenzie, George Palmer and Annabel's first flame Rupert Henley), and Annabel fell into a routine of life as a single parent. Although Jamie continued to pay the utilities on the flat, he was circumspect about his future plans and reluctant to set up any regular flow of maintenance. Consequently, Annabel was permanently short, relying on contributions from her father and loans from George, which she was embarrassed about accepting and every penny of which she vowed to repay. Jamie dropped by once a month, generally extracting a piece of furniture or a lamp while he was there. On his third visit he produced a photograph of his newborn son, Hector, and pointed out facial resemblances to Henry, which annoyed Annabel more than she could rationally explain.

It became clear that, for the sake of both her finances and sanity, Annabel needed to return to work. Her first call was to Imperial Magazines but the pressures of the corporate floor wouldn't allow for part-time or flexible working so Annabel had to resign her position. She almost accepted a four day position as PA at a city headhunters, but then the Sotheby's job came up. Poorly paid but prestigious and conveniently located in Old Bond Street, and above all three days a week: Annabel leapt at it. It was exciting to be back at work, following the near purdah of the past eight months, to be surrounded again by people and by so many beautiful paintings and objects. Nor was the work difficult, consisting mainly of selling catalogues, directing customers to the cloakrooms and summoning an appropriate expert when punters brought in a picture for valuation. She found a wonderful Portuguese au pair who lived out but arrived each morning at eight thirty a.m., so that was another problem solved. Slowly but surely, Annabel's confidence returned along with her figure, until she could begin to envisage a new life for herself, even though she still missed Jamie dreadfully. She had to work hard not to feel bitter towards him, for Henry's sake.

It became her mantra to count her blessings (Henry, chiefly), appreciate her friends, live each day as it came. She had a nice flat in Pimlico (for now), an adorable healthy son, a job she enjoyed, parents who, for all their problems, were alive and cared for her. And Flea was in a better place since her doctor put her on pills which made her allergic to alcohol; after a couple of false starts, the regime seemed to be working.

That, then, was Annabel's state of mind when Cath Fox had breezed in to Sotheby's from Harry's Bar to view the contemporary sale, and the two women compared notes after so long a separation.

Chapter Twenty-Eight

Cath sat with the three executives from the public relations company retained by Jaworski Media to coordinate tonight's dinner, while they worked together on placements. The dinner, to be held in the Orchid Room of the Dorchester Hotel, was for a hundred and twenty guests seated at ten tables of twelve. Cath was in a state of intense excitement, but she was also anxious; there were endless nuances to be considered and she knew barely half the people by name and reputation. The dinner's genesis lay in the need, identified by Jaworski Media's corporate communications director, to raise Randolph's profile in the marketplace. Despite a string of recent UK media acquisitions, including the CableCast and FlexCom cable companies and Haddon-Carew regional newspapers, he had scarcely charted in the *Guardian*'s Media Top 100.

With input from the PR company, an impressive array of politicians, media pundits, advertising chiefs and media executives had been assembled. It slightly worried her that Tony O'Flynn, her old boss at Imperial Magazines, had accepted, since she'd told Randy she'd been a main board director there and she wasn't sure he'd remember her. The *Sunday Times* editor, Andrew Neil, was coming, as was Sir David English of the *Daily Mail* and Conservative politicians Lord Wakeham and David Mellor. Discussing press coverage with the team, Cath asked whether *Hello!* was going to be there, but when they made a face Cath immediately agreed it was far better to have Londoner's Diary and someone from the Lex column at the *Financial Times*.

Nevertheless, she took particular care over her appearance that night, which she saw as her grand debut into London society. She smiled slightly as the limousine taking her to the Dorchester cruised past the Pall Mall Steam and Fitness Club on its way to collect Randy from the new Jaworski Media corporate offices in Whitehall. She blushed at the thought of Randy ever finding out about this part of her life, though he was a beneficiary of it in a way, so he should be grateful. 'Holy smoke, Kathleen, where did you learn to do that?' he'd asked her during a particularly intensive massage on board his plane.

Cath shrugged. 'I'm making it up as I go along.'

'Well, don't stop, babe, I'm telling you.'

Their relationship worked, better than it ever had with Ryan, because Randolph Jaworski was pure Alpha Male. With the exception of the decoration of his houses, he made every decision. He chose who they saw and where they ate; he would announce they were spending the months of July and August in Europe, cruising the Mediterranean on a yacht he had chartered for the purpose, or that they would be skiing next weekend in Aspen, Colorado. And mostly Cath was content with it that way, being introduced to places and situations she had only read about. From time to time a bullying edge entered his voice, if he felt thwarted or disrespected, and the muscles in his neck flexed and bulged. As Cath soon learnt, what Randy most craved was the admiration and envy of his peer group.

Randy joined her in the limo for the rest of the journey to the Dorchester. Following his usual custom where the dress code was black tie, he wore a black polo shirt under a white tuxedo, with black chinos.

'You sure we aren't arriving too early for this thing?' Randy asked her. 'I thought guests were invited for eight o'clock.'

'They said that, as hosts, we might like to come earlier and see everything before the guests arrive.'

'I thought we had people to check these things. I don't want to go round doing it.'

'It *is* all checked,' Cath reassured him. One of Cath's most useful attributes was her ability to coax him from bad moods. 'A lot of important people are coming, everything's cool.'

'And these guys really are big shots?' Randy asked. 'The names don't mean a lot to me.'

'Very big. Relax.'

'I thought they were getting former Prime Minister Margaret Thatcher along. The PR company said they could.'

'She wasn't available. They did try. She'll come next time.'

Randy shrugged. 'They should have tried harder. She goes to Conrad Black's parties.'

They arrived at the Dorchester and took up position in the small lobby at the entrance to the Orchid Room, to welcome the guests. A phalanx of waiters and waitresses stood with outstretched trays of champagne while a banqueting manager hovered about issuing final instructions. To Cath's horror, the very first guest to appear through the door was Tony O'Flynn, who approached the receiving line with no sign of recognising her at all.

She realised her only recourse was to clutch him in an embrace and say, 'Tony – my favourite man – I want to introduce you to my fiancé Randolph Jaworski. I've been telling him what an amazing boss you were, when I worked with you at Imperial.'

Tony looked confused but Randy was pumping his hand and saying, 'Kathleen's been telling me about those sweet deals you did together, and how you grew the business.'

Cath broke in, 'Tony, do you still have the largest office in London? I always found it so impressive, whenever we held our meetings up there.' And then, before he could reply, more guests arrived and Tony O'Flynn had outstayed his welcome in the greeting line.

Cath found herself relishing the evening more and more. She and Randy sat together on Table 1, surrounded by big hitters, and they were all so attentive to her, questioning her about her life and homes, and asking about Randolph and his media ambitions in England. They seemed surprised to learn Cath was English herself, and she was intentionally vague.

The only awkward moment came after dinner when she was returning from the Ladies. A journalist from the *Evening Standard* approached her, asking about marriage plans. Cath was evasive. 'Randolph and I are very happy as we are. There's no hurry. Anyway, we're too busy for anything like that.'

'But you're still married to Ryan James, aren't you? I've written about you before, when Ryan was launching his aftershave at Harrods.'

'Yeah, well, technically I s'pose,' Cath replied, reddening. The fact was, she'd practically forgotten about Ryan. 'But the divorce is going through any minute. I dunno, I've lost track.' In her panic, her new transatlantic accent slipped, reverting to an earlier default.

Randy seemed well pleased with the evening, having lobbied several members of Parliament about media cross-ownership rules and been lionised by people who counted. 'That was a worthwhile event, you did a great job with it, Kathleen.'

And Cath felt that, tonight, some social Rubicon had been crossed. She had sat at the top table at a five-star London hotel, next to her multimillionaire fiancé and surrounded by all these luminaries, and furthermore no one had considered her out of place. On the contrary, they'd been all over her. Looking back on her time with Ryan – and especially the *Hello!* wedding – she could see how tacky and superficial it had all been. Life with Randolph operated on a different level. She felt quite the toast of the town.

Cath was relaxing on the top deck of the 257-foot, seventeen-crew, nine-stateroom yacht, *Bolero Princess*, which Randy had chartered for the summer. Somewhere through the haze she could make out the coast of Sardinia, towards which they had been steadily cruising since leaving the port of St Tropez the previous evening. Just within earshot she could hear Randy and his captain trying to make satphone contact with the yacht of Flavio Briatore, the Formula One executive, who they were joining for lunch. Cath was excited to meet him, knowing his playboy credentials from the magazines.

Although this was supposed to be a holiday, it felt remarkably like work to Cath, only conducted at sea. Randy spent much of the day contacting his various business units around the world, reviewing numbers and posing questions; in taking a ten week holiday, he was anxious no one should misinterpret his work ethic. Ann Saltzman, his senior executive assistant, was in attendance, as was Maria Hernandez, his number two PA. Several of Randy's business associates were guests on board and the roster changed frequently, with different ones arriving and leaving. Each lunchtime, Randy liked to track down other large yachts in the vicinity and, if he knew the owners, join up for big lunches. In the evenings, they went ashore in Cannes, Porto Cervo or Monaco to eat in restaurants near the port, and afterwards in a convoy of cars to nightclubs where tables had been reserved in VIP areas. At all times they were accompanied by burly bodyguards in rotation, provided by a British security company, Lionbrand.

Cath relished the attention they attracted, arriving at clubs with their security detail and everyone wondering who they were while she danced the night away. Nobody looked slinkier on a dance floor than Cath, and Randy appreciated the envious stares she provoked.

Gratifying news arrived from her lawyers; Ryan was ready to capitulate on all her conditions. His only request was that Cath sign a non-disclosure agreement promising not to sell kiss-and-tell stories about their marriage to any newspapers. When Cath heard that, she went ape. 'Of all the bloomin' cheek! It's more likely *him* selling stories about *me* to the papers than the other way round. You can tell him where to put that for a start. And say I'm on a yacht in the Med and can't be contacted till the end of August.'

In Porto Cervo, Randy disappeared for meetings with Silvio Berlusconi, the media tycoon some reckoned would be Italy's next Prime Minister, about a possible joint venture in cable and satellite, and in the evening, after dinner on board the *Bolero Princess*, the entire party went ashore to a nightclub called Billionaire's. The name made Cath chuckle, because it made her think of Millionairz 'n' Playerz in Prestbury. She was going up in the world!

Four black Land Cruisers waited for them on the port, with drivers and security muttering into their mouthpieces. As they drove along the quay past the superyachts, Cath became conscious of a pair of eyes drilling in to her from the driver's mirror. She glanced at the driver and her blood went cold. She recognised that shaven, bulging scalp and thick, muscle-bound neck: *Callum*.

She made no reaction but her heart was racing. What the hell was Callum doing here, driving her car? Last time she'd seen him he'd been a bouncer at Portsmouth City Football Club. And she was alarmed at the thought of Randy speaking to him, or even hearing his name. He was always questioning her about the Callum tattoo.

She had the idea that if she acted like she hadn't noticed him, and blanked him, maybe it would be OK.

Arriving at Billionaire's, she hastened out of the car and into the club with the rest of the party. Four tables were reserved on a mezzanine balcony. Randy was in high spirits following his meetings that afternoon, badgering Cath to dance. She was conscious of Callum and two other bodyguards standing by the stairs to the dance floor, watching her. In order to reach the dance floor, she'd have to walk right past him.

The discotheque struck up 'Black or White' by Michael Jackson and Randy pulled her to her feet. 'I like this one, no excuses, Kathleen.'

As she passed him at the top of the stairs, she caught Callum's eye for the briefest instant. It was him all right. His nose had mended crooked and the muscles in his neck still resembled electrical cables.

She slipped past without speaking and kept Randy busy on the dance floor, track after track, until his face and T-shirt were soaked with sweat. She was conscious of Callum staring at her from the balcony, watching her every move.

'I'm sorry, I gotta grab a drink,' Randy said. 'I'm dehydrating. You're a great little dancer, Kathleen, I love that about you,' and headed back upstairs to the tables.

Cath didn't want to pass Callum. Instead, she wandered outside for some air. It was a relief to feel a breeze on her face, it had been stifling in Billionaire's, and all these late nights, fun as they were, were getting to her. She headed down the street to an arcade of boutiques selling Dior and Chloe, and wondered if there was anything she should buy tomorrow. Randy disliked it if she wore the same outfit too often, and two months on a yacht was a long time. She was staring at the merchandise when she caught a reflection behind her in the window. It was big and overbearing and vaguely threatening, like Bill Sykes out of *Oliver Twist*.

'Cath?'

She didn't respond, just continued peering at the designer clothes.

'I know it's you, it's no good pretending. I checked your name on the manifest.'

Cath shrugged.

'Kathleen James. That's what it says. Since when were you Kathleen then?'

'Leave me alone, Callum. I've nothing to say to you. You're supposed to be guarding your boss, aren't you? Not pestering guests on the street.'

'It's fine, Russ and Wayne are minding the principal. He's covered.'

'What are you even doing here? In Sardinia. Bit off your usual patch.'

'I work for this security outfit now, as a casual. We're protecting a midget millionaire with a head like a snooker ball. You know, the one you're shagging.'

'Callum, fuck off, or I'll get you sacked.'

'Oh, will you? And what reason will you give then?'

'No reason. If Randolph wants you out, you're out.'

Callum was standing directly behind her. She smelt his familiar smell.

'And what if I told everyone what you really are, Cath Fox? I do know you, remember. What would your rich little dwarf say if he knew we had a kid together?'

Cath said nothing.

'Well, I'm not planning on telling. Not now, anyway. But let's have no more grief about getting me sacked. And how about a snog for old times' sake?'

'Listen, Callum, I'm a different person now, right? Everything's different. My whole life. Not trying to be clever or stuck-up, but everything back in Portsmouth, Nero's and all that, I hardly even remember it. I've moved on. And I don't *want* to remember it neither. All right?'

Callum held her shoulders and manoeuvred her round to face him.

'You always were a tough little bitch, weren't you, Cath?'

'Let go, Callum. Take your fuckin' mitts off of me.'

'You may not remember, but I do. Every detail, every shag. Just be careful, that's all.'

Chapter Twenty-Nine

Jess took to Manchester immediately. She had chosen it on the grounds it was the only uni her mum hadn't got hold of a brochure for, so it felt like her own choice. It also had a good course in English and American literature, and she liked the idea of studying in a big city a long way from home. Bob and Kirsty drove her up from Bedfordshire with her stereo, duvet and kitchen utensils, which was nice of them, but once they'd located her hall of residence she longed for them to leave. It was embarrassing having her parents speak to her new flatmates.

She spent her first year living in Fallowfield at Oak House, a university hall with single-sex flats for eight women. Two of the girls quickly became friends, the other five mostly stayed in their rooms studying. As her new best friend Trina put it, it was weird how in a university with supposedly forty thousand students you met the same two hundred people again and again, in the pubs, at the students' union, at gigs. What happened to the rest of them?

Jess surprised even herself by the number of boyfriends she got through in her first year. Statistically, of course, seventeen is on the high side, even for turn-of-the-century Manchester, but she was one of those girls whose looks and personality held unusually wide appeal, making her attractive to almost every male student on campus. And after a lifetime cooped up in Long Barton, she can be forgiven for going off the rails a bit. Jess Eden quickly gained a reputation as one of the prettiest, hottest and most fun freshers. On her rare visits home to Bedfordshire, the accounts she gave Kirsty of her college life had almost no connection to reality at all.

She did, at the very least, keep up with her studies, cycling most mornings past the Asian shops of Rusholme, past the Royal Infirmary and down to the university buildings. Though she still bought a lot of magazines too and was shocked to read in *OK!* that the Man U footballer Ryan James and his wife Katie had split. She'd always liked the look of Katie James, it was a shame. In fact, one of the reasons she'd chosen Manchester was the memory of Ryan and Katie's wedding pictures.

Her second year she spent sharing digs in Levenshulme with a boyfriend, Garth, which Garth's band also used as a rehearsal studio. The lounge was permanently filled with giant speakers, mixing decks and a drum kit, and the arms of the settee covered with full ashtrays. That was the year Jess went goth and began wearing black eyeliner and black lipstick and dyed her chestnut hair black. But on her birthday, Jess still wore her locket to a gig at the Academy. She showed the photo to Garth, who could hardly see it it had faded so much, and he agreed her real mum looked cool. 'Like Patti Smith.'

She spent her first long summer vacation with Garth following the band, but when that relationship ended with the second summer term, she realised she'd better chalk up some work experience. She'd temped behind the bar at a university pub, the Queen of Hearts, but her dad had been on at her about finding an internship for the sake of her CV. 'You'll be looking for a proper job a year from now,' he reminded her. 'Employers like to see evidence of work experience, it shows initiative.'

So she wrote off to her favourite magazines requesting a summer job, and got replies back saying she'd left it too late, all work placements had been booked up months ago. She spent a couple of hours in the library doing research, then fired off more letters to TV companies and national newspapers asking if they had anything, then to regional newspapers.

The only positive reply came from Jaworski Media, who said they had an unpaid vacancy in head office for an intern for two weeks in September. Jess didn't have much idea what it was they did at Jaworski Media, but it was the only job on offer, so she accepted at once.

Chapter Thirty

Annabel was rather dreading the school reunion and probably wouldn't have gone at all if Sophie Roberts (née Peverel) hadn't been one of her year reps on the committee, and told her she simply had to be there. It was all right for Sophie, Annabel thought, she's married and has David to arrive with. The prospect of turning up at a St Mary's reunion as a single mother was intimidating.

She found a babysitter for Henry, put on her best party dress, and got a lift from Mouse to the wharf by Tower Bridge where the boat was moored. Annabel had envisaged an evening cruising up and down the Thames but the boat turned out to be a flat-bottomed barge permanently docked as a party venue. Fluttering from the flagpole was the familiar dark green and maroon banner of St Mary's, which were the old school colours.

While Mouse fed the parking meter, Annabel stared down at the party barge with its panoramic windows and could see the event was already in full swing. There must have been a hundred old girls in there and almost as many husbands and boyfriends, standing round in small, sticky groups with members of staff. She spotted Mrs Perse, her old headmistress, looking exactly the same, and Madame Renouf, who'd taught her French.

Badges were distributed at a registration table, with married names and maiden names in brackets, and the years each pupil had attended the school: Annabel Pilcher (Goode) 1976–83. 'Don't abandon me,' Annabel hissed to Mouse as they entered the room.

Everywhere Annabel looked were semi-familiar faces, several years older than when she'd last seen them. A few had been to her wedding, of course, but the majority had disappeared without trace into their own lives. A girl she'd shared a Bunsen burner with in science was now a doctor. A girl in her dorm had moved in on Mouse's old boyfriend and become Lady Arbroath and lived up in Angus. The head of the school debating society said she was on the list to become a Conservative MP, but didn't think she had much chance until John Major brought in women-only shortlists, which were essential. Virtually everyone had a man in a suit in tow. The school rebel, who'd actually been suspended for three weeks for bringing vodka into the dorm, arrived with her fiancé, a 67-year-old professor of philosophy at Queen Mary College, London. Most of Annabel's contemporaries seemed to be working as PAs in blue-chip companies, and hoping to move out to the country one day. Waiters circulated with jugs of a gin-based cocktail, which was unexpectedly powerful and loosening everybody up.

'And what about *you*, Annabel?' people kept asking. 'I heard you've married a dishy soldier. Is he here?'

'Sadly that didn't work out.'

'*No*, that's *so sad*. But there are plenty more fish out there in the sea. We must fix you up with someone gorgeous.'

Annabel and Mouse found themselves standing in a group with Mr Woodruff, the geography teacher who had once had a thing with Miss Fox. These days he was married to a different assistant matron at St Mary's, and they were lodge parents at the school. Shauna Woodruff, perky and eager with a baby buckled to her chest in a pink sling, said the pastoral care was second to none.

Her tongue loosened by gin sling, Mouse asked, 'Do you ever see anything of Cath Fox, Mr Woodruff?'

The teacher turned red. 'Er, the assistant matron who worked briefly in the early eighties, you mean?'

'The one with the tattoos. Really sexy. You were going out with her, weren't you? That's what we girls all thought.'

Now poor Mr Woodruff was scarlet, and Mrs Woodruff – Shauna – dangerously alert. 'I do dimly remember her, we haven't kept in touch.'

'You know she married a footballer? Their wedding was all over *Hello!* You missed your chance there, Mr Woodruff.'

'Yes, well, as I said, er, I haven't kept up with her.' He looked oddly dazed at the memory of Cath. Shauna was staring at him in a way which promised trouble later.

The development director made a long dull speech about the school's bicentennial appeal which aimed to raise five million pounds for a new arts and theatre complex. Afterwards, Mrs Perse gave a brisk address which reminded everyone of morning assembly, and introduced the new headmistress – who wore primitive African beads which never would have been allowed at St Mary's in Annabel's day – who spoke about widening the demographic with scholarships for disadvantaged pupils.

Afterwards, Annabel and Mouse ran into Mrs Bullock, senior matron in their day, who said she now lived with her sister on the south coast. 'We were just talking about one of your old assistants,' Mouse said. 'Miss Fox. Do you remember her?'

'I most certainly do,' replied Mrs Bullock. 'I'm afraid I didn't hold a very high opinion of her. Rather sly and untrustworthy.'

'Really, Mrs Bullock?'

'I don't want to say more but I did have my suspicions. She didn't last long. And I don't doubt she'll come to a bad end, girls like that generally do.'

Chapter Thirty-One

Cath marked her third anniversary of meeting Randolph at Old Trafford by signing off the final divorce papers from her marriage to Ryan. In the division of the spoils, Prestbury Manor was returned to the market and, in due course, half the proceeds remitted to Cath. By the time legal fees were subtracted, Cath was left with £540,000 in her own name, the largest cheque she'd ever seen. She felt a surge of pride that she was halfway to becoming a millionairess in her own right, and all by her own efforts. It was only mildly deflating when Randy mentioned the fuel bill for that year's summer cruise on the Med had come to precisely the same amount.

Divorce from Ryan implied a change of surname, and she wasn't sure whether to have her cheque books reissued as Fox or to sit it out for Jaworski. Randy often referred to marriage and Cath was, in any case, his wife already in all but name. The housekeepers and staff at the various Jaworski properties regarded her, and deferred to her, as mistress of the realm, as did the flight attendants on Randy's jet and the executives in his business. And, little by little, she was achieving a public profile, mentioned in diary columns (*Guests at last night's Cartier Chelsea Flower Show dinner in the Physic Garden included the Duke and Duchess of Marlborough, the Earl and Countess of March, Lady Annabel Goldsmith, Brigadier and Mrs Andrew Parker Bowles and media tycoon Randolph Jaworski with Kathleen James*). Randy and Cath showed up at Tate Gallery parties and took tables at fundraisers for fashionable charities. When Cath was included in a Saturday *Telegraph Magazine* feature on Britain's Twenty Smartest Young Businesswomen to watch, which described her as *American media Tsar Randolph Jaworski's secret weapon*, it provoked a flurry of requests for interviews. A media page piece duly appeared in the *Independent* with a picture of Cath coquettishly perched on Randy's desk, in which she described her life jetting round the world on the corporate plane, breathing new life into his newspapers and cable services. 'My value to the organisation is that I think outside the box,' she told the interviewer. 'I love shaking things up. Some of Randy's people probably wish I'd take a running jump but I've transformed everything I've touched.' The article reported that Kathleen began her career at Imperial Magazines *where she quickly doubled profits in her division*. It mentioned she'd attended an exclusive all-girls boarding school, St Mary's, Petworth.

In Manhattan, too, Cath joined Randolph as a bold-faced name in Cindy Adams' column in the *New York Post* and Suzy's in *W*. and *Houston Life* magazine put her and Randy on their front cover, posing on the lawn in black tie with the hacienda-style mansion behind them, and their retinue of domestic staff ranged up in chefs' toques and maids' uniforms.

They were on the Gulfstream recrossing the Atlantic when Randy looked up from his papers and said, 'You know something, Kathleen? If we're going to get ourselves wed this year, we should tell Ann Saltzman to schedule in a date. The diary's filling up fast.'

'Randy, should I take that as a proposal of marriage?'

Without looking up, he replied, 'Sure. We need to identify a date that works. Probably immediately before or immediately after the Moscow trip.'

Having agreed a prenup and established neither of them wanted a big wedding – Cath couldn't think of a single relative or friend in the world to invite, having lost touch with the Manchester girls – they settled on Westminster register office for the formalities, with Randolph's daughter by his first marriage, Candy, as the only attendant. In the evening there was a celebratory dinner in the private room at Annabel's to which two dozen of their smart new circle were invited. Cath sat alongside her husband, flashing a vast Graff diamond on her finger, and thought how much classier this wedding was than her last one.

But she was still rather pleased when *Hello!* included some pap shots of her and Randolph emerging up the steps from Annabel's, in their round-up of the week.

Chapter Thirty-Two

Jess travelled to London on the commuter train from Milton Keynes. She hadn't been up this early in the morning for ages, and couldn't get a seat until they'd almost arrived at Euston. Catching her reflection in the train window, she blanched: her hair, in transition from goth noir back to its natural chestnut, looked weird. And the business outfit Kirsty had bought her for her internship made her feel like a different, duller person.

She located the Jaworski Media offices in Whitehall which were larger and cooler than she'd been expecting, with a steel reception desk in the lobby and a wall of television screens broadcasting cable content. A backlit panel listed the global properties of the Jaworski Media Corporation superimposed onto a world map. Six steel and black leather sofas stood facing each other in a holding pen.

She was directed up to the fifth floor where the newspaper division had an open-plan office, largely devoted to marketing and advertising sales. Jess was assigned to help the deputy research director, Aditi Parab, on reader analyses for South Midland Newspapers. 'Twenty-seven per cent of SMNG readers take one foreign holiday or more a year,' said Aditi Parab. 'It's a nice positive story for the sales teams to go out with.'

For the first three days all Jess did was photocopy pages of statistics. Her boss, Aditi, was constantly excited by fresh insights into the readership ('Look, Jessica, this will interest you – fifty-four per cent of our female readers in Kettering own a cat') but Jess thought the other floors in the building – the ones housing the cable TV companies – looked more alluring, judging by glimpses from the lift doors. Each evening she travelled home to Long Barton where Bob collected her from the station, and over supper she was expected to tell them everything that had happened that day. 'It sounds like a very valuable introduction to the workplace,' said Bob. 'I'm glad they're finding useful things to occupy you.'

Each lunchtime, Jess bought a sandwich in a place off Northumberland Avenue and ate it while reading the *New Musical Express*. But on the fourth day some of the department said they were going round to the pub and did she want to join them? The Three Coachmen was the pub of choice for Jaworski Media, and Jess was soon introduced to staff from across the company. Learning she was at uni in Manchester, there was a lot of football talk, since the men were all Man U fans.

'You know Ryan James's ex-wife is married to our boss?' said a guy from CableCast.

'Katie James is?' Jess was amazed. 'She's married to who?'

'Randy Jaworski. The chairman. They got hitched a couple of months back.'

'*Really?* I remember when she got married to Ryan, they had this amazing wedding packed out with celebs.'

'Well, don't mention Ryan to her. She doesn't like it. And you don't want to cross Katie. Or Kathleen as she's called now.'

Jess laughed. 'I don't think I'm going to be meeting her in any case.'

'Well, she's in the building today. I saw her earlier. She's in her office up on the seventh floor.'

Jess was intrigued. She'd had this thing about Katie for years, ever since the *Hello!* wedding. Whenever there'd been anything about her in a magazine, it caught her eye. That they were actually working in the same building was so exciting.

'I could walk you past her office if you like,' said Steve from News. 'It's got glass walls so you can see in. I need to go up to the seventh anyway.'

On their way back from lunch, Jess stuck with Steve and they took the elevator to the top floor. The whole feel up there was different to the other floors: lighter and quieter, with fewer people about. They passed an office with mahogany doors and Steve whispered, 'That's Mr Jaworski's office when he's in town.'

Alongside was a glass corner office filled with white sofas and a television, and a white trestle desk in front of the window. As they walked past, Jess got a glimpse of Katie in a perfectly cut Prada suit with the shortest skirt, and the Manolo Blahnik mules you kept seeing featured in all the magazines. Steve strode on ahead and Jess hurried along to keep up with him.

That night, Jess told Kirsty and Bob about seeing Katie James ('I mean Kathleen Jaworski') and how amazing she was 'in this incredible glass office with all white sofas. She looked dead cool like a model out of *Vogue* or something.'

'Never mind whether or not she *looks* good,' said Bob. 'Is she effective in her job? That's the question.'

Jess had no idea. But she did know that, when she grew up, she'd like to be like Kathleen, sitting in a big, cool office like hers. Looking round the kitchen at Burdock Cottage, with its pine worktops and fridge magnets, it occurred to her how much more exciting life would be if you were Kathleen.

No offence to Kirsty, but she'd like to have had someone more like that as her mother.

Chapter Thirty-Three

It was a year almost to the day that Jess next encountered Cath, and in circumstances wholly unexpected.

Having devoted much of her first year at Manchester to random boyfriends, and her second to Garth and his goth band, Jess knuckled down to work in her final year and surprised herself and her tutors by delivering every piece of coursework on time and revealing herself as rather bright. All her old cleverness from her schooldays came flooding back. Her modules on the Literature of Emotion 1740–1814 and Shakespeare on Film only narrowly missed getting a first, and she also made time to co-edit the student newspaper, *The Mancunian*. Half her evenings were spent commissioning articles and designing pages, the other half trying to sell advertising to the city's Balti restaurants. But each morning she was in the library before ten o'clock, having crossed town in an orange bus.

She found it hard to envisage her future beyond her finals. Several of her contemporaries were applying to work in banks, or to multinationals with graduate programmes like Mars and Unilever. Bob kept talking up the advantages of Glaxo, and even posted her the application forms, but Jess could think of nothing less appealing than commuting into work every day with her dad. She half thought of staying on in Manchester and trying to get a reporter's job on the *Evening News*, but it was difficult to focus on life after exams, which loomed ever closer. As always on her birthday she wore her locket ('my lucky locket' as she called it) and her girlfriend, Trina, said, 'The lady in the photo looks just like you, Jess. Has anyone told you that?'

Jess shook her head. 'You think so?'

'I didn't notice it before, but there's a real resemblance. It could be a photo of you in there.'

'I'll take that as a compliment, thanks. Ever since I was a tiny kid I've been staring at that photo. I used to pretend it was Princess Diana. Bit sad, really.'

'Haven't you ever thought of finding your birth mother?' asked Sian, another friend. 'I read you're entitled to, once you're a certain age. You have to write to the council or something. And they contact your birth mum and ask if she wants to meet up.'

Jess shrugged. 'I don't know. I've thought about it, yes. But I don't want to upset my parents – my adoptive parents – they might take it the wrong way. And if my real mum had wanted me, she'd have kept me, wouldn't she? She could be dead for all I know.'

But Jess did sometimes wonder. The first step, she supposed, would be to ask Kirsty; presumably there were adoption papers which would give her a starting point. Perhaps they even gave the names of her real parents. But something stopped her asking. Maybe she didn't want to know the answer. There was something quite liberating about not knowing where you sprang from.

She sat her finals over two long weeks of late nights and last-minute cramming, followed by ten days of partying until the results came through. To her delight she got a 2.1, scoring a first in two of her papers. Kirsty, as a professional educationalist, was filled with pride for her daughter, and even Bob, who'd never seen the arts and humanities as proper subjects, said he was impressed, especially by the 2.1 which was better than his own 2.2 from Birmingham.

Kirsty was determined to be there for Jess's graduation, and she and Bob drove up north and made a weekend of it, staying at a B&B in Fallowfield close to Jess's third year flat, and helping her pack up her stuff. Jess planned on dumping all her lever-arch files of notes in a skip, but Bob advised, 'Best keep 'em, Jess, you never know when you might want to look something up. I've still got all mine in the garage.'

The ceremony in the Victorian Gothic splendour of the Whitworth Hall struck Jess as rather cringe-making, but her mother lapped it up. More than eight hundred students in rented gowns and mortar boards queued up for their scrolls of achievement, while parents and families clapped and cheered and recorded it all with camcorders. Students who'd left it until the last minute to get to the hire shop ended up with tiny mortar boards perched on long frizzy hair and gowns which didn't cover their bums. The vice chancellor of the university and the senior tutors sat on wooden thrones in fur-trimmed robes, and the university registrar carried a golden mace on a velvet cushion. Behind them was a second row of thrones, occupied by dignitaries and celebrities receiving honorary degrees, which would be presented immediately after the undergraduate ones.

As Jess edged closer to the front of the line, waiting for her name to be called, she couldn't take her eyes off the honorary degree recipients. The comedian Rik Mayall was there and the Labour politician Margaret Beckett, Sir Terry Leahy of Tesco, Sir Alex Ferguson of Manchester United and the newsreader Anna Ford. But she was transfixed by the sight of Randolph Jaworski who was being awarded an honorary degree by the School of Media Studies. He was sitting with Kathleen, looking massively bored, as though he couldn't understand what he was even doing there. As the ceremony of handshakes and scroll-giving went on and on, and hundreds of students filed past, Randy yawned. He'd never seen so many ugly young people in his life. He was furious with his communications team for getting him into this.

Jess collected her parchment and hurried back to her place. As she passed Kathleen Jaworski she briefly locked eyes with her, and smiled in recognition, then felt foolish; she'd never even met Kathleen. But having worked in the same office, she felt a connection.

The vice chancellor now welcomed the distinguished honorands, elaborating on Rik Mayall's contribution to the long tradition of European comedy 'from the Italian *commedia dell'arte* to the heyday of Ealing Studies and beyond' and Terry Leahy's contribution to grocery retailing. He then moved on to Randolph Z. Jaworski, 'a man who in a short period of time has established himself as a leading mogul of both traditional and the new medias. I can think of no more fitting recipient for a degree from the University of Manchester's School of Media Studies than Randy Jaworski.'

The tiny, petulant tycoon stomped up to the lectern, collected his scroll, and took the microphone for his acceptance speech. 'Listen, I don't precisely know what one has to do to get one of these things, or even what it means. The ceremony today certainly seemed long, which nobody warned me about. Anyway, I didn't go to college myself and I guess that never held me back. This is only my second visit to Manchester. The first time, I met my present wife Kathleen. It was at a soccer arena which I believe is quite well known in these parts, Old Trafford Stadium. Well, thank you for this honour, whatever it is, and I'd better be heading along now since my plane is waiting to fly me to Warsaw.'

Then all the students and their supporters flooded out of the hall into the quadrangle, where champagne was opened and photographs taken on the steps of the Students' Union. Groups of friends were forming up for mob-up pictures, or holding their gowns to their faces as masks like Zorro. Jess was made to pose between her parents with Whitworth Hall as the background, while Bob explained to a stranger how to adjust the focus on his camera. They were just about done when Jess spotted the Jaworskis crossing the quad, being escorted by their PR man.

Quick as anything, she raced over and introduced herself. 'I just want to say I did work experience at your company, Mr Jaworski, and really enjoyed it. I'm Jess Eden.'

Randy Jaworski did not seem particularly excited by the information, and scowled, but Kathleen was pleasant enough, asking which part of the business she'd worked in.

'On the fifth floor at your head office. In marketing.'

'My own London office is in the same building.'

'I saw it. Or maybe I shouldn't say that. I walked past. It's so cool.'

Cath smiled. 'Yeah, I like that office too. I don't get to use it enough. We're mostly in New York or travelling.'

'This is probably completely unprofessional to ask, but do you know if there are any jobs going at the company? Permanent jobs, I mean. I'm looking for anything in media.'

Randy was impatient to escape and pressing Cath to hurry up. 'We'll miss our take-off slot, Kathleen.'

But Cath, flattered by Jess's open admiration, said, 'Write to Human Resources and mention my name. That'll get you an interview at least. After that, it's up to you.'

'That's really nice of you. Thanks, Katie. I mean Kathleen. I mean Mrs Jaworski.'

But by then they were gone, Randy striding off ahead to the limousine.

Chapter Thirty-Four

'Annabel darling? It's Dad. Are you there if I drop by in ten minutes?'

Annabel had been reading Henry a bedtime story and just settled him down. As usual, she had no evening plans.

'Sure, how nice. Where are you?'

'Having a drink in a pub round the corner from you. With Johnnie Pev, but he's off home now for supper.'

'See you shortly. I can cook you pasta if you like.'

'Sweet girl. But don't put yourself to a lot of trouble.'

Recently, Annabel had been seeing more of her father which made her happy. He was renting a flat in Moreton Place only a few minutes' walk from Cambridge Street, and had more time on his hands these days. He often came round to Annabel's flat for supper, or occasionally to look after Henry while she did the weekly Sainsbury's shop. The previous winter, Annabel, Rosie and Tommy had thrown a sixty-fifth birthday dinner for him in a private room at the Ebury Street Wine Bar, which the Peverels, Barwell-Mackenzies and several of his old property cronies had attended, but sadly not Flea for obvious reasons.

Annabel guessed what her father would talk about because it was the one topic which preoccupied him. He was obsessed by the idea that Flea should sell Napier Avenue and move somewhere smaller. 'It's really rather ridiculous, one woman living all on her own in a huge house like that with six bedrooms. It's not like any of you children are there any more. And even in this market it should fetch over a million pounds.'

Flea was determined to stay put, not because she especially needed the space or even liked the house with all its bad memories, but because Michael wanted her to move. She felt his reduced circumstances in a one bed Pimlico flat was rightful punishment for walking out on her.

Michael arrived at Annabel's flat, as he always did, with a bottle of Rioja from the off-licence on the corner. He was still handsome in his raspberry cords with a tweed jacket. But he moved more slowly, and puffed from the stairs.

'You know your mother hasn't even replied to my last letter? I posted it through her letterbox myself, five weeks ago.'

Annabel shrugged. 'She may not have read it. She's hoping it'll go away.'

'I've set everything out, all the reasons it makes sense. I'm bending over backwards not to be unreasonable. You don't think I'm being unreasonable, darling?'

'I'm trying to stay out of it, to be honest. I'm not taking sides.'

'But you must see the logic? What does she do with all that space? Sleep in a different room each night of the week? And here you are – and I am – living like battery chickens in shoeboxes, and your mother has a hundred-foot garden.'

'I admit it's not ideal.'

'Well, your sister agrees with me. Rosie thinks it's ridiculous. So does Mark, and he's a sensible fellow.'

Mark Ellidge was Rosie's husband of eighteen months, a landowner from Burnham Market with fifteen hundred acres of peas and kale and a fifteenth-century manor with moat coming his way when his parents dropped dead. Michael was full of regard for his new son-in-law, for his inheritance and steady nature. During their short marriage, Rosie had already produced one child and was pregnant with a second. 'Mark wants at least five,' Rosie said. 'They'll all have their own houses on the estate when they grow up.'

Annabel was delighted for Rosie, and enjoyed taking Henry to Norfolk for occasional weekends, but only a saint would not compare her younger sister's good fortune with her own. Jamie was still dragging his feet over money and hadn't visited Henry in six months. Having removed the last of his furniture from the flat, he simply stopped coming. His other son, Hector, loved horses, he'd told Annabel, and had already been held on a saddle.

'My big mistake,' Michael told Annabel, 'was that I didn't leave your mother twenty-five years ago, when I could have started again with someone else. I often thought about it. But it never seemed the right time, and then it was too late.'

'Well, you did go off with Cath Fox.' It was the first time she'd ever uttered Cath's name in front of her father.

'Yes, well, I regretted that, because I knew how unhappy it made you all.' He looked thoughtful, remembering the episode.

'I saw her, you know. She came in to Sotheby's.'

'Did she? How extraordinary. Last I heard, she'd married a football player.'

'Not any more. She's married to a tycoon with a private jet.'

'Gracious me. And how was she?'

'Pretty as ever. Prettier. Dressed head-to-toe in designer stuff. Very chic.'

'She didn't mention me by any chance?'

'No, Dad, she did not. She talked about her jet and her yacht and her collection of contemporary art.'

'So, she's made it then? Good for Cath. I've never met a more determined person.'

'We were all intrigued by her at St Mary's. We'd never met anyone like her, we were so sheltered. But nobody really knew much about her.'

'Nor me, funnily enough. She scarcely spoke about her background. And didn't like it if you asked.'

'She's changed her name to Kathleen,' Annabel said.

'Doesn't surprise me. She's quite an operator, that girl. Quite an operator.'

Chapter Thirty-Five

Jess considered herself lucky. Three months after leaving college she had paid work in London in a media company, and a flat in Farringdon shared with two colleagues.

She hadn't seen or spoken to Kathleen Jaworski since that one time in Manchester at the graduation ceremony, but the advice she'd given her that day had got her the job. Jess had written in to HR, mentioning Mrs Jaworski, and a couple of interviews later was enrolled on the Jaworski Media graduate training scheme. The salary at £16,000 was rock bottom, but they shifted you about the company so you experienced different divisions: cable, newspapers, production, scheduling, even selling advertising. After a month embedded in the FlexCom newsroom, Jess had been switched to circulation, and was now writing advertorial promotions for the regional newspapers.

She sat at her computer composing eight hundred words on bathrooms: *Imagine the luxury of soaking away your cares in an easy-installation AcquaJet bathtub – or even a jacuzzi! More and more residents of the South Midlands are treating themselves to the ultimate indulgence of a new bathroom suite, many currently on display at Premier Bathroom Warehouse, where a wide selection of well-known brands are always in stock.* Jess's boss, Gloria, a sad old soak with thirty years' experience writing advertorials, had coached her in the special language and conventions of the trade, which Jess was now struggling to replicate. Once she'd finished bathrooms, she would write a promotion about nail care.

Jess got on with the job but didn't see herself doing this for long. One day, she hoped to work for the *Guardian* or the *Independent* in the newsroom. She loved the whole idea of investigative journalism, exposing big business scandals and bringing powerful corporations to heel. Another place she'd love to work was *Vanity Fair*, because it combined both her interests: gritty reporting and glamorous celebrities. But, for now, Jess was happy to be at Jaworski Media, learning all this new stuff.

It was great to be living in London with so much to see and do. She'd hardly visited the capital before, beyond a few sightseeing trips with Bob and Kirsty; it was a thrill to visit the clubs and bars she read about in *Hello!* and *Heat*. And Camden Market where she spent so many Saturday afternoons, drifting about the stalls. And going to gigs in pubs and dives where really famous bands had played before they became famous. And, at weekends, the Brixton Academy, Shepherd's Bush Empire and Twisted Melon round the corner in Farringdon.

Her two flatmates, Josh and Mia, were also on the graduate programme, and they travelled together into Whitehall most mornings. Josh was chiefly interested by the possibilities of the internet, while Mia was more into marketing. Having always shared flats in Manchester in a happy-go-lucky way, with everyone pooling everything, it was a novelty for Jess to be living with flatmates who labelled half-eaten yoghurts and cups of leftover baked beans with their names, and itemised the phone bill call by call. She saved money herself by choosing as her bedroom the smallest and cheapest of the three options, formerly a boxroom.

It was a disappointment to her that she hadn't so much as clapped eyes on Kathleen Jaworski in five months of working at the company. Apparently the Jaworskis breezed through the London office for a couple of days a month, and executive review meetings took place, but she didn't spot them. She'd like to have thanked Kathleen for helping her get the job. She'd also have liked to revisit the seventh floor, which she hadn't seen since that one time as an intern. There had been a rumour Randy and Kathleen might tour the offices, and a memo came round telling everyone to tidy their desks, but the visit never materialised. Nevertheless, photographs of the boss and his wife sometimes appeared in the newspapers, and Jess always studied them. Kathleen looked so pretty and dynamic. Jess noticed she never wore heels when she was with her husband, perhaps she was trying not to look too tall.

The eighth and ninth months of the graduate programme were spent out of London, when trainees were dispersed to different Jaworski newspapers. Jess hoped to be embedded in one of the American titles

– or an Eastern European one – but it was her luck to get Kettering. Josh, of all people, was off to Daytona Beach, Florida, to work on a freesheet, and Mia drew Warsaw. Jess felt quite disappointed taking the train up to Kettering, which rumbled through countryside near where she'd grown up, and moving in to a bed and breakfast two streets from the office.

The *Kettering and Corby Argus* had undergone substantial re-engineering since being acquired by Jaworski Media. The noble old lossmaker, with its meticulous news reporting and encyclopaedic coverage of local issues, had been slimmed down and jazzed up. These days only two or three pages were devoted to news; the remainder was given over to simpering paid-for advertorials, sections of used cars and small ads for escort services. Colour printing had recently been introduced, so the front page featured fuzzy images of the town's mayor or a prize carrot, with all the colours slightly out of register.

Jess found herself one of only eleven members of staff, and soon filing several articles a day. When she wasn't reporting the magistrates' court or a Rotary Club lunch, she was cold-calling advertisers with the classifieds team. As part of the restructure, all journalists now worked three hours a day selling small ads.

To her surprise, Jess quite enjoyed calling up strangers and selling to them. She was fearless in that regard. And she soon got the hang of making a bit of small talk, to keep it friendly, before steering the conversation to a sale. The classified manager, Patsy Bates, who'd been on the paper for ever, said she reckoned Jess was a natural.

'You don't fancy staying on and joining my team?'

'Er, thanks, but I'm on this training scheme thing.'

'I thought not. Well, if you ever want a job . . .'

Each Wednesday, as the paper went to bed, Patsy got into a panic worrying they'd miss their revenue forecast. 'I have to fax all my numbers down to head office every week,' she complained. 'It never used to be like that. Not when the Haddon-Carews still owned us. But it's all targets now. And new categories. The boss's wife was sent up here, you know, it must have been five years ago, she was a terror. Sacking everyone and changing everything. We all thought we were for the chop.'

'Kathleen Jaworski came to Kettering?'

'She was Katie then. I don't know where this Kathleen bit comes from. Oh yes, she was here several times, bossing us all about, the hard-bitten cow. I'm sorry, but that's the truth. My old boss, Roger Tibbs, he was a wonderful old man, been here for ever selling the property category, but she had him out in ten minutes flat. Wouldn't accept payment by credit card, he couldn't work the machines. So he had to go. And she introduced all these new categories – nail care, hot tubs. And if we don't carry on with them, all hell breaks loose.'

For the final six months of the graduate programme, trainees were embedded in a department as a member of the team, and Jess was pleased to get the central newsroom. A recent restructure had integrated print, web and cable news resources and forty reporters now worked from a single hub servicing all platforms. Furthermore, Randy Jaworski had decreed an upgrade of the whole news operation and several experienced journalists had been poached from rival organisations. For the first time, Jaworski Media had a political editor and foreign news editor, and there were even rumours they might bid for the *Independent* or the *Evening Standard* if they ever became available.

For Jess, it was a godsend. Instead of writing puffs for bathroom advertisers, she was given proper stories to get her teeth into. Her article about which famous person's statue should occupy the empty plinth in Trafalgar Square filled half a page of *CitiLife*, the new Jaworski freesheet, and her piece on Zone 2 and Zone 3 tube fare increases was a definite scoop. It was a thrill to be sitting at work stations only a few places along from journalists whose bylines she'd read for years, and tagging along with them for drinks at the Three Coachmen. They had so many outrageous stories about celebrities and famous politicians, and gossip about the royals and sportsmen, Jess was astounded. 'Why doesn't any of this ever get printed?' she asked. 'I mean, if it's true.'

'Oh, it's an open secret in Fleet Street. But the lawyers sit on it.'

Jess loved the sensation of knowing the real story. Whenever a TV quizmaster came on screen, or a celebrity gave an interview, she told her flatmates, 'You'd never guess he was a weekend transvestite, would you? It's an open secret.' Or, 'If I tell you her secret kink, you mustn't tell a soul.'

But what she relished most was hearing war stories of investigative journalism, about pharmaceutical companies exposed for overcharging

African mothers for essential drugs, or ostensibly reputable industrialists secretly manufacturing landmines for profit. She loved learning about the everyday tricks of the trade, intercepting emails, hacking phones and breaking into offices disguised as night cleaners.

On the evenings she wasn't drinking with the lads, she was out on the town. Her schoolfriend from way back, Bryony, was working up in London now, and they liked to go clubbing together. A trainee nurse at Lambeth hospital, Bryony had lost none of her childhood fascination with celebrities and often said how envious she was of Jess 'mixing it with the stars'. Jess slightly dreaded these outings with Bryony, who drank too much. Exhausted by long hospital hours, she was the first woman in to happy hour; by the end of the night she was often leant over the gutter, sweating and vomiting. One Saturday at Heaven, Bryony was so bladdered on vodka shots she tripped, sent her drink flying, and got into a fight with another punter. A glass smashed and then another.

Soon, a bouncer appeared. He was a meaty oaf with a mashed nose and shaven head, and a collar of muscle round his neck. He lifted the two women into the air, one in each fist, and said, 'Right, ladies. You're out, and don't come back.' Then he half carried, half bundled them down the stairs, and out on to Shaftesbury Avenue.

'Nice job, Callum,' said the doorman, as he dropped them on the pavement.

London being shockingly expensive, Jess was perpetually short of cash. She did evening shifts in a wine bar but then someone recommended a babysitting agency. 'They pay OK and it's all cash. And it's a breeze: you watch TV while the kids sleep.' Jess had her references checked out and started taking a booking a week. The majority of her bookings were in Islington or Camden, but it could be anywhere from Highgate to Tooting providing they paid her cab home. You got the run of the fridge, and Jess either chilled in front of the telly or got on with writing an article. If the kids wouldn't settle, she let them watch TV until they fell asleep on the settee, then carried them upstairs.

She hated to miss the Ten O'Clock News these days, because it was suddenly all so exciting and grim in the world following 9/11 and the Twin Towers, and she'd been busy filing stories about terrorism threats to London: real journalism. The news editor sent her to Brick Lane to take the temperature of the Muslim community: it looked much the same as usual, tandoori restaurants and corner shops, but she cranked out a thousand words just the same.

One evening she had a booking to babysit in Pimlico, at a flat in Cambridge Street. The forty-something lady who opened the door was friendly and quite pretty, but seemed worried about leaving her son with a stranger. 'I've never used an agency before. But it's a bit of an emergency.' She had prepared supper on a tray for Jess, and gave her the telephone number to ring if Henry woke up and needed her. 'He probably won't. He's a good sleeper.'

Then she said, 'I just wish I didn't have to go out tonight. One of my oldest friends has got engaged, which is lovely for Mouse, but I've had a stressful week. It looks like my son's father is off to the Gulf. We're not married any more. But it's still terrifying. His regiment's being sent out.'

'For the Iraq invasion?' The impending action to topple Saddam Hussein was all over the news.

'Yes. You can't help worrying.'

'Well, try not to, Mrs Pilcher. And have a nice evening. Everything'll be fine here, and I'll give you a bell if Henry wakes and needs you.'

'Bless you,' said Annabel. 'I'm not normally like this, I promise. Do help yourself if you want a drink or anything.'

Chapter Thirty-Six

Randy Jaworski, having amassed his fortune through low-cost, low-quality media ventures, had lately found himself hankering after respect. For years he had voiced only contempt for those proprietors prepared to indulge lossmaking newspapers because they were prestigious, or to accept low margins as the price of great journalism. 'A good newspaper is a profitable paper,' he used to say. 'A *great* newspaper is a *very* profitable one.' Jaworski Media was seldom among the prizewinners at awards ceremonies, nor did its journalists compete for Pulitzers. And Randy was fine with that.

How his conversion came about, no one could exactly say. It certainly irked him, in the early days of the war on terror, when George W. Bush did not include him in the group of media owners invited to the White House for high-level schmoozing, and Tony Blair similarly excluded him from 10 Downing Street. For all their size and scale, Jaworski's newspapers and cable channels simply didn't register.

There was a theory that his wife, Kathleen, felt snubbed by a lack of deference at industry events. At black-tie dinners, the Jaworskis did not always get top table placement and were seated alongside executives of inferior status at secondary tables. Meanwhile, directors from *The Times* and the *Observer* – who weren't even *owners*, and were working on lossmaking titles – were feted ahead of them. Kathleen was reportedly pushing her tycoon to buy something prestigious to underpin their status.

Cath may, in any case, have been pushing at a half open door. Having previously measured his success strictly by material assets – Gulfstream, yacht and art – Randy had lately entered a more refined stratosphere in which kudos is signalled by ownership of revered media institutions, rather than the shoppers and freesheets that made him rich. Randy saw the solution in hiring ambitious editors and more expensive journalists, and looking out for trophy assets to acquire.

Little by little he became more absorbed into British society, at least into the flasher, richer end of it. The Jaworskis were invited to dinners by other rich couples who saw it as a duty to entertain their peer group, and by investment bankers who hoped to secure Randy as a client. From these dinners came invitations to shoot. Randy initially turned these down – 'I don't even know what it is they hunt over here. Quails?' – but Cath coaxed him into taking lessons.

'All the big deals are done over lunch out shooting,' she told him. 'You'll miss out if you don't take part.' From her time at Blaydon Hall she remembered her shooting etiquette, and took Randy to a tailor who made him tweed suits like the ones hanging in Charlie Blaydon's wardrobe.

Slightly to his surprise, Randy found he enjoyed shooting and was good at it. Alert, accurate and sickeningly competitive, he opened fire at anything and everything, regardless of whether or not it was over his peg. And when he missed a bird, he cursed his loader, or cursed Cath, who soon refused to stand with him.

Having accepted five invitations in his first season, Randy was determined to host some shoot days himself and ordered Ann Saltzman to look into it. The next winter he rented days at Alnwick Castle, Castle Hill, Combe Sydenham and North Molton, and in August took grouse moors at Gunnerside, Bolton Abbey and Wemmergill. Price was no object. If the owners said they didn't let out their shooting, he paid and paid until they did.

Cath relished these weekends playing lady of the manor. She enjoyed presiding over butlers and housemaids and allocating bedrooms to Randy's important guests, and seating them next to herself at mealtimes. She took to it very naturally, being reminded of her days at Blaydon Hall with kinky old Charlie, except that now her status was unambiguous. She recognised paintings by the same old masters that hung at Blaydon, and told guests, 'I do so love Claude Lorrain,' or 'Nobody painted horses like Stubbs did,' or, at dinner, 'I've always admired the silver of Paul Storr, the man was a genius.' And afterwards, when they moved from the dining room into some stately drawing room, Cath gazed about her contentedly. Sometimes the actual owners of the castles were on the premises, seeing to the shoot, and Cath loved the way they treated her so respectfully, all these duchesses and countesses and whatnots.

She looked forward to the big weekends because Randy was generally bucked up by them, and behaved nicely towards her. As the years had passed, he treated her with less respect, even marginalising her in his businesses. At Davos that January, he made it clear he did not want her with him at the economic summit as he always had before, explaining he had back-to-back meetings. Cath did not believe Randy was cheating on her – he was always more turned on by business than sex – but it made her resentful.

At their big weekends, however, he played the convivial host, presiding over the table with cigar in hand, broadcasting his take on the economy and geopolitics. He prided himself on serving only the most expensive wines. His guests were the bankers and socialites he met shooting with other bankers and socialites. He loved to have cabinet ministers at his table, and certain minor members of the royal family, who are always available to shoot with rich men.

Chapter Thirty-Seven

Annabel was glued to the television. She hadn't missed the lunchtime or evening news for three weeks, since the day the regiment flew out to Dhahran in Saudi Arabia. She watched each bulletin in the hope of spotting Jamie, George or Rupert; there had been masses of footage of soldiers in battledress filing out of Tristars and Hercules transport planes, or crossing the border into Iraq, but not a glimpse of her boys.

Thus far, there had been mercifully few casualties, but Annabel lived in fear. The British had swept into Basra and the Americans were on the outskirts of Baghdad, but pundits were predicting push-back at any moment. Where was Saddam's elite Republican Guard? And what about the WMDs everyone went on about?

She wished there was some way of checking they were OK, but George warned there'd be no mobiles and no signal. He had taken her out for supper a couple of days before leaving, and it had been an emotional parting. She looked on George as her closest friend, as well as being Henry's godfather, but sometimes found him infuriatingly difficult to read. She knew he'd been going out with a woman named Charlotte, a freelance cordon bleu cook, but that had apparently ended. 'Charlotte's a lovely person, but I couldn't take second best,' he had said mysteriously. At the last supper he'd presented Annabel with a watercolour of a view across the Round Pond towards Kensington Palace, which he claimed was unfinished because his easel had been attacked by geese. It was classic George; he always said his paintings were unfinished.

Annabel worried most for Henry. Of course, you shouldn't be fatalistic, but she had this abiding dread of telling Henry his father had been killed in action. Henry worshipped Jamie. Partly, Annabel reckoned, because Henry saw so little of him. Jamie was a rotten father.

Last summer, after numerous promises which had never come to anything, he'd finally taken Henry up to Rutland for a long weekend. This had compelled Annabel to speak to Suki on the phone, which she'd dreaded but was actually fine. Henry returned to London having had a marvellous time; he never stopped talking about Daddy's sports car and Daddy's country house and riding the ponies. He'd got on well with his half-brother, Hector, with whom he shared a bedroom, and said Hector's mum had been 'really nice'. Annabel was pleased Henry had been happy, but couldn't feel entirely happy herself.

She wrote regularly to George, not knowing whether her letters reached him, but then after almost a month received a reply. It was a lovely long letter too, six sides, sent from Battle Group HQ in Basra, which George said was in an old palace of Saddam Hussein's: *You should see the bathrooms – gold taps and marble jacuzzis. Pity the water's stopped working, and the electrics come to that.* He sounded in high spirits, describing the advance on Basra and the slightly eerie sensation of taking over a city of deserted streets, with nobody about, but the feeling of being watched by unseen eyes. He made jokes about the food and how he was having dreams about the *mozzarella in carrozza* at Ziani's restaurant in Radnor Walk. *Let's go there together the first night I'm back.* He was optimistic about the war ending quickly: *We've been welcomed by the locals, they were sick of Saddam's regime*, and were already engaged in winning the peace. Both George and Rupert were majors now, and Jamie was a lieutenant-colonel and the commanding officer. 'Jamie's fine, by the way, and sends you his best. As do all your friends and admirers out here in Basra.'

Subsequent letters gave her a fuller picture of everyday life, though George was careful not to give too much detail. He said they spent part of each day patrolling the city and surrounding villages in Warriors, which Annabel knew were armoured vehicles with a gun on the roof. He said the regiment was running food and aid convoys and helping re-establish water supplies: so much of the infrastructure had been destroyed, either during the invasion or by the retreating Saddam army. *I'm sure you've seen on the news we've been getting a bit of aggro from insurgents, burying IEDs on the roads. It's* not helpful *and slows us down. Apart from that, all well here. Major Henley sends you his best, he's running a soccer league for the regiment. Jamie's in fine fettle too, getting on with the job. He sends love to my godson, as do I.*

The invasion complete and Saddam deposed, Annabel felt a definite lessening in her anxiety levels. Her job at Sotheby's still suited her though she wasn't sure she wanted to be there for ever. She saw quite a lot of her father, less of her mother, and spent one weekend in six up in Norfolk with her sister and brother-in-law at Burnham Market. It was nice for Henry to spend time with his cousins, and a bit of a rest for Annabel to be cooked for by her younger sister's legion of Norfolk retainers.

Chapter Thirty-Eight

Jess's graduate programme drew to its close and she wondered what came next. It was announced that four of the eighteen scheme interns would be offered full-time positions at Jaworski Media, and a list of openings posted for application. By now, Jess was entrenched in London life and didn't want to move elsewhere. So she was delighted when she learned she'd been given a full-time job in News plus a payrise.

With her staff job came a new brief to cover Society and Lifestyle, which meant just about everything from the homeless at Centrepoint to shiny housing developments in Docklands. Her editor encouraged her to file what he called 'crunchy' stories, full of facts, figures and salaries and preferably with a dash of healthy scepticism. All this delighted Jess, but not always her subjects. The chief executive of the Docklands Development Corporation complained she had 'wilfully misrepresented and misquoted him,' and it was lucky for Jess she'd kept her notes and her recording of the interview. Being pretty and cute, Jess lulled her subjects into letting their guard slip, or they made the error of patronising her, which they lived to regret.

The flat in Farringdon was disbanded and Jess found another place closer in, in Covent Garden, above a row of shops and brasseries in Great Queen Street opposite the Masonic lodge. Her current boyfriend, Steve, a senior reporter at Jaworski Media, told her there had once been a popular cocktail bar downstairs, Zanzibar, which he used to visit with his first wife. 'You'd have loved Zee-bar,' he told her. 'All the best-looking women in media hung out there.'

One lunchtime, emerging onto the pavement from the office lobby, she spotted Randy and Kathleen getting into a double-parked limo, and a chauffeur closing the doors for them. It was the first time she'd seen them in three years. And then, a few days later, she found herself alone in a lift with Mr Jaworski. She introduced herself. 'Hi, I'm Jess Eden, I did your graduate programme and now I'm staff.'

Randy looked at her blankly. 'Do I know you, miss?'

'Er, not really. I'm just saying hello. Though we did meet once before in Manchester. You made a speech at my graduation.'

'I did?' The door pinged open. 'This is where I get out.' And he exited the elevator.

On her twenty-fourth birthday, Steve took her to supper at a fish place, Zilli's, he was reviewing for the website. Jess, as usual, wore her locket for its annual outing, and later showed Steve the photo inside, and told him once again the intriguing story of its provenance and how it was her sole connection to her birth mother.

Steve examined it by the light of a table candle. 'She's quite a looker, your mum. Not that that's a surprise. It's hard to see properly in this light. She reminds me of someone, I'm sure I know that face.'

'She was from Portsmouth. That's all I know about her.'

'Anyway, the photo's faded, you can't really see.'

Chapter Thirty-Nine

Annabel heard the tragic news from George, who managed to call her on a satphone. He said he was ringing from the military airport in Basra, where he was about to board a Hercules with the coffin. He was flying home as part of the honour guard.

For a moment she'd thought he was referring to Jamie, then realised it was Rupert who'd been killed. He'd been out on routine patrol and his Warrior had run over an IED. The Warrior had been driving in convoy, the middle of three vehicles; the one ahead must have avoided the device by a whisker. It had been planted close to a school, in a neighbourhood normally considered safe. Major Henley was riding in the section of the vehicle directly above where the bomb detonated. George mentioned it had been a challenge to identify his remains for repatriation.

Annabel registered a succession of emotions: relief it wasn't Jamie, for Henry's sake, followed by devastation for Rupert, for his wife, his family. Annabel had never totally bonded with Rupert's wife, Pippa, but had been at their wedding, and their children were sweet, all three of them: Sacha, Freddie and Tilly. And Rupert was Henry's other godfather. At Christmas, Rupert and Pippa had taken Annabel and Henry, plus their own children, and one of Rupert's other godchildren, to a performance of *Cinderella* on ice, which had been the last time she'd seen him, or would ever see him. George said the funeral would be held at St Bartholomew's, Wootton Bassett in Wiltshire next Friday.

The service was as sad as can possibly be. Annabel was unprepared for the intensity of emotion which coursed through her, seeing Rupert's elderly parents seated in the front pew, along with Pippa and the children – Freddie so brave and the two little girls crumpled with grief – and the moving ritual of a full military funeral. The church was packed to overflowing, there must have been seven hundred people, lots of soldiers of course, but also Rupert's contemporaries and schoolmasters from Radley, from his prep school, Sunningdale, and old skiing buddies. Annabel placed herself near the back, not wanting to intrude into space meant for family or closer friends. Rupert had not, if truth be told, been a particularly intimate confidant for many years, but he was part of the narrative of her life, the man who had taken her virginity at Chalet Cheva, who had been an usher at her wedding and made godfatherly vows at Henry's christening. It struck her as unbearably random that he should now be dead. His casket was carried out of the church by George and five other officers of the Irish Guards.

Having returned to England, George was granted ten days' leave and used it to visit his parents at Mallards End and Annabel in Cambridge Street. They fulfilled their long anticipated plan to eat *mozzarella in carrozza* at Ziani's, and talked about Rupert. George had spent a couple of nights with Pippa in Oxfordshire, at Hambledon where they lived, helping her to sort out Rupert's paperwork. He had written to Rupert's old school to find out whether Freddie Henley might be eligible for a Warden's bursary since Rupert had not left much in the way of funds. Rupert's parents were keen to present an engraved bench to the regiment in memory of their son, and George was dealing with this too. He told Annabel he'd found his visit to Hambledon 'heartbreaking' and wished it had been him and not Rupert who'd copped it. Sacha, Rupert's eldest daughter, was his goddaughter and he'd told Pippa he'd pay her school fees all the way through. 'I've no one else to support.'

'Have you had any chance to paint in Iraq?' Annabel asked him at one point.

'Quite a lot. I took my paints out and have to buy some more browns and greys this leave because everything's brown or grey over there. Thanks for reminding me.'

'You should have a show. Watercolours of the Iraq campaign: a war artist.'

'Actually they're not pictures of the war. No tanks, nothing like that. Just landscapes. Which are breathtaking, by the way. Sand and mountains and minarets. The scenery hasn't changed in a thousand years, and will still be the same long after all this is over and forgotten. I did a watercolour of the Tigris. I'd love to show you.'

He said he was painting a portrait of Rupert as a present for Pippa, based on photographs. 'I'll get a copy of it made for you, Annabel. You're an old flame of Rupert's. You should have one.'

Chapter Forty

Randolph had rented Belvoir Castle from the Duke and Duchess of Rutland for his next shooting weekend and lined up a stellar guest list of guns. As he told his wife, 'There'll be two shadow cabinet politicians, three chairmen of FTSE 100 companies, a peer of the realm, and of course, David Shropshire.' He was particularly gratified to have secured the Duke of Shropshire for the weekend, who was a royal duke and an HRH, second cousin to the Queen. David was a new friend: the Jaworskis met him first at a Cartier dinner and later at an Asprey party, but had never previously invited him to anything themselves.

'How are you supposed to address the guy, anyway?' he asked Cath. '*Dook*?'

'Call him "Your Royal Highness" the first time you greet him, after that "Sir".'

Randy nodded. 'And I'm told I have to supply him with his bullets . . . cartridges. That's what I've been told. We leave them in his suite.'

'I'm putting him in the Wyatt bedroom,' Cath said. 'Emma says it's the best spare.' It gave Cath a thrill to refer to the Duchess of Rutland by her Christian name. She might have called her 'Your Grace', but why should she when they were paying an arm and a leg?

Cath was delighted by Belvoir Castle. She'd learnt you pronounced the place 'Beaver', which made her giggle for obvious reasons, and repeated it regularly to show she knew correct form. They were driven up to Leicestershire by Randy's driver through some of the ugliest parts of England, heavily built-up, and Cath wished they'd travelled by helicopter but it was apparently going to be too dark to land safely. So they'd crawled through traffic, Randy in a filthy mood, bickering all the way, until the last ten miles when the countryside suddenly became picture-perfect and they had entered the Belvoir estate.

Then the castle loomed on top of a hill, a huge fake Norman edifice with battlements and a round tower like Windsor Castle dominating the park for miles about. Even Randy was impressed. 'I reckon our guests are going to get a kick out of seeing this place. Even the dook is going to be impressed.'

They entered a vast outer hall hung with swords and shields, then an inner hall the size of a cathedral with further swords and shields and a roaring fire. Butlers and other staff appeared to carry their luggage upstairs, and Randy's guns to the gun room, and Cath was soon locked in conversation with a housekeeper about the arrangements for the weekend, and being shown the bedrooms allocated to the various guests for her approval. She had already OK'd the menus for the weekend, and Randy's wine merchant had delivered a van load of fancy vintages to the castle.

Soon the Jaworskis' guests began to arrive and were shown to their bedrooms, then congregated in the drawing room for drinks before dinner. Both Friday and Saturday night dinners had been designated black tie, and Randy stood in front of the fireplace in his trademark white tuxedo and black polo shirt. The captains of industry arrived slightly harassed from their long working weeks in London and long drive north, and privately batey at being made to put on a dinner jacket on a Friday night. But the royal Duke of Shropshire was immaculate in a perfectly cut dinner jacket and tartan trews with velvet slippers monogrammed with the lion and unicorn of the royal coat of arms. The cuffs of his dinner shirt were secured by the thickest, most beautiful cufflinks, engraved with the eagles of the Romanoffs. 'They belonged to Tsar Nicholas,' mentioned David Shropshire. 'He was a relation, actually, on both sides.'

'I love your tartan trousers, sir,' Cath said. 'Is that your personal tartan?'

'It was actually designed by Prince Albert for the family to wear in Scotland. But I allow myself the indulgence of wearing it sometimes south of the border, even if not strictly correct.'

'They look gorgeous on you, sir. You should wear them all the time.'

The duke smiled thinly.

At fifty-nine, the royal duke was an ornament of London society.

Tall, blue-eyed and aloof in manner, his appearance was often compared to Queen Victoria's husband, Prince Albert. He had been married for twenty-three years, without issue, to Princess Marina of the Balkans, but she had eventually divorced him to set up a donkey sanctuary in her own country. Deeply religious and nervy, she was widely regarded as potty.

Since the defection of Princess Marina, David Shropshire had become a fixture at the best parties and also, it was rumoured, available for guest appearances at commercial ones if the fee was right. But all that was handled with great discretion, if it was even true. What was certainly true was that he was short of money. He lived rent-free in a grace and favour apartment in Kensington Palace, gifted by the Crown, but otherwise survived on canapés and the periodic sale of heirlooms. He was permanently on the lookout for non-executive directorships from companies willing to pay £25,000 a year in return for the name HRH The Duke of Shropshire on their letterhead, and there were invariably two or three prepared to do so, for a while at least.

It helped that he was handsome and could be charming when it suited him, especially with women. Since becoming single, and perhaps even before, he had the reputation as a womaniser, his name linked to a prominent interior decorator and the English wife of an Iranian tycoon. On off-days, or if he felt his dignity too much presumed upon, he could turn frosty and distant, and people said, 'That's the royal coming out in him.'

Cath seated David Shropshire on her left at dinner and then again at the shooting lunch the next day, and on Saturday night in the state dining room and again at Sunday lunch. She felt exhilarated having royalty so close at hand and did not wish to share him with the other wives. She was surprised how attentive he was towards her, asking questions about her life with Randolph and before Randolph. In both halves of the Saturday shoot she stood with the duke at his peg for each drive, congratulating him when he shot a bird and commiserating when he missed. She found it thrilling to be standing in the line of guns next to a royal duke who was unfailingly charming, unlike Randy who became cross when he shot badly. Cath felt the envious eyes of the other women watching her with David, because people always watch royalty, openly or surreptitiously, even rich people.

And she found him easy to talk to. As they waited in bulrushes at the duck drive, she told him about her schooldays at St Mary's and her brief engagement to Charlie Blaydon when she was twenty years old and he was eighty plus.

'Lucky old Lord Blaydon,' said David Shropshire. 'I'm sure he was in clover having a pretty girl like you in his life.'

'You're telling me,' said Cath. 'I wouldn't like to tell you half the things he got up to.'

'Tell me,' said the duke. 'Really, I am fascinated.'

'No,' replied Cath, placing her hand on his arm in a gesture of caution. 'I never betray the confidence of past lovers, never. I will only say he enjoyed a bit of hanky-spanky.'

The duke's eyes lit up. 'You whipped him?'

Cath shrugged. 'Now, now. That's all private. Or we'll have to spank *your* bottom, won't we, sir?'

At dinner that night, while Randy regaled the table with an account of a White House dinner he'd recently attended and why the president really had no option but to go into Afghanistan, Cath felt the duke's monogrammed slipper rub against her ankle. And later, while smoking an after dinner cigar, his left hand rested on her lap and encroached on her thigh. Cath made no response, neither encouraging nor discouraging the overture.

And on Sunday afternoon, when making his farewells, the duke lowered his voice so as not to be overheard and said, 'This weekend has been delightful, Kathleen. Wonderful shooting, wonderful hospitality, and most of all a chance to know you better. I hope we can see more of each other in London. Would you ever be free to visit me at Kensington Palace? For tea one afternoon, or a drink? I would enjoy that . . . and to hear more of your adventures.'

'That would be a treat, Your Royal Highness. A privilege.'

'Then I shall have my people call you,' replied the royal duke softly.

Cath resolved to travel by black cab to Kensington Palace rather than take one of Randy's drivers. A single phone call to Randy's assistants would have summoned a limo, but also revealed her destination, and Cath preferred not to draw attention to this visit. So she hailed a taxi in St James's which on arrival at KP slowed at the sentry box at the gates where her name was already on the policeman's list, and she was waved on through.

The apartment occupied by David Shropshire was surprisingly small for a Your Royal Highness, Cath thought, and was entered through a small door in a wall in a pretty cobbled courtyard. She had anticipated something bigger, though the views across Kensington Gardens were nice, and the floor-to-ceiling sash windows flooded the first floor drawing room with light. She'd been expecting servants too: footmen in frock coats with powdered wigs. But David opened the front door himself and led her upstairs and poured champagne from an open bottle.

She was struck by the grandeur of the furnishings, which reminded her of that fancy china shop on South Audley Street, Thomas Goode. On both sides of the fireplace were backlit cabinets, displaying dinner plates and soup tureens, all with crests and coats of arms. David was eager to explain their provenance, this plate coming from a palace in Gothenburg where it had been part of the state dinner service of King Karl-Johan, this bowl from the Winter Palace in St Petersburg, another from the Saxe-Coburg-Gotha Schloss Rosenau. Some were noticeably chipped, and Cath reckoned they shouldn't have been on display at all, but David was delighted by them, lovingly highlighting the armorial flourishes, crowns, fleurs-de-lis and thistles.

Having detected her interest, he embarked upon a tour of the room, and the little dining salon beyond, explaining each piece of furniture, painting and knick-knack. There were tables covered with silver-framed photographs, many with gold crowns on the frame tops, and velvet mounts in scarlets and purples. David gave a running commentary, 'This one, of course, is of old Queen Mary, who I remember meeting as a small boy in a corridor at Buckingham Palace. Terrifying old lady, but much missed. And that is Crown Prince Friedrich of Prussia, whose great-niece was my first cousin. And there's poor old Princess Alice, God rest her soul. And obviously Lilibet and the Duke of Edinburgh . . . who is also a cousin through the Hellenes . . .'

Cath found it all very heady, such close proximity to royalty. She had never previously cared much about the royal family one way or the other beyond vaguely identifying with Princess Diana, but there was something about being all alone in the presence of a Royal Highness, and these autographed photos of the Queen, which left her giddy. That and the champagne, and David's being so informal and friendly, like they were old mates, you had to pinch yourself.

He poured her another glass, remarking that the champagne glasses had a history themselves, having come from Osborne House (Cath had never heard of Osborne House, but kept quiet) and belonged to Queen Victoria. It was probable the Kaiser had drunk from them. The sofa on which David and Cath were now sitting, side by side, covered in a threadbare chintz of blowsy roses, had come from Clarence House, a generous cast-off from Queen Elizabeth, the Queen Mother.

'So, you were telling me about Charlie Blaydon,' David said. 'My father, the old duke, used to shoot partridge with him at Blaydon Hall. I came across some game books. This was after the war, I think.'

'Oh, Charlie. He was a sweet man, really, sir. Used to treat me to suppers at Claridge's and Wiltons, and I was only a young thing in those days.'

David looked at her leadingly. 'And you said he liked to play certain games in the bedroom? Amusing games?'

'I shouldn't have mentioned that, just forget about it, won't you, sir?'

'On the contrary, I find that kind of activity interesting from a psychological standpoint. My mother's cousin, King Kläus-Harald of Estonia, shared a similar predilection. Every morning at noon, when he returned from riding, four Carmelite nuns from the Convent of the Sacred Heart came to his private chamber and flagellated him with birch rods until he bled. Does that shock you?'

Cath shrugged. 'Whatever turns you on, that's what I say. I mean, if that was his thing, old King Klaus-wassisname, that's his business, the kinky sod. As for the nuns, well, maybe they got a buzz out of it too. There's no accounting for taste.'

'I always found this image of the King . . . intriguing and quite exciting. But regrettably, nuns today . . . I don't think they any longer provide such a service. Certainly not in England. Which is a sadness. I have often wondered how it would feel to be soundly beaten with birch twigs from the forest. Newly cut birches. In fact, Kathleen, I have some examples of such birches in my bedchamber. Would you care to inspect them?'

'Good gracious, sir. In your bedroom?'

'Cut with my own hand. From a copse of birch trees at Swinley Forest Golf Club, where I am an honorary member. It is close to Windsor, so most convenient.'

He led her along a corridor to a large, dark bedroom at the rear of the apartment. Curtains were drawn across both windows. Suspended above the bed was a gilded coronet and there were fur-lined drapes behind the headboard.

'Yes, one has often speculated about King Kläus-Harald, and what precisely the truth was of the old stories. There are so many aspects of which one knows too little. Did they whip him across his riding breeches or scourge the naked flesh? One suspects the latter. And what of the ladies of the convent? Did they perform their daily ritual wearing the habits of the order, or disrobe as well? It is certainly possible. One cannot discount it. Anyway, here are the birches you asked to see. Go on, Kathleen, pick them up, test them out. I love the swishing sound they make. Quite evocative. Try it.'

Cath lifted a bundle of twigs and cracked it across the bed. It was like old times; she hadn't done this since Charlie's bedroom in Blaydon Hall. The sound brought it all back. She swished the birch again, this time through the air. The effect on the Duke of Shropshire was startling. He was gripped by a look of longing, and began to shake. 'Do that again, Kathleen, I love the sound. Swish it again, swish it harder.'

Cath complied. She guessed what was coming.

'You have whetted my curiosity,' David declared. 'I'm thinking this may be the time to experience at last the chastisement of the King, which I've so often wondered about. Oblige me, Kathleen. Whip me with the birch rods, whip me without mercy.'

In seconds, the duke had lowered his trousers and boxers and positioned himself across a leather steamer trunk, emblazoned with the royal arms of Hohenzollern Castle. 'Give me no quarter,' he commanded. 'Lay it on with all your might.'

Cath did as she was told, swishing the twigs hard onto the royal bottom.

'More, more,' he cried out. 'Next time you will discipline me dressed as a nun. I have the garments in a cupboard. You promise to oblige me?'

'Whatever you wish, sir. And the next six will be vicious, so brace yourself, Your Royal Highness.'

'You must promise to visit me often,' he said to her afterwards. 'Promise me that.'

'Of course. By royal command.'

'And I can trust you?'

'To the grave, sir. Our little secret.'

Cath fell into a routine of calling on David at Kensington Palace once a week. First they drank a glass of champagne together while he regaled her with stories of his royal cousins, past and present; then Cath accompanied him into his bedroom where the grey nun's habit was laid out in readiness, and Cath carried it into the bathroom to prepare herself. David then presented himself as the King of Estonia and assumed the position, and Cath whipped him with gusto across his back and buttocks.

Afterwards, she frequently accompanied him as his walker to cocktail parties and private views, and she would take him on to dinner at the restaurants he favoured. Cath invariably picked up the bill, or more accurately Randy Jaworski did, or his company did. Cath often mentioned it to Randy when she'd had dinner with the duke, but not always, in case he got suspicious. Luckily her husband saw it as a feather in his cap that Kathleen moved in royal circles.

At their dinners together, the duke never alluded to their afternoon diversions. Sometimes he sat a little stiffly, or requested a cushion for his back. His chief interests were history and shooting and he liked to discuss both with Cath. He said he had found a photograph of Crown Princess Katharina of Pless, who was Cath's virtual double, and from then on he called her Katharina. 'The name suits you better. Kathleen's too ordinary for you.'

He loaned her fat histories of the Restoration and the Hanoverians, which Cath duly took home and read, enough of them anyway, and which he liked to discuss with her afterwards. The history books he most enjoyed showcased his ancestors and contained glorious plates of monarchs on horseback or reviewing the fleet at Spithead. Having been trained by Charlie Blaydon in her formative years, Cath had no problem fanning his ancestor worship.

'I must say, it's a pleasure talking to a woman who appreciates history,' the duke said to her. 'Most women glaze over.'

As the shooting season approached, he kept in his jacket pocket a typed list of all the shoots he was invited to that year, dates, estates and hosts. 'I don't believe even my forebear Edward VII had as much shooting as I will this year.'

'I'd love to hear more about Edward VII,' Cath said. 'He sounds like a fun gentleman.'

'And he'd have *adored* you, Katharina. I imagine you and Bertie getting on like a house on fire.'

It was not for several months that Cath and the duke technically became lovers. But, once embarked upon, their affair was steamy and relentless. Sometimes they made love immediately after one of the weekly flagellation sessions; sometimes when they returned to the apartment for a nightcap after dinner. But Cath was careful always to ring Randy, wherever he was in the world, every single day, so he should not feel neglected, even when he neglected her himself.

Sex with David was satisfying, much more so than with Randy. He had a notable tool which he said had come down from the Hanoverian Georges, long but lacking in girth, and which Cath quickly got the hang of. 'Permission to suck you off, sir,' she asked, knowing his insistence on correct form at all times.

Sometimes he was prone to bitterness, feeling he was sidelined by his mainstream royal cousins, and distressed by his lack of money. In return for his free housing, he undertook certain ceremonial duties representing senior royals at funerals and greeting minor heads of state at Heathrow Airport. Or he would be asked by the Lord Chamberlain's Office at Buckingham Palace to take a salute on behalf of Her Majesty if she was overseas, or to lay a wreath. David Shropshire alternately relished the attention or felt put upon. It irked him that he was provided with no private secretary or equerry, or permanent driver from the household, and only part-time use of a secretary from the Lord Chamberlain's Office, two mornings a week.

Cath found herself constantly bolstering his morale, reassuring him how important he was – 'You're thirty-ninth in line to the throne, sir. How cool is that?' – and loving the limelight when they arrived together at a function, when all the paparazzi clustered round taking their pictures. It was like the early days with Ryan, except the duke was a royal not a footballer. Cath had never mentioned her five year marriage to Ryan James, and David never enquired.

A year after they began seeing each other, the duke still knew almost nothing about his Katharina.

Chapter Forty-One

Annabel never seriously doubted she would get the new job but it was a relief nonetheless when the confirmation letter arrived in its smartly ciphered envelope. She'd never been vetted like this before in her life. They'd contacted her old school, all her past employers, rung her parents, her doctor and three of her friends for character references. She hoped they hadn't rung Flea at the wrong time of day or there was no guessing what she'd have said. And, at the second interview, they'd asked about her divorce from Jamie and his recent posting to Camp Bastion in Helmand Province.

Now she was seated at her new desk in the Lord Chamberlain's Office on the raised ground floor of Buckingham Palace, with a view through bombproof net curtains onto an inner courtyard. Her actual job title was Lady Clerk to the Deputy Comptroller, and she was part of the team dealing with admin surrounding state visits, investitures, garden parties, the State Opening of Parliament, royal weddings and funerals. She'd been told that she needed to be efficient and discreet, and have the right attitude and values. The courtiers who interviewed her had intuited correctly that Annabel Pilcher had it in spades. Today she was double-checking a list of sixteen hundred acceptances to the fourth and final garden party of the summer and ensuring, with two assistants, that correct security passes had been dispatched to disabled guests.

As someone joked at her Sotheby's leaving party, she must be the only person ever to have left the auction house for a cut in wages. But Annabel had leapt at the opportunity to work for the monarch at Buckingham Palace, which she considered a privilege. And her background as the daughter of an army officer, and ex-wife to a Guards Officer, made her ideal material; many of the team in the

Lord Chamberlain's Office had military connections.

Starting a new job in her forties was intimidating, with numerous palace conventions to pick up. Correspondence from the royal household was laid out in prescribed ways in particular fonts and font sizes – Arial 13 pt – with every letter and envelope spaced in a particular style. And she quickly became adept at drafting briefing notes to members of the royal family in the third person as protocol required, beginning with a handwritten *Sir*, and continuing *The regiments of which YRH is Colonel-in-Chief will be gathered on Horse Guards Parade at* 10.00. *Following the Salute, should it please YRH, YRH might pause for a brief exchange with each Commanding Officer* . . .

Annabel did not herself have much interaction with the royals, but her boss, the deputy comptroller, Major-General Daubeney, did, and his boss, the comptroller, met with the monarch regularly, as of course did the comptroller's boss, the lord chamberlain. On the occasions Annabel bumped into any member of the royal family in a corridor, she'd been briefed to flatten herself against the nearest wall, curtsy, and not say a word unless spoken to.

The life suited her and struck her as more worthwhile than her previous existence selling auction catalogues to millionaires. The events she helped organise, and the people who attended them, were surprisingly varied: one day there would be a reception for commonwealth trade representatives, the next for sports personalities, ambassadors, arts mandarins, or women who worked for charities in the north-east. Henry was away at boarding school half of the time now, so it was satisfying to have something to get her teeth into.

She still saw quite a bit of the old gang – Sophie (née Peverel) and David had moved back from Hong Kong to Barnes with their kids, and Mouse Adams (née Barwell-Mackenzie) lived with her much younger husband, Josh, in Hackney, where he worked in arts administration. George completed a second tour in the war on terror, and was now temporarily assigned to Sandhurst as a lecturer in counter-insurgency. He had been promoted to the rank of lieutenant colonel and said his duties as an academic allowed him more time to paint; he sometimes took Henry into the park with easel and paintbox and taught him how to do watercolours.

Since Sandhurst was close enough to London to drive up for supper, Annabel and George spent more time together than they had for several years and both, in their diffident ways, wished their long friendship could develop into something more. But both were afraid to say anything, in case such an overture was unwelcome and spoilt things. Annabel said to herself, with a note of regret, 'We know each other too well, that's our problem,' or even, 'We're too old.'

One evening, having supper at Como Lario, the Italian restaurant in Pimlico which had become their favourite, George said, 'I'm wondering whether or not to mention this. Or perhaps you know already.'

'What?'

'Well, Jamie has left Suki. Technically, Suki's left him. I think we can say fault was on Jamie's side.'

'He's been unfaithful to her?'

George shrugged. 'I don't know all the details, but I'm afraid he's been playing away.'

'I can imagine. Oh damn him, I'd almost come round to liking Suki. Henry likes her. He spent a week up there in the summer during Jamie's last leave. Where's Jamie now? I've lost track.'

'Helmand. But coming home soon. The regiment's on ceremonial duty for the next year or two at least. So he'll be in London, round the corner from your new place of work.'

'And what about you?'

'Me?'

'What does the future hold for you, George?'

He shrugged and looked softly at her across the table. 'If only I knew. I can hope, but only a fool predicts the future with confidence. One lives in hope.' And the conversation ended on an equivocal note.

Annabel returned home feeling cross. Cross with herself and cross with George; their dinners often left her feeling that way, of opportunities flunked and things left unsaid. And she was downcast by the information about Jamie and Suki because she guessed it would make it more difficult for Henry to stay in contact with his father. She arrived back at the flat to relieve her babysitter, and found Jess writing an article on her laptop.

'What's the subject this week?' Annabel asked her.

'State education versus private,' Jess replied. 'The peg is the widening gap in exam results between London's state and independent schools. Which sort were you at, Mrs Pilcher, if you don't mind me asking?'

'Me? Er, not at all. Well, my school wasn't in London. I went to a funny girls' boarding place in the Sussex countryside, St Mary's, Petworth. A private school, rather old-fashioned.'

'And did you get loads of top grades? In your GCSEs and A levels?'

Annabel laughed. 'Hardly. It wasn't academic at all, I'm afraid. We mostly looked after our hamsters.'

'St Mary's in Petworth? I haven't heard of that one. I'll look it up on the league tables.'

'Oh, I doubt it's on any league tables. It certainly wouldn't have been then. A happy school, but I don't think education was much of a priority.'

One morning the following week, Annabel was arriving at work through the Privy Purse entrance when her boss, the deputy comptroller, stopped her and said, 'Small change of plan, Annabel. The Duke of Kent is unwell and can no longer take the salute at the parade of Commonwealth Scouts and Guides. We need a substitute and I've asked the Duke of Shropshire to stand in. He's agreed, but didn't sound too happy about it. I said I'd send someone round to brief him, and wondered if you'd go?'

Forty minutes later, Annabel went over to Kensington Palace equipped with briefing papers for the afternoon ceremony in Whitehall. Over a thousand scouts and guides from India, Canada, Fiji and Tonga would march past the cenotaph and make their salute to the royal duke, who would be accompanied by the Lord Lieutenant of London, the high sheriff and various scout movement dignitaries from Baden-Powell House, as well as the Indian, Canadian, Fijian and Tongan High Commissioners. The duke received her in his drawing room, where he sat rather stiffly on cushions in a high-backed chair. Annabel was struck by how handsome he was in a beautifully cut suit and polished brogues. His signet ring with the royal crest glinted in the sunshine.

'Your Royal Highness, it is very much appreciated that you have agreed to stand in at the last minute,' Annabel began. 'General Daubeney sends his personal thanks and good wishes.'

'Yes, well, one only ever hears from the Lord Chamberlain's Office when you people want something. One's become accustomed to that.'

'Well, it is greatly appreciated, sir. The Queen has been informed of your kindness, sir.'

'Yes, well. Let's get on with it then. Who do I need to butter up today?'

Annabel was midway through briefing HRH on the Tongan High Commissioner, who would attend the salute with three of his seven wives, when a female voice began calling from along the corridor. 'David? David?'

'Excuse me a moment.' Then walking to the door, 'Katharina? I have someone with me, I'm in the morning room.'

A couple of minutes later the door flew open, and there was Cath Fox, clutching a mug of coffee. She didn't see Annabel at first, and said, 'I've made a cafetière if you want a coffee. I'm off out. I don't know what's happened to the maid.'

'She doesn't come in on a Thursday. And, Katharina, this is Mrs Pilcher from the Lord Chamberlain's Office.'

Annabel and Cath stared at each other in surprise, until Cath replied, 'Oh David, we know each other. Annabel and I were at school together at St Mary's.'

Annabel shook hands with her old school matron who looked gorgeous, there was no other word for it, and ridiculously young, standing with her coffee on the Aubusson rug. 'It's lovely to see you. I think the last time was at Sotheby's.'

'Annabel and I were best mates at school, David,' Cath told the Duke. ' I used to stay with her family at their place in Cornwall. How is your lovely father?'

'Er, he's fine, thank you very much. Older these days, of course. But healthy.'

'Annabel's dad was the best-looking man, David. Tall and slim like you.' And she stood behind the duke's chair and smoothed his hair.

'Well, Katharina, Mrs Pilcher and I are in the middle of a meeting and need to get on. Shall I see you later?'

'I'm going over to St James's now, I need to do things at the flat, but I'll be back later. Nice to see you, Annabel. We should catch up sometime.'

Annabel left the duke's apartment in astonishment; it was all perfectly extraordinary. Only her natural discretion, and respect for her position, stopped her from telling anyone at all.

Chapter Forty-Two

Cath knew how good she was for David. Not only could she provide what he needed sexually, constantly feeding his kinky side and keeping him satisfied in bed, but she could help him in everyday life. For a start, there was the whole money thing. In the past, he'd been clueless, having no concept of his value in the marketplace. If a luxury Swiss watch brand offered him ten grand to turn up at their launch, he leapt at it, when he could have had fifty for the asking. With no one to negotiate on his behalf, he rolled over.

Cath appointed herself his agent, very discreetly of course – she wasn't doing brochures or a website or openly marketing him. But she put in a word here and a word there at the swanky dinners she went to with Randy, and it started to get out. A champagne marque was delighted to sign a six-figure contract to secure the duke as guest of honour at their polo day, as well as making two further personal appearances during the summer season. And a German car brand paid twice that to have him address their leadership summit in Hamburg, and attend an off-road driving day at Eastnor Castle for Eurozone dealerships. Everything Cath learned during her marriage to Ryan came back to help her, except you could push the fees more aggressively with a royal than a footballer. Only occasionally did David disappoint her, refusing point-blank to appear in a Patek Philippe watch advertisement, which could have set him up for years.

Most of the time he was touchingly grateful to her and daily more in her thrall, until he came to rely on her for almost everything. 'How would I manage without my little Princess Katharina?' he asked.

'I wouldn't mind being a princess, now you mention it,' she replied. 'Just kidding, sir. Obviously.'

But the idea of regularising her relationship with David did begin to take root. For all his wealth and all his efforts, Cath knew she'd never achieve top table status as the wife of Randy Jaworski, not like she got with David Shropshire. She loved being met in the foyer of the Opera House and personally escorted upstairs by the general manager, and sitting with David in the royal box, with everyone staring up at them from the stalls. And once, when David deputised for the Queen at an engagement in Newcastle, she travelled with him in a special carriage on the royal train. Truth to tell, the decor of the train disappointed her, being too plain and utilitarian, but it was a thrill nonetheless. Especially the way the train waited for them to board, and departed whenever it suited them.

A picture began to form in her mind of life after Randy. Obviously Randy was as rich as Croesus and she wasn't just going to walk away from all that empty-handed, was she? Not from a guy with a Gulfstream and a billion dollar bank balance, and all the art she'd chosen for him. The more she thought about it, the more she reckoned she'd helped him build his fortune anyway, advising him on his newspapers and TV stations, it had been a joint effort. So she was fully entitled.

And after that, their money troubles taken care of, she liked the idea of being a Her Royal Highness. It had a nice ring to it. 'Pleased to meet you, Your Royal Highness,' 'Step right this way, Your Royal Highness'. What was it they said on those hair colour commercials? 'Because you're worth it.' Well, Cath reckoned she was well worth it. She'd enjoy being curtsied to.

Without telling a soul, Cath made an appointment to visit the well-known divorce lawyer she kept reading about in the newspapers, who specialised in obtaining eye-watering payouts for the wives of rock stars and tycoons. The taxi dropped her outside a Georgian townhouse near Lincoln's Inn, where she waited in a reception like a Harley Street doctors' with piles of old magazines on a table. Some of the *Hello!*s were so ancient, she half expected to find her first wedding to Ryan James on the front cover.

Eventually she was shown to a meeting pod with nothing but a table and chairs and coffee and a plate of chocolate bourbon biscuits, and was joined by the celebrity lawyer, Angela Buchan, who looked exactly like she had in *OK* magazine standing on the steps of the courthouse with the brunette one out of Girls Aloud.

Angela could not have been more friendly, and seemed to know lots about her, having already Googled Randolph Jaworski and Jaworski Media and thus eager to represent her.

Cath explained about signing a prenup, but said she hadn't kept a copy of the document so didn't precisely know what it said. Angela didn't seem too worried. 'It sounds like you were pressured into signing something rather quickly. Unless you had full independent counsel who took you through it clause by clause, we can contest it. Do you remember when exactly it was you signed it?'

Cath shrugged. 'A few days before the wedding. Randy handed me these papers and I just signed them.'

'Did you read them first?'

'Hardly. He said "Sign there, babe" and I signed there. And I haven't clapped eyes on it since.'

'And you've played a big role in building up Jaworski Media? I noticed you're listed as editorial director on the corporate website.'

'Most of the best ideas have been mine. I repositioned all the newspapers, redesigned them, put in professional processes. I reckon I had to personally fire over a hundred people, not that I was keeping count. And Randy never paid me my market rate either, because of being his wife.'

'May I ask, does Mr Jaworski know you're seeing me today? He's aware you're considering embarking on proceedings?'

'No way. He'd go ape if he found out. He hasn't the first idea.'

'But your marriage has deteriorated. He must be aware of that? He accepts there are issues?'

'I hope not. I call him up every day, wherever he is in the world. And we still do the bedroom stuff, not that he's that bothered. He flew in for the weekend and I gave him a nice handjob Sunday morning.'

'But you are intent on going through with a divorce? I should warn you it can be a painful and protracted process, not to be undertaken lightly. I always ask my clients at the first meeting, "Are you absolutely sure?" If you decide to proceed, we will do our best to support you every step of the way, but only you can determine whether or not the marriage is irretrievable. I feel bound to say that.'

Cath stared down at the table. 'It's funny that,' she replied. 'I mean, Randy's a nice bloke, I'm not saying otherwise. And we do have good times together, going to dinners and in his plane and all that. But there's this other bloke, right, who'd better remain nameless because he's well-known, who I'd rather be with. But not if I can't get my fair shares out of Randy. What I mean is, if you can get round this prenup thing, and I end up with a hundred million quid in the bank or whatever, then that's what I want to do. But if you say "Sorry, Cath, that's a complete non-runner" . . . I mean Katharina, I mean Kathleen . . . that's a problem I'll have to think about. If you get where I'm coming from, Angela?'

'Perfectly, Mrs Jaworski. I think I understand the brief very clearly. And would be happy to represent you on those terms.'

Chapter Forty-Three

Jess was surprised to receive a peremptory phone call in the office, summoning her up to the corporate suite.

An authoritative female voice said, 'Is that Jess Eden? This is Ann Saltzman from Mr Jaworski's office. He would like you to join him immediately on the corporate floor.'

She took the lift upstairs wondering what she'd done wrong and fully expecting to be fired. 'You can go straight in,' said Ann Saltzman.

It was a relief to find Steve her boyfriend already there, along with a lady introduced as the corporate communications director of Jaworski Media. Across a vast mahogany desk sat the tiny brooding figure of Randy Jaworski, evidently in a foul mood.

'Thank you for joining us. I'm told by Steve here you're one of our red-hot young newshounds.'

'Er, well, I'm enjoying News.'

'I have an assignment for you. Steve has recommended you as his best person. I need to impress upon you this is a highly sensitive situation and somewhat personal in nature. Not a word can be shared with anyone else. Is that understood?'

'Er, yes, perfectly,' replied Jess. She felt oddly intimidated being in such close proximity to her ultimate boss and sensed his short fuse. Displayed in frames on his desk were aerial shots of his yacht and plane.

'OK, this concerns my wife of nine years, Kathleen. You may or may not be aware of her, she serves as a senior executive of this company and has played a small – factually very small – part in the expansion of the corporation . . .'

He paused and a look of fury suffused his face. 'Yesterday I received a communication from a firm of London solicitors, petitioning me for divorce. This was the first I had heard of any such idea. Furthermore, my wife is attempting to overturn a prenuptial agreement I had put in place to protect the viability of this corporation and the interests of my daughter Candy by my first marriage. An agreement which, may I say, Kathleen signed without coercion. From the tone of the letter, she plans to take me to the cleaners. She has made a number of statements relating to her role in the organisation which are inconsistent with the truth, and which I believe can quite easily be disproved . . . However, the fact of the matter is, I am now obliged to defend my interests and those of this organisation. Which is why I have asked you to join me this afternoon, so we may take the necessary steps.'

Still addressing Jess, he said, 'I've already told Steve I need to know everything there is to know about my wife . . . about Kathleen. Everything. From the moment she was born to what she ate for breakfast this morning. Who she's seeing, what she does all day, all of it. If you need to hire professional investigators, hire professional investigators. If you need to travel anywhere to follow up a line of enquiry, you can charge out-of-pocket expenses direct to this office. But no one is to know anything, is that understood? If any item appears in a newspaper, on a website, anywhere, being fired will be the least of your problems – you're going to wish you'd never been born. Now, Jess, I'm putting you onto this full-time, twenty-four seven. Steve's taking you off all other assignments to concentrate on it. Have you ever met Kathleen?'

'Not really but I've seen her here several times, getting into the car with you. And she used to be married to a footballer, Ryan James of Manchester United.'

'Yeah, sure, Kathleen was married to a football player, though that was over before I came along, at least that's what she always said . . . Good, you sound like a smart cookie. I want you to send me a confidential report once a week, keeping me informed. Everyone you've spoken to, anything you've found out, I want to know about it. Whatever it is, understood? Now, have you any questions you want to ask me?'

Jess thought for a moment. 'Well, if you have any background information, that would be useful. Such as, do you know where Mrs Jaworski was born or where she went to school, stuff like that? Or anything about her family? Don't worry, I'm not going to jump in with hobnailed boots, I'll be subtle. But anything to get me started.'

Randy sighed. 'You're going to think this strange but the fact is I've never known much about Kathleen's background. Maybe I should have asked more but she was never very forthcoming. I have no idea where she was born or raised. She never mentioned any particular city. Nor do I know anything about any family. I believe she mentioned attending college in Sussex . . . St Mary's, St Monica's . . . I forget, near a place named Petworth. And she was a board director at Imperial Magazines at one time. Beyond that, I don't know. She has a tattoo, several tattoos. One of a bug on her thigh, a spider's web on her back, and another on her arm saying "Callum". Though who Callum is or was, I cannot tell you. But I'm not doing your work for you. You're the investigator.'

'I'll get straight on it,' said Jess, feeling herself dismissed. 'My first report will be on your desk next Friday.'

'Christ,' said Steve, when they'd left the office and were safely in the lift. 'Sorry to have landed you in all that. The boss has totally lost it. Tying up the resources of the department to spy on his wife. Never cross a billionaire.'

'I'll remember that,' said Jess. 'Fancy a drink?'

Jess sat at her computer scrolling through hundreds of Google links for Kathleen Jaworski and Katie James.

The entries for Kathleen mostly related to Jaworski Media and social functions she'd attended as Randy's spouse. There was a short biog of her on the Jaworski corporate website alongside a nicely airbrushed portrait photograph, describing her as editorial director for the group with responsibilities on both sides of the Atlantic. It mentioned she'd begun her career at Imperial Magazines and consulted for South Midlands Newspapers. She served on various semi-social committees including the NSPCC development board and Friends of the Royal Academy.

Jess clicked her way through a dozen links to newspaper items, mainly in the gossip columns, saying Kathleen and Randy had been at this or that party or art exhibition. She'd certainly got around, Jess thought. There were photographs taken at the Frieze Art Fair, at Basle, at the Serpentine Gallery. There was a photograph of her and Randy standing on the steps of a magnificent Palladian country house,

Bletchingdon Park in Oxfordshire, accompanied by the multimillionaire chemicals tycoon and philanthropist Michael Peagram, as guests at a Tory fundraiser. Even a picture of her standing next to Gordon Brown at a Downing Street party.

She looked great in every shot too, from any angle. Jess was particularly intrigued by a link to *Houston Life*'s website and a long story about the Jaworski's mansion in Shadyside. Jess called Steve over to look at the pictures of them posing in full evening dress with their uniformed chefs and maids. 'She's like a modern day Marie Antoinette,' Jess said.

Later she found the old *Independent* profile of Kathleen, which Jess remembered reading at the time, but none of the articles gave much back story. Nothing about any family or her childhood or anything of that nature.

The Google entries for Katie James were more promising. All the old *Hello!* stuff was up there, loads of it. She must have featured in the magazine half a dozen times – the over-the-top celebrity wedding, the honeymoon, a housewarming party in Prestbury. Jess found it fascinating how much Kathleen/Katie had changed. She'd always been pretty, but the hair and make-up and the way she dressed was totally different since she'd met Randy and moved down to London. Seeing the old pictures took Jess back to her days in Buckinghamshire, when she and Bryony lived for the celeb weeklies, and she'd dreamt of one day having a wedding like Katie's herself. Now something that flash just seemed ridiculous. If she ever got hitched, to Steve or someone else, a register office job would do just fine, followed by a nice party for her friends. And Bob and Kirsty, obviously.

The wedding coverage gave Katie's maiden name as Katie Fox, which Jess then Googled and found several more stories, one or two of them referring to her as Cath Fox. It was rather confusing. And when she typed in the name Cath Fox, it threw up a link to the *Campaign* website which archived a mention of a Cath Fox taking over as Classified's manager at Imperial Magazines.

But the later stories all referred to her as Katie, once she'd hooked up with Ryan. The *Manchester Evening News* had mentioned her regularly at one point; it seemed she'd spent a lot of time with Ryan in Manchester pubs, which Jess couldn't really imagine, since Kathleen Jaworski didn't seem a pub sort of person. And Jess was fascinated to find a link to an old feature in *Manchester Life* which included Katie in a posed group of northern women looking really naff in designer hats. Jess thought Mrs Jaworski would die of embarrassment if that picture resurfaced anywhere. The accompanying article was as usual unforthcoming, saying nothing she didn't know already. Jess reckoned she'd have to pay a call on Ryan James, who'd surely be able to throw some light on it all. Jess thought Ryan looked rather fanciable in his wedding pictures and wondered whether he still did today. You didn't hear so much about Ryan James any more, now he'd been dropped from the Manchester squad. She made a note to track him down.

She went through the notes she'd made following her meeting with Randy, and wondered what to do next. She typed the words 'St Mary's School, Petworth' into the search engine and clicked through the site. It looked like a nice place. There were lots of photographs of happy, privileged-looking schoolgirls, studying in libraries and grooming ponies. Which reminded her: hadn't Mrs Pilcher mentioned she'd been at St Mary's? It rang a bell. Well, she was going over tomorrow to babysit Henry – childsit him, more accurately – she could ask Annabel then.

She also put in a call to Imperial Magazines and asked for their Classified department. A bit of a long shot, but nothing ventured . . .

The phone was answered by a dopey-sounding assistant who reacted to Jess's enquiry with scarcely disguised boredom. 'Caff Fox? Nah, we don't have anyone of that name in the department.'

'I said fifteen years ago. Not today. Is there anyone working there who might remember her?'

'Nah, I don't fink so. Sorry, I can't really ask around, we're short-staffed. There's this lurgy going round.'

'No one at all who was there fifteen years ago?'

'Not that I know of. Actually, my boss might have been, he's old. Do ya want me to ask him? What was the lady's name again?'

A minute later, a wary-sounding male voice came on the line. 'This is Dan Black, Classified's director. I understand you're asking about Cath Fox.'

'Yes, do you know her?'

'What's this in connection with?'

'I'm . . . an old friend of hers but we've lost touch. I'm trying to reconnect with her, and thought you might have a current contact.'

Dan replied sardonically, 'Well, good luck with that. I didn't think

Cath keeps up with old friends. She dropped us like hot bricks when she married Ryan James.'

'Were you a friend of Cath's then?'

'You could say that. She worked for me at one time and we, er, got on rather well. But she didn't invite me to the wedding. NFI – Not Effing Invited. She was moving on up, as the song goes.'

'I'd love to hear more. Would you be free to meet up for a drink one evening? Tonight or tomorrow?'

Dan sounded suspicious. 'What is this? You said you were a friend of Cath's?'

'The truth is, I'm writing an article about her. And I want to know about her true character, what she's really like. You sound like someone who knew her really well and might have interesting insights.'

There was a long pause. 'Well, I've got plenty to say, that's for certain. Plenty. And not much of it complimentary either. But whether I want to talk to you about her, that's another story. I can't have my name mentioned in print, they wouldn't like it – my employers, that is. One isn't permitted to speak to the press these days without clearing it first with the PR department. Only *directors* are *entitled* to speak to the press by edict from on high, which group does not include me, despite the millions and millions of pounds I've made for them over the years.'

About halfway through this diatribe, Jess became aware that Dan was half drunk.

'I've got a suggestion, Dan,' Jess said, speaking slowly and clearly. 'Let's have a drink together tonight at the American Bar at the Savoy hotel. They make the best cocktails in London. It will all be a hundred per cent off the record. I won't quote you or say anything which could be traced back to you. All I need is forty minutes of deep background. I appreciate it's a pain for you, so my newspaper will gladly pay you for your time. In cash. A hundred quid. And no mention of you at all. I give you my word.'

'Well, I have always liked the Savoy. Not that one's allowed to take anyone there any more. It's been put on the stop list by accounts.'

'I'll be paying,' said Jess. 'Meet you in the bar at six p.m. If you arrive first, order yourself whatever you want.'

Chapter Forty-Four

Jess arrived at ten past six, intentionally late, because she wanted Dan to get in a drink ahead of her to loosen him up further. As it turned out, he'd had two.

She found him well ensconced at a table, older in appearance than she'd expected, bloated around the jowls and wearing a suit in urgent need of a clean. 'You're her, are you?' he said. 'I'm afraid I forgot your name. I blame my PA, she never remembers a name or a phone number. Not that I remember her name either. Sharon? Shirley? I don't actually fancy her, which is a good thing or a bad thing, depending.'

'I'm Jess. Thanks so much for making time to see me at the end of a busy day.'

'Who says it was busy? I wish you'd tell that to the management consultants. We've got them *crawling* all over us. Again. And we know what they're going to say before they've even begun, because it's what they *always* say. Revenue generated by FTE – that's management speak for Full Time Employee – is lower in Classified than in Display. Well done Accenture! You've earned your million pound fee . . . again.'

Dan at this point lost his thread, so Jess jumped in: 'Tell me about Cath Fox. And order yourself another champagne. It is champagne?' She was confused by the mix of glasses on the table.

'I started with a martini, then moved to champagne and I think I would now like to revert to martinis, if you'd like to tell the chappie.'

'And Cath? She worked for you, you said?'

'This is all off the record, right? God, that girl was one fucking sexy, untrustworthy bitch. Cath Fox. She worked for me, did I mention that? I got her promoted, paid her an absolute fortune too. She was never satisfied. Whatever you paid her, it wasn't enough. And she tried to go above my head to Rich Scarsdale, and to Tony O'Flynn. She was after my job, you see. She was the most manipulative bitch I ever came across in my career, and I've seen a few. Fuck, was she good in bed though. Such a filthy bitch. Sorry, I don't mean to shock you.'

'Are you saying you had an *affair* with Cath Fox yourself?'

Dan took a long swig of his martini. 'Listen, Jill, it is Jill? Jess. Listen, Jess. None of this is going any further, can I trust you?'

'Absolutely.'

'I've got a wife at home, I don't mind admitting that, and she never knew anything about Cath, though it went on for more than a year. She was the best lay in town, Cath Fox. Bar none. Covered in tattoos. I remember the name on her arm: Callum. I used to hate that Callum and didn't have a clue who he was either. Incredible woman, Cath. Stunning. She would have married me too if I'd asked her but I never did because of Debs and the kids. Probably my mistake. You remind me of her, Jess, but Cath was better looking, no offence. Over the years I must have had a dozen girls from Classified, and some others, but none came close to Cath. Different league.'

'And do you know where she came from originally? I mean, which part of the country? Which town? Or anything about her family?'

'Nothing I can remember. I never met her folks. To be honest, most of our relationship was conducted in champagne bars. I was considered a high-flyer in those days, believe it or not. My expenses were never questioned. And then she went and ditched me for the footballer.'

'Which must have been painful?'

'Truthfully? Why should I have minded? I was her boss, it was only messing about. But I did resent the manner in which she did it. The minute she got her claws into the footballer, she was out of here. Resigned to HR and didn't work out her notice period. It caused a lot of problems for the department. If she reapplied for her old job tomorrow, I'd not take her back. Though she's the best salesgirl we ever had, I'll give her that.'

'But she did go further in the company, didn't she? I thought she became a board director?'

'*What?* Who told you that? She was my deputy, which many women would aspire to be. But Cath was never on the board of directors, no way.'

'And you've not seen her since she left Imperial?'

'Only her picture in magazines. They gave a big splash to her wedding, I saw that. A competitor got the exclusive on that one. Not that I cared. Who wants to look at a Classified slag in a celebrity magazine?'

'And having worked so closely with her, how would you sum up her personality in a few words?'

'Ambitious. Manipulative. Sex on legs. Does that help?'

'Perfect. Well, thanks, Dan. That's been very helpful.' She handed him two fifty-pound notes. 'Slip this into your pocket. And I'll settle the bill and leave you to finish up your drink.'

Annabel had been to the theatre with George and hurried back to relieve Jess from her babysitting. As usual, she found her hunched over her laptop at the kitchen table.

'Everything all right?' Annabel asked. 'Henry OK?'

'No problems. I helped him with his project for school, then we watched a bit of TV. He's a lovely guy.'

'Good. Well, we saw a very strange new play at the National. It was interesting but would have been just as good at half the length. All well in your life, Jess? Still seeing the boyfriend you told me about?'

'Steve's good, thank you. And there's something I want to ask you, if you've got a minute.'

'Sure.'

'You did say you were at St Mary's School, Petworth? Or have I got that wrong?'

'I was, yes. Years ago in the dim dark ages. Why?'

'I'm researching into someone I think may have been a contemporary of yours. Kathleen Jaworski? She'd have been called Cath Fox in those days. Does that ring any bells?'

Annabel found herself colouring. 'Good gracious, Cath Fox. Are you writing about her?'

Jess shrugged. 'Only researching at present. But I was wondering what she was like as a schoolgirl?'

'She wasn't actually at the school but I'm sure you already know that. She arrived as an assistant matron when I was in sixth form. They used to take on a few younger matrons each year to help with the laundry and so on. Mostly Australians or Kiwis. But Cath's English, of course.'

'Do you remember where she came from?'

'I do, actually. You see, we were all rather obsessed with her, we sheltered schoolgirls. We hadn't met anyone like Cath before, or Miss Fox as we called her. She used to tell us about life outside the school; she'd done all the things we longed to do ourselves.'

'Such as?'

'Oh, hanging out in nightclubs. Boys. Drinking. Miss Fox was quite worldly, we were always pestering her to tell us about low-life in Portsmouth.'

'That's where she came from, Portsmouth?'

'Yes. Sometimes she referred to it as Pompey. I can even remember the nightclub she used to tell us about: Nero's. She had a boyfriend who worked on the door as a security man, a bouncer.'

'Do you remember his name?'

'Absolutely. She had it tattooed on her arm: Callum. Unforgettable.'

'Did you ever meet him?'

'Never. The only men allowed through the gates of St Mary's were a couple of male teachers and the groundsmen. In any case, I think she'd split up from him before arriving at St Mary's. But she told us lots about Callum. Our ears were on stalks.'

'Such as?'

'Oh, how handsome he was. Actually handsome probably wasn't the right word. How muscular he was, all man. He sounded a bit of a womaniser and a bruiser. Always getting in fights.'

'And do you still keep in touch with her? With Cath?'

'No,' replied Annabel, feeling she'd said more than enough already. 'I'm afraid we lost touch long ago. But she was a breath of fresh air at St Mary's. I share a birthday with her, oddly enough, we're exactly the same age.' Annabel was too discreet to tell Jess about seeing Cath in Kensington Palace a few days earlier. And she certainly wasn't going to mention anything about Cath and her father; she wasn't digging any of that up.

So she just said, 'I think she married a footballer. I don't really follow football, but he was quite well known.'

'Ryan James,' said Jess. 'Yeah, I'm intending to interview him, once I've tracked him down.'

Jess spent the cab ride home planning her next few days. She had a lot of travelling to do: Manchester and now Portsmouth. And she had Cath's date of birth too. She was making progress.

Jess caught the train down to Portsmouth the next morning, trundling first through the prinked and manicured countryside between Guildford and Haslemere, then through open farmland and eventually a first glimpse of the sea beyond Southampton. She took a minicab from the station straight to the Portsmouth City Superintendent Registrar's office at Milldam House, Burnaby Road, where she'd made an appointment to consult their Life Events archive, which was the new PC name for births, deaths and marriages. To her delight, she located Cath's birth certificate quite quickly: *Catherine Tracey Fox. Father's name Gareth, occupation Unknown. Mother's name Pat, occupation Hospital Cleaner. Address, Flat 161 Gosport Mansions, Allaway Estate, Paulsgrove.* Yes! This was easier than she'd thought. On the off-chance, she cross-referenced Cath in the marriage register, but drew a blank.

She found a cab on Burnaby Road and asked for the Allaway estate, but the Indian driver didn't know it.

'Somewhere in Paulsgrove. Gosport Mansions? Take me to the area and we'll ask.'

'OK, but I don't know the name.' He drove on, speaking to radio control in Gujarati.

They arrived in Paulsgrove as it began to rain. The streets were deserted and the driver was unwilling to stop and ask. Jess wound down the window at traffic lights and called out to a fat boy in a hoodie, 'Gosport Mansions? Allaway estate?' But he shrugged and walked off.

A lady with a dog said sorry, she couldn't help. A Czech man said he was new here himself. She persuaded the driver to wait outside a pub while she asked for directions. The blonde behind the bar had never heard of Gosport Mansions, but the landlord had. 'It was knocked down years ago. They cleared that whole area, didn't they? Where the leisure centre is now, down past Mecca Bingo. They bulldozed it flat and started again.'

When Jess left the pub, the taxi had driven away and the rain become heavier.

She walked downhill through empty, decaying streets until she found another cab and asked to be taken to Nero's.

'Bit early for Nero's, isn't it?' said the driver. 'It doesn't open till after ten p.m.'

'I've got a meeting there,' Jess said. 'Is it a nice place?'

'Very popular,' he replied. 'Especially on a Friday and Saturday, it's heaving. Not that I'd let my daughter go there.'

'Why?'

'Very rough crowd at Nero's. It has a reputation, shall we say? You get a lot of trouble.'

They arrived outside the club, right on the seafront, but it looked closed. Some of the windows were covered with hardboard and wire grilles. The door was painted black and had no handle. But when Jess pushed against it, it opened.

Inside, the entrance stank of stale beer. The walls were painted black and purple, and she could see tables and a dance floor.

'You looking for someone?' A rat-faced youth was unpacking crates of soft drinks behind the bar.

'I'm looking for the manager,' Jess said.

'He's out.'

'Is he coming back soon?'

'Could be any time.'

'Maybe you can help me? I'm looking for anyone who was working here in the eighties. Twenty-five to thirty years ago.'

The youth made a face. 'Before I was born, sorry.'

'Can I buy a drink? Have one yourself if you want.'

'Sorry, bar's not open. Till's locked.'

Jess was wondering what to do when an older bloke in leather jerkin and jeans turned up. A few strands of lank black hair were combed across an otherwise bald pate.

'Here he is now,' said the youth. 'This lady's looking for you, Mick.'

'Yeah?' Mick turned to Jess. 'She is?'

'I'm Jess Eden. I'm looking for anyone who's been working at Nero's a long time.'

'Why? We've got all our permits and licences. If you're from the council, we've had it up to here with you people.'

'No, I'm not from the council. I'm writing an article about a lady who used to come here years ago in the mid-eighties.'

'You'll be lucky. We get a thousand people through the door sometimes. Well, who is she then?'

'Cath Fox.'

He made a face. 'Oddly enough, I do remember someone of that name. Cath . . . sexy little piece, bit of a scrubber. And what's it to you? What's she done?'

'Nothing. I just want to know about her. What was she like?'

'I thought you were going to say she'd gone and topped someone. Or been done for running a vice racket.'

'Nothing like that. But you did know her then?'

'Wouldn't say I knew her exactly. But she came here. She was Callum's bird, wasn't she? It's coming back. Yeah, she was with Callum, on and off.'

'Is Callum still around?'

'He worked here until seven, eight years ago. On the door. Useful bloke in a place like this. Any trouble and he sorted them out.'

'But he's left? Is he still in Portsmouth, do you know?'

'Haven't seen him in ages. Sorry, can't help you. He was working Saturdays up at Fratton Park, at the football stadium at one time. Last thing I heard he'd gone to London or overseas or something.'

'And Cath? She hasn't been back recently?'

He yawned. 'I doubt I'd even recognise her if she walked through the door. Well, goodbye now.'

'Oh, final question, what is Callum's surname?'

'You ask too many questions. If you are from the council, or the police, just fuck off and stop snooping about.'

Jess decided it was time to go.

Chapter Forty-Five

It proved more difficult to track down Ryan James than Jess had expected. Manchester United was unhelpful and wouldn't give her a contact number, and it seemed he'd sold his place out in Prestbury – the mansion featured in *Hello!* – some years ago. She rang the distributors of his aftershave, Kick for Men, on a trading estate in Slough, but was told the brand had been discontinued. No one seemed to know how to get hold of Ryan.

Eventually she rang a friend on the *Manchester Evening News*, who she remembered from her uni days, who asked the sports desk. 'He's really gone to ground,' she was told. 'Nobody's seen or heard from him in ages. But I've found a number for his parents in Wythenshawe if that helps.'

Jess dialled the number and it was answered by a garrulous Mancunian woman who was pleased to talk, especially when Jess asked for Ryan. 'You're not a new lady in his life, are you?' she asked.

'Er, no. I just need to speak to him.'

'Shame. I hoped you were. Well, you should meet him. He's ever so nice looking is our Ryan.'

'And you're his mum?'

'Barbara, that's right. And who might you be, luv, if you don't mind me asking?'

'I'm Jess. Jess Eden. I work for a newspaper down in London and need Ryan's help with something.'

'Oh, I'm so glad. They used to put him in the newspapers all the time. I keep all his publicity, you see, I stick them in my books. But there's not been so much about him lately.'

'Well, Barbara, it's not actually Ryan I'm writing about today. In fact, you might be able to help me here too. I'm researching his ex-wife, Katie. If you have any thoughts on her.'

There was an intake of breath. 'I see. You're interested in Katie. Well, that's not a name I like to hear. I'm not sure I want to talk about that one at all.'

'So you didn't get along with Katie?'

'No I did not! I wouldn't like to tell you half of what I think about her, the things she did to Ryan. Ruined his life. Don't get me started. I never liked her right from the start, I warned Ryan about her, but he wouldn't listen. You ask Alf, that's my other half, he's heard me often enough. Thank goodness they didn't have kids, that's all I can say. Good riddance.'

'And where can I find Ryan? I tried his Prestbury home but was told he's moved.'

'Of course he has! Katie made him sell his house and took most of his money too. He paid for that place, every penny. But she ended up with the lot. Where's the justice in that?'

'So where does Ryan live now then?'

'Back where he was before in Altrincham. Same block too but smaller than his previous place. Whether he'll speak to you, I can't say. I can ask him. He's not been well lately, not since they dropped him from the squad. And I know who to blame too. She spat him out and took him for everything. He's not been the same since.'

'So you'll ask Ryan then? I'd love to come and see him tomorrow afternoon. Thanks a lot for helping, Barbara.'

'I said I'll call him. No promises, mind. I don't know if you're planning on speaking to Katie, but if you do, you can tell her from me not to come anywhere near Manchester. Not if she knows what's good for her she won't.'

On the train up to Manchester Piccadilly, Jess made some further calls. These were to find two of the ladies who'd appeared with Cath in *Hello!*, both maids of honour at her wedding and later at the house-warming. Anita and Hayley were reportedly partners of Ryan's old teammates, Wayne Corrigan and Midge Long, and seemed to have been Cath's best girlfriends. They might know something about her, from a different perspective to her exes.

As it turned out, both ladies had long ago split up from their beaus. Anita was believed to have married a builder from Essex and was now living out in Spain, near Malaga. But Hayley was still in Manchester, partner to the owner of cocktail bars and brasseries in the redeveloped Canal Street area. Jess got hold of her easily enough, and Hayley said she'd be happy to meet Jess for a coffee at Violettes.

'I haven't seen Katie in years, though,' Hayley said on the phone. 'I heard she's with some American multibillionaire with a private plane.'

'Something like that. See you later, Hayley.'

'See ya, Jess.'

Jess took a cab from the station to Ryan's apartment block, all glass and balconies, and pressed the intercom. Barbara had warned her Ryan sometimes took a while to respond, 'but he says he'll see you, luv. I told him you sound like a nice lass.'

Eventually she was buzzed in and took the lift to the fourth floor, down a long corridor, through several fire doors, to Ryan's front door. It was opened by a thin-looking man with hedgehog hair, less handsome than Jess had expected, wearing a grey pullover and tracksuit bottoms. His appearance struck her as unwell.

'Ryan? I'm Jess.'

He stared at her in shock. 'Er, hiya, Jess, yeah, come in. Sorry, you reminded me of someone there for a moment.'

'Really? Who's that?'

'Doesn't matter. Like a coffee or something?' He seemed uneasy around her.

She followed him into a small galley kitchen with views across a car park. 'Sorry, it's a bit of a mess. Me mum's coming over tomorrow to clean up.' Pine counters were strewn with the remains of breakfast and the cardboard packaging from micro-meals. He hunted about in a cupboard for coffee granules. Jess spotted them on the counter and took over boiling the kettle. 'I'll do it.' She fixed coffee and they went together into a small lounge filled with over-large leather furniture. Various framed team photographs hung on the walls. Through the open door to the bedroom she spotted a StairMaster and Cybex weight training apparatus.

'So, I think your mum told you I'm doing some research into Katie. It may lead to an article or it may not, it's not decided. I just want to ask you about her, get a feel for what she's like as a person.'

Ryan nodded. 'I bet my mum had a right go at her, didn't she? They never got along, Katie and me mum.'

'All mothers are like that, aren't they?' Jess laughed. 'Protective of their own.'

'Yeah, s'pose. There was never any love lost there.'

'And what about you, Ryan? You loved her and lost her . . .'

'Yeah, well. She didn't behave very nicely, I have to say that. Thing is, I never knew what happened. One minute she was here and we was married and all that, the next she'd gone. She didn't say nothing. Next thing I know I'm getting these letters from lawyers down in London telling me I've got to sell the house and all.'

'It must have been very upsetting. But I don't know how you guys met in the first place?'

'Oh right, it was at a club. I forget the name of the place now, down in London somewhere. It's on a rooftop with gardens and that. They have them pink birds up there, like ostriches.'

'Flamingos? The Roof Gardens in Kensington?'

'That's it. I remember thinking "There's a cracking looking bird," and we got dancing and, well, that was it. And then she came up to Manchester and moved into my flat.'

'And what was Katie like?'

'Well to be fair, she was a great bird. Good fun to be with. Very fit. Great in the sack, and I knew what I was talking about in them days too. Nice tits. Pretty face. She looked a bit like you, in fact. Don't get me wrong, I'm not being funny. But you do look quite like her – I thought that when you arrived.'

'And what about her family?'

He shrugged. 'Never met them. They never came to our wedding or anything.'

'Previous boyfriends?'

'She didn't talk much about anything like that. She'd been with a bloke called Callum, I know that. She had this tattoo.'

'I've heard about her tattoos.'

'Yeah, she had my initials put on her back: RJ. That was a nice gesture. Not that it did me much good.'

'But you were happy together for a while?'

'Oh yeah, we had some great times. We used to go to this club over in Prestbury, Millionairz 'n' Playerz, it's still going I think. And she came to all my games, most of them anyway.'

'And this Callum guy. Did you ever meet him?'

'Never.'

'Any idea how I can get hold of him?'

'None. He worked at some nightclub, I think Katie said.'

'Nero's?'

'That's it, Nero's. But I never met Callum.'

'Cheers, Ryan. That's all been very helpful.'

At the door to his flat, he asked, 'Are you going to be seeing her? Katie, I mean?'

'I don't think so. I don't know.'

'Because if you do, say the name Ryan to her, will you? Tell her there's no hard feelings. And I'd like to meet up with her sometime, just for a drink for old times' sake. Nothing else. That's if she's ever in the area. Will you tell her that?'

'I certainly will, if we ever meet.'

'I'd appreciate it. Thanks, Jess. Oh, and don't tell my mum what I just said, will you? She'd do her nut if she heard that. She hates Katie, won't hear a good word about her.'

She identified Hayley at once, perched on a stool at the steel-fronted bar, black leather miniskirt, long red nails, sunbed brown and a cascade of fuck-me-please hair. From a distance she looked exactly as she had in Cath and Ryan's wedding pictures; closer up, her face bore the pinched, plastic sheen of cosmetic surgery.

'So, you want to know about Katie?' Hayley said. She ordered a fresh double espresso for herself from a barman in leather shorts, and a cappuccino for Jess.

'Thanks for meeting me,' Jess said. 'And this is your restaurant, is it, Violettes?'

'It's my partner's place, I virtually live here. You should meet Kabir. He's got six places in Manchester now. Drives a black Porsche.'

'Cool,' said Jess.

'To be honest, I never saw myself with an Asian gentleman but we get on really well. After Midge cheated on me and all that ended, I thought, well, why not? He's a successful bloke. You should put him in your newspaper.'

'Maybe we should. But you were saying about Katie . . .'

'What do you want to know about her? As I said on the phone, I haven't seen her in ages. Once she left Ryan, that was it, none of her mates ever heard another word. She'd met this billionaire American.'

'But you were close friends before then?'

'You kidding? We called each other up every day, met up for coffees, shopping, girls' lunches. Katie, Anita and me, we was like this little gang, three naughty girls about town. We were all in relationships with football players and had a whale of a time. They loved us in the boutiques because when the new designer handbags came in, we were like, "Right, I'm having that one, that one's mine, you have that one, Katie, you have that one, Anita," we were terrible. She was a great girl, Katie. I miss her. I was maid of honour at her wedding and we was all over *Hello!*. I'd like to catch up with her again and have her meet Kabir. I've told him about her and how we was best mates.'

'And what about boyfriends? Before Ryan, I mean. Did she ever mention anyone?'

'It's funny, she was always quite secretive, now you mention it. She didn't say a lot, not like some people who never leave off talking about their exes. There was one bloke she mentioned: Callum. She'd been with him when she'd lived down south. Portsmouth she came from originally. She used to make us laugh, talking about him. She said he was the ugliest bloke with cauliflower ears and a broken nose. But he must have had something, mustn't he? Wonder what that was?' And she roared with laughter.

'Did you ever meet him? Callum, I mean?'

'Never. But it's funny you should say that because I did wonder whether I'd seen him the one time. This was in Portsmouth, I'd gone to watch Midge play in an away game. And Katie was talking to this big bloke like a security guy, and it looked like they knew each other before. They seemed to be having a right ding-dong about something. And he looked just like she'd described Callum, all muscles and shaven head. But she didn't introduce him. I remember thinking at the time, "I bet that's Callum."'

'And what about her family? Did she ever talk about them?'

'I'm trying to remember. I think she said she had kid brothers, I'm fairly sure she said that. And her dad, of course. He sounded like bad news. She only mentioned him the one time. We'd been having lunch in this Italian place – Katie, Anita and me – and we were talking about our childhoods growing up and Katie suddenly said, "I never knew my dad that well, he was usually inside, doing time." She said he'd been in and out of prison all through her childhood. She'd never said anything about it before, and never did again. It was probably the wine. We were really into Chardonnay in them days, it was all we drank, that and bubbles.'

On the train back to London, Jess wrote up her notes and drafted her first promised report for Randy Jaworski. She found it rather difficult to know what to put. Randy had told her to include everything, but it was awkward. She was hardly going to tell her ultimate boss that his wife was 'such a filthy bitch' – Dan Black, and 'A bit of a scrubber' – Mick, manager of Nero's.

So she listed her interviews and the various people she'd spoken to in Portsmouth and Manchester, and the details of Cath's birth certificate from the Portsmouth archive.

It appears Mrs Jaworski may not have been a board director at the Imperial Magazines Group, she wrote, *but I need to check that out further.*

Later she wrote, *There is an unsubstantiated rumour Mrs Jaworski's father may have served time in a British correctional facility.*

Having finished the report, she addressed it to Ann.Saltzman@jaworskimedia.com, pressed Send and headed home to Steve for the weekend with a sigh of relief.

Chapter Forty-Six

Jess spent most of Saturday morning in bed with Steve. Steve's idea of a perfect Saturday was to drink his way through a pot of coffee in bed, read the newspapers, fuck, and eat a plate of waffles with bacon and maple syrup . . . in that order. Afterwards, they had a long hot bath together. Steve liked to smoke cigarettes with the ashtray balanced on the bath rack. Sometimes he got through three of four fags in a single bath, which Jess considered his sole truly disgusting habit.

Steve got dressed in his trademark jeans and long black overcoat, and set off to watch his son, Danny, play football in a schoolboy league in Dulwich, close to his ex-wife's place. The existence of Danny, and the fact that Steve was in his late forties, were two reasons Bob and Kirsty could never quite approve of him. Whenever Jess saw her parents on her own, on home visits to Long Barton, they asked whether she was still seeing Steve, and Jess knew how happy she'd make them if she ever replied no.

But she had no plans to leave Steve. No plans to marry him, no plans to split up from him, no plans period, which is why their relationship worked. Jess loved being with Steve because he'd done so much in his life and been to so many interesting places and knew stuff. He'd been a reporter on music magazines and toured the States with bands like Pulp and Oasis. He'd lived in Cambodia and Tehran working on English language newspapers. He'd had a contract with the *Independent* before joining Jaworski Media as chief news reporter, which was where Jess had met him, in the aftermath of his failed marriage. He was the most relaxed, laid-back guy she'd ever been with, except when he was working on a big story when a different side to him came through, resourceful and obsessive. Jess knew she'd learnt a massive amount from Steve about how to research and construct real journalism.

Jess would have the whole afternoon to herself, since Steve wouldn't be back until the evening. It was his habit to take Danny out for a hamburger after the game, or sometimes a movie. Sundays she normally had Steve to herself, though tomorrow she was making him come with her to Long Barton for lunch on a long-standing engagement. She wanted Bob and Kirsty to get to know him better and like him better; that was the objective. But now the day was almost upon them, Jess was rather dreading it and wished she'd never suggested it.

She was wondering what to do with herself that Saturday afternoon when she saw an email ping on to her computer. It was from Randy Jaworski, not even sent by his PA, but direct from his BlackBerry. The message was full of typos. *Thanks for your breif report, nice start. Pls follow up on new info you mention. Two other leads – K was once engagged to an older guy – Lord Blaydon/Baydon? Big place in Nottingshire. Check that out. Also K is friends with some royal – David Duke of Shropshire. What are they up to? I am in transit between Chicago and Houston but my office can locate me. RJ*

Jess sat at her computer and searched for both Lord Blaydon and Lord Baydon. The Blaydon title was reportedly extinct, having terminated with the death twenty years earlier of Charles Blaydon, the thirteenth Lord Blaydon of Blaydon Hall in Northamptonshire. Jess clicked onto his obituary in the *Daily Telegraph* archive and skimmed through it. No mention of Cath Fox, though there had been a wife, Betty (née Throckmorton) who predeceased Lord Blaydon by eighteen years. In his photograph, Charlie Blaydon looked like a typical old toff in trilby hat with a watery eye. Could Cath really have been engaged to him? It seemed unlikely; he looked a hundred years old. His obituarist described him as a backwoods Tory peer, a former Deputy Lord Lieutenant of Northamptonshire, educated at Eton and Corpus Christi, Oxford, a member of White's Club. In later years he was reported to have become a partial recluse, living virtually alone at his hundred-room house, designed by Hawksmoor.

She typed in Blaydon Hall, hoping to find a photograph, and was surprised to discover it was now a hotel. The Blaydon Hall Spa Hotel and Golf Club, according to its snazzy website, promised the highest recreational facilities as well as a conference centre and spa treatments, including hot stone massage. There were photographs of golfers in golf carts parked in front of the enormous façade of the house, and a sommelier pouring wine in the hotel dining room. The hotel was part of the Von Essen luxury hotels group and apparently no longer belonged to the Blaydon family.

Jess returned to the obituary, this time reading it more carefully. Lord Blaydon's sole heir had been a daughter, the Hon. Rosemary Savill, who Jess promptly Googled and struck gold. A Rosemary Savill was named as a former Hon. Sec. of the Chelsea Ladies Luncheon Club, which met monthly at the Sloane Club in Lower Sloane Street. She was married to Hugh Savill, a retired solicitor. Her address was given as a flat in Warwick Square, Pimlico, and furthermore her telephone number wasn't withheld.

'Hello, please may I speak to Mrs Savill?'

'Who is this please?' The voice down the phone was peremptory.

'My name is Jess Eden, I'm calling you because . . . '

But the voice cut in. 'I hope you're not trying to sell me anything? I don't speak to cold callers, I'm sorry.'

'I'm not a cold caller, Mrs Savill. I need to talk to you about something important to do with your late father, Lord Blaydon.'

Now Jess had her attention. 'About Papa? What about him?'

'I think it would be easier if I talked to you in person, Mrs Savill. Would it be convenient for me to come round today?'

'On a *Saturday*? At the *weekend*? I call that most odd.'

'I have some information about someone called Cath Fox.'

There was a sharp intake of breath. 'Well, I suppose so. We are here this weekend. You may come after tea at five o'clock.'

Jess had never been in such a grand flat before. It occupied the first and second floors of a high-ceilinged stucco mansion on a garden square, with four long windows in the drawing room. Every inch of space was crammed with antique furniture and paintings, many of them vistas of the stately home Jess recognised as Blaydon Hall.

'What amazing things you've got here,' Jess said, looking around her.

'They're just family bits and pieces,' said Rosemary Savill. 'Mostly from Blaydon or from my father's flat in Chelsea.' Rosemary stared suspiciously at the young girl in jeans and a Peruvian jacket. She was pretty enough but scruffily dressed and her hair was a mess. She couldn't imagine what she might want.

Jess perched on the edge of an uncomfortable sofa, facing Mr and Mrs Savill who sat in armchairs.

'Well?' said Mrs Savill.

'Thank you for agreeing to see me,' Jess began. 'I wanted to talk to you about Cath Fox – I'm researching her for a possible article I'm writing.'

'You're not a *journalist*, are you?' said Hugh. 'We would never have invited a journalist into our home. You should have said.'

'I'm sorry, but it's in connection with Lord Blaydon. I think he was a friend of Cath Fox.'

Rosemary's pug eyes bulged and her lips pursed. 'No, I can correct you there. My father was *never* a friend of Miss Fox. Miss Fox was *in service*, she was my father's nurse. He became rather old and frail towards the end of his life, and Miss Fox was one of the team of ladies who took care of him.'

'I see. And can I ask what she was like?'

'Good heavens, she was my father's nurse. I hope you'll forgive me when I say one didn't take all that much notice of her, not as a person, one simply hoped she did her job properly, for which she was paid. I'm not sure I could tell you anything about her.'

'I heard she became engaged to Lord Blaydon and they were going to get married.'

'Stuff and nonsense. Absolute rubbish. I don't know where you heard that but it simply isn't true. Tell her it isn't true, Hugh.'

'My wife's absolutely right, there's no substance to that whatever. And if you ever say so in print, we shall sue you *and* your newspaper. I was a lawyer for forty years so I know what I'm talking about.'

'OK, but I did hear—'

'I don't mind *what* you've heard. I'm telling you now, quite categorically, that Lord Blaydon was not of sufficiently sound mind to become engaged to anyone, let alone his twenty-year-old nurse. No court in the land would dispute that.'

'But it sounds like they did at least have a special friendship?'

'*No!*' exclaimed Rosemary. 'I will not have that said. I cannot allow that. Miss Fox and my father had nothing in common, nothing whatever. We recognised what sort of person she was at once, we saw straight through her. Papa became lonely in his old age and she took advantage of that. All his lovely real old friends were dying, one by one. And that manipulative minx took full advantage, fluttering her eyelids and making herself agreeable.'

'How did they even meet? Was she sent by a nursing agency?'

'If only we *had* used an agency. No, my father suffered from mild arthritis and used to visit a health clinic close to White's, his club. Somewhere in Pall Mall. I don't know where exactly. They used to massage his hands and legs. And that's where he came into contact with that girl. She was employed as a therapist, apparently.'

'And you haven't kept in touch with her since your father's death?'

'Gracious, no. She's not on our Christmas card list, I can assure you. There was a photograph of her in the newspaper years ago, with a football player. Which was about her level. I hope we shall never see nor hear from her again. And my husband is quite right. You will not, repeat *not*, include my father's name in any newspaper article. Is that understood? You do not have our permission.'

Jess and Steve travelled up to Long Barton by train, Bob collecting them both from the station. It was one of Steve's eccentricities that he wilfully refused to drive, and Jess couldn't afford to keep a car in London. Bob, recently retired, kept himself busy helping organise his former company's staff sports programme, as well as sports and social activities for other retired alumni. He said he was currently planning a fun run for all ages 'eight to eighty' in aid of Help for Heroes, and was busy as ever. Kirsty, meanwhile, was on the steering group for a Long Barton Royal Wedding street party being planned for Prince William and Kate Middleton's wedding in April. Kirsty did not entirely approve of the Royal Family but all proceeds were going to Stoke Mandeville hospital, so she was swallowing her principles.

Whenever Jess returned home to Burdock Cottage, she was struck by how unchanged her childhood house was. Bob had recently extended the garage to incorporate a small workshop, but otherwise it was identical. Jess could have sworn the fridge magnets hadn't moved one centimetre in twenty years. She recognised every scratch on the worktops in the kitchen and the burn mark on the lino where she'd spilled hot cooking oil half a lifetime ago.

Bob and Kirsty were, as ever, thrilled to see their daughter of whom they were so proud. They half hoped she might one day find a job on a Jaworski local newspaper closer to home but recognised she was enjoying life up in town, even though the media world, and particularly the new media world of internet and iPad and heaven knows what else, remained a mystery to them. Bob took the *Guardian* but couldn't see himself reading it on a computer, which he used only for email and eBay.

'So, still working hard at your newspaper, are you, Jess?' Bob asked. 'Getting your name in lights, I hope?'

Jess laughed. 'I dunno about lights. But I'm writing lots, for print and digital. Lots of London stories.'

'And your bosses like them, I hope?'

'You'll have to ask Steve that, won't you? He's my boss.'

'Ah yes,' said Bob doubtfully. 'Well, I hope that doesn't create any difficulties. Because of your . . . friendship, I mean. Most big companies don't like it.'

'I'm sure it's fine,' Jess said. 'Steve, tell Dad about the political stories you're working on, he'll be interested,' and Steve told Bob how Jaworski Media was viewing the new coalition government. Randy Jaworski had a lot of time for David Cameron but hoped his policies wouldn't get sabotaged by his Liberal partners. Steve added that personally he had voted Labour at the last election but without his old conviction, feeling they'd lost their way, and he was now afraid they'd lurch further to the left which could only lead to a generation out of power. Bob, however, found himself becoming annoyed by his daughter's clever, articulate, over-sophisticated, too-old, previously married lover, and declared that Labour should return to its working class roots without delay and start sticking up for the working man again rather than cosying up to the rich and to the newspaper owners. The more reasonable Steve was in his arguments, the more agitated Bob became. It took all the combined efforts of Kirsty and Jess to calm him down, before they went through to the kitchen to eat.

Over lunch, Jess watched Steve do his best to present himself as a desirable human being, but Bob and Kirsty picked him up on whatever he said. When he spoke of his job, Bob said, 'I always think journalism's such an unpredictable business. One minute you're cock of the walk, the next you're out of a job. I'd have hated the uncertainty myself. Not the sort of life where you can settle down and start a family.'

'You're right,' Steve replied. 'The media's unpredictable. That's what keeps you on your toes. But I'd rather that than a thirty year sentence as a salaryman in a multinational.'

'I was at Glaxo for thirty-one,' said Bob, taking umbrage. 'And a perfectly good life it was too, most of the time.'

'I didn't mean that,' Steve replied, rapidly backpedalling. 'I'm not dissing Glaxo. I'm just saying there's a lot of variety in the media and it helps keep you young.'

Kirsty nodded, but with an expression which said, 'Not young enough.'

'Anyway,' Steve went on, 'it's great seeing Jess's childhood home. She often talks about this place and I can see why, it's an attractive part of the country.'

In fact, Jess seldom spoke of Burdock Cottage. She loved her adoptive parents but had never especially liked Buckinghamshire.

'Oh yes,' said Bob. 'I always say we have the best of both worlds here. If you want peace and quiet or a nice country walk, you've got it all on your doorstep. But if it's the high life you're after, you've got Leighton Buzzard and Milton Keynes. And you can be in central London in an hour if you choose the right train.'

Bob had been following the recent phone-hacking scandals and quizzed Steve on how much of it had gone on at Jaworski Media.

'I'm not actually aware of any,' Steve replied. 'Our papers are positioned slightly differently, more comment and journalism, fewer exposés.'

'Oh, I'm sure they're all saying that now,' said Bob. 'I've heard the whole of the media was rife with it from top to bottom.'

'Not at Jaworski. Isn't that right, Jess? You've not come across any phone hacking?'

Jess agreed she had not, but Bob looked unconvinced. 'That's how they get half their stories, listening in on people's private conversations. They call it journalism but there's nothing very clever about it. Whatever happened to old fashioned *reporting*, I ask myself?'

'Actually, Dad, I've been doing old-fashioned reporting, as you call it, all week. Trawling through records offices, tracking people down in Manchester and Portsmouth, travelling all over the place.'

'Then I take my hat off to you,' said Bob. 'What's the story you're working on?'

'I'm afraid I can't tell you. Sorry, Dad. I'm sworn to secrecy. But it involves trying to find out about someone, a lady, very rich, and her secret life story. She's a bit of an enigma and a gold-digger, been with lots of different men, all yachts and private planes. So that's what I'm up to, good old-fashioned reporting.'

'She sounds horrible,' said Kirsty. 'I don't understand how women like that can face themselves in the mirror in the morning, living off men in that unscrupulous way. Where's their self-respect? Where are their feminist principles?'

'You're right, Mum. But maybe she wasn't taught any better. Her family sounds quite rough, her dad in and out of prison. She was brought up poor. So it's quite a journey she's been on, like the heroine in a Victorian novel.'

'Well, one shouldn't be judgemental,' Kirsty said. 'But I wouldn't be happy if you ever did that, jumping from one sugar daddy to another.'

'No danger of that,' Jess replied, laughing. 'Steve may not be twenty-five but I don't think you could exactly be described as a sugar daddy, could you, Steve?'

Chapter Forty-Seven

Jess spent a frustrating morning at her computer in the office, trying to locate the elusive Callum. But without a surname there was little to go on, and after an hour she'd achieved very little, beyond flicking through websites for companies supplying security and close protection.

Instead, she decided to read up on HRH the Duke of Shropshire, who Randy Jaworski had mentioned was a friend of Kathleen's. Having been raised in a household with little interest in the Royal Family, Jess was rather vague about them herself. She knew about the main ones, of course, like the Queen and Prince Charles, and Princes William and Harry, but once you got onto the minor ones, the second and third cousins, she didn't have a clue.

David Shropshire was a handsome guy, she could see that at once. A bit arrogant with a superior expression on his face, but well dressed and fit looking. She scrolled through several hundred photographs on Google Images of the duke at parties, on polo fields, at Trooping the Colour wearing full military uniform and medals. There were several pictures of him cutting ribbons at official functions, but mostly he was out socialising. He always wore wonderfully tailored suits with a silk handkerchief spilling from his breast pocket.

In several of the most recent pictures, Cath was photographed standing alongside him. They'd evidently been spending a lot of time together. Sometimes Cath was tagged in the captions, sometimes not, but you could spot her in the background two steps behind him, arriving at the opera and visiting the Chelsea Flower Show. Cath certainly looked relaxed in his company, almost proprietorial in some pictures.

Jess clicked her way through royal and genealogical websites trying to figure out the duke's lineage but became confused by his German,

Danish and Prussian ancestors. The Queen seemed to be his cousin through Queen Victoria, and he'd been married to, but was divorced from, some princess from the Balkans. It mentioned on www.royal.gov.uk that HRH the Duke of Shropshire would tomorrow evening be opening an exhibition of Sèvres porcelain at the Wallace Collection in Manchester Square, and Jess made a mental note to be there: it would be interesting to see him in the flesh, and Cath might be there too. She rang the Wallace Collection Press Office who agreed to bike over an invitation for her at Jaworski Media.

At lunchtime, on a whim, she decided to try and track down the health clinic that Rosemary Savill had spoken about, the one where Cath had apparently worked as a therapist and first met Lord Blaydon. She strolled up Whitehall, crossed Trafalgar Square, and up on to Pall Mall. Chances were the place would have shut down years ago, but it was a crisp spring afternoon, the sun was shining, and you never knew your luck.

She walked past the Institute of Directors and up past the façades of several imposing gentlemen's clubs. She'd heard that very few of them accepted women as members, which struck her as outrageously sexist – not that she wished to join, even if she could. When she reached St James's Palace, having passed nowhere remotely resembling a health club, she crossed Pall Mall and retraced her steps on the opposite side. Here there were wine merchants, fishing tackle shops and companies chartering yachts, but no health clinics. Then, in the window of a townhouse, she spotted a sign for the Pall Mall Steam and Fitness Club.

A dingy flight of stairs led down to a basement and Jess wondered if she was in the right place. It didn't seem the sort of joint Lord Blaydon would have frequented. She arrived in a long, low room with a reception desk and black leather settees. Half a dozen ladies in white spa tunics were sitting about awaiting clients, and an older lady with peroxide hair looked up from behind a bar. 'Can I help you, dearie?'

'I was, er, just passing. I saw the sign and wanted to see what it's like down here.'

'That's all right, dearie. No need to be shy. I'm Mona, by the way, I'm the manageress. And you've come at a good time because we *are* hiring.'

Two men in towelling robes padded past from the locker room to the sauna, and Mona called out, 'Don't be too long in there, Tony. I'm giving you Katrin in cabin nine.'

'Thanks, Mona,' replied Tony, eyeing up Jess with a greedy stare. 'Is she a new girl?' he asked, nodding at Jess.

'You behave, you,' warned Mona.

Returning to Jess, she asked, 'Ever worked in a place like this before, dearie?'

Jess shook her head. 'Actually I'm not looking for a job.'

'They all say that when they first come in,' Mona replied. 'You'll get the hang quick enough. The girls will show you. Anyway, you're a grown-up lass, it won't be anything to shock you. How old are you anyway?'

'I'm twenty-nine.'

'Gracious, I thought you were younger. Well, you can say you're twenty-two if anyone asks, which they will. Magda? Come over here a minute, I want to introduce you to, er . . .'

'Jess,' said Jess.

'Jess then. That's nice, we haven't got a Jess at the moment. Magda's an old hand, she'll take you under her wing. I give all my new girls to Magda. She gets the biggest tips, the gentlemen love Magda and her special tricks. The older ones especially. She always gets the oil pumping,' and she cackled at her joke.

Jess felt more shocked all the time. The place was a virtual brothel. She couldn't believe Mrs Jaworski had once worked here, sat on those leather sofas, and done that sort of thing. And what about Lord Blaydon? Pug-faced Rosemary Savill would die if she ever found out.

'I'm serious, Mona, I'm not looking for work. Really I'm not. I'm trying to find someone who I think once worked here, years ago. Cath Fox? Does that mean anything?'

Mona thought. 'Cath? Cath? We've had a lot of Caths over the years. Give me something to go on.'

'What can I tell you? She was apparently very pretty. Came from Portsmouth . . . and became friendly with one of your members, Lord Charles Blaydon.'

'Charlie Blaydon! Well, there's a name from the past. He loved this place, Charlie did, couldn't keep him away, the dirty old bugger. And I know exactly the girl you're speaking about. Kelly! Kelly Fox. I think she *was* a Cath too, but we made her a Kelly because of having a Cath already. One of our best girls. His Lordship always asked for her. She did very well, Kelly, we're all very proud of her, aren't we, Magda?' Magda nodded, sharing the pride.

'She ended up married to a footballer, I forget his name now, but their wedding was all over *Hello!*,' Mona said. 'We kept that issue in the club for ages, several of the members remembered her, and it was inspiring for the other girls to see how well Kelly's done for herself. She's our most successful old girl.'

'Was she working here a long time?'

'Oh, a year at least, maybe longer. She was making a fortune, all the members asked for her, and got quite annoyed if she wasn't available. I don't know what it was she did for them. Best not ask! But they kept on coming back for more.'

'Well, that's all very helpful,' Jess said. 'Thanks for that. And have a nice afternoon, everyone.'

'Sure you won't reconsider?' Mona asked. 'You'd do well here, my gentlemen would really go for you. You've got the look. A bit like Kelly, only you're older than she was, which is a pity.'

Jess was so astonished by what she'd discovered at the Pall Mall Steam and Fitness Club she almost forgot she'd been booked that night by Annabel Goode. Henry was sixteen these days so didn't really need a babysitter but Jess tutored him in English literature when his mother went out for the evening. She remembered just in time and hastened over to Pimlico to find Annabel already changed to go out to dinner, while George Palmer and Henry played on an Xbox. Jess had met George several times round at Annabel's but found their relationship ambivalent. Was George her boyfriend or wasn't he? In some ways he acted like he was – and Henry got on well with him – but there was no evidence of him ever staying over. None of his clothes lived in the flat nor shaving tackle in the bathroom. Jess found it strange. She knew he was an army officer, but sometimes he seemed too gentle and unaggressive for that to be plausible.

Annabel looked particularly pretty that night, Jess thought. Often she seemed a little middle-aged and staid, especially when she'd come from work at Buckingham Palace, but tonight she was glamorous in a red dress with her hair up and make-up nicely done.

'I hope you had a nice day,' Annabel said. 'Busy as ever?'

Jess smiled. She was tempted to spill the beans about Cath's naughty stint at the massage parlour – she was sure Annabel would be fascinated by her matron's exploits – but restrained herself. She wasn't even sure how she was going to tell Randy Jaworski about it; it was a tricky one. He'd said he wanted all the scoop on his wife but did he really want to know that?

She replied, 'I've been in Portsmouth and up in Manchester. All over. Still researching my possible article about Cath Fox.'

'This is an old matron from my boarding school we're talking about,' Annabel explained to George. 'She first married a footballer, followed by a media tycoon.'

'And now she's a close friend of a member of the royal family,' Jess said. 'The Duke of Shropshire. He's a Royal Highness.'

'Absolutely,' George said. 'David Shropshire. He's taken the regimental salute a couple of times. Looks good on a horse.'

'And have you met Cath?' Annabel asked, curiosity getting the better of her.

'Not yet. But I'm keen to. I've become rather obsessed by her having interviewed Ryan James and several of her friends. But the person I really want to speak to is her first boyfriend, Callum. But it's difficult, I can't find him. I went down to Nero's in Portsmouth but he left there a few years ago. They said he's a professional bodyguard now, but I don't know where.'

'Does he work for a company, do you know?' George asked. 'There are loads of them here in London providing close protection. Mostly ex-military. Security for Middle Eastern sheiks and Russians. And for Red Sea shipping sailing close to Somalia, because of the pirates.'

'You're well informed,' said Jess.

'My father's in the risk management business. He's a partner in Lionbrand, one of the older ones, been doing it for years since coming out of the army. If you want, I can ask him to do a quick computer search for you. He's got hundreds of guys on his database, thousands probably. Mostly freelancers.'

'I don't have a surname to give you. Just Callum. Is that enough?'

George shrugged. 'No idea. I can ask. I'll ring the office tomorrow and see what they can do, and let you know.'

*

Jess had never previously visited the Wallace Collection. She enjoyed museums and art galleries but had never much fancied the look of this one with its fussy French oil paintings and rococo furniture. As she walked through an enfilade of galleries to the room where the royal reception was taking place, she could see she'd been right to avoid it. The furniture and porcelain on show were too elaborate and covered in gilt, the paintings by Fragonard and Watteau of ladies in frilly dresses reclining on swings made her think of the pictures on the lids of wooden jigsaw puzzles.

She arrived at a gallery filled with guests drinking champagne and circulating around glass cabinets displaying pieces of Sèvres china. Not recognising a single person in the crowd, she wandered around the exhibits, peering at the porcelain and thinking how ugly it all was. There were scallop-shaped fruit dishes – *compotiers* – decorated with rose petals and foliage, and far too much gold, and a hideous Madame du Barry dinner service with plates and soup bowls with serpentine rims. There was a Sèvres inkstand covered with cherubs and crowns which she wouldn't have paid a pound for at a car boot sale, and a pair of wine-bottle coolers dated 1754 glazed with vegetables and fruit. All the other guests were scarily smart and posh in suits and cocktail frocks, and Jess felt seriously underdressed. A lady from the press office bore down on her, pleased to have a journalist from Jaworski Media at the opening, and insisted on escorting her round the show and introducing her to the curator. 'We're so looking forward to your review,' said the press officer. 'When do you think it will come out?'

At that moment there was a frisson of excitement and several flashbulbs went off, and the press lady said, 'Sorry, Jess, got to go. Our guest of honour has arrived.' And across the gallery Jess could see HRH the Duke of Shropshire entering the room, accompanied by the director of the Wallace Collection, and Cath. The duke was taller than she'd expected, walking stiffly from glass case to glass case, almost as though he had a broomstick down his spine. The ladies were all dropping curtsies to him and the men bobbing their heads in respect. Cath stood just behind him and seemed very much part of the royal party. She looked gorgeous in a black cocktail dress with a diamond and gold necklace round her neck. Her look had become even more sophisticated, almost regal.

*

Cath followed David around the gallery, half inspecting the china, half surveying the guests. She could see at once they were a dull lot, not A-listers; as David had warned her, you didn't expect an exciting crowd at the Wallace Collection. From time to time Cath caught the reflection of her necklace in a glass case and smiled. She'd borrowed it for the evening from Bulgari and reckoned she'd hang on to it for as long as possible, ideally for ever. After all, she was bringing them loads of valuable publicity by wearing it.

Although porcelain fascinated her much less than jewellery, she nevertheless found herself a bit of an expert these days, just through spending so much time with David. Two years ago, she couldn't have told a Sèvres plate from a Woolworths one, but now she identified the Bolingbroke dessert service without reading the label. The director of the Wallace Collection said he was very impressed by her eye.

The fact was, Cath had quickly acclimatised to life in royal circles. She kept reading articles in the newspapers speculating on how Kate Middleton would adapt once she'd married Prince William, but Cath could have told her: it's easy. Once you've attended three royal film premieres, cut three ribbons, been greeted by three mayors, you've seen it all. She'd soon got accustomed to people bowing and scraping, opening car doors for her, and meeting and greeting her on the front steps wherever she went. Cath sometimes thought how strange it would feel to arrive at a gallery or a theatre and not to be escorted by the director and the chairman. Or to step onto a pavement without a strip of red carpet.

Life with David felt almost routine. She stayed overnight at KP several times a week now, though she had to be discreet about it. She helped him plan his schedule, secured his sponsorships, organised his social life and his shooting weekends. She'd even sent off to a mail order sex shop specialising in S&M gear and had a parcel of whips, gags and restraints posted to KP in bubble wrap.

If one thing irritated her, it was that David hadn't yet introduced her to any of his royal cousins. He kept promising to, and she'd been giving him a hard time about it because she wanted to meet the Queen, but David said it was complicated because of the protocol. Aside from that one niggle, and the fact she couldn't yet marry him because of the divorce from Randy not being resolved, she was feeling good. After a lot of nagging, David had secured her an invitation to the royal wedding later in the month and to the reception afterwards at Buckingham Palace. She'd insisted on being seated right next to David in the abbey too, in the royal pews, not shunted away somewhere at the back, thank you very much. Cath regarded her royal wedding invitation as the breakthrough she'd been working towards, the first important step in her campaign. The next was to meet the other royals, become accepted by them, get a juicy big pay-off from Randy, and then marry David. She reckoned a few more months would do it, once the William and Kate thing was out of the way and forgotten.

Across a display case, she noticed a girl she half recognised, who seemed to watching her. Not that there was anything particularly surprising in that; you got used to being stared at in royal circles, it was something she enjoyed. She wondered if she'd met the girl before somewhere. She was rather scruffy with badly cut hair, so probably not. She was surprised anyone would turn up to a reception where royals would be present without making more effort.

Jess, meanwhile, was trying to figure out the precise nature of the relationship between Cath and the duke. Whenever he looked at her, which he frequently did, he seemed more than affectionate, almost needy, as thought he was dependent upon her. The two were having an affair, no doubt about it. Which was another awkward fact to report back to Mr Jaworski. And why on earth did the duke keep calling her Katharina?

Jess couldn't take her eyes off Cath, knowing everything she now knew about her. She tried to visualise Cath drinking with Ryan James in Manchester pubs, hanging out at Nero's in Portsmouth, working at that sordid massage club – it was way too bizarre. Cath looked more like a film star or a royal princess, which she virtually was.

Hers was an extraordinary story, a genuine rags to riches tale, which Jess longed to write. The more she thought about it, the more excited she became. It could be the article of her career, the biggest and best thing she'd ever done. Five thousand words minimum, even ten thousand words, a real *Vanity Fair*-style blockbuster. From the backstreets of Portsmouth to the British royal family . . . the story had the lot. They could call it 'The Girl with the Callum Tattoo'.

*

Jess returned to her flat to find two new emails waiting on her screen. The first was from Randy Jaworski, sent in the middle of the night from Shanghai, asking how she was getting on. The tone was vaguely accusatory as though he suspected her of dragging her feet. *My wife's lawyers are pushing me for a settlement. Essential you provide information detrimental to K's character – and fast. When can I expect this?*

Jess started composing a reply, informing him about her discoveries at the Pall Mall Steam and Fitness Club, but something held her back. She didn't like the idea of blowing her scoop and handing it to Randy's lawyers on a plate. Nor did she feel like reporting the details of her visit to Rosemary Savill, and the light it had thrown on Cath's relationship with Lord Blaydon. So she sent Randy a schedule of her various interviews and excursions of the past few days, mentioned she'd seen Kathleen with the Duke of Shropshire at a gallery private view, and that she was trying to track down Kathleen's first boyfriend, Callum. *Rest assured, I'm on the case.*

The second email was from George Palmer and filled her with excitement. *If you still need a contact number for Callum, I think I may have found one*, he wrote. *There were quite a few Callums on the Lionbrand database, it's a popular name in the bodyguard fraternity apparently (!), but only one with a Portsmouth connection. Callum Michael (Mike) Dodd. Did freelance jobs for Lionbrand between 2007–2009 but nothing since.* He gave a mobile number. *No guarantee it's still in use though.*

With fingers crossed, Jess dialled the number. She heard it ring three, four, five times then go to voicemail. A gruff recorded voice said, 'This is Callum, leave a message. I'll get back to you if I can be arsed.'

Jess left him a purposefully vague message. 'Hi, Callum, this is Jess Eden. I need help regarding your line of work. Please ring me back.'

Forty minutes later, just as Jess and Steve were turning in, her mobile rang. 'It's Callum. You called me.' There was a lot of background noise, it sounded like he was speaking from a pub.

'It's difficult to hear you,' Jess said. 'Can we please meet up tomorrow somewhere, I need to speak to you.' They agreed to meet at Davy's wine bar in Crown Passage, just off Pall Mall, at one o'clock.

'That works,' Callum said. 'I'm on a job tomorrow night, but the day's free.'

Chapter Forty-Eight

Jess identified him the minute he walked down the basement steps: thickset and pugnacious, below average height with no neck at all, broken nose, and scars on his face consistent with an ancient glassing incident. His head was close-shaven and he was dressed in black jeans, black Adidas trainers, Bench T-shirt and bomber jacket. She guessed he was mid-fifties but he looked strong and fit. To Jess, he faintly resembled the actor Ross Kemp, Grant Mitchell out of *EastEnders*.

'Callum? I'm Jess.'

Closer up, she noticed a big skull ring on his index finger and a gold flat-linked chain round his neck. He stared at her with a half-aggressive, half-predatory expression she found intimidating.

'I've kept us a table over here,' Jess said. The place was already filling up with a lunchtime crowd of office workers, who came for the olde England ambience and sawdust on the floor.

Jess and Callum settled into round-backed carver chairs and ordered steaks and red wine from the waitress. After she'd left, Jess said, 'Thanks for coming, Callum. You're a difficult man to get hold of. I've been searching for you for quite a while.'

'Yeah? Well, I prefer it that way. It's not anyone's business where I am. You're not from the CSA, are you?'

'No, I'm definitely not from the Child Support Agency. Why? Are they after you?'

'You could say that. Not that they have any reason or proof, not over Michelle. With Connor and Shane, OK, I held my hand up, but I haven't got the cash to pay more. And Michelle's not mine, not definitely. Her mum was seeing several other blokes.'

'Well, that's not why I wanted to meet you today. There's a lady I'm interested in, who I think you used to know a long time ago.'

'Yeah?' He looked suspicious.

'Cath Fox. From Portsmouth. I think you knew her when you were working at Nero's.'

'You know a lot about me. Nero's and that?'

'I tried to find you there. That's where I began looking.'

'Haven't been in ages. Not since I got into protection work. I've been living all over since then. Oman, Bahrain, you name it.'

'What about Cath? Seen her lately?'

His eyes narrowed. 'Why the sudden interest in Cath Fox? You sure you're not CSA?'

'Promise. Listen, I'm a journalist, I'm writing an article about Cath – or Kathleen Jaworski as she is now. I'm trying to get a feel for her. What she was like in the old days. Who her friends were. What she got up to before she became rich and famous.'

Callum laughed. 'I could tell you some stories, I'm not joking. We had a larf in them days, Cath and me. She was a wicked bird, Cath. Very wicked.'

'I know she's got your name tattooed on her arm.'

'It's still there? That's nice. I thought she'd have got rid of it. Yeah, she had that done at the parlour by Clarence Pier. We was both off our heads at the time, she just walked in and said, "Put Callum on me arm."'

'And tell me about your time together. I don't even know how long you were an item?'

He shrugged. 'To be honest, it was a bit on-off. We had a lot of fun, Cath and me, and we were younger in them days, Cath was anyway. I probably shouldn't say this but we shagged a lot in the toilets at Nero's. We had to be quick, mind, or the boss would have gone crazy. And then I went and did something silly and she did a runner and that was it really.'

'What happened?'

'I might just tell you if you buy me another wine.'

With a fresh Beaujolais in hand, Callum said, 'Well, Cath's mum, Pat, starting coming on to me when I was over at hers. I was an idiot and, well, I gave her one. More than one. And Cath caught us at it and totally lost it, and left Portsmouth the same day. Never saw her mum again, never saw the kid, never saw me. Not for ages anyway.'

'The kid? What kid?'

'Oh, didn't I mention that? Cath went and got herself pregnant, silly cow, and didn't realise till it was too late. So she had a baby girl to look after.'

'Was it *your* baby?'

'If I find you're from the CSA, I'll break your fucking neck. And I'm not kidding neither.'

'Where's the child now?'

Callum shrugged. 'Cath's mum put her up for adoption. Which was a liberty, because she shouldn't have done that without asking me. Probably for the best though. Cath didn't want her.'

'And you haven't seen the baby or Cath since?'

'Not the kid, no. I do sometimes wonder what happened to her. She'd be a teenager now, I reckon.'

'More like late twenties. Cath left Portsmouth back in the eighties, didn't she?'

'Yeah, you could be right.'

'And Cath? You implied you've seen her since then.'

'I've seen her, yeah, on a couple of occasions. She came to watch a match at Fratton Park the one time. That was a memorable reunion.' He laughed dirtily. 'And then I was doing security for her new bloke, the Polish midget with the yacht. So I ran in to her in Sardinia, the snooty bitch.'

'She wasn't happy to see you then?'

'Not happy at all. Pretended she didn't know me.'

Callum had begun eyeing Jess up in a way she found uncomfortable, and which she did her best to ignore. 'What about Ryan James, then? Did you ever get to meet Cath's footballer?'

But Callum just replied, 'Tosser. Manchester tosser,' and gave Jess a hard stare.

Then he said, 'Did I tell you I was in the SAS?'

'Really? I didn't know that.'

'Yeah, I was out in Iraq with Andy McNab. I'm mentioned in his book, *Bravo Two Zero*, but not by name.'

'Wow, when did this all happen?'

'A few years ago. I was in Afghanistan too, and Kuwait. Undercover surveillance behind enemy lines.'

Jess realised he was making it up, part of a misdirected macho seduction technique. So she asked, 'Tell me more about the baby. The one you had with Cath.'

'What's there to tell? She got pregnant, had a baby. It happens.'

'Were you present at the birth?'

'I was working that night. But I did go over to the hospital, to visit her and that.'

'And?'

He shrugged. 'Cath was OK, and the kid.'

'But you think Cath lost touch with her daughter?'

'I told you. Her nan put her up for adoption. Cath had scarpered. No one knew where she was. She wasn't bothered, was she?'

Then he said, 'Doing anything afterwards, Jess? We could go for a drink.'

'We've *got* a drink. And I have to go back to my office.'

'Aw, come on, sweetheart. We could have fun, you and me. You're a nice-looking bird.'

'Callum . . . no. Seriously.'

'What's your problem? You frigid or something? I've got a room near the Elephant, we could go there.'

'Sorry, Callum. I'm already seeing someone, I've got a boyfriend.'

'So? I've got a ladyfriend . . . several in fact.' There was something menacing in his voice, and the muscles in his cheek were starting to twitch. 'You come with me, you snooty cow. You'll enjoy it. I've not had any complaints.'

Jess pushed her chair back. 'I'm going to pay. Thanks for making time to meet me. But I've got to go now.'

He grabbed her wrist, so firmly it almost snapped. 'How fucking dare you? You've been giving me the come-on all afternoon, fucking tart.'

Jess snatched a fork from her plate with her spare hand and drove it into Callum's arm. He yelped and released his grip.

'Goodbye, Callum,' said Jess, and went over to the bar to settle the bill.

The letter she composed that evening required half a dozen drafts because she knew the tone had to be pitch-perfect. Having finally completed it to her satisfaction, she made a fair copy on office writing paper, then handed it to Steve for his comments.

'This is good,' Steve said, having read it through twice. 'It's the most greasy, flattering letter I've seen in my life. No one would say no to it. She's going to say yes for sure.'

Jess was unconvinced. 'Royals never give interviews, do they?'

'Mrs Jaworski isn't royal.'

'But she thinks she might become one. Which makes it even more unlikely.'

Jess reread the letter one last time before putting it in an envelope.

It began: *Dear Mrs Jaworski, I am a journalist working for the* Daily Telegraph *and am desperate to interview you for the paper. I am a huge fan of your personal style. I saw you at the Sèvres exhibition at the Wallace Collection last night when you were accompanying HRH The Duke of Shropshire, and I know you are also an accomplished expert on porcelain and art. It would be the greatest honour . . .* and so on for two more sides.

Having addressed the letter c/o Kensington Palace, Jess took a taxi to the sentry box at the palace gates and handed it over to the policeman on duty.

Chapter Forty-Nine

'Happy birthday, angel,' said Steve, reappearing in their bedroom with a cafetière of coffee and a birthday *pain au chocolat*. There were three cards on the tray, which from the handwriting on the envelopes Jess reckoned were from Steve, Bob and Kirsty, and Bryony. Steve's card had a badge pinned on the front saying *9 Today*, which he'd amended to read *29 Today*.

'Do you have to rub it in?' Jess asked.

'Count yourself lucky,' said Steve. 'I can hardly even *remember* twenty-nine.'

The newspapers arrived and they spent an hour together in bed, drinking coffee and reading the latest guff about the royal wedding, now only two days away. Steve said he couldn't stand it, having to generate fresh stories and angles day after day for Jaworski Media when there was nothing new to say, but Jess said she was really getting into it. There was a plan of Westminster Abbey in today's papers showing where all the royals and politicians would be sitting in the north transept, and the friends of William and Kate, and Elton John and the Beckhams. Jess found it oddly fascinating, despite herself. She located David Shropshire's seat alongside the Kents and Gloucesters, and wondered whether Cath had wangled herself an invitation. Well, she could ask her that soon enough.

It had been five days before Cath finally responded to her letter. Then an email arrived, direct from Cath herself, saying she didn't normally do publicity but might be prepared to grant an interview under certain conditions. She demanded full copy approval with the right to remove anything she didn't like, and picture approval over the choice of photographs. Furthermore, she would answer no questions on certain subjects: she wouldn't talk about her friend the Duke of Shropshire, nor about her marriage to Randolph Jaworski, nor about Prince William and Catherine Middleton. And she reserved the option to pull the entire interview if she considered it unfavourable. However, she would be happy to speak about her personal style, the jewellers and fashion designers and charities she supported, as well as her transformation of Jaworski Media. It would be convenient for Jess to visited her at Kensington Palace at three p.m. next Wednesday, when she had an opening in her diary.

Ever since getting the summons, Jess had been in a slaver of excitement and apprehension, going over and over her notes and refining her interview strategy. She now knew so much about Cath, she hardly knew where to begin. And how was she going to approach the interview in any case? She could hardly just go in and say, 'So, I hear you gave great handjobs at the Pall Mall Steam and Fitness Club?' She'd be flung out on her ear. There was so much she needed to ask her: about Ryan, about Callum, Lord Blaydon and Randy Jaworski. And why she'd kept on changing her name; she'd been Cath, Kelly, Katie, Kathleen, Katharina . . . it was all so fascinating. And the baby in Portsmouth. How was Jess going to broach that particular subject? Before or after the massage parlour?

There was no question about it, the interview was fraught with pitfalls. She'd be sitting there in a royal palace, probably with Beefeaters and soldiers in bearskins outside the door, with one hour maximum to ask her questions. And if she called it wrong, she'd probably end up in the Tower.

The only thing to do, she reckoned, was play it by ear. She'd start off with easy questions about jewellers and fashion designers to put Cath at her ease, then lob in some awkward ones. It was a nerve-racking prospect, she'd have to steel herself. As she'd reminded herself again and again, a story this good doesn't come along very often. She mustn't flunk it.

At ten minutes before three o'clock, Jess presented herself at the Kensington Palace barrier. Greatly to her relief, her name was on the list and the policeman rang through to the apartment to announce her arrival. While she was waiting, Jess checked her appearance in the glass reflection of the sentry box. She had put on a suit and her prettiest blouse, and her lucky birthday locket, of course. She needed all the luck she could get.

A policeman escorted her through a courtyard and into a smaller cobbled courtyard beyond, where he rang a doorbell. The door was opened by Cath herself, which took Jess aback, and the policeman said, 'Miss Jess Eden for you, ma'am.'

'Thank you, officer,' Cath replied and shook hands with Jess. In her presence, Jess felt uncharacteristically shy, fazed by Cath's beauty and sophistication. She was impeccably dressed in a pale violet dress, with three strands of pearls at her neck. The sleeves of the dress covered any traces of tattoo. Her skin was flawless, Jess noticed, her hair specially done for the interview.

'Would you like to follow me upstairs?' Cath said. 'I thought we'd talk in the morning room, it's my favourite room in the apartment, full of light.'

'Great,' said Jess, carrying her notebook and tape recorder upstairs.

They entered a room of comfortable sofas and cupboards filled with china, and small tables covered with royal photographs in silver and gold frames. A pot of tea and cups were set ready on a tray.

'I do so love this little room,' Cath declared. 'It's a wonderful place in which to sit and read. And we hold some of my charity committees in here too. One can just about squeeze ten ladies in, if we don't mind being cosy.'

Jess was struck by Cath's voice which was faultlessly grand, exactly like the toffs in *Downton Abbey*. And everything about her was so gracious and ladylike, the way she perched on the chintz sofa and poured the tea, offering a choice of milk, sugar and sweetener. The tea ritual complete, Cath said, 'I don't normally give interviews. But your letter was so charming, I didn't feel I could disappoint you.'

'It's very kind of you.'

'But you will respect my conditions, won't you? One has to be so careful, as you appreciate.'

'As a friend of the Duke of Shropshire's, you mean?'

'I'm afraid I can't talk about him at all. But, yes, when one's in royal circles.'

'And, if you don't mind me asking, you are still married to Randolph Jaworski?'

Cath gave a polite little smile. 'Randolph and I remain great friends.

What I'm telling you now is not for publication but we are in fact in the process of separating. It is all very amicable and civilised. But I'm afraid I can't speak about it, I'm sure you understand. Randolph will remain a treasured friend of mine and of the duke's. They shoot together regularly. We are all the greatest of friends. Now, what is it you would like to ask me about for your interview? I greatly enjoy the *Daily Telegraph*, it is the newspaper I read every morning with my first cup of tea.'

Jess blushed. She had chosen to pretend she was from the *Telegraph* because she guessed Cath considered it respectable.

'Er, I'd like to ask you first about your jewellery. I noticed you wearing the most wonderful diamonds at the Wallace Collection the other night.'

'Ah, my favourite Bulgari piece. They are such artistes at that house. Like Van Cleef and Arpels, their workmanship is exquisite. To see those very old men, the craftsmen, at their benches surrounded by precious stones, is a wonderful sight. I love the way the traditional skills have been preserved, passed down from master to apprentice. It is the same at Hermès . . .'

'Did you grow up with wonderful jewellery?' Jess asked.

Cath frowned, but replied, 'I was very fortunate. My mother always wore lovely jewellery. My earliest memories are of her visiting me in my night nursery to kiss me goodnight, and my little fingers playing with her pearls. And later, even when I was a schoolgirl at St Mary's, I developed an appreciation for beautiful pieces.' Cath then mentioned several other jewellers and dressmakers she said she admired, keen to seed as many plugs into Jess's article as she could. But she was also anxious to project an image of sophistication. She hadn't told David she was doing this interview but hoped it might accelerate her acceptance by his family. If they read a positive article about her, saying how posh she was, they'd get a favourable first impression.

For half an hour, until she knew her cowardice could continue no longer, Jess wrote down all Cath's musings on life and luxury goods. 'We are so fortunate in this country to have wonderful brands like Burberry and Smythson,' Cath declared. 'And wonderful British institutions like Wiltons and Ascot races.'

Taking a deep breath, Jess asked, 'And presumably you became quite a football expert too, during your marriage to Ryan James?'

Cath turned pale and a look of panic crossed her face. Jess could see her wondering how to reply: whether to deny the marriage and pretend there'd been some mistake, or own up to it.

Eventually she said, 'Ah yes, lovely Ryan. I was far too young to have got married, of course, someone should have stopped us . . . but you do impulsive things when you're young . . . we just grew apart, which was so sad.'

'And what about Lord Blaydon? Rumour has it you were engaged to him, despite a sixty-year age gap.'

Cath stared at her, aghast. 'I thought I told you, I won't discuss personal matters. I made that a condition.'

'You met him at the Pall Mall Steam and Fitness Club, I believe. When you were working there as a massage girl.'

'Who told you that? It's not true, I wouldn't dream of working anywhere like that. In fact I've never heard of it.' She was visibly panicked.

'Lord Blaydon's daughter told me, since you ask. And I visited the place myself to check it out. Mona sends you her love, so does Magda. Mona says you were her best girl.'

'I don't know who that is. This is complete rubbish you're talking. I'm sorry, this was not in our agreement. I'm stopping the interview. You can turn your tape recorder off, go on, switch it off right now. Otherwise I'll call the police and get them to throw you out.' Cath's voice had lost all trace of gentility, she was bawling at Jess like a fishwife. 'The interview's over. Get the hell out of here, I'm telling you. And if you write one word of any of this, I know people who can make your life very uncomfortable. You understand me? I'm warning you.'

'People like Callum, you mean?'

Cath turned deathly white. 'Callum? Who's Callum? I don't know any Callums.'

'Well that's strange. He certainly remembered you when I talked to him last week. He told me all about you – your classy little nights together at Nero's . . . in the toilets. I've visited Nero's, just in case you're wondering.'

'This is ridiculous. Even if I did know a Callum, it would have been years ago. I've forgotten. I can't be expected to remember everyone I've ever met.'

'Try rolling up your sleeve, Cath. I think you'll find a reminder on your arm, where you see it every single day. And I'm surprised you've forgotten him, he's a forceful guy. He practically tried to rape me in a wine bar last week. I'm sure it'll come back to you, if you think hard. And here's another clue: you had his baby back in Portsmouth. Ringing any bells now? You had his baby and then your mother had Callum.'

Cath rose to her feet, eyes blazing, and grabbed hold of Jess by the neck. She started to shake her. 'What the fuck do you want from me? You want to ruin me? Is that what you want? Why? What did I ever do to you? I've a good mind to fucking kill you.'

She began squeezing at Jess's throat, throttling her, when she suddenly stopped and released her grip.

'What's this? Where did you get this?' She was clutching Jess's locket which had snapped from its chain and fallen open. Cath stared mesmerised at the photograph of herself inside. 'Go on, where did you get it, you thieving cow? This is my necklace, my picture's inside, look.'

For a moment the two women stared at each other in stunned silence as the enormity of the revelation sank in.

Jess was the first to speak. 'I've had it since I was a baby. My mother gave it to me, my mother who adopted me. It belonged to my real mother . . .' Jess stared at Cath in shock as she absorbed the words she'd just said.

She remembered Ryan saying how she resembled Katie, and Mona from the massage club saying she was like Kelly. And then another thought hit her, sending her spinning: *Callum was her dad.*

'Well,' Cath said at last. 'I don't suppose either of us expected this when I agreed to give an interview. Weird. It must be twenty-plus years. How old are you now, anyway?'

'Twenty-nine.'

'Yeah, that figures. You should do something about your hair, Jess. You won't find a nice feller if you go out looking like that.'

Jess regarded her mother in dumb astonishment. 'I don't think I need any advice from you, Cath, Katharina, Mrs Jaworski. Not on men. I know rather a lot about you, remember. You're scarcely a role model.'

'Mind if I have a drink?' Cath said. 'You could probably do with one yourself. David has a cupboard full of them. What do you fancy? It's all here. Gin? Champagne?'

Jess found herself accepting a glass of white wine, poured into a glass engraved with royal ciphers.

'I suppose we ought to drink to our good news,' Cath said. 'It's not every day you're reunited with your long-lost daughter. Cheers!'

'It's a shock,' Jess stumbled, her head reeling. 'I've spent the past three weeks researching your life. But it seems I missed the most interesting fact. I've been down to Portsmouth, up to Manchester. I saw Ryan James . . . Rosemary Savill . . .'

'No! You saw Rosemary Savill? That toxic old witch! I bet she didn't have much good to say about me.'

Jess laughed. 'Not a lot, no, actually.'

'Go on, who else have you seen then? I noticed you at the Wallace Collection, stalking me round the room.'

'Er, I met your friend Hayley in Manchester. She asked to be remembered to you.'

'Good girl, Hayley. I feel a bit bad, not keeping up with her.'

'Ryan wants to see you again too. He asked me to say that, if I ever got the chance.'

Cath made a face. 'He'd better not hold his breath. Because I don't see that happening.' She continued, 'So you saw Callum and he tried it on, eh? Well that's typical. He's a brute, Callum. I hope you slapped him?'

'Actually I dug a fork into his arm.'

Cath screamed with laughter. 'Good for you, girl. I love that. I hope you dug it in deep too. He was always low-life scum, Callum.'

'I'm surprised you say that. I thought you two went out together? I guess he must be my dad?'

'Since you seem to know so much about me, yes, I did go with Callum for a bit, years ago. He was a sexy guy in those days. But an animal. That was half the attraction. Plus he could get you into Nero's without paying at the door.'

Jess stared at Cath with incredulous fascination. The whole thing was so surreal, she could hardly take it in. Here she was in Kensington Palace in a room filled with royal portraits and photographs, and she'd just discovered this woman sitting opposite was her mother.

Cath, meanwhile, stared back at Jess. Now she was looking for it, she could see a faint family resemblance. Jess and she had the same nose. At least she didn't look too like Callum, that was a mercy.

In her quick-witted way, Cath had already sized up the new situation. Obviously it was uncomfortable, having this girl knowing so much about her. For decades, Cath had compartmentalised her life, doling out her back story on a need-to-know basis. But now it was all coming home to haunt her. She felt no maternal instinct towards Jess but it was interesting to see her, she had to admit. She'd occasionally wondered what became of her daughter.

'So, tell us all about you then, Jess? What've you been up to, since I last saw you in Gosport Mansions?'

Jess started to tell her about her childhood in Long Barton in Buckinghamshire with Bob and Kirsty, and what nice loving parents they'd been, and the church and choir and Bishop Ottley's School for Girls. 'Just an ordinary middle-class upbringing really.' But even as she described it, Jess felt waves of resentment towards Cath for abandoning her, and never once making contact, while she cavorted about the place with famous footballers and royals and billionaires with private planes.

'Well, I'm glad you had such a happy time,' Cath said when she'd finished. 'That makes me feel a lot better about everything.'

'Actually,' replied Jess, 'you have no reason to feel OK about anything. I can assure you, I don't feel OK about it myself, not at all. I don't know what I think, to be perfectly honest, I'm in a state of shock. For several weeks I've been thinking about you night and day, interviewing all these different people and hearing all these stories. Ryan's mum. Dan Black at Imperial Magazines . . .'

Cath made a face. 'Blimey, you really have got around, haven't you?'

'Mona at the Steam and Fitness Club . . . and I'd formed a very negative view of you, to be honest. And then today, out of the blue, I suddenly discover you're actually my birth mother. And I'm the daughter of this . . . completely amoral gold-digger who worked in this really seedy disgusting massage parlour and had affairs with all these different rich men . . . and it's just very difficult to get my head round . . .'

Cath gave her a hard look. 'What a judgemental girl you are, Jess. I wonder where you got that from? Not from me. Must be from those church-going adopted parents.' She tipped more wine into her glass, then refilled Jess's. 'Let me tell you a few home truths, Jess. We're clearly different people, you and I, but we're also flesh and blood, so probably not quite so different as you think. I'm sorry you're angry with me. OK, I did leave you with Callum and my mum. I had my reasons, you know. Maybe I should have stayed put? Maybe I should still be there in Portsmouth on the Allaway estate, you too, all of us, living there in the flats? But I didn't, I moved on. And it doesn't sound like you had too bad a time of it, living in a comfortable home with a well-off family. I'm not that sorry for you, not really. You had a better start than you would have had in Pompey; all the advantages. I never got an education like you got. I couldn't even read or write properly when I got out of school. I never went to college. There were no choirs round where I lived. Everything I got, I got for myself, every inch of the way. And had a very nice time doing so, thank you very much. I'm not asking for anyone's sympathy, I've had a very interesting life, way more interesting than most people's. I've been with some great blokes. Not Callum, though we had our moments. But I was with this nice guy, Michael Goode, I learnt a lot from Michael. And old Charlie Blaydon, he taught me about art and architecture and how to appreciate it. And Ryan – you've met Ryan – he was a lovely guy in his way, we had this place out in Prestbury, outside of Manchester, and travelled all over the country watching matches. And then Randy Jaworski came along and that was something else again, a whole new experience. Randy and me flying about in his Gulfstream and giving fancy parties in New York and meeting all these fascinating people. But that relationship started to lose its mojo in the end, as things do, and then David came along.'

'I work for Mr Jaworski.'

'Never! Well that's a coincidence.'

'Actually, it was you who helped get me my job. I came up to you after my degree ceremony in Manchester.'

'Well I'm glad I've been able to do something for you at least. Anyway,' Cath went on, 'I've had a great life. It's not all been easy, mind, but I have enjoyed it. Even that massage place which shocks you so much had its moments. Some nice blokes used to visit, you'd be surprised. Judges and Members of Parliament, all sorts. You could have interesting conversations. But whenever I began to get bored,

I moved on; it's nice to see what else is out there. Some people stay put with the same man, doing the same job, living in the same place all their lives. Well, good luck to them. What about you, Jess? Had plenty of nice fellers? Or maybe you're married, you didn't say?'

'Er, well, I did have a few boyfriends at uni. But I've been with Steve – my current boyfriend – for a few years now. Four, I think. He works at Jaworski Media. We share a flat.'

'Nice guy, is he? Interesting to be with?'

'Er, yes. Steve's great.' Jess was wondering how she was going to break all of this to Steve, about Cath . . . and Callum . . . all of it.

'I'm sorry,' said Cath, settling back into the chintz sofa. 'We seem to have lost the thread of our interview. It took an unexpected turn. It might be rather tricky for you to write it up now, I don't know.' She gave Jess a coquettish little smile and cocked her head questioningly.

'I don't know either,' replied Jess. 'I need to think . . . about lots of things, it's all very confusing right now.' Then she said, 'I think I should leave. It's OK, I can find my own way out. Goodbye . . . Mrs Jaworski. See you.'

And she recrossed the courtyard to the KP barrier, her mind in turmoil.

Chapter Fifty

Annabel had been in the abbey since seven o'clock that morning, rechecking arrangements for the twentieth time. The whole of the Lord Chamberlain's Office had been on red alert for weeks, finalising the seating, the order of service, the arrival times for foreign diplomats and heads of state and British and foreign royals. Outside in the streets she could hear the roar of the crowds, many of whom had been camped out on the pavement all night and now cheered everyone and everything that went past, even the bin lorry. In less than two hours they really would have something to cheer, Annabel thought, when the VIPs began arriving.

Annabel had a seat in the sixth row of the south nave, alongside other colleagues from the LCO. Part of her would be relieved when today was over; she'd thought of nothing but the royal wedding for months. She was dressed in a pretty pleated skirt with a pink jacket, and a big hat with flowers: the outfit she'd worn twice before to friends' weddings. Well, nobody was going to be looking at her today, were they? She was glad she'd elected to wear flat shoes because she'd be on her feet for hours to come. She felt an enormous sense of responsibility that it should all go off smoothly . . . for the royal couple, for the department, for Queen and Country. The eyes of the world were on Westminster Abbey today.

She did a final recce of the church, taking in the flowers, the service sheets and the small television monitors so the congregation in the nave could watch what was happening at the altar, up beyond the organ screen, where the royal families and closest friends of William and Kate would be seated. All the time, she had half an eye open for Jamie, her ex-husband, who would be in the abbey in his capacity as

Colonel of the Irish Guards. And George would be there too, in full ceremonial dress with sword and spurs.

She had already double-checked the name cards on the seats of the royal families, to ensure nobody had been missed. She still found it difficult to accept that Cath was going to be there, actually seated in the royal pews, when she was only unofficially engaged to the Duke of Shropshire. It broke all the rules of protocol, but David Shropshire had insisted. So there was the card with Cath's name on it – Mrs Katharina Jaworski – in the fourth row, several rows ahead of Prime Minister David Cameron, and ahead of the kings and queens of Spain, Denmark and the rest of them. Annabel considered it incredible, as did her whole department.

Twice in the past week Annabel had woken up after uneasy nightmares of a job left undone. Which Swedish royals were travelling to the reception at Buckingham Palace in which minibus? Would the deposed King of Albania mind sitting in the row behind the deposed King and Queen of Greece? Once she'd got them all safely back to Buckingham Palace, Annabel's own duties were over. Then she was going home to Pimlico to watch it all over again on TV; she'd asked two dozen friends and neighbours round to join her. Her father was coming over too, and her old babysitter Jess with her boyfriend Steve had promised to drop by for a drink.

Cath, meanwhile, was feeling thoroughly hassled by David, who kept telling her to hurry up and get dressed. The car taking them from Kensington Palace to Westminster Abbey was waiting, and David was in a panic. It always surprised Cath how stressed he got about little things like arriving late at royal functions. After all, he was royal himself. He hardly needed to worry.

Cath examined herself critically in the mirror. Yes, she looked good. She'd given considerable thought to her wedding outfit and called in lots of choices from different designers before settling on the royal blue fitted Chanel coat with gold buttons and matching Chanel skirt and sunglasses. Her hat, selected with the help of a personal shopper at Harrods, was by Philip Treacy with three black swan's feathers. It was a strong look, on-trend and classy. Cath wondered what Victoria Beckham would be wearing today.

As they approached the abbey, Cath began to feel ever more

excited. Hundreds of thousands of people lined the streets, waving flags and cheering the cars and limousines dropping off guests at the abbey doors. Banks of television cameras and temporary studios had been erected in Parliament Square for TV stations from across the world, and on the pavement in front of the abbey stood ranks of Coldstream Guards to attention, and Yeomen of the Guard in their scarlet doublets bearing their staves of office. As members of the royal party they'd been given a precise time to arrive at the Great West Door. Cath knew Princes William and Harry had arrived already, followed by the foreign royal families. Then the bride's mother and brother would arrive and then, at ten thirty a.m., David and Cath and the first wave of British royals.

A great roar of cheering erupted when she and David stepped out onto the pavement, welcomed by the dean of the abbey, and they were escorted by army officers with clanking spurs all the way to their seats in the south transept. As she processed up the aisle she felt the eyes of the congregation upon her, watching her every move, and Cath felt a little surge of triumph. Outwardly, she did her best to look calm and composed but inside she felt quite stirred by the pomp and ceremony, and by how far she'd come in her life. Who would have thought little Cath Fox from the Allaway estate would be arriving at a royal wedding with an HRH, and nearly an HRH herself?

As she progressed further up the aisle, past all the establishment types in their morning suits – lord lieutenants, ambassadors, dignitaries and field marshals – Cath relished the feeling of having better seats than all of them. She spotted David Beckham and Posh Spice relegated to the south nave while she was escorted on and up to the royal enclosure. How sweet it felt.

They were shown to their places and Cath looked round, craning her neck to see who else was there. She spotted the Middletons across the aisle, and there was Prince Harry, all in blue and gold braid, and various famous politicians several rows behind her, and a phalanx of foreign royals she didn't know the names of but vaguely recognised from *Hello!*. Wasn't that naughty Boris back there too, the Lord Mayor of London? And David Cameron and his hatless wife? Way above her in the rooftops she spotted the booms of television cameras moving to and fro, scanning the congregation, and realised her face would probably be shown on TV. The prospect made her happy.

'Don't keep turning around, Katharina. Sit still,' David warned her. But it wasn't easy. The Prince of Wales and Duchess of Cornwall arrived and were ushered to their seats in the front row, swiftly followed by the Queen and the Duke of Edinburgh. Cath hoped she'd get a chance to be introduced to them later on, maybe at the reception. She'd been on at David about it all week.

The organ was playing music Cath didn't recognise, and now a procession of clergymen was advancing up the aisle, all sorts of bishops and archbishops and canons. Cath was slightly surprised they arrived after the Queen. And finally the procession of the bride herself, with Kate Middleton in a beautiful lacy wedding dress on the arm of her father, followed by bridesmaids and pages and Pippa Middleton, the bride's sister, as maid of honour. Cath couldn't avoid a fleeting twinge of jealousy at the sight of Pippa Middleton on centre stage, and was glad she was wearing sunglasses so no one could see her face.

From her seat in the south nave, Annabel witnessed Cath's arrival and had to admit she looked fabulous. Annabel probably wouldn't have chosen that exact Chanel outfit herself, even if she could have afforded it, but Cath did look very striking, though the sunglasses were a definite breach of protocol. For the briefest of moments Annabel recalled the hideous occasion when she'd disturbed Cath in bed with her father in the holiday bungalow in Rock, a memory she'd tried to suppress for almost thirty years. How extraordinary it was to see her old school matron with the royal Duke of Shropshire. You had to hand it to Cath, she'd come a long way.

Across the aisle, Annabel spotted Jamie, red-faced and jowly round the chin. Since splitting up with Suki, he'd had a string of girlfriends, each more unsuitable than the last. When he'd taken Henry out for Sunday lunch three weeks ago, he'd been accompanied by a Stringfellow's pole dancer who looked nineteen. According to George, Jamie's bosses in high command were unimpressed.

Cath disliked hymns. She never knew the tunes and found it difficult to sing along. 'Guide Me, O Thou Great Redeemer' left her completely lost; the words were gobbledegook. It worried her they might show her on TV getting it all wrong, so she moved her lips as best she could. Then the dean embarked on his welcome and introduction, which gave Cath time to think. Ever since the encounter with Jess two days ago, she'd been tense. It scared her that Jess knew so much about her, all her little secrets; secrets which Cath had never even faced up to herself. She approached life like a mountaineer on a sheer rock face, edging her way from foothold to foothold, ledge to ledge, always alert to any means of advancement. And now, just as she was so close to the summit, everything could crumble away.

That Jess had the power to ruin everything, she had recognised at once. David was entirely unaware of most of her life story. She had never discussed Ryan with him, and her days as a footballer's wife. She'd certainly never told him about Callum or the baby or that massage place. If any of that came out she didn't know how he'd react, but the marriage would be off for sure. Her divorce from Randy and her attempt to overturn the prenup would be fatally undermined too. She wasn't going to look good in court, with all that to pick over.

As the Archbishop of Canterbury conducted the exchange of vows between bride and groom, Cath longed more than ever to become a full member of the royal family. It would be the ultimate fulfilment of a lifelong quest for respect, for security, for self-esteem. She wanted to be Her Royal Highness the Duchess of Shropshire – she thought about it all the time. And it was within her grasp.

Would Jess expose her? It was more than possible. Jess was a journalist and had been working on the investigation for weeks. Cath could see it was a good story. The thought made her feel sick. To lose it all now when she was so near to her prize was more than she could bear. But conscious of the television cameras swinging overhead, panning the pews for recognisable or attractive faces, Cath continued to smile serenely.

Sprawled across the sofa in the sitting room of their Covent Garden flat, with mugs of coffee in one hand and flutes of Tesco champagne in the other, lay Jess and Steve. They had switched on the TV at six a.m., just for a quick squint at the wedding preparations, and been strangely transfixed by the vacuous interviews with royal experts which told you nothing, and the vox pops with crazy people camped out on the streets, some of them face-painted with Union flags. Inside the abbey, the cameras kept switching between Elton John and David Furnish and David and Victoria Beckham, and back again to the royal pews. Several times they focused on Cath, and Jess had a strange feeling, knowing it was her mother.

In the past three days, she'd done nothing except think about her.

Uncharacteristically, she hadn't yet told Steve about it; the story was too raw and personal. She felt quite exhausted going over and over it in her head, about how she felt and what to do. Though she had relived every second of the interview at Kensington Palace, before and after the cataclysmic revelation of the locket, Jess still felt confused. The knowledge that she was Cath's daughter disturbed her profoundly, undermining and altering her sense of self. Although she had always known Bob and Kirsty weren't her real parents, she had absorbed many of their values, even when they irritated her. The altogether dodgier reality of her biological parents had shocked her.

She was surprised how ambivalent she felt about Cath; there had been something feisty and almost persuasive about Cath's self-defence. Cath had indeed led an exciting life – much more exciting than Jess's own, now she thought about it. She had to slightly admire her, in spite of everything. The cameras panned back across the royal pews and Jess thought, 'That's my mum sitting there a couple of rows behind the Queen,' and it was impossible not to feel slightly proud.

If she wrote up the story it would be a sensation when it was published. She might even win an award, or get a book contract.

But Jess wondered. The fact was, she didn't know what she thought about anything at the moment.

The service over, Cath and David climbed into one of the people carriers waiting to ferry minor royals from the abbey to Buckingham Palace. It was mildly disappointing to be transported by a van with side-sliding doors rather than in the golden carriage she'd hoped for, but Cath at least relished being seated knee-to-knee with members of her future clan. All along the route, well-wishers cheered them on their way, and Cath waved back in response, in the polite little acknowledgment she observed the other royals giving. At the gates of the palace, guardsmen in bearskins presented arms, and the convoy of people carriers crossed the courtyard and pulled up underneath a porched entrance. Television cameras filmed them all entering the reception and Cath made sure she was fully on view, walking between the Duke of Shropshire and the Princesses of Norway and Lesotho.

Seated on one of her stiff-backed sofas at her flat in Warwick Square, Rosemary Savill almost had a seizure. She and Hugh were watching the wedding on television, with a glass of sherry to toast the occasion, when there, clear as daylight, Cath appeared on screen, actually mounting the steps of Buckingham Palace in a group of bona fide guests. Rosemary gave a little cry of distress. 'Hugh, Hugh, that *couldn't* have been . . .' But Hugh had spotted her too, there was no mistaking her. 'I simply cannot bear it,' Rosemary exclaimed. 'It's utterly beyond belief.'

Cath was loving almost every aspect of the party. The palace was everything she'd hoped and more: red velvet plush and acres of gold leaf, and uniformed flunkies circulating with trays of drinks and canapés. There was a string quartet playing violin music and a harpist plucking away in the corner, and posh-looking courtiers in morning coats being super-courteous. At one end of the great room was a little area where the Queen and other senior royals had assembled, not actually roped off or anything, but most of the guests were steering well clear. 'Go on, introduce me,' Cath kept telling David. 'Now's our chance, let's go over and say hi.' But the duke was reluctant and didn't wish to intrude, which Cath considered very peculiar and annoying. And when she said, 'There's the bride and groom, look, let's get in quick,' he shook her off.

Cath hissed, 'I'm giving you such a thrashing tonight, David, if you keep on like this.'

She couldn't feel discouraged for long, however, not at a royal wedding. There was Princess Michael of Kent, looking very chic, and the royal carpenter with the furniture shop, Viscount Linley. And she liked the look of some of Prince William's ushers, they were very fit. One way and another, her eyes were on stalks.

Before she knew it the long sash windows on to the balcony were thrown open and the royal family were being collected by footmen to go outside to the cheers of the half-million people standing in the Mall, all waiting for the first public kiss from William and Kate.

'Wait here, Katharina, this won't take long,' David said, abandoning her inside. But Cath soon got fed up being all alone and listening to the cheering from the crowd, so she boldly stepped out onto the balcony and joined the line-up. It was such a sight to behold, thousands of tiny faces wherever you looked, and people climbing up onto the Victoria Memorial for a better view, with thousands more pressing up against the railings. As a fly-past of Spitfires and Hawker Hurricanes roared overhead, and everyone stared up into the sky to watch them, Cath sidled along the back row until she was standing right next to Zara Phillips and Princess Beatrice, gazing out between the shoulders of the Duke of Edinburgh and Princess Anne.

Rosemary Savill, still tuned in to her television set in Warwick Square, was so disturbed at seeing Cath's devious little face for a second time, she had to go and lie down. Callum, meanwhile, who was providing security for the day at a royal wedding pub function in Bermondsey, spotted Cath on the big plasma above the bar, and was quite unable to reconcile the elegant person on the screen with the bird he used to shag in Pompey. While in Wythenshawe, Manchester, where Ryan had gone over for dinner to watch the wedding on TV with his parents, only his mum, Barbara, recognised Katie on the balcony and thought it best to say nothing, since Ryan was still a bit funny about her, if her name ever came up in conversation.

Annabel had set up a table of drinks in the sitting room of her flat in Cambridge Street, laden with bottles of assorted champagne and wine and jugs of elderflower cordial. George, meanwhile, had changed out of his uniform and headed round the corner to Oddbins to pick up some ice. Annabel felt supremely upbeat, almost elated, the events at the abbey having gone off without a single significant hitch, delay or terrorist incident. And the new Duke and Duchess of Cambridge looked genuinely happy and in love, which further boosted the feel-good factor. Now she could relax, have a few drinks with friends and family, and watch it all over again on television.

Henry had arrived home for an exeat weekend from school and was laying out bowls of nuts and crisps and platters of hummus and taramasalata with sticks of carrot and celery. Josh and Mouse Adams were helping in the kitchen opening bottles. Then Annabel's father, Michael, turned up with several more bottles, full of compliments for Annabel for 'putting on such a splendid show in the abbey today. The whole thing was faultless, darling, from start to finish'. Soon the little flat was bustling with friends, the doorbell ringing every other minute as more and more rolled in clutching bottles and presents of cheeses and cupcakes. The big TV on the bookcase was broadcasting highlights from the wedding on a continuous loop, and Annabel had moved her little portable set from her bedroom into the sitting room, setting it up on another table so everyone had a clear view. Whenever the screens showed Kate and Wills saying 'I do', the whole party broke into applause and further corks popped into the air, and the room was filled with goodwill. At some point in the evening Jess turned up with her boyfriend Steve. Annabel had never met him before but liked the look of him. Jess had warned her he was older than she was, but the age gap didn't feel unnatural, they seemed like a good match. Nevertheless, Annabel thought Jess seemed tense tonight which was unusual. After such a long time having Jess as their babysitter, Annabel felt rather maternal towards her.

They were watching the balcony scene all over again when Michael Goode suddenly turned white, and said to his daughter, 'Annabel, that woman standing behind Prince Philip. It *couldn't* be . . . it looks just like her.'

And Annabel, replied, 'Actually, Daddy, it *is* her. She's the girlfriend of David Shropshire these days.'

'Well I'm blessed!' He stared at the screen. 'She's good looking, no question about it. But then she always was.'

Jess, who had overheard the exchange, asked, 'Mr Goode, did you know her? Cath Fox?'

He laughed. 'You could say that. It was all a very long time ago now – centuries, it feels like – and it's not an episode I'm particularly proud of either. Jolly nearly ended my marriage too, but that's another story.'

Annabel said, 'Jess is researching an article about her, Daddy, but I didn't say anything about you. Sorry, Jess. I just couldn't.'

Jess smiled. 'Nothing surprises me any longer about Cath. One day I might tell you about it. I went to interview her earlier this week. At Kensington Palace.'

'Really? Now that is interesting. I wonder whether the Buckingham Palace Press Office knows about that.'

Jess shrugged. 'I doubt it. I didn't approach her through official channels. I don't even know if I'm going to write the piece actually, I keep changing my mind.'

Steve gave her a little hug and said, 'I keep encouraging Jess to hurry up and write it. I think she should, she started to uncover some amazing material.'

'I don't know,' Jess said. 'Don't pressure me, Steve. This is something I need to take at my own pace.'

'And what did you think of her when you met her?' Annabel asked Jess. 'If you don't mind my asking. What was your assessment of Miss Fox?'

'I've been pondering on that all week. Well, where do you start? Be autiful . . . feisty . . . and she's got some interesting philosophies on life too, which I wasn't expecting. She's almost post-feminist in some ways.'

'That's a kind way of putting it,' said Annabel. 'Some people consider her a sly little gold-digger.'

'She's probably that too. But she told me something which is so true. How in life you can't just wait for things to drift by. You have to go out and make your own luck, decide what you want and then make it happen. If you don't do it, no one else will.' Jess coloured. 'Well, something like that anyway. I haven't yet got my head around everything she told me.'

'I see,' said Annabel. 'It sounds like a good theory to me.' And she glanced across the room at George who was sitting on the sofa with Henry, deep in happy conversation. Well, she mused, I did always rather hang on Miss Fox's opinions, didn't I?

Epilogue

Cath sat alone in her boyfriend's Gulfstream G650 being flown from Shanghai back to Hong Kong. For three days, the trade talks had made good progress and the senior representatives of Apple, Google and Microsoft now had a much clearer understanding of the Chinese government's priorities, and the terms by which they would be allowed some limited access to the Chinese market. Cath knew her networking skills had been instrumental in the success of the talks, and Benny Leung was pleased with her. This was the second time in a year Cath had pulled off a significant trade deal between the People's Republic of China and Western business interests, with Leung Industries benefiting both times.

Already her short marriage to David Shropshire felt like a distant memory. They had wed in a private ceremony in the Queen's Chapel, which wasn't exactly what Cath had hoped for, but at least she'd got him there. And it was the best feeling being an HRH; it gave her a little glow each time she thought about it. She still used the title now, of course, and always would, even though it was nearly three years since she'd dumped David for Benny.

Looking back on that marriage, which she scarcely ever did, Cath knew what had gone wrong. She'd resented the way David expected her to pay for everything, every little thing: their holidays, his new suits, all of it came down to her. He was such a sponger. Once her settlement had been agreed with Randy Jaworski, and the two hundred million dollars hit her bank account, David started acting like it was his own cash. Cath regarded him as a gold-digger, and suspected he'd only married her for her money.

Furthermore, the joys of living in a seven-room flat in Kensington Palace quickly lost their allure. There were so many neighbours living cheek by jowl in a confined area – other royals, courtiers, privy purses – you got no privacy at all; it reminded her of the Allaway estate in Portsmouth. And David kept slipping further and further down the royal ranks as new royal babies were born, closer than him in line to the throne, so it was rather pathetic; he was something like fiftieth in line these days. She got fed up with seeing his bare, needy bottom bent over the whipping bench. She'd lost all respect for him.

And then she met Benny Leung at a state banquet at Windsor Castle, when he was part of the Chinese delegation. The Lord Chamberlain's Office, which never found HRH The Duchess of Shropshire particularly easy to seat on these occasions, had placed her next to the billionaire Chairman of Leung Industries. Within a few days, they'd embarked upon an affair. Soon afterwards, she moved out to Hong Kong to be with him. It was surprising how effective a British HRH could still be in the twenty-first century in helping open doors in China and sweet-talking the Chinese authorities.

Annabel always felt she had reason to be grateful to Cath. On the night of her royal wedding party, when everyone except George had gone home, she took Cath's advice (as transmitted by Jess) and plucked up the courage to make a move on him. George was instantly receptive, overcome with relief that Annabel had taken the initiative, kissed her back passionately and stayed the night. From there on, the road to the altar was swift and natural. Within five months, they were married from George's childhood home in Berkshire, Mallards End, at a small church service in the local village. The Palmer parents were delighted to welcome Annabel into their family, and tactfully never reminded her that they'd witnessed her first engagement in their house to Jamie Pilcher, all those years ago. 'If you'd been a bit quicker off the mark,' Colonel Palmer told his son, 'you could have bagged her the first time round.' Everyone agreed that Annabel could not have looked more gorgeous or appropriate, processing down the aisle on the arm of her father, wearing an ivory-coloured dress with matching calf-length coat. Annabel's one sadness was that her mother, Flea, was not well enough to make the wedding. For over a year she had suffered from acute cirrhosis of the liver and was confined to St George's Nursing Home in Pimlico. In recent months there had been a partial rapprochement between Flea and her ex-husband, and Michael strolled round to the nursing home at least once a week to visit her and bring her grapes and that week's issue of *The Lady*.

A year after the wedding, following much badgering from Annabel, George finally agreed to put on an exhibition of his paintings, but only on condition that some of Henry's pictures were included in the show as well, plus one or two by his mother, Mary. Henry had absorbed a lot of his stepfather's talent, and was regarded as one of the most gifted schoolboy artists at Bryanston. More than a hundred and fifty of George and Annabel's friends attended the private view in the upstairs space at the Sladmore Gallery in Bruton Mews, and by the end of the evening 90 per cent of George's watercolours of Iraq, Afghanistan and Berkshire had red stickers on them. But the paintings which impressed everyone the most were his fourteen portraits in oils of Annabel, executed over fifteen years, mainly from photographs. George had never shown them to anyone before, and there was something deeply poignant and romantic about the whole idea of them, the product of so much unrequited love. 'I hope it doesn't make me seem like a stalker,' George remarked, when people praised them.

Within a few months of the great retrospective, Colonel Palmer died of old age, followed six months later by his wife. Mallards End was sold for an unexpectedly large sum and this windfall enabled George and Annabel to quit London altogether, give up their respective jobs, and buy a manor house in Dorset with a studio in the garden for George to paint full time. Flea had died of liver failure over the winter, and Michael moved down to Dorset to be closer to his favourite daughter; almost too close in fact, occupying the coach house belonging to the manor itself. Henry was delighted by his new home, and spent all his holidays there painting with George. Twice a year, he went on a duty visit to Rutland to stay with his father; in a deftly handled manoeuvre, Jamie had been encouraged to take early retirement from the regiment. He now ran his mother's riding school and drank too much.

As for Jess, she did sometimes wonder whether she'd made the right decision in never writing the article about Cath. She'd tortured herself about it for weeks, but in the end had chickened out: it just didn't feel right to expose your own mother; it wasn't the sort of journalism she believed in. Even Steve agreed with her in the end when she told him her secret. It would have made a sensational story, but could she have lived with herself afterwards?

Randy Jaworski was furious with her for finding out so little information about Cath – Jess had been rather economical with the truth – and partly held her to blame for the giant payout he was required to make to his ex-wife. Jess took the hint and quit Jaworski Media soon afterwards, rapidly followed by Steve who rejoined the *Independent*. Jess took up a freelance career as a television documentary researcher for *Dispatches*, which suited her perfectly, especially when Scarlet came along. Slightly to everyone's surprise, Jess was a natural and devoted mother and only too happy to put her career on hold for a few years, until Scarlet reached school age.

It was a sadness to Bob and Kirsty that Jess and Steve had no plans to get married, but they did at least agree to have their daughter christened in the church at Long Barton, followed by a lunch at Burdock Cottage. Jess had long ago decided never to tell her adopted parents about the existence of Cath and Callum, which she felt would only disturb them without gaining anything. She did, however, send messages to both of Scarlet's biological grandparents informing them of her birth. It just felt like the right thing to do.

She never heard back from Callum. Later she was told he'd returned to Portsmouth, back to his roots, and was working on the door of a new club named Cock T's, close to Clarence Pier.

On the morning before Scarlet's christening, however, a package arrived by DHL from China in which was a small turquoise box from the Shanghai branch of Tiffany & Co. The box contained a solid silver locket by the designer Elsa Peretti, on a solid silver chain.

On a tiny square of card inside the box was written the following message: *This is a present for your daughter. Please put your own photograph inside it. Every girl should have a nice picture of her mum in a locket.*

The card was unsigned, but was inscribed with two big XXs.